A Lady Who Knows What She Wants

Sunshine and Specter Paranormal Agency #2

Dan Ackerman

Supposed Crimes LLC • Matthews, North Carolina

For David

October 1, 2016
Saturday

Waking up next to Felix still dazzled Sunshine a little bit. The warmth of his skin, the quiet wheezes of his breathing, the smell of his hair first thing in the morning. He woke naturally and rolled over, unimpeded by the body that should have lain next to him. He sat up and looked around.

Felix's clothes scattered where he'd drunkenly strewn them last night. His phone plugged in on the nightstand. A shadow of teal dye on the white pillowcase, proving he'd slept there.

Sunshine got out of bed and started thinking of perfectly good reasons why Felix wouldn't have stayed in bed.

He always woke earlier than Sunshine did, for one, except he usually stayed in bed with Sunshine until he woke up. He might have gotten up to make coffee or breakfast, except the apartment didn't smell like food or coffee.

He found the demon in the living room, surrounded by papers and wearing Sunshine's coziest sweatshirt and possibly the world's tightest pair of briefs.

"I'm figuring it out," Felix told him as he shuffled through a few more papers in the case file.

Sunshine knew better than to interrupt his train of thought. He put on coffee and opened the fridge, trying to figure out what to make for breakfast.

"Toast," Felix ordered. "I'll throw up anything else."

Sunshine presented him with coffee and a plate of dry toast. He settled into the floor beside him. "Can I ask?"

"No. But you can go next door and get my computer. And then you can call Shay—"

"It's the weekend."

Felix waved dismissively. "Call Shay and tell her *not* to go to talk to the Mumford woman."

"Not to talk to her?"

"Mmhm, she said she'd do it today while the kids were with her mom, but it's looking dicey."

"Alright."

Before Sunshine could stand, Felix gave him a pat on the shoulder. "Thank you."

Sunshine almost teased him about finally using his manners, but he knew Felix had made a real effort lately to be nicer to him. His therapist seemed to think it was important. Sunshine wasn't a therapist, he hadn't even gone to school, so he didn't think it his place to weigh in.

He fetched the laptop and made the call. Shay seemed to take it personally. She wanted to know if they were putting someone else on the case and he had to talk her down from taking offense.

Felix burrowed into the couch with his laptop, deep down whatever rabbit hole of research he'd gotten himself into.

Sunshine sat on the floor and looked through the papers he'd thrown around. A series of suspicious suicides unlinked except that the victims belonged to the Community and a similar piece of jewelry had been found on all the victim's bodies. Always half of those charms that made up a heart when put together. Not high-quality metal, nothing more than costume jewelry, but they'd all had them and always the right half.

One woman had survived her attempt. Alfrieda Mumford. They'd wanted Shay to interview her.

"What changed?"

"I couldn't stop thinking there was something weird about the fact that Ally had dated *three* of the victims. Like, damn, even I haven't fucked that many people who've offed themselves," Felix said.

"Ah."

"So, I went deep. Mumford is her married name, except she's divorced, *and* they were swingers."

"And?"

"I'm looking into the ex. Uh. Gimme a couple hours."

Sunshine took a bite of the toast Felix hadn't finished. "Shay seemed upset."

"She's not off the case. I just don't want to upset the balance right now."

Sunshine glanced through the photos. He set aside half a dozen, one from each crime scene. "You should shower at some point."

"I will."

Sunshine scooted closer to the couch and placed his chin on Felix's knee.

Felix glanced down. He combed his fingers through Sunshine's hair. "What's your favorite cake?"

Sunshine thought for a minute. "I love a butter pecan cake, actually. I haven't had one in forever, though..." He tried to remember the last time he'd had butter pecan cake and could only come up with a Christmas about twenty years ago.

"Okay."

Sunshine kissed Felix's knee.

"Don't."

"No?"

"No, I'm disgusting. I need to shower, and I haven't brushed my teeth, and also I may actually vomit if you try to put your dick in my mouth."

"So. Romantic."

Felix put a foot on his chest and pushed him away. "You're in the wrong goddamn place if you want romance."

Sunshine didn't allow himself to fall back. He pulled himself onto the couch. "Liar." He kissed his temple, then went to shower.

Ten minutes later, he heard Felix come in to brush his teeth. When Sunshine was clean, they switched places.

Sunshine went back to look at the pictures he'd selected before. The shower had cleared his head. He stretched out on the couch with them, flipping between them.

Something was here.

Felix came out of the shower without a stitch on and asked, "Do I have clothes here?"

"Uh. Not clean ones."

He groaned and went into Sunshine's room. He came back out in only a pair of sweats that were too large and hung incredibly low on his hips, even when cinched all the way.

"Dude, I can see your fucking pubes," Sunshine said.

Felix grinned and glanced down. "I know, I'm letting myself go, aren't I? I haven't shaved in ages," he said as if he were proud.

"Those are my favorite sweatpants."

"I know."

"You're a wretched person."

Felix grinned. He pulled Sunshine's favorite cozy t-shirt over his head.

He looked extra scrawny in those too-big clothes. His hair stuck up and he finger-combed it. "I used your toothbrush."

Sunshine didn't react. He flipped through the pictures some more.

Felix straddled him but did nothing else.

Sunshine sighed at one picture in particular. He stared, then turned the picture around so Felix could see it. "Do you see that?"

"See what?"

"There's a clean spot."

Felix took the picture.

It wasn't a photo of the actual scene of the death. It was the victim's bathroom. On their vanity, there was a small space among the clutter of other items. It stood out to Sunshine for some reason. Around it, the other items grouped together more tightly, like something had pushed them out of the way when it had been set down.

He knew the pattern well. It was how his desk looked. Half the time when he put something down, he accidentally pushed something else off.

He showed Felix the clean spots on the other photos. Some in the bathroom, some in the kitchen. A spot where something had been and was no longer.

"Might be something," Felix agreed.

"Might be."

Felix took the photos out of his hands and placed them on the coffee table. He leaned forward. "Halloween at the Black Diamond."

"What about it?"

"It's a big deal."

"Oh."

They went to Halloween at the Black Diamond every year. Sunshine didn't know what would be different about this one. The only difference between this year and every other year was that he and Felix were...well, they were together in whatever capacity it was that they were together.

A few things about their relationship had changed, but those were more additions than real changes. They could touch each other now, big addition there.

A nice addition.

"I'm still thinking. I'll let you know what I decide," Felix told him.

"Sure."

"What was Garfield doing when you went over?"

"Sleeping."

Felix smiled. "He's such a good boy."

Garfield made the perfect pet for Felix's present state. He spent most of his days lazing around. He didn't, as far as they'd seen, use the bathroom, and he didn't appear to need to eat, although he did enjoy eating things like glass, sand, and woodchips. He could also spit fireballs.

"He harrumphed at me when I checked on him."

Felix's smile turned into a grin. He kissed Sunshine, then

rolled off him. "I need to lie down. You keep figuring out what those empty spots are."

Sunshine went through the other pictures again.

He could hear Felix playing a game and watching videos on his phone. He re-emerged in time for a late lunch.

Sunshine put a series of pictures in front of him.

The six photos of the clean spots and a photo from the Mumford woman's bathroom. He tapped a paper cup with the tag of a teabag dangling out.

"What am I looking at?" Felix asked.

"Look in the garbage."

In either bathroom or kitchen garbage was a non-descript disposable paper cup. The clean spaces in each area were about the size of the cups.

"Okay."

"I don't know. That's weird, right?"

"Could be something," Felix agreed. "Too bad those are all probably in a landfill by now."

"But Ally might know."

Felix rubbed his eyes. "Well. I guess call Shay back. Damn, she's gonna be pissed, though."

"You call her."

"You're better with people than I am."

Shay, as predicted, was not pleased with the change of plans. She told him it would have to wait until Monday at this point and he told her he'd email her the updated case notes.

Felix spent the rest of the day digging up more dirt on Ally Mumford's ex and making the connections between the various players in the case.

Sunshine cleaned up around the house, did laundry, and took Garfield for a walk, just in case he did need, or want, to go out.

As he walked out of the Weller, he passed Amity Sage on the way back in. The young man worked for the owner of the building in a capacity that Sunshine didn't understand, even after years.

"How's Ms. Weller doing?" Sunshine asked.

Amity glanced towards the little terrier at his side; she belonged to the owner. He looked back up at Sunshine, his face a perfect mask of polite subservience. "She's having a good day today. Much stronger than last week."

Sunshine made himself smile. "Well. Let us know if you need anything."

"Thank you, Mr. Sunshine, I'll certainly pass that along to Ms.

Weller."

"Have a nice night, Amity."

"You as well, Mr. Sunshine." Amity took the dog up the staircase.

Sunshine took Garfield outside. The elemental ate a few pieces of broken glass it found on the street. He brought it back to the apartment with him, where it sprawled out on the tile of his kitchen floor.

Felix had parked himself on the couch again.

Sunshine spent the rest of the evening stepping around the two laziest creatures he'd ever encountered as he tried to do his weekend chores. He managed. He'd gotten a lot of practice doing things with Felix being in the way in the most unhelpful way possible. He seemed to actively enjoy distracting Sunshine by making lewd comments or lounging in overtly sexual positions.

Presently, he had tied up his t-shirt like a crop top and made no effort to keep the sweatpants in an appropriate location on his body. He noticed Sunshine looking at him and rolled onto his stomach, lifting up his ass ever so slightly.

Sunshine continued vacuuming.

Felix wiggled.

Sunshine, as he passed the vacuum by the couch, slapped Felix's ass, not as hard as he could, but definitely harder than Felix would have appreciated.

Felix screeched, flipped over, and climbed over the back of the couch.

Sunshine danced out of his way and put the vacuum between him.

"What am I, a nervous fucking Yorkie?" Felix demanded.

Sunshine kept the vacuum between them.

"Turn the vacuum off."

"No, I'm not done yet."

"Turn it off."

Sunshine didn't. "Make me."

"You know I can," Felix warned.

Sunshine raised his eyebrows, then continued to vacuum.

Felix swatted at him once, then seated himself on the back of the couch. His eyes followed Sunshine as he finished and put the vacuum away. "Come here."

He said it in exactly the right way.

Sunshine went over. He almost couldn't help himself. Better than that, he didn't want to help it. He stood in front of Felix.

"That was too hard."

Sunshine started to worry.

"I'm not some filthy degenerate like you. I don't like being hit."

Sunshine couldn't tell which way this would go. Was he really in trouble? He hoped not. He hadn't smacked him that hard. "I'm sorry."

Felix stood up, his chin tilted up so he seemed taller than Sunshine.

"Am I in trouble?"

"Absolutely. Pull down your pants and lean over the couch."

Sunshine sighed with relief. Not in *real* trouble, thank God. He did as he was told, anticipation and desire bubbling in his stomach. He didn't know exactly what Felix was about to do to him. They were really still figuring a lot of things out, finding what they liked, as well as their limits.

He tried not to worry as he waited, his fingers digging into the couch.

Felix slapped him across the ass, not hard at all. Playful more than anything.

He drew in a breath. "Harder."

Felix hit him harder, hard enough to sting this time.

His insides started to warm. He rolled his hips forward, pressing his cock against the couch. He let out a slow breath and closed his eyes. "Harder, please."

Felix didn't hit him. He cleared his throat.

Sunshine couldn't see him. At this point, the anticipation was just about killing him. It took everything he had not to turn around.

"Fucking. Christ," Felix breathed. "Potatoes."

Sunshine glanced behind him. That was the safe word they'd chosen, but he hadn't thought Felix would be the one to use it.

"I'm sorry, I can't, I'm done."

Sunshine pulled up his pants and turned around.

Felix couldn't look at him. He had his arms wrapped around himself. "I'm sorry, I just, I can't."

"That's fine."

"Shit, Sunshine, I really don't want to hit you."

"That's alright." He approached Felix and offered a hand to him.

Felix took his hand then cuddled up to Sunshine's chest. "I tried," he insisted in a pout.

Sunshine squeezed him. "I know. It was nice."

Felix snorted.

"Thank you for trying."

"Fucking useless."

"No," Sunshine insisted. He kissed his temple. "I can think of a thousand and one uses for a fellow like you."

"Would it be terribly indulgent of me to ask you to name them?" Felix asked.

"All one thousand and one?"

"Maybe just one or two."

"As a very good friend to have in general," Sunshine said, "And as a wonderful partner to try things with."

"It hurt my hand."

Sunshine giggled. He took Felix's hand and kissed his palm. "You're such a *baby*." He kept his arms around him so he couldn't get pouty and squirm away.

"I told you, I'm not a freak like you are."

Sunshine nuzzled into his throat. "Call me a freak again," he purred.

"Can we put the TV on?"

"Sure."

Felix slipped out of his grip then. He pointed to a damp spot on the back of the couch. "You got precum on the couch."

Sunshine got a Clorox wipe and took care of the spot, knowing he would think about it nonstop if he didn't.

Felix teased, "You're lucky I'm not good at this, you know."

"How's that?"

"We'd never get anything else done."

He sat on the couch next to Felix, whose hand immediately found his inner thigh.

"I did like looking at you like that, though," Felix told him. "And I liked that noise you made." Felix's hand found Sunshine's cock through his pants.

"You don't have to—"

"But I want to."

Sunshine licked his lips and pressed against his hand.

"Don't you want me to have what I want?"

"Everything you want."

"Then give it to me."

Sunshine hurried to undo his pants and give Felix better access.

Things had gone so sideways since Heaven had sent him to Earth. There was no way he was supposed to be living in Manhattan or getting spanked by a demon who had the potential to become the Antichrist. He hated to think what his life would be like if things had gone any differently.

Felix teased him and toyed with him. He climbed onto Sunshine's lap and buried his free hand in Sunshine's curls, pulling his head back.

Maybe he didn't want to hit Sunshine, but he'd figured out other perfectly adequate ways to inflict the right kind of pain.

Felix tugged down the band of the sweatpants and wrapped his hand around both of them. He looked proud and relieved all at once.

Sunshine smiled.

Felix grinned and chuckled. "Don't fucking smile, you're going to ruin it."

Sunshine knew he wouldn't. He urged him closer so he could kiss him. "I love you."

"Shut up or I'll stop," Felix threatened between kisses.

He didn't stop, he made them both cum, and he stayed on Sunshine's lap for minutes afterward, just kissing him, sweet and soft.

They spent the rest of the night cuddled on the couch. They ate leftovers from last night and tossed balled up napkins to Garfield when he came over to investigate.

Sunshine scratched the creature behind its nubby ears, and it gurgled at him. He hadn't decided if that meant he'd pleased or irritated Garfield.

"I think he likes us," Felix said.

The elemental looked up at them, rasped a bit, then went to lay down on the bathroom floor. It liked to lay in cool places. It had spent the whole summer parked under an AC vent.

"What do you want to do tomorrow?"

"I don't know," Sunshine said.

"What do you want to make me for dinner tomorrow?"

"What do you want me to make for dinner tomorrow?"

Felix stretched and sighed; he draped himself across Sunshine's lap and looked up at him. "Teach me how to make something."

The idea sent a tingle of fear down Sunshine's spine. "Really?"

"Yeah. I'm at like, grilled cheese and Kraft dinner. Bring me up a level."

"A level past Kraft dinner?" Sunshine asked, faintly terrified at the whole enterprise.

"Yeah. Something with a vegetable and a meat and a bread.

You know. The food groups." Felix made a triangle with his forefingers and thumbs and used it to frame Sunshine's face.

"I'll think of something. What's the occasion?"

Felix dropped his hands. "Thirty days."

Sunshine thought, then put the piece together. "Clean?"

"I mean." Felix looked away. "Nothing serious. No uppers or poppers, although, like who counts poppers, really? Or benzos, except for that one time that I actually took one for a panic attack and not because I was bored. No sleeping pills. And you know I don't fuck with opiates anymore and I never *liked* molly anyway. None of that kind of stuff."

For decades, Sunshine had maintained a general awareness of all the various drugs with which Felix entertained himself. He recognized when the drugs became (more) problematic and had fished Felix out of the deep end enough times that he wouldn't be sad to see any of them go. Hearing them laid out in a list like that made him wonder if he should have done or said something sooner.

"You're looking at me."

"I'm proud of you," Sunshine told him.

"Oh." Felix picked at his cuticles. "It's the longest I've gone without in a while. It's the only time I've actually, uh, *tried* not to when I wanted to use something."

Sunshine smoothed the teal locks back from Felix's forehead. He couldn't stop thinking that he should have done more to help.

"I, uh. You know. You can't make someone get clean. It only works if they want it. So, get that look off your face."

Sunshine tried to change his expression, though he wasn't sure what had given his feelings away. Maybe they just knew each other's expressions too well.

In a nearly accusatory tone, Felix told him, "And I didn't do it for you, either."

"Oh." Sunshine hadn't thought he had.

"Last year was. Uh. Trying to feel something or feel nothing and taking *way* too much. It was the first time I really felt like I wasn't in control of what I was putting in my body. It wasn't fun and I don't..." Felix swallowed. He couldn't look at Sunshine. "I don't want to feel like that again."

"Let me know what you need."

Felix scowled. "Can't you say something shitty for once?"

"No."

"Why the fuck not?"

Sunshine thought about giving a blasé answer. "I'm an angel," he could have said, "We're made of better stuff." He considered that Felix had shared something with him. He took hold of Felix's hand and kissed his knuckles. "I think I'm too dumb to think of shitty things to say."

Felix sighed and tightened his fingers. "You really aren't dumb. Which isn't fair. That He made you beautiful and kind and strong and smart."

He didn't make me kind, Sunshine thought but didn't voice it.

Felix yawned and stretched. He rolled onto his side to watch the TV. They had seen this movie already, but they'd decided to do a horror movie each night of October. They had carefully curated the list of horror essentials and shared it with friends. They'd even started a group chat.

Tonight, the list offered them *Carrie*. Their viewing mostly consisted of Felix murmuring, "What a bitch," or "Good for her."

They didn't do much for the rest of the night, or much that morning either. They went to the grocery store in the afternoon.

Sunshine trailed behind Felix with a grocery basket as Felix chose ingredients from a list which he had carefully curated based on a two-hour long affair with *How to Cook Everything*. It had taken him ages to pick a recipe. At first, he'd deemed anything with more than five steps 'too complicated' until Sunshine had assured him that nothing in *How to Cook Everything* would be too hard for them to make together, no matter how many steps.

Felix only burned himself once while they cooked. Steak, baked potatoes, roasted broccoli, most of which Felix cooked independently.

Sunshine couldn't force himself to totally cede control of the steaks, though. An over-cooked potato was one thing, but a well-done steak was an affront.

After they ate and cleaned up, and watched their movie for the night, Felix gave him a kiss and said, "Get me in the morning."

"Sleeping at yours?"

"Mmhmm, I have some things I need to do. Laundry, mostly." He smiled. "Unless you think I should start wearing your clothes everywhere."

"You hate my clothes."

"I hate them for me. They're fine for you. You know, also on the topic of things I hate: I hate showering here. You need to up your toiletries game if you expect me to keep staying over."

"Why don't you bring some of your stuff over?" he suggested.

"Why won't you stay at my place?" Felix asked.

"Because you don't change your sheets."

"Ugh. Whatever. Get me in the morning." Felix went back in for another kiss, then called for Garfield and saw himself out.

A few hours later, he snapped a picture of Garfield sleeping inside the toilet bowl with the caption *So now I need to give this fucker a bath.*

Sunshine responded with a dozen laughing emojis and did not offer to help.

October 5
Wednesday

Shay had interviewed the Mumford woman, ruled her out as the cause of the suicides, and found out a little bit more about her ex, Dan Mumford. She'd passed that information on to Sunshine, who'd passed it on to Felix.

Felix had given it to Rose and demanded, "Dirt."

Rose had turned up that the man worked at a witchy café that specialized in different herbal teas. He'd also found him on a few dating apps looking for a woman to join him and his girlfriend in the bedroom.

Felix sighed and rubbed his eyes when Rose had told him that. "I honestly can't with people these days. Can you fucking believe this shit?"

Rose glanced at Sunshine.

Sunshine mouthed, "You're fine," to the young man, who'd become much more nervous around Felix lately.

Felix squinted at the fairy. "You eyeing my man?" he asked.

Rose widened his eyes. "No," he whispered.

Felix's face sobered. "I was joking."

"Sorry."

"Did I do something to you?" Felix asked.

"No."

Felix looked at Sunshine.

Sunshine had no answer to give.

Felix scowled, sighed, then waved his hand at Rose. "Nice work, anyway, kid. Gen Z triumphs yet again. You're dismissed."

Rose scuttled out of the room.

"Did I do something to him?" Felix asked.

Sunshine shrugged.

Felix dwelled on that for a while, then had Tate come up to their office, even when Sunshine asked him not to. He gestured for her to sit.

"What's up?" she asked as she sat.

"Did I do something?"

She glanced at Sunshine. "What kind of something?"

"To Rose. He's been nervous."

"Oh." Tate smoothed down the hem of her shirt against her leggings.

"Around me specifically," Felix pressed.

"Uh. That's...Uh." She squirmed. "I don't know if it's my

business to tell you. I also already told him it's not a big deal."

"Tate."

"Come on, Specter, I'm not...It's not my business."

Felix insisted, "Can you at least tell me I didn't do something?"

She sighed. She evaluated Felix, her eyes scanning over his furrowed brow and hunched shoulders. "Promise you didn't hear it from me?"

"Fucking cross my heart."

Tate tucked a bit of hair behind her ear. "He's dating your ex."

Felix squinted. "Which one?"

"Uh, Cassie? Cassandra?" she guessed.

Felix frowned, then his eyes widened, "Cassandra Gains!"

"I think so."

"She's *way too old for him.*"

Tate snorted.

"No, like, she's like two thousand years old. He's such a *baby.*" Felix leaned back in his chair. "Fuck."

"It's, uh, it's not a big deal, right?" Tate asked.

"No, what, I don't care. I didn't even think Cas was dating anyone she's been..." Felix trailed off. "Oh."

"Oh what?" she asked.

"Not important. Anyway. Thank you."

"You didn't hear it from me," Tate reminded.

He nodded.

When she'd gone, Sunshine asked, "Cas has been what?"

"She's been sugaring all these little...you know, those Titanic-Leo looking skinny, pretty boys with no body hair. Like *barely legal* peach-fuzz types."

"Cas always did have a type," Sunshine said. He flicked his eyes over Felix's thin frame and smooth cheeks.

Felix opened his mouth to agree, then narrowed his eyes and flipped Sunshine off.

Sunshine giggled to himself.

Felix self-consciously rubbed his face. He had such pale, fine hair that he didn't even need to shave every day. Sometimes, Hiram teased him about it, saying he hadn't needed to teach him to shave until he was nearly twenty.

Felix cleared his throat. "Let's go get tea."

"Hmm?"

"Yeah, let's go. Let's poke around."

"I don't want to go to Brooklyn."

"It's barely Brooklyn. Twenty minutes."

Sunshine huffed but got his jacket anyway. It was never twenty minutes. Knowing the MTA, it could be (*would* be) twice that. Or they could die in a subway tunnel. Sunshine didn't have any proof of it, but he really believed the MTA wanted to kill him personally. "I thought this was Shay's case."

"Yeah. It is. But, uh, I'm bored and it's this or help Emil take sneaky pictures of that mage who's banging his secretary."

"I don't know, you went through that photography phase in the seventies."

Felix scoffed at him and walked out the door.

Sunshine followed him.

Much more than twenty minutes later, Sunshine followed him into a café called Tearapy, which Sunshine understood as a pun but wasn't sure how to pronounce. He hung back a little when Felix gave a subtle flick of his wrist.

He scanned the shop. A few young people worked the counter, a girl with a blue mohawk and a boy with a handsomely messy flop of blond hair. A handful of patrons sat cozily in armchairs or tables for small groups.

The whole place smelled herby and spicy and grassy all at once, three dozen smells that pinged off each other and melded together. Behind a glass display sat dozens of fat, happy muffins sparkling with pearl sugar.

Felix surveyed the menu, then approached the counter. He addressed the young man, "Uh. Dan Mumford works here?"

The youth glanced up. "Uh."

"It's, uh, it's not anything weird," Felix assured, "I, just. I've kind of had a hard time getting ahold of him."

The youth's eyes widened, then he fixed his face. "Oh."

Sunshine approached the display case and inspected the muffins a little more closely. Scones and donuts sat a few racks lower, and those big cookies.

Sunshine had mixed feelings about big cookies. They didn't always cook right, too hard on the edges and unpleasantly gunky in the middle.

These ones looked good, even all the way through.

"Can I help you?" the girl with the mohawk asked.

"I'm just looking. I might be a minute."

She nodded and left him alone.

"He does work here, right?" Felix asked.

"Yeah."

"My name's Felix."

"Kev," the youth answered.

Sunshine went to look at the refrigerated drinks.

"Do you know Dan at all?"

"Sure. A little bit." Kev shrugged. "We all work together. You know Dan?"

Felix gave a shrug, but it was a flirty, shy kind of shrug. "Just a little bit."

What an excellent liar. Sunshine lied, but not well. He couldn't keep track of the things he said well enough. Felix lied with his whole body.

"He won't really message me back. This must seem super desperate! I was just...already in the area, you know. I thought I'd swing by..."

"No, no," Kev supplied awkwardly.

"Anyway...Uh. I guess." Felix looked back up at the menu. "Any of that stuff good?"

"I like the pumpkin spice one."

"Great, can I get one of those? Uh. Small I guess?"

"Any sweetener?"

"Uh. A little sugar. And a splash of milk?"

"Sure thing."

Felix dithered around while the kid made his tea and then requested, "Listen, uh. I'm kind of embarrassed. Don't tell Dan I stopped by."

"No, I won't. Don't worry."

"Thanks."

"A lot of people come by to see him," Kev assured. "He's...pretty popular."

Felix gave a sheepish smile. "He is cute, though, right?"

Kev blushed and chuckled. "Yeah, I guess," he said with a smile.

Sunshine bought a bottle of kombucha, whatever that was, and a muffin, and then went to sit at a corner table.

When Felix had his tea, he approached Sunshine's table. "This seat taken?"

Sunshine played along, for appearances and for fun. "No, I think I got stood up."

"Oh, bad luck for you. Good luck for me."

"You want to sit?"

Felix slid into the seat. "Felix."

"Sunshine."

"Oh, nicknames already?"

Sunshine rolled his eyes but couldn't help the smile.

"If you did have a name, what would it be?" Felix asked, dropping the farce, but keeping his voice low.

"I do have a name."

"I mean, a, uh. You know. A whole name."

"Um." Sunshine tried to think of something to say. "I like my name the way you gave it to me."

Felix let out a hard sigh, seeming impressed and kind of riled up, in a good way. "You're something else."

Sunshine smiled back at him.

Felix sipped at his tea. He nodded towards the kombucha Sunshine had bought. "Heard that makes you poop."

Sunshine glanced down. He didn't know how he felt about the flavor. "I guess we'll find out. You want to try it?"

"No." He slid one hand across the table. "You want to get out of here?" he asked.

"Anywhere with you." Sunshine placed his hand in Felix's and grinned when Felix curled his fingers around his hand.

Felix smiled back.

Instead of heading back to the office, they got lunch. Sunshine threw away the rest of the kombucha. He normally never threw away food, but he really couldn't adjust to the taste.

Felix finished the tea over lunch.

They survived the ride back to the office but got off a few stops early to walk and enjoy the weather.

At the office, Sunshine went upstairs to get some work done.

Felix stayed on the first floor to talk to Shay.

Sunshine had gotten about halfway through reviewing and approving overtime hours for the week when Rose clattered into the office.

He sucked in a breath. "You should. Specter. He...He said he was going to jump in front of a train."

Felix made those kinds of threats all the time, idle and joking. Dark jokes, and maybe sometimes too close to serious, but never with any real intent. "He says that sometimes."

Rose shook his head. "No, but...His face, Mr. Sunshine! He got weird first. And he walked out and he, he really *pushed* Tate when she got in his way. Knocked her over."

Sunshine stood up immediately.

He didn't know what had happened, but he knew that Felix would never push Tate like that.

Rose stepped out of the way as Sunshine hurried downstairs.

"Which way?" he asked Tate.

She pointed down the street towards the subway station. "I called the—"

Sunshine ran as hard as he could and leaped the turnstile. He bowled through at least half a dozen people who couldn't get the fuck out of his way in time. He kept his eyes peeled for Felix, unmistakable in any crowd. Moon pale, teal-haired, and almost certainly dressed in black.

He saw him on the subway platform, near the mouth of the tunnel. Away from the others who waited for the next train.

"Felix!"

Felix stared down at the tracks, his head bowed and cocked to one side.

Listening.

Listening for the next rain.

His posture straightened.

People on the platform shuffled forward.

Sunshine ran over and grabbed him by the wrist. "Hey."

"I'm sorry."

"No, it's alright."

Felix squirmed his arm around. "Let go."

"No."

"Sunshine, just. Just let go."

"You know I can't. Step back."

Felix squirmed harder. He was skinny but he was so goddamn strong. He writhed out of Sunshine's grasp and stepped away. "Leave me alone."

The train rattled on the tracks.

Sunshine grabbed Felix around the waist this time, hauling him back as he tried to step forward.

People around them gasped and murmured.

One person screamed.

Someone always screamed during things like this.

The train rattled to a stop.

Felix kept bucking and twisting as Sunshine hauled him back.

Over and over, he demanded, "Lemmegolemmego."

Sunshine dragged him as far as he could until he had to stop and bring them both down to the floor. He wrestled his way on top of Felix. He half-crouched, half-knelt over him, and held on to his hands. "Felix, relax," he insisted stupidly.

Felix didn't relax.

He did seem to get tired, but Sunshine was afraid to get up.

Sunshine tried to breathe and draw up enough of his power to calm down Felix. Normally he could do it without much of a problem, but this had him rattled.

People crowded around and tried to ask him questions.

Sunshine closed his eyes, took a deep breath, and prayed. He tightened his grip on Felix, held down one of his arms with one hand, and grabbed his face with the other. "Look at me. I'm trying to help but you have to let me."

"Sunshine," Felix whined. He balled his free hand in Sunshine's shirt.

"Look at me. Just look, okay? It's me and I'm trying to help you."

Felix squirmed less. He stared up at him, his eyes red-rimmed and wet. His breath came in sad little whines.

"Breathe with me." He let go of Felix's arm and clasped a hand over the one balled in his shirt. He drew up as much calm as he could and drew in slow steady breaths. He needed it as much as Felix did.

Felix stopped fighting him. He gripped Sunshine's shirt even harder, then started to keen.

Sunshine adjusted himself, keeping a grip on Felix the whole time. He settled back and pulled Felix into his arms. "You're okay."

People still crowded around, watching.

Taking videos.

At least half a dozen phones pointed towards them.

"Could you fucking not!" Sunshine barked at the nearest person filming them.

The girl, maybe thirteen, flinched and stowed her phone.

If Sunshine had had something to throw, he would have thrown it.

A few police arrived, too, and at least they dispersed the crowd.

They started asking questions, staring down at Sunshine and Felix. One of the cops took charge, crouching to get on their level. She asked, "What happened?"

"He tripped." The lie came out instinctively. He mistrusted other people with Felix too much and he couldn't imagine handing him over to anyone else right now. He knew the procedure after a suicide attempt and in his line of work, he'd facilitated it a few times. But without a doubt, there was no way he was letting anyone take Felix.

This wasn't like him, not even at his worst, and he needed something other than a hospital gown and enough Valium to keep him quiet.

She raised an eyebrow. "He seems pretty upset."

"We were fighting. He wasn't paying attention to where he was going and he stepped too far. He gets, uh, it must have really scared him. He has panic attacks."

Felix let out a pathetic whimper.

"It was a pretty bad fight," Sunshine added.

"What were you fighting about?"

He glanced up at the other officers huddled around.

She waved them back.

They receded but didn't leave the area. They stood there, hands on their belts, watching them. Sunshine already knew how he'd incapacitate each of them if they tried to put a hand on Felix.

Felix sniffled and snorted, then wiped his face on his shirt, leaving a big wet smear. He straightened up a little.

"I really need a better picture of what happened," the officer told them, her voice low and kind. "We got a call—"

"I fell. I wasn't looking," Felix said. "He...Holy shit." He pressed a hand to his mouth. He sucked in a breath. "Oh, shit, holy fucking shit." He swallowed. "He just...He couldn't..." A sob escaped instead of words. He pressed his hands over his mouth, sucked in a breath, then said, "I'm trying to plan this wedding and he doesn't care about a single thing, just 'do whatever you want' and he can't..." Felix fanned his eyes. "He can't take half a goddamn day off to go try the fucking cake..." He sniffled. "So, I just said, 'fine, I'll go by myself' and I turned around too fast and I almost..." He wiped his eyes with a trembling hand.

"Alright," she soothed.

Sunshine used his sleeve to wipe a few tears Felix had missed.

"You fucking asshole," Felix accused quietly. He glanced at the woman. He squinted at her uniform. "Officer...Medina?"

She nodded.

"Thank you."

"Oh. You're welcome."

Felix crooked his fingers, his hand held by his side. He flicked some spell or another towards the woman. "All those people looking at us! God, I'm so embarrassed. Do I look awful?"

"No," she assured. She blinked a few times, then her face smoothed. She smiled a vague, pleasant smile.

"A little," Sunshine said.

Felix let out a weepy laugh. "You see what I have to put up with? Are you married?"

"Yes."

"Did your husband go to the cake testing?" he asked.

"I said I'd go," Sunshine told him, petulant and quiet.

"Yes," the officer answered.

"See?" Felix insisted. "And he's straight. What's your excuse?"

"I'll go," Sunshine promised. He tightened his arms around Felix. "Wherever you want, I'll go. I promise."

"Yeah?"

Sunshine nodded. His throat tightened. Not from their fake reconciliation, of course, but from how close he'd come to watching a train flatten Felix.

"Let me up. I have to go, I have to change! God, is my face awful?"

"You're perfect," Sunshine assured.

They all stood together.

Felix, either because he felt fragile or for the sheer drama of it all, threw his arms around the officer. "Thank you. So much."

She seemed startled.

Felix found out her station and her badge number and insisted that he would talk to all her superiors and let them know what a good job she was doing. He laid it on so thick that Sunshine almost laughed; Felix worked with cops if he had to, but the Community preferred to monitor itself.

She told him it wasn't needed. She seemed actively relieved when they parted ways and somewhat confused, like she'd couldn't remember if she'd left the stove on, or if she even had a stove.

Sunshine kept his arm firmly around Felix's shoulders the whole time, not sure he wouldn't bolt or collapse.

Felix still shook. He tripped a few times up the stairs and leaned against Sunshine the whole time.

Sunshine wanted to bring him home, but Felix said, "The office is closer. And I have too many drugs at home."

"I thought you weren't using."

"I...I might have a few rainy-day stashes. And things I have a prescription for. But I want to make sure this is worn off."

"What *happened?*" Sunshine asked.

"So fucking stupid. I started...You know, I was talking to Tate and Rose and I started, getting really, uh, dark. Like, in a bad place. Circling the drain, worse than it's ever been. It was like I couldn't breathe that's how miserable I was. It kept getting worse and worse and then I just...It was like ten years of depression crammed into thirty minutes, Sunshine. Jesus. So stupid!"

"You're not stupid."

"I drank the goddamn tea!"

Sunshine blinked.

"The tea. I thought Dan must have been poisoning people. Tea at the scenes, he works at a tea shop, he dated all those people, but...Fuck. It must be that little shit! Kev. Kevin. Whoever it was. *Fuck*, I need a drink."

"I don't think you should drink," Sunshine suggested softly.

Felix didn't argue or agree. He didn't say much until they got back to the office and when he did talk, it was only to tell Shay to go to the restaurant where he'd thrown his tea away, rifle through their garbage, find the disposable cup, and bring it back for testing.

She looked angry but went anyway.

"For someone who's late every day, you think she'd have a better attitude," Felix mentioned once she'd gone.

Sunshine stared at him.

He'd been staring at him.

"What?" Felix snapped.

"I want to ask if you're okay, but I know you'll get mad."

"Well." Felix scowled. "I'm not okay."

"I know. Can I hug you?"

Felix nodded.

Sunshine squeezed him as hard as he could. He wanted to squeeze him hard enough to make them one body so nothing like this could ever happen again.

"If you cry, I'll start again," Felix warned.

"I don't know what I'd do without you."

"You'd be fine."

Sunshine shook his head. "I would never be fine again, not even in a million years."

"And I'm the dramatic one?"

He hugged him even harder. "You're my best friend. Ever."

Felix scoffed. "Can't be better than all those other pretty boys you lived with in that big swimming pool."

"A hundred times better."

"Better than Heaven?" Felix asked. He pulled back to look at Sunshine, disbelieving and almost hurt, like he thought Sunshine had lied, said it just to make him feel better.

Sunshine nodded.

A sadness claimed Felix's face.

"What's wrong?"

"That's so pathetic, that I mean that much to you."

Sunshine swallowed.

"What would you *be* without me?" Felix asked. He asked it gently and touched Sunshine's cheek.

Sunshine didn't know how to answer. He wouldn't become nothing. He wouldn't lose all the interests and hobbies he'd garnered in his time on Earth. The few friends he had would remain. Things would taste the same, the sounds of birds in a meadow would still soothe him, he would still enjoy long walks and the smell of fresh coffee. "I'd..."

He met Felix's eyes and he knew. He felt that familiar stirring deep in the core of his being. Not lust or love, not tenderness or camaraderie, all of which he'd felt towards Felix before. This was adoration.

"I would be lost. Without covenant. I would have no one to—"

"Don't," Felix breathed. "Don't say it. You'll make it true."

Spoken, it would become a pledge. He would serve. He would give Felix everything he had and break the ties between him and Heaven. He would fall and Felix would ascend.

"I can never go back," Sunshine murmured.

"I know."

"Without you, your father would take me."

"He'd have a field day with that. If there was ever a reason for me to stay alive, it's imagining what my dad would do to you," Felix said. He leaned back into Sunshine's arms.

"It was just the tea," Sunshine hoped aloud.

"Just the tea," Felix assured. "I've got a whole wedding planned. Weren't you listening? I wouldn't want to miss it."

"If you really wanted to go to a cake tasting, I'd go."

Felix chuckled. "I already picked a bakery."

Sunshine wondered how many years would pass before Felix got tired of joking about their engagement. A one-off comment had turned into a months-long farce.

Felix stayed in Sunshine's arms for a while. He didn't say much and neither of them got any work done.

They watched their movie for the night early. They pushed together their chairs behind Felix's desk and pulled up *Sleepaway Camp* on his laptop. Felix kept a hold of one of Sunshine's hands throughout the movie.

When they went home, Felix didn't stop at his own apartment.

Sunshine waited until he fell asleep, which meant waiting until four or so in the morning, before he went to Felix's apartment and scoured it for hidden drug stashes. He didn't flush them, though he desperately wanted to.

He hid them under his own kitchen sink, though he didn't actually know that it would keep Felix from finding them if he wanted to.

He slid back into bed.

Felix immediately rolled over and latched onto him, his usual octopus-style of bedsharing. He scooched up in the bed and murmured, "That's a really bad hiding place."

"You're crushing my windpipe," Sunshine breathed.

"Yeah? Do you like it?" he asked with a hint of a growl.

"Uh. Not presently."

Felix shifted his arm and kissed his cheek.

"Do you feel better?"

The answer took a while. "I mean, I feel...worse than usual. But not as bad as before."

"Yeah?"

"Yeah."

Sunshine proposed in what he hoped was a tone of casual tenderness, "Stay here a couple of days?"

Felix said, "Yeah. But you're gonna have to flush those drugs in the morning."

"I will."

"Mhm. Thank you. By the way."

Sunshine rolled over and gathered up Felix for a tight hug. "Go back to sleep."

Felix feigned a snore, then peeked one eye open.

Sunshine smiled.

They giggled.

In the morning, Felix didn't let him flush the drugs. At least, not all of them. He woke up early, retrieved them, and carefully sorted them into two piles. He pointed to the small, less colorful one and said, "Just in case I need them."

Sunshine looked at the pills. He had many responses, but none of them would help anything. He felt no disgust or resentment toward these pills, or towards Felix. Mostly he felt worried. Worried about what that tea had done to him, and what the world had done to him, and how whole and healthy Felix could be and had ever been.

Traveling in the crowds they had, Sunshine had known a lot of partiers and addicts, people who got messy and people who got hurt. He had never managed to summon the anger or hate others had found. He'd always just...cleaned people up, taken care of them if he could, brought them to a hospital if he couldn't. He had rubbed so many backs, wiped up blood and vomit and sometimes worse, fed and watered them, and put them to bed. He'd told them, "It's okay, you'll be okay," to every person, even if he knew it wasn't true.

He'd been called an enabler more times than he could count.

Had he *let* this happen to Felix?

"That's not enough of anything to kill me. I'd have to take all of those and drink a lot and I'd still probably just get really sick," Felix insisted.

"Okay."

"Okay?" Felix demanded, half-whine and half-glower.

"Okay." Sunshine scooped up the bigger pile and flushed them. The *plink* of the pills against the water of the toilet sounded almost pretty.

He swept the smaller pile into a small Tupperware he usually used for nuts or trail mix. He tried to hand it back to Felix.

Felix shook his head. "No. Put it somewhere."

He nodded and put the Tupperware back down.

Felix tapped the top of the container, then drummed his fingers on it once. He took his hand back, rubbed his nose, and ruffled a hand through his hair. "They're just in case."

"I understand." He didn't really, not about the drugs, but he understood it in the way that he kept a knife in his bedside table 'just in case' too. He didn't *want* to use it, but someday he might need it more than he didn't want it.

A different kind of need altogether, but one all the same.

Felix sighed and crossed his arms.

Sunshine looked at him. He didn't know what else to do.

Felix glared. "What?"

"I love you."

The demon bared his teeth, showing pointy little fangs.

Sunshine wrapped him up in a hug. "I do. So much. No matter what. You can tell me anything."

Muffled by Sunshine's chest, Felix said, "I know." He sounded exhausted and relieved and miserable.

Sunshine hugged him harder.

Felix squirmed his arms free and clutched on to Sunshine. "I really do know."

October 13
Thursday

For two hours straight, Felix had stared at his computer and made a variety of dissatisfied sounds. Sunshine felt relatively sure it had nothing to do with work and more to do with Halloween.

Sunshine left it alone. He'd made a few suggestions that Felix had summarily executed with a cool viciousness. Sunshine still thought calling Superman and Wonder Woman 'an utter fucking travesty' had leaned towards extreme, especially since it played into Felix's interests.

Sunshine dared to ask, "Lunch?"

Felix answered, "We're fucked."

"No, I don't think...I don't think it's that bad."

"I've had literally zero good ideas."

Sunshine took a big chance and suggested, "We could be Dorothy and the Scarecrow. Cause, uh..."

"You're the stupidest person I've ever met and I'm a mentally ill drug addict with low self-esteem?" Felix sniped.

"No, just I..." He shrugged. "We could find like, two other people to be the Tinman and—"

"The point of a couple's costume is *not* to have other people involved," Felix practically snarled.

Sunshine left at that point.

Felix called something nasty after him as he went down the stairs.

He ignored it. He offered to buy Rose lunch, even though Rose technically didn't work enough hours to take a lunch. He spent an hour talking with the young fairy about the concert Rose would attend this coming weekend. They looped around the block before they went back to the office.

Sunshine tried not to act like something was bothering him.

Rose, to his credit, also tried to pretend that they hadn't both heard Felix call Sunshine the most basic and uninteresting excuse for a fag he'd ever met.

Sunshine headed upstairs, set a sandwich on Felix's desk, and said, "It was the first movie I ever saw. You made me go and said if I was going to stay on Earth I'd have to learn to act like a person."

Felix glanced up but couldn't hold Sunshine's gaze. He picked up the sandwich, put it down, and then organized a few papers on his desk. He glanced back up. "Why are you still standing there?"

"Because you were rude to me."

"You like it," Felix sulked.

"Not like that. And you know that."

Felix huffed and groaned. He threw himself back in his chair and stared at the ceiling. "Fine, you're a remarkably interesting fag. *Wizard of Oz* is a very original costume idea in the East Village."

Sunshine went back downstairs.

He stayed there for the rest of the day. He spent a lot of time on the phone with one of the witches who worked for the NYPD and helped get the more dangerous criminal magic users managed. For a while, the Community had managed itself with extrajudicial punishments, but in the more aware and connected society of today, it had become more difficult. So, Community members had started working for the government.

Sunshine didn't like to think of it as an infiltration so much as representation for a historically disenfranchised people.

Ten mages, a few werewolves, and probably dozens of witches worked for the FBI. A lot of vampires worked for the CIA; apparently, they flourished in that field of work.

He left without Felix and didn't go home.

He got dinner with an old friend, Paula Boyd. They'd all gone to a lot of shows together back in the 70s. Paula and Sunshine had spent a lot of time together because Felix and her boyfriend at the time had been close. She lived in Long Island with her husband and kids now and had been in the city today for a business meeting of some kind.

"Where's Specter?" she asked as soon as she'd hugged him and they'd both sat down.

"I'm mad at him right now."

She laughed. "Uh-oh. What'd he do?"

He waved a hand. "The same thing he always does. I don't want to talk about it. How's Mark?"

"Good. I mean. Pre-diabetic, but we're working on it. He's a real beast without his snacks, though," she shared.

He listened to stories about her daughter getting ready for college, her son on the soccer team, and Mark's weight loss journey. He shared a little about work.

Finally, she said, "So."

"Hmm?"

"You haven't said a word about Specter in two hours."

He shrugged. "What's to say? He's selfish and rude and viciously unkind."

"You two break up?"

He raised an eyebrow. He had not, once, mentioned that he and Felix had started that sort of relationship.

"What, you're still not out? It's twenty-sixteen, I figured you'd be..." She made a vague gesture. "You know. By now."

"I..." He rubbed the side of his nose to banish an itch. "I was never *not* out."

"Okay. So those girls you never slept with, they were really your girlfriends?" she asked.

He pressed his lips together.

"What? You leave girls alone, they're gonna talk," she said defensively.

"I didn't never have sex with them."

She put up a hand. "You know what, forget I mentioned anything. It's your life. I'm sorry."

He didn't understand the entire coming out process, no matter how many times he'd witnessed it. Who was he supposed to tell and what, exactly, should he have told them?

"We didn't break up," he settled on saying. "I'm just mad at him."

"I'm sure he deserves it. He always was a bitch."

Sunshine didn't say anything.

"What? Am I not supposed to say that either?"

"No, he's still a bitch."

On the train ride home, he scrolled through his phone. It suggested a lot of memories, mostly photos he'd taken of Felix slaving over some costume or other over the years. He'd always painstakingly make couples' costumes if he was seeing someone or go all out on something for himself.

He'd still been cursed last Halloween and had stayed home, likely drugging himself to sleep.

Every other Halloween meant a small party while the children of the Weller trick-or-treated, then heading to the Black Diamond for the rest of the night, no matter the day of the week.

Sunshine huffed and put his phone away.

It didn't give Felix any right to act the way he had.

Sunshine went into his apartment without stopping over to say hi. He locked his door, which he never did if he was home and awake. He started to cook dinner, chicken thighs roasted with herb butter and assorted vegetables. He heated up a little bit of leftover rice to go with it.

The doorknob rattled.

He ignored it.

Someone knocked.

Someone.

Felix knocked. No one else would try to let themselves in.

The door rattled again. "Sunshine?"

He stared intently into the microwave, watching the rice.

"Sunshine, come on, open the door," Felix demanded, irritated.

The microwave beeped.

Sunshine checked the rice, then put it in for a little longer. He peeked into the oven.

Felix slammed his fist on the door. "Come on!" A little while later, he threatened, "You know I can open the door!"

He took the chicken out of the oven, plated his meal, and went over to the couch to eat. He turned on the TV and turned up the volume much louder than he would have normally. He turned it down after he felt reasonably sure Felix had gone back to his apartment.

The chicken had come out exactly right.

Work would be undoubtedly awkward tomorrow. He tried not to think about it.

He didn't sleep well and decided to go in early when he woke up for the fourth time that night around five a.m.

The silence of the office first thing in the morning had a strange quality. A place between worlds, a workplace without workers.

The stray cat that everyone had come to call "Specter's Dad" eyed him from where it had stretched out on the rug. The cat hadn't yet come to trust anyone but Rose, who had an unfair advantage as a fey. Felix resented that.

The cat stretched and yawned, then leaped to the top of the bookshelf. It liked to watch the office happenings from there.

Sunshine made himself a cup of coffee then went upstairs to check his email.

Later, people trickled in.

Felix showed up around ten. He knocked before he came into the office, which unsettled Sunshine.

"What?"

He stepped halfway through the door. "I'd like to make an apology if you'll have it."

Sunshine raised an eyebrow.

"If you'd like, I can go."

Sunshine almost told him to stop being ridiculous, but he

looked so somber. He'd even dressed up, a button-down, jacket, and trousers, a far cry from his usual casual office wear of jeans and combat boots. "Come in."

He stepped inside, closed the door, and presented Sunshine with an envelope made of thick, high-quality paper and sealed with wax. "I apologize for what I called you. I crossed a line saying that. I knew it would hurt you and I did it on purpose. It was wrong."

"What's this?" Sunshine looked at the envelope. Embossed with his personal seal, the mark of a prince of Hell, the only heir to the Reinhart-Queen dynasty, and an Antichrist, though Felix denied that part of himself. A crowned serpent curled around an orb, a stag standing atop the orb with flowers draped in its antlers.

Someone had drawn it for him long ago, a human friend from his childhood.

"A written apology. The promise I won't do it again."

"Sometimes I forget your parents raised you to have manners."

Felix didn't smile. "I realize that the way I behave toward you is...unbecoming. You tolerate me so much better than I deserve."

"Felix, come on."

"No, I mean it, Sunshine. I treat you poorly and you have the grace to let me."

Sunshine tapped the envelope. He placed it in the drawer of his desk. "I'll read it later."

Felix nodded. "Do you accept my apology?"

Apologies from Felix came rarely, and apologies of this sort came almost never. And he looked so sad. "I accept."

"Thank you."

Being called a fag didn't have such a profound impact on Sunshine that he couldn't recover from it; it had happened hundreds of times. It was that he'd asked Felix not to call him that and Felix had agreed not to.

Felix stood with his hands clasped in front of him. He nodded, then headed to his desk.

Sunshine came around and met him before he could sit. "You know why I was mad, right?"

Felix nodded.

"Say it."

"I said I wouldn't, and then I did. I said I'd be careful, and I wasn't."

Sunshine nodded. He swallowed.

"I just...I really...I don't want to fuck this up. Any of it."

"Including Halloween?"

Felix raked a hand through his hair. "Don't get me started on Halloween!"

Sunshine rubbed his arm. "You see the email from NY-AM?"

Felix shook his head and turned on his computer.

"Burglary in the Obscure Artefacts wing of the Holtzman Gallery."

Felix rolled his eyes and threw back his head with a groan. "Again? We just did this last year."

"Oh, they already caught them, that charm you set up worked like a...well. Like a charm." Sunshine smiled. "It's just a thank you."

"Undergrads?"

"Undergrads," Sunshine confirmed.

"No one's so uniquely stupid and reckless as teenagers away from home for the first time," Felix mused.

Sunshine returned to his desk.

When Felix went to get lunch, Sunshine read the note, a sincere apology in Felix's best handwriting, a Spenserian script almost identical to his father's. Phaedrus had an elegant but distinctly atypical hand and the Devil's spidery scrawl bore no influence on Felix's penmanship. He returned the letter to its envelope and placed it in the most recent photo album on the shelf.

Rose came upstairs while Felix was out. "Jen wanted me to bring you the mail," he said as he handed over a fistful of envelopes.

"Thanks, Rose."

"You guys going somewhere special later?"

"Hmm?"

"Mr. Specter's all dressed up."

"Oh. No."

"Oh." Rose shifted. He cleared his throat. He looked like he wanted to say something and kept glancing toward the door like he expected an interruption.

"Go ahead," Sunshine encouraged.

Rose raised his eyebrows. "Hmm?"

"Whatever it is you're not saying."

Rose sighed and twisted the end of his braid around his fingers. His periwinkle-blue cheeks darkened to a purplish hue, surely from the effort of not speaking honestly. "Fairies can't lie, you know, and it...it might not be my place to say anything, but do you know how hard it is to *not* say something?"

"Then say it."

"Mr. Specter is not...He's *not* nice to you, Mr. Sunshine."

"No," Sunshine agreed.

"You deserve someone who treats you well."

"I appreciate the concern, Rose, I do. But there's nothing to worry about."

Rose pressed his lips together.

"If you knew where we had been, you'd understand that this is...appropriate, perhaps, is the right word," Sunshine assured. "Growing pains?"

Rose rubbed the back of his neck.

"You can rest well knowing you've done your due diligence. It's good to watch out for other people."

The young man gave the smallest smile. "I've just, I've had boyfriends that weren't nice to me either...They always say sorry."

"Apology is best measured by whether the offense is repeated. Specter's apologies are rare but reliable."

Rose nodded. "I didn't mean to be nosy."

"It's fine."

He scuffed his toe on the carpet. "Anyway..."

"Of course," Sunshine said. He almost said thank you, but fairy manners prohibited it. Rose only had one fairy parent and Sunshine hadn't figured out how much he adhered to Court etiquette.

Rose went back downstairs.

Felix took an unusually long time getting lunch, considering the deli he'd gone to was only three blocks down. He returned with a paper bag and a small bouquet already in a vase. He set down the bag and offered the flowers to Sunshine.

No one had ever given Sunshine flowers before. He stared at them. Half a dozen pink and white roses with a few sprays of baby's breath, not ostentatious or obsequious. He glanced up at Felix.

Quietly, Felix admitted, "They didn't have what I wanted, but I...I wanted to get you something."

"Oh."

"It." Felix licked his lips. "It seemed like a good idea, but now it feels weird."

It was absolutely bizarre. "No, it's...it's very sweet, Felix."

"Red felt too overt. Like a proposition more than an apology. Pink and white was a little softer but still affectionate."

"No, I understand." Sunshine glanced around the room looking for somewhere to put them. He cleared off a spot on his desk and placed them down. He'd given people flowers before, but those situations had always been clear cut: a recital, a date, a funeral. He couldn't call to mind a single clear instance or how the receiver had reacted. "Am I...Should I...What do you when you get flowers?

No one's ever given me flowers."

"I don't know, I think you just say thank you."

"Oh. Thank you."

Felix opened the bag and handed over Sunshine's share. "They were out of pastrami."

"What!"

"I know! Anyway, I got you roast beef."

Sunshine took the sandwich, not devastated by the change.

Felix handed him a packet of latkes. "They're fresh."

Sunshine grinned. He devoured all three without out condiments, his sandwich forgotten. The latkes gone, he returned his attention to the sandwich. "Out of pastrami?"

"Listen, I don't know, I don't ask questions. Elsa said 'nisht mer pastrami' and I said, 'okay, Elsa' and ordered something else."

"You remember the time she threw you out?"

Felix scowled. "I don't think wanting white bread is such a crime."

"It gets soggy."

"Maybe I want a soggy sandwich!"

"Deviant," Sunshine accused.

Felix flashed a smile. "Would you like me otherwise?"

Sunshine ate his sandwich instead of answering. He stared at the roses as he chewed, deciding how he felt. Finally, when he'd eaten and cleaned up, he leaned over to sniff them. He sighed. "You remember how they used to smell?"

Felix nodded.

They spent the rest of the day finalizing their notes and evidence to hand over to the police for the tea shop case. The right police, of course, who'd direct the case to the right judges who knew the Community and would trust the report of a reputable paranormal detective agency.

A few times, mundane police had come to Sunshine and Specter Paranormal Detective Agency as a last-ditch effort on a desperate or long-cold case, but they always had trouble stomaching any evidence provided to them by unorthodox means. Usually, they turned those cases down now.

They sent over all they had gathered. An uncomfortable feeling settled over Sunshine when he caught another glance at the crime scene photos. If Tate hadn't gotten in the way, if Felix hadn't pushed her, would he have taken Felix's statement as anything other than the need to blow off steam?

Instead of deciding if he liked flowers as a gift, he would have been surrounded by them at a funeral. Antichrist or not, a train would have squashed him like a bug.

He dropped the case file into their archive, not caring if it went in the wrong spot, and went over to wrap his arms around Felix.

Felix flinched, then relaxed, and leaned against him. "What?"

If Felix had tried to jump in front of a train last year, Sunshine would have burned him till he bled trying to pull him back. "You know you're the world to me."

"I shouldn't be."

"You're uniquely positioned to hurt me more than anything in any realm. You know that's why...you know I had to be firm with you."

Felix giggled nervously. He knotted his fist in the front of Sunshine's shirt, curled against him. "I know."

Sunshine squeezed him harder. When the tightness in his chest passed, he asked, "So you're going to take me to dinner, too, right?"

"Do you ever think about anything other than food?"

"Food is, without doubt, the most exquisite thing this realm has to offer."

"You haven't done enough drugs, then."

Sunshine snorted.

"Or been fucked right."

He rolled his eyes at that. He pulled away from Felix. "Do you ever think about anything other than drugs and sex?"

"Sure, sometimes I think about blowing my brains out."

"Specter, you can't joke about stuff like that right now."

"I have to. Where'd you want to go to dinner?"

"I was just teasing."

"Hmm." Felix looked him over, then went back to his desk. "Can you fix that file you threw in there? It doesn't go in that section."

"Of course, master. I live only to serve."

Felix flipped him off without looking at him.

They didn't go out for dinner. Sunshine didn't want to make a big deal out of this. He didn't want acts of kindness to become restitution for poor conduct. They walked home together, hand in hand for the whole five or so miles. They wandered through Central Park.

"Remember when all the *Times* did was write about murders here?" Felix mused as he looked around the park.

It had gotten dark already.

Sunshine nodded absently. "You think Rose's mom is one of the fairies that held court here?"

Felix shook his head. "He's from Connecticut."

Sunshine couldn't help but wrinkle his nose.

"Oh, you never thought about retiring to a nice little town in Connecticut? We could afford a good piece of land, you know. No neighbors. No hustle or fuss or crowd."

"You'd wither away."

Felix made a face. "You've seen Pickering."

"And you were restless there. Imagine how antsy you'd get holed up in a cute little Colonial with me." He realized he'd assumed that Felix meant for him to come along. They'd never talked about moving in together.

"That farmhouse in New Avondale was still for sale last time I looked."

"The haunted one!"

Felix shrugged. "I'm not afraid of ghosts."

Sunshine shook his head. "There were like ten people in that whole town."

"It was dirt cheap."

"'Cause it's *haunted*."

"*Was* haunted. We got rid of the ghosts. And they did nice upkeep on it. It doesn't need work or anything. Maybe a little landscaping! Didn't I say there was a great space for a garden? On that slope in the back? Imagine how it'd look with a terrace and a little patio."

"Felix..." Sunshine started to worry. A quiet, domestic life in rural Connecticut would not sit well at all with Felix.

"I put in a bid and...uh. You know, they took it."

"You bought a house!"

"It's not done yet! You're the one who always wants to get out of the city!"

Terror that Felix had bought the house for him overwhelmed him. "I've never said that!"

"You do, you always want to go on vacation."

"I said that like...twice. Vacations are *normal*."

"So is buying a house! Now, you know, we can go for a weekend whenever we want. And I thought..."

"Hmm?" Sunshine prompted.

"I thought Papa and Bibi might...Might need somewhere to go. Somewhere quiet. Calm. Papa should be resting, not running a university. And we'd be closer to each other."

Delight replaced terror. "You're such a *daddy's boy*."

Felix scowled.

Sunshine wrapped him up in a hug and lifted him off his feet. He nuzzled against his throat. "You *are*, you love them so much."

"Shut up."

"You're such a nice boy!" Sunshine cooed.

"I'm not. I'm an awful degenerate."

"A total bitch."

"An addict."

"A slut," Sunshine added.

Felix giggled. "You know if anyone else said that I'd—"

"Already be fucking them?" Sunshine guessed.

"Oh, and I'm the mean one!"

Sunshine smiled.

"Put me down."

Sunshine placed him on the ground. He twisted his fingers with his. "I don't have anything for you to eat at home. I didn't take out enough to defrost for two people."

"With the way you cook, there's definitely enough for two."

"I mean it. I was planning on staying mad at you."

"I'll figure something out. I wasn't going to come over."

"No?"

"I have to do laundry."

"You did laundry last week," Sunshine said. Felix's laundry got done once a month, at best.

"Then I'm doing something clandestine and disreputable."

Inside, Felix lingered at the doorway of Sunshine's apartment. He didn't let go of Sunshine's hand. He jangled his keys in the other. "We're okay?" he asked.

Sunshine leaned in as though he'd kiss him, then blew a raspberry against Felix's cheek.

Felix smacked him. "Fuck you."

Sunshine laughed.

"No, fuck you, Sunshine!" Felix declared. He stomped back to his apartment without a glance back.

Sunshine made himself another solitary dinner. He tried not to dwell on the accusation that he only thought about food. He didn't think Felix meant it in a serious or displeased way, but he'd had partners who'd made similar statements and meant them unhappily.

It wasn't that he didn't like sex, he did, or that he didn't think about it, he did that, too. Something about it, though, didn't exactly consume him the way people expected it to. His affections tended to run warm instead of hot, more prone to cuddling and handholding than passionate lovemaking.

Not that he couldn't!

Though some people had accused him of impotence.

Or of being in the closet.

Or sometimes even of being straight.

Normally, it didn't bother him. In fact, it almost never crossed his mind to wonder if he didn't like sex enough, but sometimes certain things sparked the thought.

Tonight, he wondered more about the unfairness of things: that he could perform with ease but didn't always see the need, and that Felix desperately wanted sexual gratification but struggled to achieve it.

He lay awake with his hands folded over his stomach wondering what, if anything, to do. Resigned to a second sleepless night, he spent hours on his phone attempting to better educate himself on the matter overall.

Around three a.m. he let himself into Felix's apartment and headed toward his bedroom. The lights were off, but he could see the blue glow of his phone. And, not to mention, Felix had woken him up enough times that this seemed fair play. He pushed open the bedroom door.

A glass dart whizzed toward him, whistling faintly.

He closed the door in time and heard it *thunk* into the wood. "What the fuck!"

"I'm sorry!" Felix rushed the door and threw it open. He danced around the broken dart and threw his arms around Sunshine. "Oh, I thought...! You know, don't scare a girl like that, living all alone in this city!"

Garfield appeared and gobbled the glass from the floor.

Sunshine rubbed his back.

"What are you doing here? It's the middle of the fucking night," Felix said into his chest.

"I wanted to talk. Check in."

"About what?"

Sunshine hadn't played this scenario out well in his head. "Uh."

"Well?"

"You know what? Never mind. This is stupid." Somehow, he'd thought Felix would be three steps ahead of him, that he'd already know what Sunshine wanted to talk about.

"Of course it's stupid, it's three a.m. Tell me anyway." Felix pulled back and yawned into his elbow. He stepped around Garfield and headed back to bed.

Grunting and snorking, Garfield followed him. The elemental paced around the bed, over Felix, sniffed his phone, then headed to lay on the tile floor of the kitchen.

Sunshine remained in the doorway.

Felix conjured a small orb, a smudge a fuzzy golden flow. "Darling, please, it's nearly my bedtime."

Sunshine sat cross-legged at the end of his bed. "I just was thinking."

"Dangerous. About what?" Felix encouraged from where he'd nestled into his pillows.

"Sex."

Felix wrinkled his nose. He blinked a few times. "Oh. That's...not like you."

"I know. It's sort of, well, you know, you remember how you said that you've always just been a little slow to get going and I just, I felt bad thinking that I could whenever I wanted and you can't and I know you said that it...You know, you make it seem like it's so important to you and it never has been to me. I did a lot of reading—"

"Sunshine, the point, if there is one to be had, is eluding me."

"I don't know, I feel weird about it. I thought I should check in."

"About our sex life?"

"What there is of it."

Felix opened then shut his mouth. "I know you didn't mean that the way it sounded."

"Am I doing enough?" he asked, then clarified, "To help."

Felix composed himself, eyes closed, breathing in then out, a mask of serenity. He opened his eyes. "Yes."

"I didn't know if I should be doing more."

"More than being gorgeous, attentive, honest, and mindful?"

Sunshine shrugged. "I don't think I'm good at this. At sex stuff. Like, I always just...do it. Like, without thinking about it much or trying to be good. I haven't been with a lot of people."

"You know, you get like this when you don't sleep. All..." He waggled a hand toward Sunshine. "Weird and sincere. Do you want a lude?"

"No."

Felix sighed. "Ambien?"

"No."

"An honest expression of my feelings?"

"Please."

"I've already given you one of those today."

"Please," Sunshine repeated.

"Fine, alright, soooo…Yes, I've always been like this, yes, I get a little touchy about it, and yes, when it's good, I have a great time fucking. But also, *maybe*, you know…maybe what was once simply *how I was*, a…hmm, leisurely yet mostly functional bedmate escalated into something I did to myself. Like, maybe I did a fuckton of drugs and slept with a bunch of shitbags and maybe that…had a marginal impact on my psyche and performance."

"Oh."

"So it's a work in progress, this harm-reduction thing, our sleeping together thing, but I think it's going well."

"Okay."

"Did you understand that, or do you need smaller words?"

"I think I understand."

Felix patted the pillow beside him. "The offer for a sleeping pill still stands. Tomorrow is Saturday. Won't matter how long it knocks you out for."

Sunshine shook his head. He stood to leave.

Felix flicked back the covers and rubbed his hands over the sheets, an exaggerated seduction. "Ohh, look, fresh sheets." He bit his lip and waggled his eyebrow.

Sunshine got into bed with him.

"Tell me more about what you read," Felix requested. He did it with softness and sincerity.

"I don't know." Sunshine lay back.

Felix twined around him and kissed his shoulder. "None of this is like you. You don't overthink things. I can count on one hand the number of times you've woken me up to tell me something."

Sunshine didn't know what to say. He'd swallowed a lot of information already tonight and didn't know how much of it he could digest.

"Can I tell you what I think?"

"Please." His voice cracked.

"Sunshine."

"No, I. Just."

Felix ran his fingers through Sunshine's hair. "You are steady, Sunshine. You are serenity personified. You don't usually care what people think about you. I've never met anybody so even in all my life. A person who didn't know you as well might think that means you never worry. You do though. You..." Felix kissed his shoulder. "You don't belong here. You know it. It scares you."

"That's not what I read about."

"I'm getting there," Felix assured. "You never felt like you belonged. Not among humans or creatures. You don't belong with the angels anymore either. And there's another community now that you're not quite belonging to either. You never told anyone you dated men. Never had a boyfriend that you took out like you took out girls. It's not shame, though. It's because when you look at the queer community, it's just one more place you never saw yourself."

Sunshine sniffed and rubbed his nose.

"It wasn't so bad back in the day, you know, when all these things were hush-hush anyway. But now it's...loud and it's proud and holy shit is it sexual. And you aren't. Oh, you *can* and sometimes you even want to. But you know, Sunshine, darling..."

Sunshine's eyes hurt. He wasn't crying. His face was just wet. "What?"

"It's not about sex. It's not about your partners. It's about *you*. *You're* queer. Or bi or pan or demi or ace, or however it is that you identify if you identify at all. You belong here. I see you and you belong."

"Thanks."

Felix squeezed him. He said, "You're...No. Never mind."

"What?"

"You'll get mad."

"No, go ahead."

"Ah. Are you sure?"

"Specter, before I die from anticipation," Sunshine insisted weakly, his voice still a little congested.

"You really are a remarkably interesting fag."

Sunshine snorted.

"Absolutely my favorite one."

"Shut up," Sunshine told him. He turned onto his side and looped an arm around Felix. "Thank you."

"Yeah, I kind of..." Felix sighed. "You know, I thought it was weird. You taking it so hard. Not that...not that I was right to do it. Or that you were wrong to be upset. It's just that mean names never bothered you. Water off a duck's back. This...this makes sense. It wasn't me calling you a fag that struck such a nerve. It was that I said you weren't a good one."

"Are these new sheets?"

Felix had the grace to accept his abrupt change of topic. "I only had one set and you made such a thing out of me not changing them."

"I'm flattered."

"You should be."

"I'm also concerned."

Felix clicked his tongue. "Pish-posh."

"Mary Poppins and Burt."

"Why do you want me in drag so bad?"

"I could be Mary Poppins," Sunshine offered, "But only one of us is practically perfect in every way."

Felix groaned. He rolled out of Sunshine's arms. "Fucking Christ, Sunshine."

Sunshine followed him and gathered him close. He blew a raspberry against his throat.

"Ugh, don't, don't get me worked up. It's time for bed."

October 29

Saturday

Sunshine didn't know what Felix had gotten into, but he'd gotten into something for sure. He had thrown things all over his apartment, knocked over chairs, flipped his coffee table.

Sunshine had heard him flip the coffee table. It had woken him up and prompted him to go next door.

Garfield cowered in the kitchen sink.

Sunshine went over to pat the elemental on the head. "Good boy. You're okay."

Garfield didn't look so sure.

Something crashed in the bedroom.

Sunshine headed that way. "Specter?" He stepped inside to see clothes and shoes scattered everywhere.

Felix emerged from his closet and threw a shoe at Sunshine. "What do *you* want?"

"Uh. I...You're making an awful lot of noise in here."

Felix threw the other shoe.

Both shoes had missed, probably because of how shaky Felix was. He looked about ready to rip himself out of his skin.

"Felix."

"No, I...! What do you want?"

"I wanted to check on you."

Felix threw a hanger at him. "Check on me! Fuck you *check on me*."

Sunshine crept closer.

"Check on me! What the *fuck* do I need you to check on me for!"

"Take a breath."

"I can't!"

Sunshine nodded. "Okay." He'd gotten within arm's reach of Felix. "Come here."

Felix backed toward the closet. "No. I. I need to get this done."

Carefully, Sunshine asked, "Get what done?" He looked at the clothes strewn around the room.

Felix swatted at him. "Not a single fucking good idea."

Sunshine reminded, "Felix, we talked about Halloween."

"Bullshit we talked about it."

About a week ago, they'd still had no good costume ideas. They'd agreed not to worry about it this year. Try again next year, they'd said. A whole year to think of something good.

"Fuck you we talked about it."

"Felix, just come here."

Felix pushed him then grabbed onto the front of Sunshine's sweatshirt. He gave him a shake. "Fuck you."

Sunshine wrapped his arms around him and drew him close. He didn't have to drag him or keep a tight hold on him.

Felix folded against him.

"What's wrong?"

The demon let out a cracked sob. "I don't want to wait another year."

Sunshine rubbed his back. "Why didn't you say anything?"

Felix pressed his forehead against hard against Sunshine's chest. "All the good couple's costumes are for straight people."

Sunshine bit his tongue to hold in a laugh. He took in a deep breath. "I told you I'd do drag if you didn't want to."

"I don't want either of us to do drag."

Felix had never shied away from a dress and he had never let gender get in the way of a really good costume.

"Why not?" Sunshine asked.

"I don't know. I don't. I just." He burrowed his face harder against Sunshine and balled his fists in Sunshine's sweatshirt.

Sunshine kept rubbing his back, letting all the calmness he could gather flow from him into Felix. It wouldn't kill his high, but it would settle him.

"You're like a human benzo," Felix mumbled.

"I'm not human. I'm like a divine benzo," Sunshine corrected.

"Must be why it works faster."

He got Felix into bed and started to clean up around the apartment. He didn't put everything away, but he righted the furniture and put everything into piles so Felix would have an easier time of it tomorrow. He helped Garfield out of the sink. He settled in next to Felix for the night.

In the morning, he woke to an empty bed.

He found Felix crying in the bathtub. A weak, whimpering sniffle that indicated he'd been at it for a while.

Sunshine sat on the bathmat. "You ready to talk?"

"I didn't...I shouldn't have." Felix sucked in a breath. "I didn't *want* to do that. Take those. I just." He sniffled. "I had to."

"Okay."

"I."

"Go ahead."

"These *fucking* Halloween costumes."

Sunshine dipped his fingers in the bathwater. "Tell me."

Felix shook his head.

Sunshine pulled off his sweatshirt, then scooted out of his boxers. "Make room."

Felix pulled his knees up to his chest and slipped toward the back of the tub.

Sunshine slid into the tub. He placed a hand on Felix's knee. "Hon, you can tell me."

Felix put his hand over Sunshine's. "I. You know. Maggie just came out. And she's trying so hard and she...How...How am I gonna put on a dress and pretend to be a girl when she's...she *is* a girl and it been so hard for her."

Sunshine clucked his tongue. Maggie was more a friend of Felix's than of his, which could be said of most people. Felix went out and chatted and danced, and Sunshine sat and watched and made sure everyone got home. He did feel safe saying, "Maggie probably wouldn't mind. She loves drag shows."

"It just...It felt wrong. Rude. And I..."

"And you...?"

"And is it *so* fucking awful that I want to do a couple's costume where we aren't a man and a woman?"

"No," Sunshine assured.

"I don't want to do weird pedophile Batman and Robin, either."

"Okay."

"I just...I want like a normal couple that is also men and isn't like...fucking. Fucking gross or obnoxious." Felix pulled in a shaky breath. "I don't know. I don't. I know it's stupid."

"Frog and Toad."

Felix looked up like Sunshine had cussed him out. "What?"

"Frog and Toad. They're a couple."

"You...you were just sitting on that this whole time?"

Sunshine shrugged. "I didn't know you wanted to do two guys."

"Get out of the tub. I'm going to drown myself."

Sunshine splashed him gently. "Next time maybe just tell me what's bothering you."

"I prefer to crush up and snort a bunch of pills, thank you very much."

"You look like shit by the way."

"I feel like shit." He raked a hand through his hair, making it stick up. He pointed out, "We don't have time for Frog and Toad."

"Bert and Ernie."

"They're not a couple."

Sunshine made a face. "They're a couple."

"Tell that to the Sesame Street people. They almost sued someone over it."

Sunshine said, "Kirk and Spock."

"Real couples, Sunshine. Some...some goddamn representation!"

"Okay, so what, like *Brokeback Mountain?*"

Felix groaned.

"You're right, you'd make a terrible cowboy," Sunshine said. "Renly and Loras? Achilles and Patroclus."

"Notice how many of those people die," Felix said.

"Bert and Ernie are still alive. And screw what Sesame Street says. I know a queer relationship when I see it."

"I don't want to paint myself yellow."

"You don't have to. We can just do the shirts. Lowkey, easy, cute."

Felix sighed. "I hate you."

Sunshine said, "You should have told me what was wrong."

"You know I'm irrational!"

"Did you talk to Dr. Reza about it?"

"I haven't gone."

"Specter!"

Felix sunk lower in the tub. "I haven't been since the thing with the train. I don't know how to talk about it. How do you talk about that?"

"Specter, you can't...You." Sunshine sighed. He made himself stop to gather his thoughts. Scolding him wouldn't do any good, it would just make him defensive. "We're okay. And you're okay, too. This was just...kind of a funny spell. We'll go get shirts and do Halloween and then you'll set up a session with Dr. Reza, okay?"

"I thought you were the stupid one."

"Well, congratulations, now we're both stupid," Sunshine told him. "Okay?"

"Fine," Felix sulked.

"I love you."

Felix pinched him.

Sunshine smacked his hand.

"I love you, too," Felix grumbled.

Felix moped through the rest of their bath, barely ate, and

came close to starting a scene in three different stores as they looked for Bert and Ernie shirts. They had no luck and ended up buying plain shirts and fabric paint.

Felix stopped painting his about halfway through, locked himself in the bathroom, and wept for about an hour.

Sunshine finished painting the shirts.

When Felix emerged, he didn't want to talk about it.

The shirts, Sunshine thought, came out really good.

Even Felix admitted that they'd be fine. He stared at them, eyes red and runny, his cheeks blotchy for a while after that.

"I'm sorry," Sunshine said.

"Hmm?"

"I didn't...you know, I didn't think it was such a big deal."

Felix glanced at the shirts. "It's not."

"You almost got us kicked out of a store today."

"Yeah."

Sunshine waited.

"That's...it's not about the shirts. Or Halloween." Felix glanced around the room, at everything except Sunshine. "I just. I've been trying, you know! Being nicer, not doing drugs, all that. But...how does something so *stupid* set me off?"

"Shit happens, Felix."

"I've never tried not to use before. Sometimes I think...Sometimes I think I can't. That I'm really just...you know. An addict. That it's pointless to try to be anything else."

Sunshine squeezed his shoulder. "You've never let anyone but yourself control your life."

"I guess that's what happens when you have a murderous stalker for the first two and a half decades of your life."

"Yeah, and you dealt with that pretty effectively. If you're not going to let the ire of Heaven determine your path, then I don't think you'll let a couple of crushed up Ambien get in your way either."

Eyes still on the shirt, Felix said, "You know I've done meth, right?"

"I might remember what you've done better than you do at this point," Sunshine said. "You could go to a support group."

"I'd rather die."

"You might."

Felix glared.

"Have you talked to Dr. Reza about it?"

Felix shrugged.

"Maybe start there."

"Does any of this bother you?"

"It bothers me that it hurts you."

"That's a half-truth if I ever heard one."

Sunshine answered, fully aware of how delusional he sounded, "If something ever happened to you, your father would wind up with me. You know it, I know it, so part of me...I just...I can't rationalize a world without you, so I choose to believe you'll always be here. Because you would never do that to me. You'd never give me to your father like that."

"Maybe you should go to therapy, too."

"That or we can go out in a blaze of glory together. I bet we'd do something heroic. Don't you?"

Felix put an arm around his waist and leaned against him. "I want to take another bath."

"Go ahead."

"Come with me."

"I was going to make something to eat," Sunshine said. He regretted it immediately. All he thought about was food.

"Come in after. I'll be in for a while." His arm slipped off Sunshine's waist and he shuffled toward the bathroom.

Sunshine ate, then joined Felix in the bath.

Felix reached over, rubbed his stomach, and asked, "When are you due?"

"Don't be a bitch."

Felix grinned at him and sloshed closer. He took both of Sunshine's hands in his. "Why aren't you fat? How do you eat the way you do and stay the way you are?"

Sunshine shrugged. "He made me this way. Besides, I've gained a little weight."

"Oh, yeah, what? Ten pounds? Over how many years? You still look like a fucking statue."

Sunshine sighed. The first thing he'd ever eaten on Earth he'd found in the trash. He'd lived like that for years, decades, before Felix had captured him.

Phaedrus, bless their heart, had given him his first taste of a home-cooked meal.

Felix kissed his palm. "What'd you make me for lunch?"

"Nothing."

Felix pouted.

"I had a grilled cheese. You know those don't last. I'll make you one later."

Felix kissed his palm then his wrist. "With bacon?"

"You don't have any bacon."

"You smell like bacon."

"That's because *I* have bacon. At *my* apartment."

"So then you can make me one with bacon."

Sunshine scooped up water and dumped it over his head.

"Oh, don't! Don't, you *know* the color washes out!"

Sunshine combed the wet hair out of Felix's face. It had faded to a washed-out greenish-blue over the month. "You were going to make me redo it tonight anyway."

Felix hadn't asked but Sunshine knew he'd want to look his best for Halloween. He ran his fingers through his hair. "Do you think I should let it go back to normal?"

"It's your hair."

"I don't know, it's a little...I don't know. Isn't it a little much?"

"Felix, you are the definition of a little much. I don't think it's the hair that does it," Sunshine said.

Felix sighed.

Sunshine made him a grilled cheese, with bacon.

Felix never did ask him to redo his hair. Even when Sunshine offered to do it, he only sighed and shrugged.

Halloween night, about a dozen friends came to Felix's to assist in the ritual of giving out candy to the children of the Weller Building.

The kids in the building treated the day like Christmas and the Fourth of July. The whole Community did. The one day of the year where they didn't need to hide their least human parts. The little girl in 3A could drop her glamour and show her wings. The twins in 7D could take off their hats. The teenage huldra in 4B could finally wear that cute backless top she's bought in the summer.

Felix had spent the last week curating the best candies stores had to offer, always full-sized and never some half-assed brand like Hershey's. Chocolates and confections that a child couldn't appreciate.

He'd talked Sunshine into making cookies and homemade caramels. "Like the ones Bibi used to bring home," he'd begged.

Sunshine hadn't needed much talking into. He'd wrapped the cookies and candies in the little festive bags Felix had bought and piled them into a bag beside Felix's fancy chocolates.

More than enough for all the kids in the Weller, so Sunshine didn't say anything when James Kelly dipped his hand into the bowl.

June saw Sunshine watching the vampire and smiled. He came over to stand beside Sunshine, who'd stationed himself at the counter to set out snacks. "You know any other vampires with a sweet tooth?"

"Can't say I do."

Everyone they'd invited had shown up.

Sunshine left the snacks. He kissed Felix's cheek and said, "Babe?"

Felix gave him a funny look. "Hmm?"

"Can you do me a favor?"

"What?"

Sunshine put an arm around him and pulled him close. "We don't have any napkins."

"What?" Felix frowned.

"Please, hon, they're all finger foods and you know, your couch is new..."

"Are you serious?"

"Please, just, real quick, run out and grab some. Please, please," Sunshine pleaded softly. He tightened his arm around Felix.

Felix groaned. "Fine!"

"I love you."

Felix grunted, grabbed his jacket, and headed out.

Once Sunshine knew he'd left the hall, he cleared his throat and called, "Hey!"

Their guests turned toward him.

"I need three things from all of you."

They shifted and looked at each other.

"You're gonna tell Felix our costumes are really cute, and that Bert and Ernie are a great gay couple. You're gonna tell him how nice it is to take things easy this year. And third, if single fucking one of you offers anything stronger than an aspirin, I will absolutely end you."

The whole room shuffled and coughed.

Sunshine directed a few pointed looks.

June took a large sip of his drink and subtly tucked something into James Kelly's pocket.

James Kelly quietly hissed, "I told you."

June looked a little embarrassed. He took another sip of his drink and stared at his shoes.

"I appreciate it. Uh, everyone has a drink, right? Soda and juice in the fridge if the bar's not interesting. Plenty of snacks, too!" Sunshine added cheerily.

People fell back into their conversations.

Rose came over to get a snack and asked, "Are you sure it's okay for me to be here?"

"This part of Halloween is usually tame. I just...I want to set Felix up for success."

Rose gave a nervous nod.

Sunshine assured, "Ask Tate. She came last year. She'll tell you we're harmless."

"They're absolute deviants!" Tate called from across the room.

Rose chuckled.

Sunshine offered him a plate. "Snacks." He nodded towards the carved fruits with cream cheese dip; he'd never met a fairy that could refuse a treat like that.

Rose immediately took a heaping serving, then looked at Sunshine. His cheeks darkened.

Sunshine offered him a smile. "I made extra."

Rose smiled back.

Sunshine took his drink, a little proud that his smile worked on fairies and humans alike. Despite Felix's denials, Sunshine would have bet the smile worked on him, too.

He felt very sure of it when Felix came back with napkins.

"Here," the demon handed them over.

Sunshine tilted his head toward the island.

Felix set out the napkins, first carelessly tossing them down, then going back to straighten them out.

Sunshine grinned at him. "Thank you."

Felix looked at his shoes.

Sunshine kissed him. "You didn't miss any trick-or-treaters."

They played a movie in the background while they handed out candy and when the stream of trick-or-treaters dried up, they started to plot their next move.

Not everyone went to the Diamond. June and James Kelly had other plans. Rose and a few others called it a night and headed home. Half a dozen of them, though, set out to the Diamond. The Village Parade had ended, but that didn't mean people weren't still out.

Sunshine placidly followed Felix around and got compared to a faithful hound a few times. He sipped his drink and smiled. He smiled the most at people he knew would offer Felix something he shouldn't be taking right now, or people he knew saw Felix as a hookup and little else.

They all gave him the same nervous smile back and slunk away after a short conversation.

Not, of course, that Felix couldn't have gone with them if he'd wanted, but the line between having a good time and getting used tended to blur for him.

Felix elbowed him. "Stop with that."

"Hmm?"

"You're scaring everyone away."

Sunshine smiled.

"Stop!" Felix insisted. "Just because we're...doing our thing doesn't mean you get to loom behind me and scare people away."

"If you're going to sleep with other people, you should at least pick people who will be nice to you," Sunshine said.

Felix rolled his eyes. "Sure, and that's not jealousy?"

"Uh. In the sense that I'm protective of your general wellbeing, yes, I have long felt a mild, possessive resentment toward the people who don't treat you well. In a sexual sense, no."

Felix smirked. "But you wouldn't, would you?"

"Don't get mean."

Felix leaned against him. "On that note, and in a serious kind of way...I do think I need to sleep with someone else."

"Need to?"

"Uh. Yeah. Like. Being with you is the only good, healthy sexual experience I've had in years, and I don't want to, to make that correlation into a causation. Like. I don't want to over-associate you with the *only* good sex I've had recently. You know? Like. It's not *you*, it's how you are with me, and I don't want to get it in my head that you're the only one I can get off with, or you know, get off and not feel like shit after. Cause that seems dangerous, psychologically speaking, to make that association. In both directions. I don't want to do that to you or to fucking," Felix rambled. "Cause I do like to..."

His eyes sort of glazed over and he stared out over the dance floor, crowded with every kind of costume known to man.

Not concerned but slightly confused, Sunshine asked, "Do you want to see other people?"

"No. Not really. I'm not interested in dating presently. Uh. We're still settling into what we have. And I don't think I could balance more than one committed relationship at a time."

Sunshine didn't think Felix could either. He felt a little relieved, which surprised him. He hadn't expected to feel that way about the idea of Felix dating other people. He didn't feel possessive of Felix in that way, but maybe this feeling came from being overprotective. Felix had been sort of delicate lately.

Maybe more than lately. Maybe it had just taken a long time for Sunshine to realize it.

"I was, uh. I was thinking of hiring someone. Just to make sure." Felix shrugged. He rested his head on Sunshine's shoulder. "I don't know." He wiggled his shoulder into Sunshine's armpit.

Sunshine put an arm around him.

"Well?"

"Hmm?"

"What do you think?"

"I think if that's what you want to do and it will make you feel better about yourself or us, then you should do it. I think if you're scared and trying to figure out why, but you're not really sure, you should wait."

"It really wouldn't bother you?"

"I don't think so. I mean. You're being honest and open and we're discussing it ahead of time. I think I'd be kind of hurt if you did it without letting me know, or if I thought it was because I'm...I'm not as active as you'd like."

People had gone behind his back before, and Felix had done loads of other kinds of things without telling Sunshine. He tried not to think of how much it would hurt to find out Felix hadn't told him how he'd felt.

Felix hugged him hard. "I can never tell if I want to rebel against society's cishet monogamous patriarchy that treats submissive partners like property, or if I want to rebel against the stereotype that queer men are only in it for the sex and can't commit to a loving, stable relationship."

"I'm sure there's a balance in there."

Felix tightened his arms. "There is. I just don't know what I want. I mean. I know what I want."

"Which is?"

"A kiss. And another drink."

Sunshine pecked him on the mouth. "Finish that drink first."

Felix brought the straw up to his mouth and slurped the dregs of drink and melted ice as loudly as possible. He handed Sunshine the glass. "Thank you."

Sunshine kissed him again. His mouth was cold and tasted faintly of Sprite. "Same thing?"

Felix nodded.

Sunshine headed toward the bar.

Felix found someone else to hang all over. He had his hands

folded on Maggie's shoulder and his chin on his hands. Together they sort of looked like a modeling shoot, since Felix had skin as pale as the moon and Maggie's was a deep, cool brown.

Then, suddenly, Sunshine realized why the image looked familiar. The rock star and the model, the saturation turned up to extremes.

Maggie had inched her way out of the closet, one slightly feminine detail at a time. Testing the waters with manicures and growing out her hair, then dabbling in makeup and flirting with a more colorful wardrobe, until she had told everyone her name.

Sunshine didn't blame her for treading carefully.

He tried to hand Felix his drink, but he leaned over and sipped out of the straw instead of taking the glass.

"Maggie, did you want something? Sunshine can go get you something."

She looked at Sunshine, her eyes lined with dramatic neon blue. She'd dressed as some anime or cartoon character that looked familiar, but Sunshine couldn't name. "No, thanks. You shouldn't let him boss you around like that."

"Sunshine likes it when I boss him around," Felix half-purred.

"Is that what you two get up to when you play ghost hunters?" she asked.

"First of all, we are paranormal detectives, and second, Maggie, haven't you heard? Mr. Sunshine and I are engaged to be married."

"Bullshit." She looked at Sunshine, waiting for him to deny it.

He wished he could tell her one way or another, but he had no idea if Felix intended to marry him. He had drawn out jokes like this for decades. He'd spent most of the seventies and up until eighty-three telling new acquaintances that Sunshine's full name was Jürgen Wolfgang von Sunshine the Fifth and that his uncle was a well-to-do count in Bavaria.

Not many people had believed him, thankfully.

"Believe it or not, Sunshine and I have stepped out together rather officially," Felix insisted.

"Look at you, living the dream. You caught yourself a straight."

Sunshine didn't know what to say. He sipped Felix's drink. He could tell her that he'd been queer for longer than she'd been alive, but that probably wouldn't get anywhere productive. He thought about asking about her ex, but that was downright cruel and perhaps evidence that he'd spent too much time with Felix.

"Hope it lasts," she said, a little bitter, a little wistful.

"You know, you get *mean* sometimes, darling," Felix chided.

"Nice coming from you," she pointed out.

"Yes, well, my therapist says I should stop. I have been working on it. Haven't you noticed? I didn't even say anything about the lipstick all over your teeth."

She shrugged him off her shoulder. "You really are a bitch." She rubbed at her teeth.

Felix made a 'what did you expect' face. He took his drink from Sunshine. As a consolation, he offered, "It's just a little, really. Let me see if you got it."

She glared.

He insisted, "Let me see."

She showed her teeth.

He smiled. "Look at you, perfect again. Let me buy you a drink."

"I was going to head home anyway."

"I'll call you a cab."

She raised an eyebrow.

"Or an Uber or whatever it *is* people use to get around this city these days. Come on," he said.

They walked out together and stayed outside for a long time. It probably took forever to get a ride on Halloween, first of all, and they did get to talking for hours sometimes. They were both academics and unrepentant nerds, so Sunshine didn't mind at all not being privy to their conversations. He found a table and waited for Felix to find him.

A few people stopped by to say hello. Most of them asked where Specter had gotten to now.

He wondered if he should make more friends, not at all for the first time.

One of their original party came to sit with him. "Specter ditch you again?" Lana asked.

"Ditched is not exactly the right word."

She twitched one eyebrow and rolled her eyes. "Okay. So, where is he? Follow someone to the bathroom?"

"Even if he did, that's between him and me."

"Oh, no, sorry. To powder his nose," Lana clarified. "I asked him a million times if he had a thing for you, you know. He denied it every time."

Sunshine shrugged. He'd gotten used to these kinds of statements from their friends and acquaintances. He had, honestly, gotten sick of finding out how much people had talked about him and Felix behind their backs. "I think if you got all our exes together in a room, all they'd talk about was whether or not Specter and I had a thing for each other, when it started, what exactly it was, and whether it's one-sided."

She snorted.

Sunshine swished around the ice in his drink. He tried to think of a way to change the topic, couldn't, and resigned himself to sitting in silence.

Another person came to sit and fell into conversation with Lana.

Sunshine sat there until Felix came back and snuggled up to him.

"Miss me?"

Sunshine put an arm around him. He'd watched a good handful of Felix's partners squirm out of his grasp, complain about how clingy he got when he slept, say they felt suffocated by him. He understood that not everyone wanted the level of physical affection that Felix doled out. He wondered if he'd ever get sick of it.

Felix kissed his cheek. "Get me another drink."

"You have to move."

Felix whined.

"I can't phase through your body."

Felix didn't move. "I'm sorry I broke you like that."

"Hm?"

"You used to be able to use the in-between places. I ruined that."

"Oh. I don't miss it. I hated touching the strings."

"Dad hates it, too," Felix murmured. He sniffed. "Let's go home."

Sunshine looked at the time. A pretty early night, by Felix's standards. "You sure?"

"Mental breakdowns really take it out of me these days."

"Okay."

Felix stretched, yawned, and paid his tab. He linked pinkies with Sunshine and nodded off against him on the train ride home. Once inside the Weller, he straightened up and started to fiddle with his keys.

"Hmm?"

"I should go say hi."

Sunshine raised an eyebrow. "To who?"

"Elisa."

"Oh." Sunshine didn't like the Devil's firstborn. She had a malicious streak twice as wide as her father's and sort of reminded him of Hannibal Lecter. She behaved so badly that Devil had put her under house arrest.

"She is my sister."

"Be careful."

"Oh, Daddy would be furious if she hurt me. I don't have anything to worry about," Felix assured. "I'll meet you at home."

"Yours or mine?"

"Mine. Garfield likes the company."

They parted ways on the third floor. Sunshine headed up to the fifth floor and tidied up the remains of the party. Not too much to do, their guests had been considerate. He snagged one of the remaining caramels from the fridge. He'd hidden a few, just to make sure he'd have one for later.

Garfield slept in the bathtub and didn't stir when Sunshine turned on the light to check on him.

It felt strange, getting into Felix's bed without him, but he fell asleep soon enough. He stirred, hours later, when Felix crawled into bed and curled up against him.

"Hmmm?" Sunshine asked.

"Go back to sleep."

Sunshine went back to sleep.

November 3
Thursday

Rose rapped quietly on the door before he poked his head into the office. "Excuse me?"

A little guilt flashed over Felix's face. The upcoming election had put him in a spectacularly foul mood and Rose had stumbled into the brunt of it. They both seemed determined to leave it behind after Felix had explained himself and the two of them had wept together.

Sunshine had stood and watched, hideously uncomfortable with his friends worried about something he couldn't do anything to fix. He couldn't even vote, so short of organizing an assassination he was out of ideas.

He might have had the skills to do that, in all honesty, and the idea had more than idly crossed his mind a few times. He wasn't sure if he was hatred for the man himself or the fact that he made Felix so upset. Either way, plotting an assassination might not have been the most angelic solution to the problem.

"Come in," Felix said.

"Mr. Specter, there's someone here to see you."

Felix glanced at the clock. "A walk-in?"

"No, someone else. He says he's a friend. Robert Tanaka?"

Sunshine's head jerked up. He hadn't heard that name in decades.

Felix had already clambered around his desk and headed downstairs, squeezing past Rose and crowing, "Bobby!"

Sunshine followed.

Two people, a woman in her late twenties and an older gentleman, waited in the pair of chairs near Jen's desk. The woman looked remarkably like Bobby had in his younger years. The same wideset brown eyes, broad cheekbones, and strong jaw. Sunshine couldn't see much of the man because Felix had his arms around him.

"You're going to strangle him," Sunshine warned mildly.

The man pulled back. He at once looked too old and too young. Sunshine hadn't seen him in thirty years, at least, so he expected him to look both twenty-five and elderly at once. A slight thinness to his golden-brown skin, wrinkles around the eyes and bags under them, a few age spots, and a lot of gray in his hair, but Sunshine had almost expected him to be shriveled and hunched.

Bobby still stood up straight, though. He smiled at Sunshine.

"You two haven't changed."

Sunshine gave him a quick hug.

Bobby gestured to the woman at his side. "This is my daughter, Carrie."

Felix shook her hand when she offered it. "Felix Specter. Nice to meet you."

"You say that now. I've heard a lot from my father..." She glanced around the office, her eyes lingering on Rose, who ducked into the kitchenette.

Sunshine offered his name and shook her hand as well.

"She thinks I'm losing it," Bobby shared readily.

"Dad," Carrie scolded.

"Oh, you did," Bobby assured.

"What are you guys in town for?" Felix asked.

Bobby spread his arms and gestured around. "This. Are you taking cases?"

Felix's mouth opened, then he smiled. "Anything for you, Bobby. Come upstairs, come on. We'll talk about it. What kind of case are we talking?"

"Dad thinks our place is haunted."

"It *is* haunted," Bobby insisted. "Or something. I know something's not right."

"The house is just old."

"The house has *been* old the whole time I've lived there."

"Alright, come on upstairs," Felix said and ushered everyone toward their office. He bounced up the stairs, his step lighter than usual. He glanced back over his shoulder once with a grin.

Before he sat down, he headed over to the photo albums and tugged one down. He placed it on Bobby's lap. "I bet you remember those!"

Bobby peeked inside the cover, closed it, then subtly looked toward his daughter.

Felix noticed that then looked over at Sunshine for confirmation.

Sunshine barely tilted his head and twitched his eyebrows.

Felix cleared his throat. He sat at his desk. "So. A haunting?"

"It has to be. Noises I've never heard in the house before, things moving around—"

Carrie said, "Lots of people come through, Dad. They move things around."

"Oh, yeah. How many guests did we have last week? How many do you think went into my bedroom and moved things?"

Carrie sighed. She looked at Felix. "There's no such thing as ghosts."

Felix shrugged. "People used to say that about mermaids and now there's one living in California."

She asked, "You're really going to take advantage of an old man like this?"

Bobby's cheeks flushed. "Hey!"

"What? You pretend you're going to help, nothing changes, then we get a bill? Isn't that how it works? My friend works in computer graphics, I know every single one of those ghost hunting shows is faked," she insisted.

"It is not my job in life to convince the unbelievers," Felix said.

"No, it's to scam old people and idiots."

"It's to help people who've asked for help," Sunshine said before Felix could defend himself, or more likely, lash out at Carrie.

She looked at him.

"And we don't charge friends," Sunshine added.

She rolled her eyes at that. "Friends. Sure. You and my dad are friends."

"Bobby." Felix nodded toward the photo album.

Bobby looked at his daughter. "Give us a minute."

"So you can get talked into—"

"Give us a minute, Carrie," he repeated. "Go."

His daughter went but looked displeased with her arms crossed and her mouth twisted into a scowl.

"They pulled my license a few years ago. I would have come on my own if I could have…"

"Eyesight?" Felix guessed.

Plenty of older friends of theirs had gone through the same thing. Eyes, it turned out, could be a real pain.

Bobby let out a mournful chuckle. "Nah. Diabetes. Kept having blood sugar crashes." He waved away concern. "Got it managed now. Don't worry. I'm not going to faint on you."

"Good for you," Sunshine said.

Felix fidgeted, then asked, "So…your daughter?"

"She thinks I'm losing it. Dementia. But I know something's not right. I'm not just misplacing things. They're moving. I've seen them move."

"We believe you," Sunshine assured.

"Did you tell her what we are?"

"A demon and an angel? So she'd really think I'd lost it?" Bobby scoffed.

"And I don't figure you told her how we knew each other, either?" Felix guessed.

Bobby finally opened the photo album.

Felix had at least three albums for the seventies. He probably still took just as many pictures with his phone and sometimes he had a bunch of good ones printed up and started a new album.

This album contained pages and pages of their life from the seventies, stuffed to the brim with queers and punks and all the other artsy weirdos they'd hung around with then. Felix had come to better accept himself among these people, stopped hiding and worrying about being looked at. They weren't just nightlife pictures of bars and clubs and grindhouses, but dozens of people on the streets, hanging out in parks, and cooking each other dinner.

They'd had people over all the time back then. Potlucks and rooftop parties. Picnics and beach days. There had always been new faces coming around then, people running away from their old selves, their small towns, their disappointed parents, sometimes their spouses.

Sunshine had to ask, "How's Peg?"

"Passed in oh-nine," Bobby said.

"Oh. I'm sorry."

Bobby nodded. "Bad heart." He sighed. He ran his fingers over a photograph. "She'd had problems with it...You know how it goes."

Sunshine could only nod.

Felix cleared his throat. Gently, he asked, "So you never told your family?"

"Peg knew. And...and it wasn't like that. I loved her. She was my best girl. I never had any secrets from her. I never went behind her back or any of that. It was...it was just so nice to be around people like me for once," Bobby said. "But the kids...what was there to say? At what age do you sit your kids down and tell them dad likes boys, too?"

"Hey, no judgment," Felix assured.

"And now I'm just too old."

"That's just silly," Felix said. He went over to the bookshelf, picked out another album, flipped through, and pulled out a picture of them all at the beach. A dozen young people in swimsuits, hanging off each other. He brought it over to Bobby. "Look at that *body*, honey. Everyone was so mad when you got a girlfriend."

Bobby chuckled.

"Here. Keep it."

Bobby stared at it a while longer, then put it on the breast pocket of his button-down. He put his hand over Felix's. "Thank you."

Felix clucked. "Oh, you're welcome. Now tell us more about this ghostie of yours."

Bobby related the details of what sounded like a fairly standard haunting. Out of place sounds, moved or missing objects, seeing things that others didn't, smelling odd smells.

"What kind of building is it again?" Sunshine asked.

"Oh. A bed and breakfast."

"You're in Mass, now, aren't you?"

"On the Cape."

Felix gasped. "Thirty years and you never wanted to tell any of us! You'd have had every fag in the city trying to get a room."

"Oh, they all make it to the Cape anyway."

"True. Aren't you just living the dream?"

"Peg's dream, actually. She loved it. I mean. The day she died she was out making everything perfect. She planted this beautiful flower garden behind the house, all native plants for pollinators...Put in a beehive and everything," Bobby said.

"Sunshine, how soon can we get out there? What have we got to wrap up?" Felix asked.

"We should be set."

"Really?"

"Emil finished up that thing with the rats yesterday."

Bobby said, "I can't have this stuff keep happening when the tourists come back."

"Might be a fun attraction," Felix said.

"You know how often people lose things and get it in their head someone took it?" Bobby asked.

"Fair. Fair. So. You head home. Uh. No. Give me your number, and I'll call you when we're on our way. Probably..." Felix looked at Sunshine.

"After you vote."

"What's that, the...the eighth?" Felix asked.

Sunshine nodded.

"But right now, let's do lunch. You haven't done lunch yet have you?"

"No. No."

"Gio's is still there. Come on. Let's go. Show Carrie one of our family friend haunts," Felix proposed. "And if I'm giving too much away just pinch me."

Bobby nodded. It took him a minute to get up from his chair.

Felix hugged him again, then bounced over to Sunshine and hung off his shoulders. "How long has it been since we've had a visit from an old friend!"

Sunshine made himself smile. A lot of their old friends had died. Age, illness, substances, suicide...so many ways for the world to take people away. He kissed Felix's temple. "Oh, people have better things to do than hang around us their whole lives."

"Yes, why stay and be fabulous in the most marvelous city in the world when you could move to New Jersey and be a plumber?" Felix asked. "And I did look into that, you know. He is retired. And bald."

Bobby looked between them.

Felix peeled himself out of Sunshine's arms and headed downstairs, calling, "Rose, we're going out!"

He chattered happily although lunch, asking Bobby a hundred and one questions, and trying his best to be nice to Carrie, too.

Sunshine felt like he'd fallen into a dream. Not a surreal one, but some idle fantasy of Felix's, who was prone to the idlest of fantasies.

Or, at least, he had been, before the business with the fairy curse.

He seemed so much more himself lately, even with the election looming overhead. Bobby's visit had at least distracted him from that.

Sunshine reached across the table and took his hand.

Felix nestled their fingers together without interrupting his story about the time they'd seen a whale at Jones Beach.

The story didn't impress Carrie very much, but she'd grown up on the Cape. Whales must have been a dime a dozen there. She also didn't like Felix's stories about the Mudd Club or how he'd spent the 1965 blackout trying to follow a murder suspect. By the time the waiter asked them if they wanted dessert, Felix had given up trying to amuse her and had fully fallen into reminiscing with Bobby. They did the dead-married-moved rundown of all the people they'd hung around with.

Eventually, they parted ways, Bobby and his daughter back to their hotel, and Felix and Sunshine back to the office. Bobby left his address and phone number.

At home a week later, Felix started to pack like they were taking a tropical vacation until Sunshine reminded, "Hon, it's not gonna be any warmer in Massachusetts."

Felix looked at the sundry shorts and swimsuits he'd gathered.

He sighed, scooped them up, and shoved them into one drawer. He had to force it shut.

Sunshine cringed.

"Oh, don't." Felix flapped a hand. He delved into his closet and dumped some clothes on Sunshine's lap. "Fold those for me."

Sunshine started to fold, laying the garments neatly into Felix's bag. "What are we going to do about Garfield?"

Felix frowned. "Ah, shit..." He looked around for the elemental. "I bet he'd love the beach, though! All that sand?"

"I don't think he'd love the ride to the Cape."

Garfield had spent the ride from Pennsylvania to New York huffing and pacing around the backseat. He'd started belching smoke at one point.

"Mmm." Felix abandoned packing, flopped onto his bed, and held his phone above his face, scrolling through his contacts. He dropped his phone onto his face, swore, then rolled onto his stomach. He glanced at Sunshine.

"What?"

He put his phone to his ear. "Hi. Do you want to do me a favor?"

Lucifer appeared beside the bed.

Felix startled. He sighed and hung up his phone. "This is why I never call."

The Devil looked a little embarrassed. "I may have some absentee-father guilt to work through. What did you need?"

"I just wanted to ask if you'd watch Garfield while I'm away."

"Oh, did you get a cat?" Lucifer looked around the apartment.

"Not exactly."

Sunshine fidgeted. He tried his hardest to stay still and look comfortable, but Felix's father made his skin crawl.

Felix pushed himself up and gestured for his father to follow. "Garfield is an elemental. Fire, I'm pretty sure. I keep meaning to look into it but well, you know how I get."

Sunshine followed but not too close.

Lucifer noticed him anyway. He snaked an arm around Sunshine's shoulder. "How is my favorite angel?"

Conscious of how warm his face felt, Sunshine looked away. "Fine."

"You know, when you marry Felix, you can be my favorite son-in-law, too. I'd even let you be a prince."

"We're not getting married," Felix told his father.

"Then you should stop telling everyone that you are. Word's

starting to get around and I'm feeling terribly out of the loop. You know how sensitive I get." Lucifer pulled away from Sunshine and caught up with his son.

"This is Garfield."

Lucifer peered down at Garfield, who lay in the kitchen sink. "Oh, a salamander. If I find out you've sent out invitations and I didn't get one, my heart will absolutely break."

"I haven't sent out invitations for anything! Are people saying they've gotten an invitation?" Felix asked.

"No. But people are really talking about it," Lucifer said.

"It hasn't even been that long!" Felix protested. He looked at Sunshine.

"I don't even know if we *are* engaged, you're the one who's been telling everyone!" Sunshine said.

Lucifer held out his hand for Garfield to sniff. "You want me to watch this?"

"He doesn't do much. Just keep an eye on him until we get back," Felix said. To Sunshine, he continued, "You don't know if we're engaged?"

Sunshine shrugged. He looked at the floor.

Lucifer had lifted Garfield into his arms and held it the way people held small dogs. "Why are you keeping a salamander in your apartment?"

"He's good company."

"Do you know how big salamanders get?" his father asked.

"I...no. About three feet, right?"

"You'd better hope he isn't a giant salamander."

"I...Well." Felix put his hands on his hips and sighed. He glanced at Sunshine, clearly torn between two conversations. "He hasn't grown at all since I brought him home."

"It takes giant salamanders hundreds of years to grow up. By the time you've figured out if he's too big to keep, he'll be too domesticated to send home...It's likely too late even now," Lucifer said. "But I'll watch him for you if you don't mind me bringing him home. Is he okay with cats?"

"He's fine with dogs," Felix said.

"Ira will get a kick out of this. Do you want to come home with me?" Lucifer asked Garfield.

The salamander made a gurgling wheeze.

"Sounds like a yes to me," Lucifer said. "Are we entering into a formal contract or is this one of those informal parent-child arrangements that people do?"

"It's a parent-child thing," Felix assured.

Lucifer smiled proudly. He snuggled Garfield more comfortably into his arms. "We should do dinner when you get back. My place. And bring that one." He nodded toward Sunshine.

Felix nodded. He hugged his father and then the Devil was gone. He turned back to Sunshine. He scuffed his foot against the floor. "Are you mad at me?"

"No."

"Do you want to talk about it?"

"Not really," Sunshine said.

"Oh, good, because I don't know either."

"Let me know if you figure it out."

"I...Well. If I did want to get married, would you do it?"

"Yes."

His eyes slightly widened, Felix asked, "Do *you* want to get married?"

"No. Well. Not as such. Marriage doesn't mean anything to me. Being your husband wouldn't...it wouldn't change anything for me. I'm already yours in the fullest sense I can be without crossing a line you don't want to cross. Marriage wouldn't change that," Sunshine explained.

Felix went quiet and serious for a moment, then he smiled and said, "But it could be fun to have a wedding!"

"It could be fun," Sunshine agreed.

"I also like telling people we're engaged. If I were going to marry anyone, it would be you. That counts, doesn't it?"

"I'll consider myself your intended if it pleases Your Highness."

"It pleases us. It would also please us if you finished packing our bags."

Sunshine couldn't keep in his smile. He turned back to the bedroom.

Felix launched himself on his back and secured himself. He nestled his cheek against Sunshine's face. "I'm so hyped to go to the Cape. What if we retired from the agency and just became...you know, wealthy jet setters?"

"You'd kill one or both of us if you retired."

"Mmmm. Maybe."

Sunshine leaned one shoulder toward the bed.

Felix rolled off his back and onto the bed. He gathered the pillows into his arms and watched Sunshine finish packing. A funny sort of melancholy settled over him, as it had on and off for the past week or so. He waffled between confidence that Trump would lose, terror that he wouldn't, and bitter disillusionment with the system as a whole. Sunshine had heard rants on all scenarios.

In the morning, Felix called for Sunshine to come outside to the car he'd rented. Sunshine loaded their bags and waited for Felix to get out of the driver's seat.

He didn't. He rolled down the window. "Come on. Get in."

"You're driving?"

Felix rolled his eyes.

"I'd like to make it there alive."

"I've never been in an accident!"

"You drive like a maniac."

"Get in the car."

Sunshine groaned but climbed in. He made a show of buckling his seatbelt and making sure the passenger airbag was on.

Felix smacked him in the arm. "Stop it."

"I'm surprised they gave you your license back."

Felix locked the doors. "They didn't. I bought a fake."

"Specter!"

Felix grinned and tore away from the curb.

Sunshine grabbed onto whatever he could find to secure his position and didn't relax until they'd made it out of the city. A stop at a polling station provided a temporary respite from Felix's driving but left a strange stone in Sunshine's stomach. In the back of his mind, he recognized it as dread. The future could be vicious. They'd survived this hideous political cycle before, and they would again if that's what it came to, but so many hadn't.

He wanted to be hopeful. At least Felix could vote, he had been born in Vermont and had the birth certificate to prove it. Sunshine, though, waited in the car.

On the highway, he flinched with upsetting frequency as Felix zipped along, weaving and cussing at other drivers even more venomously than usual. At one point, Sunshine gasped loud enough that Felix looked over.

"When'd you get so jumpy?"

"Around the time I had something to live for."

Felix clucked his tongue and rolled his eyes. He eased up on the speed and settled into one lane. He took his hand off the shifter and placed it on Sunshine's thigh. "Do you think Garfield's alright with Dad?"

"I'm sure he's fine."

"Probably, right? I mean. Things are probably going to be fine, right?" Felix asked. "With Garfield."

"I'm sure your father will take good care of him."

"But also like, in general, things will be fine. Honestly. Who would vote for that asshole? Just other assholes. And...uh. You know. I do like to believe that most people aren't assholes," Felix said without sounding convinced. "Right?"

"I hope so."

Felix tightened his grip on Sunshine's leg.

Sunshine put his hand over Felix's and gave it a squeeze.

"On the other hand...!"

"Let's not do this right now."

"I know. I just...You know! I can't stop thinking about it. There's nothing I can do except what I've done and I just...I want there to be something more. And...you know. If I was..." Felix swallowed and glanced at him. "If I were who I could be, I could do something. But that's not my choice to make. To decide that for everyone. You know?"

"I know."

"I can't stop thinking about it."

"Have..." Sunshine trailed off. He'd almost asked if Felix had talked to his therapist about it but ascending to become a quasi-deity in order to change a country's political landscape couldn't have been within Dr. Reza's scope of practice.

Felix shook his head. "She still thinks I'm delusional. I think telling her I'm the Antichrist would just be the edgelord version of telling her I'm Jesus."

"You can talk to me about it if you need to talk about it. I'm not sure that I'll have any good advice, but sometimes it helps to just say everything out loud."

"Thanks." Felix went quiet for a few minutes, then proceeded to talk for an hour straight about all his various fears and hopes, not just for the election but for the planet in general.

Sunshine listened. He didn't know what to say. He'd been created to follow orders, not to give opinions. He could recite events exactly as they'd occurred in a pitched battle or make tactical predictions for a war, but politics required a level of duplicity and cunning he'd been made without. He could only guess based on what he'd learned and witnessed since he'd come to Earth, which was about as much as any other person could do.

Felix didn't seem to want an opinion for him. He needed to give a voice to his worries.

He concluded by saying, "And everyone tells me I don't have to worry but I'm worried, Sunshine! I'm *fucking scared*."

"Me, too."

Felix let out a long sigh followed by a groan.

"Do you want me to drive?"

"No, I need the distraction. Besides, I like to scare the Connecticut drivers."

"You give the whole city a bad reputation."

Felix flashed him a grin.

The drive through Connecticut kept Felix in a fairly sprightly mood, in that he seemed to actively enjoy terrorizing the other drivers. Oh, he didn't target people indiscriminately. He somehow knew which people he could enrage with minimal effort.

He pissed off one person enough that the car he'd cut off followed him for miles, honking viciously.

Felix glanced in the rearview mirror.

"Whatever you're doing..."

"Ooooh, Sunshine. Give me some credit. My days of cathartic brawls are several decades in the past." He changed lanes, getting all the way to the right, and taking an exit advertising food and gas once he made sure the person he'd angered hadn't followed.

"You really go too far sometimes, you know."

Felix tutted. He pulled into a gas station. "Snacks?"

"Mmm."

Felix kissed his cheek. "Be right back."

Sunshine hunkered down in his seat and closed his eyes to wait. About two minutes later, he jolted upright when someone pounded on the window.

An unreasonably well-muscled man in a tight shirt stood outside the door.

"Can I help you?"

"Where the fuck do you get off driving like that?" the man demanded. "What the *fuck* is wrong with you?"

"Sir, I am not even in the driver's seat."

"Fucking smartass."

Sunshine sighed. "Listen, I wasn't driving. I don't know what you want me to do or say."

"Get out of the fucking car."

Sunshine frowned. "I have no intention—"

"Hey!" Felix called. He had enough snacks to feed six in a bag he dangled over his shoulder. He carried a large soft drink in his other hand.

Sunshine saw the corner of his favorite kind of chips poking out the top.

The interloper turned toward Felix's voice.

"What the fuck are you doing? Get away from my car."

The man sneered.

"Yeah, I hope you fucking fight better than you drive, you slab of meat," Felix called before the other man could retort.

The man headed over to Felix.

Sunshine got out of the car and stood on the doorstep. "Felix, get in the car."

Felix's eyes flicked over the man who strode toward him. He grinned at Sunshine and cocked one eyebrow. "Alright, beefcake, I'm gonna give you one warning. Get back in your car and go."

"Or what, fucktard?"

"Specter, get in the car!"

Instead of listening, Felix let out a bloodcurdling screech, more bestial than human, as the stranger moved within arm's reach.

The man flinched then stumbled back. "What the fuck?"

Felix grinned and it was his father's grin, hideous and too wide. "Ivan Roberts, flee now or look upon your death," he intoned. Smoke curled out of his mouth and from his nostrils. "I give this warning but once. Linger and the beasts of the Pit will feast upon your soul."

Sunshine sighed and rested his forehead against the car, waiting for Felix to finish with his display.

It didn't take long.

The other man outright screamed and fled before Felix could even really show off the scariest tricks he'd perfected over the years.

Felix hopped back into the driver's seat. When Sunshine got in, he deposited the bag of snacks in Sunshine's lap.

Sunshine rolled his eyes at him.

"What?"

"You're gonna get us in trouble one of these days."

"I get us trouble all the time," Felix pointed out. He swooped in for a kiss.

Sunshine dodged it. "Your breath tastes bad when you do that thing with the smoke."

Felix took a sip of soda, swished it around, then went back in. He didn't go all the way and raised an eyebrow. "Hmm?"

"Fine."

Felix pecked him on the lips. "Would you have fought him for me?"

"Do you need to ask?"

"I just like to hear you say it."

"I would fight the world for you," Sunshine said.

Felix kissed him again.

"I'd also really appreciate it if you could drive like marginally less of a maniac."

"Hmmm. Maybe."

Felix pulled out of the gas station and kept it reasonably tame on the road for the rest of the drive.

November 9, 2016
Wednesday

The clock showed a few minutes before three a.m. and Felix hadn't come to bed yet. By now, he'd usually at least brushed his teeth and crawled under the covers.

Sunshine had tried to get him to lay down a few times, but he just sat in the armchair staring at his phone. The blue glow of it illuminated his face, the only thing Sunshine could see in the darkness of the room.

He'd sat there with his lips pressed into a thin line.

"Babe, come lay down," Sunshine called quietly.

"I'm watching his victory speech."

"You don't need to watch that." Sunshine got out from under the covers and went over to the chair. He crouched next to Felix and saw the shine of tears on his cheeks, dribbling off his chin. "Come lay down."

"I won't be able to sleep." He kept his eyes fixed on his phone.

Sunshine sat on the floor. He rested his head against Felix's leg.

Felix twisted his fingers through Sunshine's curls. "You should go to bed. We've got a case to figure out tomorrow."

"I'll stay with you."

Once they did make it to bed, neither of them slept well.

Bobby and Carrie didn't look any better off at breakfast.

Felix took about two bites of food and pushed the rest around on his plate.

Sunshine guiltily refilled his plate, but all the eggs and toast in the world couldn't fill the pit in his stomach.

Felix pushed his plate toward Sunshine.

Sunshine ate that too and felt awful afterward, somewhere between heartburn and nausea.

No one talked much as they cleaned up. They made some attempt at small talk and even tried to talk about the case, but no one could stay focused for much of a conversation in any direction.

Sunshine and Felix split up to check out the areas where Bobby had reported the highest levels of activity. Neither of them found much, but hauntings could get tricky like that. Spirits might target specific people or wait until specific times. Some spirits didn't have much control over what they did. Others got downright nasty.

He found Felix sitting in the backyard garden with his knees pulled up against his chest. He sat next to him.

Felix pointed to a butterfly hovering around a cluster of pansies.

Sunshine watched the butterfly with him.

"You find anything?" Felix asked.

"No. You?"

Felix shrugged. "Not really."

Sunshine put an arm around him.

"I think I need a day."

"We all do."

"Can we go for a walk?"

"Sure."

It took Felix a while to uncurl himself from the bench.

They walked aimlessly down the streets of the small town, which after so many years in New York felt like they had fallen into one of the Otherworlds or a foreign land. They passed gift shops and restaurants, all of them empty, and ended up standing on a bridge staring over a salt marsh.

It reeked, not the urine and trash reek of a city neighborhood, but the rotten smell of low tide, the scent of all the dead plants and animals bubbling up to meet their noses, carried in on a gentle breeze.

Sunshine could only imagine how much worse it would be on a sweltering August day.

"We should stay up tonight, see if we can find anything," Felix suggested. "I won't be able to sleep anyways so we might as well be productive."

Sunshine hummed his agreement.

They wandered around for a while longer, then headed back to check on Bobby. They found him in the backyard pulling up weeds.

Felix sat on the grass beside him. "Bobby, darling, I hate to see you working like this."

"I'm old, not dead."

"Would you like help? Sunshine can help. Sunshine, come help Bobby."

Bobby sat back with a quiet groan and wiped his hands on his pants, leaving smears of dirt. He looked at Sunshine. "You're still letting him talk to you like that?"

Sunshine smiled, unable to stop his eyes from going to Felix. "I live only to serve His Majesty."

Bobby shook his head.

"Oh, he means it, he does!" Felix insisted. "Sunshine, tell him how much you like me."

Bobby sighed.

"What?" Felix asked.

"Help me up."

Felix popped to his feet and helped Bobby stand. He hovered at his side as Bobby walked to the bench. He handed Bobby his water bottle as soon as he looked at it.

"Thanks."

Felix beamed at him. He noticed Sunshine smile at him and immediately his face clouded. "Don't smile at me."

"But I like you so much."

"Well, stop."

Sunshine gave a small bow. "Of course, I am but a worm. I live to serve."

Bobby shook his head again. He sighed and huffed.

Sunshine couldn't figure out if he was disgruntled or simply making the various noise that old people made.

"You two really haven't changed," Bobby said.

"People never change. I mean. Superficially, they do, their looks or energy may change with age or circumstance, but people never really change. We just look the same, too," Felix offered. He looked over Sunshine. "I mean. We are...We are differently involved than we were before."

"Differently involved," Bobby repeated.

"Physically and openly, instead of that...star-crossed emotional entanglement we had for so long," Felix said. He made a vague gesture between himself and Sunshine. "I'm surprised you haven't asked. Literally everyone else has asked about it."

"Ah, not my business to ask." Bobby waved a hand. "Although..."

When Bobby didn't say anything else, Felix asked, "Although what?"

"What took you so long! It was *so* obvious," Bobby said.

Felix glanced at Sunshine and raised an eyebrow.

"Oh, you tell him, you like to talk."

Felix blew a raspberry. He settled on the bench next to Bobby. "You want the long or the short version?"

"Short?"

"Uh...Sunshine's terrified of my father so he put on a protection spell against the Devil, but it affected all his bastards, too. Well. And probably Elisa, but Sunshine wouldn't touch her with a ten-foot pole. So, he actually *couldn't* touch me without hurting me," Felix said.

Sunshine leaned close to Bobby. "Ask him for the long version, you know how much he loves to hear himself talk."

Bobby laughed. "Tell me the long version, Felix."

Felix gave Sunshine a sour look.

Sunshine winked. "Tell him the long version."

Felix rolled his eyes. He started his story though.

Sunshine ruffled his hair. He wandered away after a while. It had gotten past his usual lunchtime. He found Carrie in the kitchen, standing over the legs of someone who'd wedged themself beneath the sink.

A few minutes later, a comfortably built, olive-skinned man struggled out from under the sink and back to his seat. He had to be about sixty and had thinning, brown hair shot through with gray. He wore filthy, ripped jeans and a tight wifebeater. "Pipe needs to be replaced," he told Carrie. He glanced at Sunshine, then did a double-take. He raised a hand. "Howdy. You on vacation?"

"Oh." Carrie rolled her eyes. "That's a 'friend' of Dad's, I guess."

"My name's Sunshine."

"Vinnie."

They shook hands.

"Didn't know Bobby had..." Vinnie looked over Sunshine again. "Friends. Like you."

"I'm older than I look."

Vinnie let out an awkward kind of chuckle. He gave Sunshine another once over.

Sunshine spied an interlocking pair of Mars symbols hanging from Vinnie's necklace, nearly obscured by a healthy amount of chest hair.

Vinnie reached up to touch it when he saw Sunshine looking. He fiddled with it.

"I came into see about lunch," Sunshine told Carrie. "Do you mind if I use the kitchen? I don't want to wear out my welcome."

"You did that when you decided to scam an elderly man," she told him. She walked away.

"Spitfire, that one," Vinnie noted. "You're scamming Bobby?"

"No. We're...Felix and I are paranormal detectives. Bobby got in touch because he believes the building is haunted."

"Oh. That. You guys can do something about that?"

"You've had experiences, too?" Sunshine asked.

"Well. I never. I never figured myself for superstition, but you know. I believe there's more to the world than what we see. Grew up Catholic, all that. Something...Something's going on here."

"Do you have a little time?"

Vinnie frowned.

"To talk. About the haunting," Sunshine said. He offered, "We can chat over lunch."

Vinnie said, "I guess so, yeah."

Sunshine had figured that would get Vinnie's attention. "You think Carrie would kill me if I raided the fridge?"

"Oh, she's all wind and piss. But there's a good place down the street if you don't want to ruffle any feathers."

"I simply deplore ruffling feathers. Let's go."

They passed through the backyard on their way out.

"Felix, Vinnie and I are getting lunch. Did you two want to join us?"

"What do you say, Bobby?" Felix asked.

"Oh. I. We could."

"Good, good, let's go." Felix helped Bobby stand.

Bobby glanced at Vinnie.

Vinnie watched Felix take hold of Bobby's arm.

"Mr. Tanaka, I have to say, I'm so flattered. It's not every day a girl like me has such a handsome escort to lunch," Felix said. "I've grown so used to the riffraff of the city." He shot a venomous look over his shoulder at Sunshine.

Sunshine said, "Don't mind Felix. He plays fast and loose with reality."

"Oh, god, he's *following us*," Felix hissed to Bobby.

Sunshine and Vinnie hung back.

"Honestly, what is this city coming to?" Felix asked.

"If he tries to bite, you just have to smack him on the nose," Sunshine told Vinnie.

Felix turned around and poked Sunshine in the chest. "How dare you!"

Sunshine took a quick step forward and looped an arm around Felix. He crushed him close. "Stop showing off."

Felix growled.

Sunshine nuzzled his throat. "Vinnie thinks there are ghosts, too. You should play nice."

Felix hummed. "Okay."

Sunshine released him but twisted their fingers together. "We're working, need I remind you."

"I said okay."

It took about fifteen minutes to walk to the restaurant, but the hostess seated them as soon as they walked in. They shared the restaurant with an elderly couple and a young man in a far corner booth, but no one else.

The menu listed a handful of Italian American staples.

Felix eyed the menu. "Which one is piccata?"

"You like it."

"It's not the one with peppers?"

"No."

Felix set down the menu and didn't glance at it again.

Bobby and Vinnie hemmed and hawed a little about what to get, but mostly they sat as far away from each other as they could get in the booth and glanced away from each other every time their eyes met.

When the waitress came, Sunshine ordered for him and Felix because Felix had casually flapped a hand in Sunshine's direction with the waitress asked him. He'd gotten caught up reading some article and had pinched Sunshine's arm when he'd tried to take his phone away.

Once their food came and Felix had finished obsessing over the article, Felix asked, "So. Vinnie, right?"

Vinnie nodded.

"You've had unexplained experiences in the bed and breakfast, too?"

"A few times."

"Can you tell us more about what you saw or heard?"

Vinnie nodded. He fiddled with his necklace again. "Uh. It was just a few times. I do work around the place a lot, have for years, but this...this stuff is all new. I'll put something down and find it somewhere else. Or...Sometimes I feel something. Like something touching me, but when I turn around, there's never anything there."

"It gets worse at night," Bobby said. He chased a noodle around his plate.

"Do you ever hear anything?"

"Laughter," the men said together.

"Like giggles," Vinnie said.

Bobby nodded. "Like children."

"Huh. No, uh, no kids have died in the building, have they?" Felix asked.

"Not that I know of. Not as long as I've owned it, and before that...The people we bought it from didn't mention anything, but I don't imagine they would have. Or even if they knew. It's an old building," Bobby said.

"We'll have to look into the property records," Sunshine said.

"Still, if kids died there, it must have been a while ago...I wonder what got them bothering people now?" Felix mused. "But things like this, they come and go sometimes. But anyway...what else?"

"Just, stuff like that. Nothing ever...scary. I mean, not like a horror movie. You know? Just...naughty," Vinnie said. "It never hurt me."

"No, no, they've never hurt me," Bobby said. "If it wouldn't put off the guests so much, I'd...I'd leave it alone. But it's not just my home, it's my business. But you know tourists. They're always losing things, putting things away in the wrong place, their kids leave things at the beach."

"Yeah, people are terrible," Felix agreed.

They fell into silence through lunch.

Felix speared a piece of chicken. "So. Vinnie. You, uh...You have family around here?"

"Oh, no. Not really. Not." He touched his necklace. "Parents moved down to Florida years ago anyway."

"Tough being that far. Mine are up in Canada."

"Ah, I never saw 'em much when they were up here," Vinnie said. "Not..." He made himself stop touching his necklace. He cleared his throat. "Not like you're thinking. They don't care one way or another about that. About me being gay."

Felix grinned.

Bobby cleared his throat. He excused himself to the bathroom.

Vinnie watched him go with a sad sort of embarrassment.

"Somebody's got a crush," Felix accused lightly.

Vinnie's olive skin flushed dark red all the way down to his chest.

"You should ask him out," Felix said.

"Specter," Sunshine scolded.

Vinnie shook his head. "No. No. I don't...Bobby's not. He's not."

"Ask him, the worst thing he can do is say no," Felix said.

"We've been friends for years, I don't want to...to do anything to ruin that. To change his mind about me. I know he...You two are young, you know. You don't get it. People are tolerant, you know, but they don't want to know. They don't want to talk about it. It's not the same as how your friends feel about you."

"Ah," Felix said.

"Things have come a long way, it's trendy now."

"It's not trendy, people just feel safer than they used to," Felix corrected gently. "Even if it's just a little safer."

Sunshine idly wondered how old he looked.

"I mean, you're what? Maybe twenty-eight, thirty?" Vinnie asked Felix.

Felix laughed. "Oh, goodness, now you're trying to flatter me! I am quite spoken for at the moment and dear Sunshine does get *so* jealous."

Bobby returned and Vinnie went quiet for a while.

After lunch, Felix went upstairs to lie down for a while.

Sunshine followed close behind and snuggled up to him before he got comfortable enough that it would irritate him to be disturbed. He could function fully without a good night's sleep, but that didn't mean he didn't enjoy being well-rested. A nap would help make tonight more productive and tolerable, too.

He kissed Felix.

"It's not happening," Felix said.

"Hm?"

"I'm not in the mood."

"Okay." Sunshine gave him another kiss. He'd had no intentions in that direction anyway.

Felix pinched him. "What's wrong with you?"

"Ow! What was that for!"

"I said I didn't want to do anything."

"I wasn't *trying* to do anything." Felix's moods flipped so wildly sometimes. "I just..." He stopped before he started trying to defend himself. That would just get Felix riled up. "I'm sorry."

"Well, keep your mouth to yourself next time." Felix huffed and rolled over. He let out a long sigh a moment later.

"Do you want me to go?"

"No."

Sunshine thought about what to say. He couldn't say it was just a kiss. Plenty of people had gotten kisses they didn't want, and no one should have to deal with that. He stared at the ceiling, trying to figure out what to say and how he felt. "Are you upset?"

"Yes."

"You...I'd never. You know that. Right?"

Felix huffed again. He didn't roll over.

"Felix?"

Felix rolled over and groaned. He looped an arm over Sunshine's waist and curled up against him, his knees somehow in

Sunshine's ribs. "Stop trying to apologize, just let me be upset. I'm not mad at you, I'm just mad."

Sunshine licked his lips. "But you know?"

"Course I know." He said it so practically, like Sunshine had asked him if he knew the letters of the alphabet. Like he'd asked a stupid question.

He felt better after that. He dozed for a few hours and woke to find Felix still beside him but lying on his belly watching something on his phone with the volume turned low.

"Nice nap?" Felix asked.

"Mmhm. Were you watching something?" He vaguely recalled bits and pieces of some show.

"Oh. Yeah. I ended up watching Dr. Phil clips on Facebook, but you kept making these weird, semi-lucid comments, so I switched over to something else. Your solution to a lot of problems is making someone a nice meal."

Sunshine's cheeks warmed.

Felix kissed him on the cheek. "You're cute when you're embarrassed."

He felt overwarm and slightly sweaty, which happened if he took a nap sometimes. "I'm...I think I'm going to jump in the shower."

"I'll be here."

A quick shower and a change of clothes had him feeling better.

Felix looked wonderfully mussed from his rest, wrinkled and twined in the blankets. Sunshine reached over and finger-combed his hair into an attractive disorder instead of a comical one.

It didn't take long for darkness to fall. Once it did, they went to nose around the same spots as before.

Around eleven, when they'd split up to do rounds of the house separately, Sunshine heard a door open. He made his way to the nearest window and saw an orb of light bobbing around in the backyard, as well as a dark figure moving about.

It could have been anything from Felix to a spirit, or even another person awake at this hour. It wasn't so late that it would be unusual to find others out of bed.

He watched a little longer, decided it was probably a living person and not a ghost, and went back to his perusal of the attic. He found, as he expected, nothing unusual. Decorations, old furnishings, labeled cardboard boxes that seemed to hold old toys or clothes. Some exposed pipes in the attic, more than he'd expected to find, but he guessed they had to do with the bathrooms in all the guest rooms.

A few boxes said 'Peg' on the side.

Sunshine had liked Peg. He thought she'd like him, too, not that they'd spent much time together. Bobby hadn't kept his life strictly separate, but he knew that Peg hadn't exactly felt welcome at the queerer gatherings. He'd gone out of his way to be nice to her, though, because he knew so well how it felt to be out of place.

Most of the people they'd hung out with understood that too, but some had narrowed their perspective too much to appreciate Peg's situation.

Sunshine ultimately left the boxes alone, though. He hadn't come here to snoop, and he highly doubted anything in the boxes would help unravel the haunting.

The attic ultimately yielded nothing helpful, no creepy doll or vintage photos of little children, no old journals with fortuitously detailed entries about dark happenings. It would have made his job a lot easier if things had come together so neatly as they did in movies.

A trip to the library tomorrow might at least give them some information about previous residents of the bed and breakfast. Bobby said it had been a family home before it had converted to a bed and breakfast.

He sat for a while on the attic floor in the dark, but even presenting himself as such an easy target didn't yield any results.

He headed back downstairs. He sat for a while in various locations, trying to keep himself open to experiences without making himself vulnerable. At one point, he laid down on the parlor floor, listening to the house creak and the pipes groan. After about ten minutes, he heard something that sounded like skittering or scratching in the walls.

Probably mice. Old houses like this always had mice and the cold weather would have them wanting to be inside.

By four o'clock, he and Felix had met back up, reviewed their limited experiences, and called it a night when neither had something interesting to share.

As they got ready for bed, Sunshine noticed dirt and dew on Felix's boots and remembered that he'd seen someone outside. "Did you find anything when you went outside?" he asked.

"I didn't go outside." Felix pulled his shirt over his head.

Sunshine frowned at him. "I saw you. Or I saw someone at least. And your shoes are dirty."

Felix looked down, then tossed his shirt on the floor. He ran his fingers over the side of his boot then rubbed them together. He frowned. "I didn't go outside."

Sunshine sat on the bed. "It looks a lot like you did."

Felix huffed and started unlacing his boots. He kicked them off, wiggled out of his jeans, and crawled under the covers. He pulled his pillow close. "Then I don't remember. And I don't like that."

Sunshine climbed in next to him. He pulled him close and kissed the top of his head. "Maybe you're getting senile."

"Or maybe we're in a haunted fucking house."

"Mmm. I didn't take you for the sort of fool who believes in ghosts, Mr. Specter."

"I must be the greatest of fools if I've found myself in your bed again."

"Do you want me to go look outside?"

"No. We can look in the morning. What time was I out there?"

"A little after eleven."

Felix huffed.

"Your shoes wouldn't still be wet."

Felix huffed louder.

"Stay here."

"Don't go out."

"I won't, I'm just going to the window. Stay in bed."

Sunshine went out into the hall and down to where he could see outside. He didn't see much out there, but the moon was waxing past the first quarter, so it wasn't totally dark. No signs of anything untoward, no disturbances or out of place items.

He went back to bed, reported that he'd seen nothing, and snuggled up to Felix. He slept better with Felix next to him. Normally, beds that weren't his own gave him a hard time. Even at home, he sometimes still needed his meadow recording to rest peacefully.

It wasn't anything about the recording, it was the familiarity. The same thing every time.

He hated to compare a living person to an old recording, but Felix had that same comforting quality. He smelled the same, breathed the same, felt the same every night, and he felt more familiar than any partner Sunshine had slept beside.

Of course, that tracked.

"Do..."

"Hmm?" Felix asked.

"Nothing."

"No. Tell me."

"You liked me back them. When we first met. Not...not like you like me now, but you flirted with me," Sunshine said.

Felix tittered. "You're gorgeous. Even when I didn't want anything to do with you, I could see that."

"But if we could have...If we could have touched...Do you think we would have?"

Felix let out a laugh, a silly sort of startled giggle. "Are you asking what I think you are?"

"Well?"

"Well...Yes. I think I would have tried, at least. I think you would have wanted to, too. I mean, what else would two like-minded fellows have gotten up to under the same roof for all those years? I mean, I didn't know then if you were like-minded, but I would have tried harder to find out if we could have touched. Some rainy day when the radio wouldn't come in...Yes. I think we would have," Felix quietly concluded.

Sunshine tightened an arm around him. "I..."

"Stop trailing off."

Sunshine sighed. "I think if we had, it wouldn't have worked out the way it did. It would have been so different."

"Of course, it would have."

"I think you would have dumped me."

A surprised snort escaped Felix. "What!"

"I just...I don't know."

"I'll have you know, Sunshine, that I've never once turned out a stray I took in. I'm deeply insulted that you think I would have."

"Oh, no, no, not...Not like that. I think we'd be friendly still. I just think the other thing wouldn't have lasted. It was so one-sided, our relationship then. I needed you so much and you didn't need anything from me."

Felix surged up to kiss him. "You don't know how much I needed you, darling. You never had any idea how badly I needed exactly you. You've done so much for me, so much, and I'm sorry I made you think that you mean less than everything to me."

He nestled closer and could only manage to say, "Ah, I figured it out after a while." Felix's open and sincere affections always made him flustered in the most delightful way. He liked the teasing and mild bullying, but he liked it even more when Felix made him feel special.

"Do you wish we could have?"

"I don't know," Sunshine admitted.

"Me neither." A few quiet minutes passed. "Are we doing this late-night chit-chat thing?"

"Not really."

"Mmm." Felix burrowed beneath the covers. He yawned.

Sunshine nodded off and slept late. He found Felix still beside him, reading on his phone. He nudged him. "Hi."

"Morning. What time is it?"

"Ten-ish."

He yawned and looked at the time. Nearly half-past ten. "Do we have to go to the library today?"

"Mmm. Town Hall, too, if we can."

He yawned again.

Felix put down his phone and rolled over, half on top of Sunshine. "You still sleepy?"

"No."

"Then let us away, my love, with happy speed."

Sunshine knew that line from somewhere. Maybe a movie, but he could almost recall Phaedrus saying it. Maybe it was one of their poems. "Is that one of Bibi's?"

Felix smiled. "No."

Sunshine tried to think where he'd heard it before.

"There are no ears to hear, or eyes to see."

"Something, something, something mead?"

"Drown'd all in Rhenish and the sleepy mead: Awake! Arise! my love, and fearless be, for o'er then southern moors I have found a home for thee," Felix said.

Sunshine felt pretty good about getting one word right.

"It's Keats, by the way."

He at least knew that Keats was a poet and could have sworn he'd read something by him. Halfway through his shower, it occurred to him that Bibi had used to read them all poetry sometimes at night when they didn't care for anything on the radio. He didn't think Felix's parents even owned a TV, or if they did, never watched it.

Phaedrus had a lovely speaking voice, one that surely must have been crafted by the Almighty specifically for the storyteller.

Their trips to the library, town hall, and local historical society turned up little. People had died in the house, of course, it was bound to happen in a house that old, but no children aside from an infant too young to laugh. They found no history of occult or untoward happenings in the house later, no one ever accused of black masses or child sacrifices, no nasty uncles or fathers inclined toward abuse.

Nothing that made the house seem like a child had any right to haunt it.

They ordered a late lunch from a deli and went to the beach to eat.

The beach in the off-season had a unique beauty. The wind that blew in ruffled their hair and slapped a little color into their cheeks, bringing the scent of salt this time instead of the stench of low tide.

A few birds shuffled and fluttered about the beach, the waves lapped in and out, and about a quarter of a mile away, Sunshine could see another person. Just a speck really.

Felix wiped excess mayonnaise off his sandwich.

Sunshine peeked at his and saw that it had received the same treatment. He gave it a try, decided it was too much, and smeared some off onto a napkin.

They ate without saying much.

Felix had stretched his legs under the picnic table and had one foot hooked around Sunshine's ankle.

When the sandwiches and chips had disappeared and they were both slurping the remains of their drinks, Sunshine asked, "Now what?"

"Do you think I should stop dyeing my hair?"

"What did you read that made you think dyeing your hair is problematic?" He hadn't dyed it in a while, but a greenish tinge clung to the pale strands. It looked almost intentional.

Felix's pallid cheeks flushed blotchy red. He reached over to pinch him.

Sunshine caught him by the wrist. Felix didn't make good use of the speed and strength granted by his father's blood. He was next to useless, really, in serious hand-to-hand combat. Oh, sure, he could hold his own in a scrap against a human but when in real danger, he relied on magic.

Felix tried to tug his hand back.

Sunshine didn't let go. "You've exceeded your pinch quota for the month."

He yanked his hand out of Sunshine's grip. "You've exceeded your stupid question quota," he sulked.

Sunshine gave his mood a minute to settle, then asked, "Do you like dyeing your hair?"

"Yeah, but people always ask me about it. Like...I don't know, I never wanted my hair to be another thing people have questions about. And they're always pointing out when it's faded or saying something about the new color. I'm over it."

Sunshine gathered up their garbage. "Well. You can tell people to stop asking about it."

Felix grunted.

"Let's go for a walk."

They shed their shoes and socks, cuffed their pants, and walked at the edge of the water. Waves rolled over their feet, cold but not freezing.

They discussed next steps on the case until it started to get dark, then went home for a hot bath to warm up. They shared their lack of progress with Bobby and Carrie. Carrie seemed vindicated by their reports.

November 13, 2016
Sunday, Early Morning

Felix shook Sunshine out of a deep sleep, the best sleep he'd gotten in a while. Life at the bed and breakfast agreed with him and though they'd made little progress on the case, Sunshine didn't mind that.

"Hnng?"

"Shh. Listen," Felix whispered.

It took Sunshine a second to settle and he couldn't hear much past the echo of his own heartbeat in his ears.

"Do you hear it?"

Sunshine closed his eyes and listened. Faint, maybe coming from outside, he thought he heard laughter and maybe something else. Hushed voices and quiet music. He rolled out of bed and went to check the window.

Felix stayed right beside him.

They couldn't see anything in the yard, but the sounds had definitely come from outside. They headed out, their feet bare and wearing nothing more than underwear and sweatshirts. Sunshine regretted coming out as soon as he caught sight of a handful of dark figures not in the backyard but just beyond the wooden fence. A breeze brought over some kind of stench. Ghosts came with bad smells sometimes, rot or sulfur.

Felix gripped the back of his sweatshirt and walked so close their legs bumped together a few times. He conjured a light and tossed it toward the figures.

They did not react as ghosts would, instead throwing up hands and turning toward the light. One, in the cracking voice of a teenager, demanded, "What the fuck!"

Felix immediately yanked the orb back and extinguished it, switching it out for his phone's flashlight.

The light revealed a pair of teenagers.

Sunshine now recognized the smell as bad weed.

"Hey, what's the idea?" the girl demanded.

Felix came to stand in front of Sunshine. "Isn't it a little late?"

Sunshine covered his mouth to keep in a laugh.

"People are trying to sleep!" Felix scolded.

Sunshine wrapped an arm around his waist and said, "Come on, before you get arrested for exposing yourself to minors."

Felix scowled. To the teens, he said, "Just try to keep it down."

"Or what? You'll call the cops?"

Felix demanded, "What? Do I look like some kind of fucking fascist? Keep it down to demonstrate you have some modicum of common courtesy. Or at least get better taste in music, you little shit."

"Fucking tourists," the girl grumbled.

"Alright, come on," Sunshine said. He pulled Felix back inside before he could chew out the teens any further. "When did you turn into such a grumpy old man?"

"I thought they were ghosts."

"You're not scared of ghosts."

Felix huffed. He wiped his feet and trudged back upstairs.

Sunshine thought about calling after to tease him, but he knew Bobby and Carrie were asleep upstairs, too. He headed upstairs but stopped in front of the kitchen. The cabinets and fridge were opened. Dozens of boxes and jars lay spilled on their sides. Some had been torn or smashed open, but others remained relatively unscathed.

He turned on the light. Something yanked his hair, hard, but he didn't see what, and it only happened once. "Specter."

Felix came to stand beside him. "Fuck." He started to take a step inside.

Sunshine caught his arm and pulled him back. "There's broken glass."

Felix edged more carefully inside, taking pictures, then poking around.

Carrie came downstairs not too long after, her hand held up against the light. "What are you doing?"

"We found it like this. You didn't hear anything?"

"Like what? Ghosts?" She glared at the mess. "You really smashed all this up to con an old man?"

Felix let out a small growl.

She grabbed a broom and pushed it into Sunshine's arms. "Well. Now you can clean it up, too." She looked around again. "I *just* bought that!" She pointed out a smashed jar of honey. "You two are un-fucking-believable."

Felix watched her stomp away. "You think she's gonna feel like an asshole with we solve this case and set her dad up with a boyfriend?"

"Don't start playing matchmaker."

"Oh, but Bobby deserves something nice and they *so clearly* have a thing for each other."

"Meddlesome," Sunshine accused.

Felix immediately shut up and started cleaning, though pretty inefficiently in Sunshine's opinion.

Sunshine joined in, getting the kitchen as tidy as could be and double bagging the garbage bag full of broken glass. He even taped a note to it so the garbage collectors would know to be careful.

Back upstairs, he said, "Seems like something a little kid would do. They're always getting into things they shouldn't."

They went back to bed for a few hours. They couldn't sleep in much because they could hear Carrie and her father fighting downstairs. She thought he needed to go to the doctor and he told her he'd been to the doctor, that there was nothing wrong with him. She accused Sunshine and Specter of being conmen and Bobby got really upset at that.

Sunshine and Felix waited upstairs until they finished having it out with each other. One of them stormed off, probably Carrie by the sounds of it.

They gave it another few minutes, then went downstairs. They couldn't very well sit around upstairs all day.

They found Bobby sitting at the kitchen table with his head in his hands.

Felix edged back into the kitchen. "Bobby?"

Bobby rubbed his face and shook up. "Don't get old, Felix."

"Oh, baby, I could tell you stories..." Felix sat next to him and took his hand. "You're a man, honey, and nothing good hardly ever comes to men who stay young for too long."

"Don't have kids, either," Bobby said.

Felix laughed. "Oh, goodness, you don't need to tell me twice. Can you imagine me with kids? Fuck."

Bobby sighed. He rubbed his face again. "So what exactly happened last night?"

Felix slid his phone across the table.

"Bobby, do you mind if I cook?" Sunshine asked.

"Make yourself at home."

Sunshine saw to breakfast while Felix went through what they'd found in the kitchen and answered a few of Bobby's questions about ghosts.

Most of the answers amounted to things like 'sometimes' and 'maybe' and 'some can.' Several institutes and universities, as well as individual researchers, had investigated the various phenomena involved in hauntings. The causes and spirits came in so many varieties that no one had found any hard and fast answers.

He set bacon and eggs on the table, unable to cook much else with the kitchen so devoid of sweet ingredients. No jam, chocolate, sugar, or syrup, which had put a damper on his plans for pancakes. He hadn't even been able to find any butter for toast, so he served it dry with an apology.

In the picture, he noticed the jar of honey Carrie had pointed out as new, though it had surprisingly little mess around it. Not nearly as much as a mostly full jar would have created.

In fact, looking again at the picture, most of the jars and boxes seemed mostly empty.

He noticed it and had no idea what to do with that information.

He tuned into Felix telling Bobby he wanted to set up cameras around the house that night just in case something like this happened again.

Bobby gave his blessing.

Felix swept up their breakfast dishes, produced a sheaf of cash, and tucked it into Sunshine's front pocket. "Go to the store for me, darling."

"Which store?" Sunshine said, not able to think much beyond Felix's hand in his pocket.

Felix wiggled his fingers. "To replace dear Robert's groceries, of course."

"Oh, don't—" Bobby began.

"Hush, now," Felix said. "Sunshine, go." He pecked Sunshine on the mouth.

Sunshine went without thinking about it. He'd already skipped down the front steps before he realized that he didn't have his jacket, phone, or a grocery list. He didn't run back, of course. It wasn't too cold and he had on a sweater, he could live without his phone, and he had a pretty good idea of what Bobby needed from cooking breakfast.

He felt sort of free and light as he made his way to the grocery store. He wandered contentedly through the aisles, filling his cart, too aware of how much cash Felix had tucked into his pocket.

It wasn't until he'd made his way through the checkout and had walked his overfull cart outside that he realized he'd made a mistake.

He stared at the bags. The walk back was only about thirty minutes, but he didn't think he'd make it home with all the bags intact. He glanced around the parking lot.

He'd stolen things before, but not in a long time and never a shopping cart. He took a tentative step toward the parking lot exit.

"Hey there."

Sunshine glanced toward the voice. "Vinnie!" He grinned.

"That's a lot of groceries for a man on vacation."

"Oh, we had a...an incident in the kitchen." Sunshine looked at his overfull cart. "I may have gone a bit overboard."

Vinnie held a coffee and a pre-made sandwich.

Sunshine had never considered himself prideful, which made it easy to say, "Can I ask you for a huge favor?"

"What'd you have in mind?"

"You think you could give me a ride back to the house? I might have gotten overly ambitious."

Vinnie laughed. His belly jiggled a little. "Sure. Come on. I'm parked over here."

Vinnie talked most of the ride back. He asked a lot of questions about New York. Apparently, he'd never been.

"I almost ran away from home," Vinnie said. "Good thing I didn't, though, I...I don't think I'm cut out for a big city like that."

"No?"

"Small town like this does me just fine. Maybe a little lonely..."

Sunshine said, "A city can get lonely, too."

"Oh, yeah, I know...You know, I said you young fellows didn't understand how it was back in the day but damn if I understand what's going on these days either."

Sunshine laughed. "For all the things that change, the basics never do."

"Basics? Like what?"

"If you like someone, you should tell them."

Vinnie chuckled. "Your, uh, your boyfriend there, he's a pistol, isn't he?"

"No. He's...He's one of those guns they use to take out elephants," Sunshine said. "But he's...you know, he means well. Felix almost always means well and honestly, if he didn't, we'd all be fucked."

Vinnie glanced over at Sunshine, concern scrunching his face.

Knowing he approached sounding legitimately delusional, he said, "He's a being of immense power."

"Uh."

Sunshine cracked a smile to break the tension. Vinnie was not ready for any Community revelations, no matter how much Sunshine liked him. He had a settled feeling to him, a little rough, but pleasant and warm. "He's got rich parents."

"Oh." Vinnie chucked. "That." He pulled up in front of the

house and insisted on helping Sunshine bring in the groceries.

Bobby and Felix had a show on in the living room.

While Sunshine unpacked, Vinnie went in to say hi. Felix immediately started to put on his Hollywood Glamor airs, so Sunshine called for him.

Felix appeared, seated himself at the kitchen table, and did not help put anything away. When he saw the bag of chips he flopped over the table, stretched out his arms as far as they would go, and made grabby hands.

Sunshine gave him the bag. "You're an absolute child, you know that?"

Felix flashed him a smile and peeled open the chips. He only ate a few before he sealed the bag with a bit of heat. He only ever ate a little junk food at a time these days. When he'd been cursed, he'd gorged himself on so many terrible and cheap foods that he couldn't stomach much of them anymore. "What are you making for dinner?"

Sunshine shrugged. He heard Vinnie's laugh and suddenly, an overwhelming urge for spaghetti and meatballs overcame him. Something about Vinnie's laugh reminded him of an old flame.

"What's that look?"

"Nothing."

"Oh, no, it's something. You look sad."

"I was just thinking about someone," Sunshine said.

"Who?"

Sunshine hesitated to answer. "You remember Anthony DiMarco?"

Felix narrowed his eyes. "What about him?"

Sunshine shrugged. Felix had never liked Anthony even before things had gone sideways. In fact, if Sunshine thought about it, Felix had never liked any of the handful of men Sunshine'd had those quiet affairs with. He'd never liked any of his girlfriends, either. He wondered if he'd gone for people Felix didn't like or if Felix had somehow known subconsciously that Sunshine was involved past the point of friendship.

"Oh my god. Him, too?"

Sunshine shrugged. "He taught me how to make meatballs."

Felix's eyes widened. "Have you been feeding me Anthony DiMarco's meatballs for fifty fucking years?"

"Not...not exclusively. Sometimes I use other recipes. And besides, it was his grandmother's, so, really, it's her recipe."

"Like I give a fuck about his nonna. You know he put a hit on me."

"Well, yeah, we broke up after that," Sunshine said.

"Sunshine, he was in the fucking mob."

"And you're the goddamn Antichrist. He was nice to me and he...You know, he was only trying to scare you off the case. He was in over his head with them."

Felix crossed his arms. "Anthony fucking DiMarco. And fucking Cantamesa, too. You really have a type, don't you?"

"People who let me take care of them."

Felix let out a disgusted scoff. "People I can't stand. Who's next, Alby Coal?"

Sunshine kept his mouth shut. He found something else to put away.

"Alby Coal!" Felix demanded.

Alby had never done anything illegal, but he and Felix had engaged in one of the most famous academic rivalries the Community had seen for a good part of the eighties. It had ended with Coal's posthumous rebuttal on the ethics of magical noninterference in non-Community issues with specific regards to the AIDS crisis.

"Only a few times. Not...not anything serious," Sunshine said. "It was before."

"I can't believe you."

Coal had maintained that lives mattered more than secrecy. Felix had taken the stance that secrecy kept Community members alive. He insisted Coal was human and didn't understand the danger that floated above the heads of the creatures in the Community, or what would happen if they were exposed to the wider world. Coal responded that Felix was immortal and didn't understand the danger that humans faced from something as small as a virus.

The debate flared up every time something wildly unfortunate happened in the human world. Health crises always saw a lot of pressure on the University of Triviai, the only arcane university with a medical branch, and a flare-up in vampires turning people. Most of the vampires Sunshine knew had been turned during a pandemic or war.

Of course, Felix hadn't been able to publish anything refuting Coal's paper without looking absolutely heartless since Coal had passed away in Yale-New Haven Hospital, bone-thin and unable to speak.

Felix had even gone to visit him as he'd died. Before ethics and illnesses had come into play, they'd been good friends. Their discussions and debates had turned into ugly arguments, insults that couldn't be walked back. Before Alby had died, they hadn't seen each other in person for a good two years.

Now, Felix examined his nails and finally admitted, "I might have, too." He spoke more to his hands than to Sunshine.

Sunshine shook his head, not surprised in the least. "Then you can't be that mad at me."

There had been too much emotion between the two for it to not have spilled over somewhere. He didn't know if it had come before or after they'd started to argue. Sometimes Sunshine thought that if Alby hadn't gotten sick, if they hadn't started fighting, then he and Felix would have ended up together.

Felix didn't like to get too serious with humans, but he might have made an exception for Alby.

Instead of arguing or listing reasons he had to be mad, Felix sighed. "We...we were both wrong. Or, you know, we were both right. There is no good answer to a problem like that. I wish." He glanced up for barely a second. "I wish hadn't fought with him about it. I wish I'd been a better friend. He was dying and scared, and I was healthy and safe, and yeah, I was sad, it hurt to lose people like that, but who was I to say what was right or wrong? The Community might have had to go underground but we could have saved millions of lives."

"But nothing, Felix. You don't know what would have happened. All the lives saved for one thing might have cost just as many lives on another end. Humans have done hideous enough things with sciences of their own devising, what would happen if magic got involved in wars or dictatorships?"

"I don't know."

"You don't know if it would have been better. You don't even know if the Community could have done anything."

"Sounds like apologist ideology if you ask me."

Sunshine said, "The answer to human illnesses is human medicines, not a small, relatively secret community of supernatural creatures who can barely manage their own crises. It's not turning a generation of sick people into vampires or having them strike deals with the Devil. It's not the medical magics that Triviai holds hostage. The answer to human problems is humans."

"I just wish..."

"You're miserable at healing people, you couldn't have saved anyone without becoming something you don't want to be."

"What the fuck do you know anyway?" Felix snapped.

"I know you."

"You don't know shit."

"Felix—"

"I don't know what I wanted to talk to you about this anyway for. You wouldn't understand. Didn't the guy who made you wipe out the world with a flood? Ask a guy to kill his son? Gives a good perspective on how you up there feel about humans."

Once, those accusations would have easily led Sunshine into an argument. He'd had love for the home he'd left behind, but more than that, he'd had blind obedience. "Abrahamic mythology and actual events are often vastly different."

"I just think the person who made the world should take care of it," Felix sulked. He was right to sulk. A creator should care for its creation.

Sunshine licked his lips. He thought of what to say and whether he should say it. He'd gotten close to revealing such truths before but had always held back. "The world exists, and every culture has its own story of how it came to be. Just because the Almighty made your father, and your father made you, does not mean He is the answer to everything. Your view narrows so much when it comes to these things. He is real but the Bible is not the truth. It is human stories based on a few interactions thousands of years in the past, rewritten and translated a hundred times over."

"I know. Big bang, evolution, all that."

"So then don't blame the world's problems on an infinite, genderless being with no real concept of time or human morality just because it fucked around and created a couple of humans a few million years ago."

"Jesus Christ," Felix breathed.

"*That* was a weird period in Heaven, I think He was going through something then. Your father probably did something to put him in a mood," Sunshine said.

"Don't get all cosmic and revelatory on me, we're supposed to be working and I can't do that if you throw me into an existential spiral."

"So you don't mind if I make meatballs."

"Fine, make Anthony goddamn DiMarco's meatballs. Christ. What the hell do you think normal couples talk about?"

"I think they fight about their in-laws and who does more housework," Sunshine said.

"At least we don't do that. Any other Heavenly truths you'd

like to lay on me?"

Fully joking and hoping it showed in his tone, Sunshine said, "It was really weird when the humans all started fucking those monkeys. Those poor chimps. But a man will fuck anything if you leave it alone with it long enough."

"You're a bad person."

Sunshine grinned at him. "You'll help me cut up onions later?"

"If I must."

"Go see if Vinnie wants to come to dinner."

Felix traipsed out and Sunshine could hear him say, "You're Italian, aren't you? Come over for dinner. Sunshine's making meatballs and you should come tell him what he's doing wrong."

"Oh, well, I..."

"What time!" Felix hollered toward the kitchen.

"Six!"

"So you'll be here at six, Vinnie?"

"Oh, well," Vinnie began again.

"I have so come to enjoy your company," Felix said.

"I suppose...I can come by after my last call today. I, uh, I might be a little late," Vinnie said.

"Wonderful!" Felix crowed. He came back to the kitchen, shoved the remaining groceries willy-nilly into the fridge and cabinets, and grabbed Sunshine's hand. "Come help me with the cameras, I won't want to do it later."

It took a while to charge and set up the handful of cameras they'd brought. One for the kitchen, one in the bedroom hallway, and one pointing outside. They skipped the basement and attic because they hadn't noticed anything down there.

Dinner proved a cozy affair. Vinnie offered no critiques of the meatballs or sauce and Felix accused him of just being polite.

Once Vinnie left and Bobby went to bed, Felix seemed to deflate. He oozed into one corner of the couch and wrapped a blanket around his shoulders. Sunshine turned on the TV and rested his head on his lap. One of Felix's fingers twirled around one of his curls.

"If you're tired you should go to bed," Sunshine said after an hour of no sounds but the ones from the TV.

"It's not that kind of tired."

Sunshine had suspected as much. "Do you need anything?"

"A lot of things. I need so many things, darling, but mostly I just need you to stay on the couch with me for a while."

Sunshine took his hand and pulled it to his lips. He kissed his palm, then returned it to his head.

Felix wiggled his fingers briefly. "Will you change the channel?"

Sunshine flipped through until Felix found something he liked.

Carrie found them on the couch. "At least the frauds on TV actually pretend to do something. What's your excuse?"

Sunshine rolled onto his back to see Felix's reaction.

Felix looked at her.

"You know this is my home, too. I run this business with my father. It's not just *his* money he's throwing away."

"I don't want your father's money," Felix said.

She let out a disgusted scoff.

"You've never experienced a single thing in this house that gives you pause?"

"No. I'm not an old man with dementia."

Felix let out a long, slow exhale. He lifted his hand and extended it palm up. He conjured a flame to sit in his palm.

Carrie stared.

Felix said, "Come touch it if you don't believe it's real."

She didn't move.

Felix extinguished the flame and when he opened his hand again, a piece of glass sculpted into the shape of a maple leaf rested there. He floated it over to Carrie.

She stepped back.

"Take it," Sunshine advised, propped up on one elbow.

She touched one finger to it, then grabbed it when it started to fall.

"We're not here to scam your father, ghosts are real, and I'm a hundred and one—"

"Two," Sunshine murmured.

"Hundred and two years old," Felix concluded.

Carrie hadn't spoken yet. She stared at the glass leaf in her hand.

"You can use it as a Christmas ornament," Felix offered. "If you do Christmas."

"We do Christmas," Carrie whispered.

"Slap a little ribbon on that bad boy..." Felix trailed off and seemed to lose interest in Carrie. He settled back into the corner and patted his lap. "Get comfy."

"This is insane."

Sunshine felt a little bad for how Felix had dropped the information on her. "It takes time to adjust to the idea of magic."

Carrie looked up.

"It is magic," Sunshine assured.

She walked away.

Sunshine laid down and stared up at Felix. "I can see your nose hairs."

"Well. It'd be weird if you couldn't from that angle."

"You need to shave. You're getting all peach fuzzy."

"It's not peach fuzz!"

Sunshine reached up and ran the back of his finger across Felix's jawline. "I've always wanted a beard."

"What?"

"I don't know, I think I'd look good."

"You'd look great no matter what, short of your actual entire face and scalp being peeled off."

"Well, that's...sweet."

"You're welcome."

They lazily traded ideas back and forth about minor tweaks they would make to their physical appearances, given the chance. Felix had more on his list. Sunshine just wanted a beard and to be less identical to the other soldiers.

"I wish my eyes were a different color," Felix said quietly, like he knew he shouldn't have said it.

"You have beautiful eyes."

"I've got demon eyes."

Sunshine clucked his tongue. "Your eyes are beautiful."

"They...Just. They're red."

Sunshine had never thought of Felix's eyes as red. True, they were but it only ever became apparent in direct light. Any other time, they looked black. The red indicated Felix's parentage like a brand. All the Devil's children had red eyes, but the Devil's eyes had not held red until after his fall. Sunshine saw how that could play into Felix's complicated relationship with his identity and father in general.

"Your eyes are beautiful," he repeated. "And I'll keep saying it."

Felix pressed his lips together and squirmed.

Sunshine sat up and blew a raspberry against his cheek. "Let's go to bed."

"I'm really...I'm not in the mood, Sunshine, I'm sorry. It's..." He sighed.

"I'm tired, too," Sunshine said.

"I guess we could lay down."

They curled up in bed together.

Sunshine fell asleep.

He woke up alone hours later, but long before his Monday morning alarm. The spot where Felix had lain still felt warm when he touched it. He wasn't in the bathroom unless he was standing perfectly still and not breathing.

Sunshine got out of bed to look for him. If they'd been at home, he wouldn't have worried, but they were in a haunted house. He found Felix standing outside in his underwear and Sunshine's sweatshirt, barefoot and staring up at the sky.

He had conjured an orb of light, except it looked wrong.

After decades, Sunshine had a pretty solid idea of what Felix's magic looked like and it didn't look like that.

"Felix?"

No response.

"Specter!"

Still, he didn't move.

Sunshine went over and touched his shoulder.

He didn't move.

Sunshine circled in front of him and found his eyes blank. Not just empty, but cloudy gray and devoid of intelligence. He gave him a firm shake.

Felix's eyes widened. He sucked in a slow breath then fixed his gaze on Sunshine's face, the gray haze draining away from his eyes. He blinked.

"Hon, what...what are you doing?"

"I was...I was at a picnic." He smiled and licked his lips. "Cherries and..." His smile faded. He looked around and began to frown. "What time is it?"

"About three a.m."

Felix ran a hand through his hair. He sighed. "Fucking ghosts."

Sunshine hugged him.

Felix nestled his face against his chest. "I swear, I tasted it."

Sunshine squeezed. "Come back to bed."

Felix held his hand as they walked back. Before he crawled into bed, he used the belt from a bathrobe to link their hands.

"What...?" Sunshine began to ask but realized he would have agreed to this no matter what reasoning Felix provided.

"I don't like sleepwalking."

Sunshine cuddled up to him and held on extra tight.

"You're squishing me."

Sunshine squeezed him tighter.

Felix grunted, then whined, so Sunshine loosened his arms,

kissed his shoulder, and didn't let go, for once the clingier of the two. They woke up twisted and tangled together like scraps of yarn at the bottom of a knitter's purse.

While the video footage from last night uploaded to their laptop, Felix insisted on a walk along the beach. Sunshine had eyed the heavy gray clouds and tried to direct him to another activity, but he had said, "I'll go on my own, then."

That had worked.

Carrie hadn't spoken to them or her father when she'd seen them at breakfast.

Sunshine didn't particularly care what Carrie thought of them. Bobby was an old friend, but they hadn't seen him in decades and probably wouldn't stay in touch. It happened with each generation. They made friends with humans around the ages they looked, then as the humans got older and moved on with their lives, Sunshine and Felix stayed behind.

At least they had each other and a few other core friends who also had extended lives.

Felix didn't say a word as they walked across the beach.

Sunshine asked, "You feeling okay?"

"I don't like this sleepwalking thing."

"No, me neither."

They lapsed back into silence until Felix said, "Does this feel like a haunting to you?"

"Not really."

Felix grumbled for a while under his breath.

"We'll have to see what the cameras got."

"If they got anything," Felix huffed.

Sunshine looped an arm around him and pulled him close. He pressed a kiss to his temple. "We'll figure it out."

"And if we can't?"

"Uh, you can buy the bed-and-breakfast like you bought that haunted house in Connecticut and Bobby can retire somewhere warm."

That at least got a chuckle out of him. A funny feeling came over Sunshine. A weird, itchy feeling on the back of his neck. He glanced around and saw nothing except waves, sand, and seagulls.

They sat in the sand for a while, watching the waves. The clouds cleared up enough that Sunshine didn't want to ask to go back. He eyed a persistent patch of thunderheads further out to sea and hoped the wind would blow them away instead of inland.

The feeling got worse the longer they sat.

Finally, he stood and did a more thorough search.

There! A way off, but something glinted in the distance. He squinted toward it, trying to figure out what it could be. It sent an uncomfortable quiver of familiarity through his guts.

"What?" Felix asked.

"Something's wrong."

"What do you mean?"

"We should go, we've..." His mouth when dry when he realized what he saw. It was the gleam of sunlight on armor. He would have seen it before except the clouds had dimmed the sun too much to make it reflect off metal.

He grabbed Felix and pulled him to his feet.

Felix peered around him. "What's got you...oh." His eyes widened a little but more than surprised he looked resigned. He'd always expected this to happen.

"Go."

Felix touched the ring he always wore, a plain band on his left forefinger. It was meant to shield him from Heaven.

Sunshine didn't have time to think about how the angel had found them, not now. He grabbed Felix by the wrist and pulled him along, practically dragging him through the sand.

"Stop, stop, Sunshine."

Sunshine didn't stop. He nearly picked him up and threw him over his shoulder. "We have to go."

"Go where!" Felix demanded, digging his heels in. "Back to Bobby's? We can't have an angel follow us there."

"Anywhere but here," Sunshine said. "He...his mission isn't Bobby, it's *you*."

Felix refused to move. "I'm not a scared kid anymore, Sunshine. I'm not running away."

Sunshine gave his arm one more tug.

Felix yanked his arm back. "I'm not running."

Sunshine looked down the beach. The other angel had progressed steadily, close enough now that Sunshine could no longer hope he was mistaken.

"And I need to know how he found me."

"Felix, please."

"No."

He grabbed Felix by the arms. "I don't want to kill him."

The hard resolve on Felix's face softened. He touched Sunshine's cheek. "I wouldn't ask you to."

"I don't want you to kill him either."

Felix smiled. "Since when have either of us taken to murder as our first course of action? I talked you into leaving me alive, didn't I?"

Sunshine still almost picked him up and ran away. He tightened his grip. "Please be a little more sensible than usual."

Felix looked toward the angel.

The angel wore a golden chest piece and a golden leather skirt and carried a sword across his back. He hadn't drawn a weapon yet. He hadn't even loosened his sword in its sheath. He walked steady, implacable, but didn't seem to be on the offensive.

He didn't even look defensive, honestly.

Assured and haughty, but not angry.

Sunshine said, "Let me talk to him first."

"I guess."

"And stay here."

Felix rolled his eyes and crossed his arms but didn't argue.

Sunshine squared his shoulders and walked out to meet the other angel. He tried not to look nervous, but he could feel his sweater start to stick to his back.

They stopped about three feet away from each other.

The other angel smiled at him.

Sunshine frowned.

"Are you so long from Heaven you cannot recognize the face of a friend?"

Hearing his own voice from another person's mouth made Sunshine's skin crawl. It sounded exactly like him but in so many ways, it didn't. His cadence, tone, and vocabulary had changed so much as he'd more fully integrated into society.

"The face I recognize, but your intentions remain unknown."

The angel smiled again, broader and warmer. "Intentions? You are our lost soldier. What could my intentions be but to resolve our mission and bring you home?"

"Lost," Sunshine echoed. He licked his lips. The wind blew through him and send a horrible coldness over him, making his sweater lay cold and damp against his skin. "I'm not lost."

"More than a century you've been away. We felt your loss, all of us, when the son of the Beast bound you to this realm."

"I'm...I'm not bound anymore."

His own face smiled back at him, except it wasn't his anymore. The newcomer's face was sharper featured and revealed less of his internal state if he had one at all. Sunshine recalled how purposefully empty he'd been upon coming to Earth. "I know. We could feel you again. We knew you'd won your freedom somehow, but you didn't return to us. I came to find you. To lead you home."

Sunshine shifted. He tried not to look over his shoulder. So far, the other angel hadn't noticed Felix, which confirmed that he'd come for Sunshine and not the Antichrist. The ring still worked. Felix could hide. That was all that mattered.

The angel's eyebrows knitted ever so slightly. "I thought I'd find you...poorer. Unfit somehow. You seem hale enough. Why haven't you returned home?"

"I can't go through the in-between places anymore."

The angel nodded. "Of course. We wouldn't want that power in the wrong hands. I can take you." He extended his hand.

Sunshine swallowed.

"What?"

"I...I have...My mission. What of the Antichrist? Aren't I supposed to be hunting him still?"

"Do you know where he is? We can do it together."

Sunshine shook his head. "No." Fear made his voice waiver. He wanted to look behind him. He hoped Felix had run away all the way back to New York. No, back to Pickering. He hoped he was on his way to Hiram and Phaedrus now.

The angel embraced him. "Your time here cannot have been kind. The Beast does not treat his captives well. I cannot imagine his son does any better. Come home. Rest."

Something inside Sunshine broke. He started to weep. Not just cry, but weep like someone had died. He had not seen another angel since he'd left Heaven, he'd had no contact with the Almighty, and he had yearned for his home in the worst way. He curled himself into the other angel's arms and sobbed.

The angel soothed him. "Come home. It's over."

Sunshine pulled himself back together enough to say, "I can't."

"Why not?"

Sunshine pulled back. He scrubbed his sleeve across his cheeks and under his nose. "I...I have people here."

"People?"

"Friends. A..."

The angel guessed, "You've taken a mate."

"Not...no. Not a mate. We don't have children," Sunshine hurried to correct.

"Good. Angels aren't meant for such things."

Sunshine didn't argue. He didn't want to argue with someone who had nothing but Heaven's word to go on. He remembered how he was then. "But I'm here, I'm in this town because I said I'd help someone. An old friend."

The angel nodded. "I see. I'll help with what I can. Lead on."

"You don't—"

"What one of us can do, two of us can do in half the time. Tell me of your friend's troubles," the angel insisted.

Sunshine stared at him.

"The beach is empty. Your friend is not here, I assume."

Sunshine licked his lips, but that only made them sticky. He nodded, cleared his throat, and tried to get enough spit to swallow. He said, "Uh. This...This way."

He turned and made eye contact with Felix. "Go," he mouthed.

"Go where?" Felix mouthed back.

"Bobby's."

Felix's face scrunched. "What?"

"The bed and breakfast," Sunshine said louder and made a pointed face at Felix.

"A what?" the angel asked.

"It's a type of human lodging. My friend owns it."

"Ah."

Felix scurried ahead of them, texting furiously.

Sunshine received a message that read, *What the actual fuck do you expect me to do right now!!!!*

Go to our room and wait.

Wait for what.

Just go and lock the door and wait.

Felix didn't answer, but he threw a poisonous look over his shoulder.

Sunshine kept a slow pace and walked beside the angel. He knew his next question could be taken poorly, but he had to ask, "Do we have names yet?"

"The Almighty has no need to name us."

"The people here, they all have names. I needed one to live among them."

"And you live among them?"

Sunshine shrugged. He'd gone pretty native, all things considered. "People call me Sunshine."

The angel wrinkled his nose.

"Have you been on Earth long?"

"I've experienced several seasonal cycles, but I can't tell you an exact count of the days."

"Well, uh. Do...do you know anyone? I mean, have you made acquaintances or anything? Or friends?"

"No."

Sunshine had expected as much. "What should I call you, then?"

"You don't have to call me anything."

"Well, I mean, we're not telepathically linked liquid anymore. It might be helpful to have something to call you."

The angel gave him a funny smile. "I'll think on it."

Their walk back to the bed and breakfast passed quietly. Sunshine had a million questions he wanted to ask, but he needed to think of what to tell Bobby and how to get Felix as far from the angel as possible. He also had to explain why he couldn't go back to Heaven. He didn't see Felix when they went inside and asked the angel to have a seat in the living room.

The angel stood beside the couch with his hands clasped behind his back.

Sunshine hurried to find Bobby, offered the quickest and easiest explanation he could, which was that he'd run into his brother and that's who was in the living room. He asked if the angel could stay in one of the rooms and insisted on paying for it.

Bobby, he thought, only agreed because Sunshine must have looked about as harried as he felt. Bobby kept asking him if he was okay.

"And don't tell him Felix is here."

"Why not?"

"He can't know. He'll try to kill him."

"Literally?"

"Literally," Sunshine said. "I'm...I just." He raked his hand through his hair. "I'm sorry to bring this into your house. What...I just. I didn't know what else to do. I don't...I don't even know how he found me. I didn't know he was even *looking* for me."

"Honey, are you in trouble?" Bobby asked. He put his hand on Sunshine's arm.

"I really hope not."

"You sure you want him to stay here? There are a dozen other places he can stay in town."

"I..."

"You want me to make a phone call?"

"Do you mind?"

"No, course not. You go get yourself settled. I'll find a place for him to stay," Bobby promised. "Check on Felix. He went upstairs in a mood. Can't say I blame him."

Sunshine squeezed his hand. He went to tell the angel, "I've got to do something upstairs, but then...uh. I'll find you a place to stay for a few nights."

"This issue can't be resolved today?"

"No, I'm. I'm sorry."

The angel shrugged. "A few more days makes little difference."

Sunshine forced a smile, then had to stop himself from running upstairs.

Felix sat on their bed not fidgeting or playing with his phone, but stone-still. "Well?"

"I'm trying to buy a little time."

"Time for what?"

"Time to make him understand I'm not going back."

"He's downstairs?"

Sunshine nodded.

Felix patted the bed.

"No, I'm all sweaty."

That made Felix smile. "Come here. I don't mind."

He sat beside him. "I don't know what to do."

"If he's anything like you were, you can put him in a hotel room, show him how to order room service, and come back in a week."

He tried to smile.

Felix leaned against him. "He couldn't see me at all?"

"The ring still works."

"At least there's that."

Sunshine put an arm around him and dragged him close. "Will you stay in here though, until he's gone?"

"The videos are uploaded. It will take a while to look through them."

"Thank you."

After a quiet minute, Felix asked, "Are you okay?"

"I'm scared."

"I've never seen you cry like that before."

His throat tightened again. "I'm sorry."

"Don't be sorry, you idiot. I'm trying to be nice to you."

"I'm so sorry."

"Sunshine, it's not your fault."

"He came looking for me. They think...He said I was lost. How...How do I tell him I can't go back? That I won't go back?"

"I don't know."

He grabbed Felix's hands. "Felix, let me be yours. Make it so I can't go."

Felix shook his head. He pressed his lips together. "I..."

Sunshine knew he couldn't. He knew it wasn't fair to ask. But still, he knelt before Felix and said, "Please."

Felix's jaw trembled. He drew in a shaky breath. "Sunshine."

He stared up at Felix, ready to fall, not in adoration, but out of fear. He knew, somehow, if he asked again, Felix would do it for him, he would become something he never wanted to be because Sunshine had asked.

This wasn't how Sunshine wanted things to go. He wanted to be Felix's out of love, not because he was too afraid to tell another angel the truth.

He let go of Felix's hands and stood before Felix could agree. He had hidden from Heaven as much as Felix had, not out of fear for his life, but because he feared their judgment. "I shouldn't have asked you that."

"If you need help, I can—"

"No. I shouldn't have...I'm scared. I need...I need help but not like that. I shouldn't be trying to make you do something you don't want."

"Sunshine, you..." Felix looked away. He started picking his nails. Sulkily, he said, "You always just do whatever I tell you. If you want something back, you should go ahead and say it."

Sunshine sat next to him and nudged Felix's shoulder with his. "Forget I asked, honestly. You're rubbing off on me, I'm getting dramatic."

Felix leaned against him. "Well, stop. One of us has to be sensible."

"I'll be back later. Stay put in here, okay?"

"I've got to watch those videos anyway."

"Text me if you need anything."

Felix nodded.

Sunshine took another minute to compose himself then went back downstairs to see the other angel. He found Bobby attempting to communicate with him and it made him wonder if he'd been that hard to talk to.

The angel didn't understand why he couldn't stay here or what exactly it meant for the building to be haunted.

"You." The angel turned to look at him. "You're lodging at this place, yes?"

"I am but—"

"Then why wouldn't I?"

"It's haunted."

"An angel has no need to fear a spirit."

"Yes, but..."

"And how can I help you solve this problem if I'm elsewhere?" the angel pressed.

Sunshine looked at Bobby.

"We haven't got any other rooms ready," Bobby tried.

The angel smiled at Sunshine. "Thousands of years as part of the same infinity, sharing a room wouldn't be such an imposition."

"You know what? I'll go...I'll go get some sheets out of storage, I'll get a room ready," Bobby said, clearly having read the panic on Sunshine's face.

The angel had seen it too. Looking somewhat hurt, but mostly confused, he asked, "Is it an imposition?"

"There's only one bed," Sunshine offered lamely.

"And that is...too intimate?"

Sunshine wanted to say yes and give an easy answer, but it wouldn't have been true. In some ways, he wanted nothing more than to be in Heaven again, linked and formless, and bedsharing got pretty close to that experience. "There's just not room. It would be uncomfortable. Physically. Not emotionally."

"I see." The angel looked relieved.

"Here, uh...Really, come sit down." He sat on the couch.

The angel sat beside him. "Tell me more of your undertaking here."

"Oh. It's...I told Bobby I'd help him get the ghosts sorted."

"That shouldn't present much of a challenge."

"I hope not."

The angel smiled at him. "How do we begin?"

"Uh. I kind of wanted to catch up."

"How so?"

"Tell me about Heaven. About the others. I haven't been there in more than a century."

"When you rejoin us, you will know all that has passed."

Sunshine said, "But I don't know it now."

"You will."

Sunshine looked at his hands like they could tell him what to do. "I'm not who I was when I left."

"All you need is rest—"

"No. It's...It's not just that I'm different. I don't want to be who I was."

The angel blinked. "Come home. It's worse than I thought, but once you rest, once you're with us again, you'll forget all the things done to you here."

"I don't want to forget them."

"There's no reason to hold onto pain. Lay down your burden. Forget this place. Whatever happened while he had you, Heaven will wash it away."

Sunshine took the other angel's hand. "I'm not in pain. He never did anything to me."

"He stripped your powers, bound you from Heaven, held you prisoner—"

"No. Not. Not the way you're thinking of it. He only did those things to keep himself safe. He never hurt me. I chose to stay here."

The angel pulled his hand back and stood. He looked down at Sunshine. "Come home now."

"I'm not going."

The angel grabbed his arm and pulled him to his feet.

Sunshine wrenched out of his grasp. "I don't want to go back. I'm not lost, I don't need saving. I have a life here and I'm not leaving."

The angel reached for him again.

"No. I'm not leaving."

"This is worse—"

"It's not worse. Just...Just stay. For a little while. I haven't seen anyone from home in a century and...I missed you. I miss home, I do, and I missed being together. Stay. Let me show you my life before you decide it's not worth living."

The angel frowned.

"Please. It's a good life and I know it probably sounds crazy to you but just...Give a me chance. Please." Sunshine put his arms around the angel again. "Please, it's been so long, I don't want to fight about this."

As much as he worried about what would happen if the angel found out about Felix, he wanted him to stay. Maybe he could convince him that Felix wasn't a threat. After all, Sunshine had accepted it within a few days of meeting him and he and this angel had been made to be the same.

The angel patted his back. "You're not ready. You've been through so much. We'll take the time you need."

Sunshine hugged him harder. "Thank you."

Bobby cleared his throat. "Room's all set. End of the hallway."

Sunshine pulled back. "Thanks, Bobby. I really owe you one." To the angel, he said, "I'll show you up. Get you a change."

"Why?"

"Of clothes? It's...You're not exactly discrete dressed like that."

The angel narrowed his eyes, then seemed to resign himself to playing along with Sunshine. "Very well."

They walked upstairs together. Sunshine tried to duck into his room, but the angel stayed close and stood in the doorway.

Felix froze as he lay on the bed, on his stomach in front of the laptop.

Sunshine tried not to freak out.

The angel moved closer to the bed. "I've seen other people with these."

"Oh, the laptop?"

Felix tried to edge off the bed as the angel came closer. He rolled off with a thud, his eyes huge.

The angel's head jerked up.

Sunshine let out a nervous laugh. "Haunted house, am I right?"

"It is disconcerting," the angel agreed.

Sunshine knelt beside the bed, pretending to go through his bag. "You okay?" he whispered.

"What are you doing?" Felix whispered.

"Getting him clothes."

Felix sighed. "You only *brought* one pair of shoes."

Sunshine ran a hand through his hair.

"Go ditch him. We'll go shopping."

Sunshine stood. To the angel, he said, "I, uh. I need to do laundry, actually. It won't take forever. Come on, I'll show you your room."

"I can come with you."

Sunshine took him by the arm and gave a tug. "No. I remember what it's like to have a mission, to search for someone. Come get some rest."

"I'm not tired."

"Have you ever slept in a bed?"

"No."

"Then you're tired," Sunshine promised.

He showed the angel the shower and the bed, both of which the angel claimed to understand but Sunshine knew understanding couldn't be had without experience. He prompted him to take a shower and a nap, then promised they'd get something to eat later.

Felix waited for him outside their room, arms crossed. "We need to talk anyway."

"Nothing on the footage?"

"No, there's a lot on the footage. Orbs and static and

manifestations like I've never seen. If I never hear a giggle again it'll be too soon." He took Sunshine's wrist and tugged him down the stairs. "I thought you were getting rid of him."

Sunshine looked at his feet.

Felix raised an eyebrow. "Well?"

"I don't know, Specter. It's been a hundred years—"

"A hundred and two years."

Sunshine smiled.

"You're not going back, are you?"

"No."

"You'd tell me if you were."

"I'm not."

Felix kicked the bottom step and didn't look at him. "I've never been abandoned but I don't think my psyche could handle it right now."

Sunshine wrapped his arms around him and lifted him off his feet. "I'm not going anywhere."

Felix nuzzled against his neck. "Promise."

"I promise."

He pulled away and headed toward the door, Sunshine's sleeve grasped between his fingers. "Are you alright, darling? I know this is probably a bit much, even for someone as unflappable as you."

"Whenever I stop to breathe for a second too long, I feel like I'm going to cry."

"Then you should probably cry."

"Can I do it in the car?"

"You can absolutely cry in the car. I will park all the way in the back of the Target parking lot, and you can cry as hard as you want. I'll even get out if you want to cry alone."

Crying alone sounded horrible. He shook his head.

Felix pecked his cheek and took him to cry in the Target parking lot, all the way in the back like he'd promised. Afterward, he bought him a coffee and a huge cookie from a nearby café, then proceeded to act like nothing had happened while they found something for the new angel to wear.

When Sunshine brought the clothes and shoes into the angel's room, Felix peeked over his shoulder. He stared at the angel's collapsed, nude body on the bed and said, "You're right, you have gained weight."

The angel looked chiseled even in his sleep. Sunshine could see immediately the differences, nothing extreme but enough to make them no longer identical. Ten or fifteen pounds, a tattoo, and a haircut separated them, but it felt amazing to realize he was no longer one of sixty identical men. He was their slightly softened brother, a version pampered by the Antichrist and Earth.

Felix kissed his cheek. "That's alright. I don't like a man with too many muscles."

"Go back to the room."

Felix went but he let his hand slide all over Sunshine, from his shoulder to his thigh, on the way out.

Sunshine set down the bag by the bed and wondered if he should wake him. He looked so comfortable that Sunshine decided to leave him alone. He probably hadn't gotten a good night's sleep in years. He left the bags and headed back to his room.

Felix had moved the laptop off the bed and lay on his side, sprawled out and looking luxurious.

Sunshine lay down beside him. He expected him to ask why Sunshine thought he had permission to invade his bed, but instead, Felix scooted closer and softly kissed him.

"We should talk about the case," Felix said and kissed him again.

"Okay."

"But first..."

"Hmm?"

Felix sort of shrugged. "I don't know, maybe you could take your pants off."

Sunshine couldn't help but smile. "Yeah. I could do that."

Felix tugged at one of his belt loops and kissed him again. He didn't wait for Sunshine to take his pants off, or even for him to pull them down all the way. As soon as he had his fly undone, he had his mouth around Sunshine. He moved with an intentional sort of tenderness. It wasn't like he was trying to be nice or acted out of pity. It felt more genuine than that. It felt like Felix loved him.

It was a lot to assume based on a blowjob, but Sunshine had worked for years to interpret Felix's actions. He couldn't help but read into things at this point.

It also helped that Felix snuggled up to him afterward, at least for a little while.

After about five minutes, he smacked Sunshine's leg and said, "Put your dick away, we're supposed to be working."

Sunshine let out a huff, not surprised.

"Honestly, you're a disgrace."

Sunshine rolled on top of him. "You're going to give a fellow the wrong idea."

"And what idea is that?"

"He might start to think you like him."

"I don't like anybody, least of all big dumb sides of beef like you."

Sunshine kissed him. "Sides of beef, that's new. You've never called me that before."

"Get up or I'll think of something worse to call you."

Sunshine drew back.

Felix kissed him, then slid out from under him and grabbed the laptop. They spent an hour or so reviewing all the strange footage Felix had flagged.

In all the haunted houses they'd investigated, they'd never gotten so much evidence on tape.

November 15, 2016

Tuesday

Felix dragged Sunshine out of bed much earlier than he would have liked and brought him out to stand in the backyard. Now they stood in underwear and sweatshirts in front of Peg's butterfly garden.

Felix paced back in forth in front of it while Sunshine stood sort of uselessly off to the side, not sure what Felix wanted from him other company.

"You don't smell that?" Felix asked.

"Smell what?" Sunshine smelled flowers, mulch, and dew.

"You don't think it smells like..." Felix quieted and turned. "Company." He nodded behind him.

The angel hadn't woken up since he'd laid down yesterday. He walked over toward Sunshine with a bounce in his step and a smile. He'd pulled on the clothes they'd gotten for him and he looked almost normal, though his face still held some of that focus and serenity that made him look strange. "I saw you from the window." He pointed to the hall window like Sunshine might not know what a window was. "You like flowers?"

"I. Yeah. But...but that's not why I'm out here."

"Why are you out here?"

Sunshine glanced over his shoulder at Felix. "It might have to do with the case."

"Really? Do flowers and hauntings often accompany each other?"

"No."

The angel put his hands on his hips.

"Did you pick a name yet?" Sunshine asked.

The angel looked around.

"Oh, don't, you'll end up with a name like Bench."

"Is Bench a name?"

Sunshine smiled.

Felix huffed.

The angel looked toward Felix and squinted. "Do ghosts usually make that noise?" He moved toward Felix.

Felix scurried away, his face twisted into a horrible scowl. He pinched Sunshine on his way past.

Sunshine forced a straight face.

Felix headed back up to the house.

"This is concerning, these noises...And it smells. Do you smell that?"

"Smells like what?"

The angel took a deep breath. "I don't know."

"Anyway. A name?"

The angel shrugged. "I knew a man named Jeff once."

"Jeff," Sunshine repeated, trying to withhold judgment.

"I think it will serve its purpose for the time we remain here."

"Are you sure?"

The angel nodded.

Sunshine almost wished he hadn't picked a name. Jeff. Jeff the angel. Then again, who was he to judge? Sunshine was barely even a name. "Alright. Well. Jeff. How about breakfast?"

"I don't yet require—"

"Listen, this is kind of like the bed. Trust me. You're hungry." He headed back inside. "You ever have pancakes?"

"No."

Felix sat in the kitchen and let out a disgusted sigh when Sunshine came in with Jeff in tow.

Jeff looked right at Felix.

"I swear, it's like they're trying to get caught," Sunshine said and gave Felix a pointed look.

Felix huffed and stomped upstairs. A few minutes later he threw Sunshine's phone over the railing.

"The spirits here must harbor great discontent."

"Oh, yeah, they're pissed alright," Sunshine agreed as he went to retrieve his phone. It buzzed with texts a few minutes later, full of Felix sulking about the angel, to which Sunshine had the great pleasure of responding, *Actually, his name is Jeff.*

Felix didn't text anything back after that.

Jeff ate everything Sunshine put in front of him. He didn't coo or rave over the pancakes, but he admitted they were better than what he usually could find to eat. When Jeff excused himself to the bathroom, Sunshine brought a plate upstairs to Felix.

Felix sighed, took the plate, and said, "Thanks."

"Why'd you bring me out to the garden?"

"Oh. I don't think the house is haunted anymore."

"What do you mean?"

"I don't want to talk where they might overhear. Get Jeff taken care of and meet me down the street in a while?"

"Alright."

Sunshine headed back downstairs and asked Bobby to keep an

eye on Jeff. He similarly found Jeff and asked him to talk to Bobby about the haunting and check out the various areas of the house.

He met Felix at the bridge over the marsh after explaining to Jeff that ghosts did tend to slam a lot of doors to cover up the sounds of Felix's exit.

"What didn't you want to talk about?"

"It's not ghosts," Felix said. He'd hopped up on the railing of the bridge and faced out over the marsh.

Sunshine stood beside him and rested his head on his shoulder. "Then what is it?"

"I think it's fucking fairies."

Sunshine stopped to think. It made sense. The missing food, the laughter, Felix's sleepwalking. "I hate dealing with fairies."

Felix's face twisted. "Well. It explains why we can't figure out anything about a dead kid or a reason for a haunting."

"Babe?"

"Hmm?"

"Can you..." He had no idea how Felix would take his request, but he made himself say, "If it's fairies, I want you to stay somewhere else. Or go home."

Felix rolled his eyes.

"Hon, I really mean it."

Felix scoffed.

"Hey, please. Can you turn around and look at me?"

Felix turned.

Sunshine moved in front of him and pushed between his knees so he could wrap his arms around him. "Please, Felix, I just got you back and I don't know what would do if something happened. Just. After what happened with the train last month—"

"Was that only last month?" Felix murmured.

"And the sleepwalking...and the absolute shitshow that was that curse, I just...You asked if you could be fragile and I really think you are. I think you need to be careful. Please."

Felix rested his chin on the top of Sunshine's head. "Are you playing the 'I never ask for anything please give me this one thing' card?"

"If I have to."

"I'm not scared of fairies. And I won't sleep with any of them, so it shouldn't get as bad as it was last time."

"Will you make me a promise?"

"I don't know, ask."

"If you sleepwalk again, will you find somewhere else to sleep?"

"Nnng."

"Is that a yes?"

"I guess so."

Sunshine hugged him a little tighter. "Thank you."

Felix huffed. "Finding somewhere else to sleep will be easier to deal with than you hovering all the time. I still think you're overreacting. Have you always been this much of a worrier?"

"I'm cautious when it's tactically appropriate."

Felix repeated what he said mockingly and under his breath.

Sunshine pushed him, not hard enough to send him off the railing, but hard enough that he yelped and grabbed on to Sunshine.

"What the fuck!"

He pulled Felix off the railing. He put an arm around him and started to walk. "What are we going to do about the fairies?"

"Put out an offering, see if they'll talk to us, I guess."

"Should I make something?"

"Yeah, a stick of butter coated in jelly should do it."

"I'll make cookies."

"Any secret lovers with really good cookie recipes that you wanna tell me about?"

Sunshine thought for a minute. He hadn't had many secret lovers. He hadn't had many lovers at all. Maybe a dozen through all the years. "I don't think so."

"You sure, cause you waited a few decades to drop that meatball bomb on me."

"Like you haven't slept with people who wanted to kill you."

"That's my prerogative. I've never slept with anyone who wants to kill you," Felix pointed out.

"No one wants to kill me."

"You think that smile is so *potent*. Christ, just because you're an angel doesn't mean you're immune to people hating you," Felix grumbled.

"Yeah, and being a demon doesn't make you immune to people liking you. You let your abrasive personality and weird complexes do the heavy lifting on that."

"Rude!"

Sunshine brought him closer and kissed his temple. "Despite all that I have always found you far too likable."

"How likable?"

"It teeters heavily toward adoration."

Felix let out a pleased little hum and burrowed against

Sunshine's side. "Sugar cookies?"

"Okay."

"The soft kind. With frosting."

"Okay."

"And sprinkles."

"Is this for you or the fairies?"

Felix bumped his hip against him. "Isn't everything always really for me anyway?"

Sunshine kissed his temple again. During the walk home, he let himself pretend that they really had taken a vacation.

Felix made himself surprisingly useful in the kitchen while they baked, at least until Jeff appeared in the doorway and pointed out the bag of sugar floating back into the kitchen. After that, Felix sat in the living room and Jeff scrutinized the process of cookie making.

He also stared down at Sunshine's phone for a while every time it buzzed. "Tell me more about these," he said.

"The phone?"

"Yes."

"Uh." Sunshine tapped in the password and handed it over to him. "Knock yourself out."

"Why does it keep buzzing?"

"Oh, it's just a notification."

"What are you being notified about?"

"It means someone sent me a message."

Jeff narrowed his eyes at the device and cautiously tapped a few things. "You get a lot of messages."

Thoughtlessly, Sunshine said, "It's just Felix."

"Who's that?"

Sunshine's stomach flipped. He tried not to freak out, so he focused on making the rows of cookie dough perfect while he said, "He's...uh. He's my partner." He licked his lips and forced a smile. "My other half."

Jeff shook his head. "You've been halved?"

"No, it's just, it's a saying. It means we go together well enough that we might be two halves of the same whole." Sunshine shrugged. He put the tray in the oven. "I mean, most people would probably just say he's my boyfriend, but he's more than that."

Jeff frowned. "You said you hadn't taken a mate."

"That's because animals take mates. It's about reproduction. Felix and I aren't animals, we aren't reproducing."

"A half-lie is still a lie. You're in a carnal relationship with a human."

Sunshine debated letting that go uncorrected, but ultimately said, "He's not human."

Jeff set down the phone and crossed his arms. "Then what is he?"

"It doesn't matter."

"It matters. How far from the Almighty have you strayed?"

Sunshine shrugged. "Not far enough to fall." He took his phone to see who'd texted him. Mostly Felix, but some from the office. He tapped out a response.

Jeff kept staring at him.

"It's my life, I can do what I want with it."

"It is not your life. You were made to serve—"

"It *is* my life."

"No. You are an angel. Your will is not your own."

Sunshine said, "If the Almighty wants to enforce His will upon me, He is certainly welcome to come and make it known to me. Until then, I do as I please."

Jeff shoved him with such force that the counter knocked the wind out of Sunshine.

Sunshine crumpled to the floor with a hard wheeze. In all their years of existence, none of the soldiers had ever done violence to another one. It took him so by surprise that his first instinct was not to fight back or even defend himself. He stared up at the other angel, who had a hand raised.

"You cannot speak that way of the Almighty," Jeff warned.

Sunshine pressed his lips tight and ground his wrist into his eyes, but that didn't stop them from hurting.

"What the fuck happened?"

Jeff whirled around.

Felix shouldered past him to crouch next to Sunshine.

"The ghost!" Jeff cried.

Felix touched Sunshine's face. "What happened?"

"Just go," Sunshine whispered.

"The ghost, where did it go?" Jeff demanded, sweeping his hands around wildly.

Felix shoved an open hand toward Jeff and sent the angel tottering back with a blast of power. He also let out a horrible growl that had Jeff scurrying out of the room. Not a theatrical, showy growl but a truly beastly, possessive one.

When Jeff had fled, Felix asked again, "What happened?"

"He pushed me."

Felix stood.

Sunshine caught his wrist. "Where are you going?"

"To make him wish this place really was haunted by a malevolent entity."

"Don't."

Felix glanced after Jeff.

"Please."

Felix sat down next to him. "You're okay?"

"No one's ever pushed me like that before."

"You haven't had enough boyfriends," Felix suggested lightly. His face fell, but he fixed it a second later. "I will actually kill him if you want."

Sunshine shook his head. "I don't want you to kill him."

"Maim?"

"I..."

"What?"

"I just want..." His voice warbled. "I want him to like me."

Felix tsked. "Oh, Sunshine."

His voice cracked as he said, "Don't tease me."

Felix took his hand and kissed it. "Maybe we're both a little fragile."

"I'm not."

"You've been crying a lot."

"I'm not crying."

Felix wiggled a little closer. "You can if you need to."

"No, I just want to stand up, the oven is making me sweaty but only on my right."

Felix stood and helped Sunshine up. He gave Sunshine a squeeze and a kiss on the cheek. "Darling, you know you weren't exactly keen on unfamiliar ideas when you came here."

"I hate who I used to be."

Felix squeezed him harder. "Stop it."

"I was a coward."

"You were lost. Anyone would've been afraid in your shoes."

"I'm still a coward."

"Me, too. Being brave is overrated," Felix assured.

Jeff returned with Carrie, dragging her in by the arm and insisting that an evil spirit occupied the room. He looked genuinely unnerved.

Carrie kept trying to yank her arm back. "Let go."

"The thing is *here*, I heard it. It spoke to me."

Felix pressed his fingers to his lips and shook his head at Carrie.

"What the actual hell is going on in here?" Carrie asked. She finally wrenched her arm away from Jeff. "Sunshine, what's wrong with your brother?"

"I guess he's afraid of ghosts," Sunshine said.

"You heard it too. That sound," Jeff insisted, moving toward Sunshine. "You heard it."

Felix sat at the table and sighed.

The timer went off and Sunshine hurried to check the cookies.

"Aren't you going to do anything?" Jeff demanded.

"I am doing something. Unless you have an as-yet unrevealed stash of occult knowledge, I'd appreciate it if you could let me do it."

Felix let out a snigger.

Jeff stared in that direction, his orange eyes wide.

Sunshine wondered what it was about ghosts that had him so spooked.

"What have cookies got to do with ghosts?" Carrie asked.

"Oh, sorry, are you also an expert on the paranormal?" Sunshine asked. He knew he was being mean, but he'd had about enough. He set the cookies atop the oven to cool and put in the next batch. He said, "Keep an eye on those."

Felix gave a thumbs up.

Sunshine headed to the backyard, tugging on Jeff's sleeve. "We should talk."'

Jeff followed.

They sat on the bench.

"You've lost your way," Jeff said without looking at Sunshine.

"No. I've found a different one. That doesn't make it wrong."

"The Almighty—"

Sunshine said, "You can accept it, or you can leave."

"This is not the life an angel was meant for."

Sunshine shrugged. "What I have here has value."

"Only if you trade in false currency."

Sunshine felt ridiculous. He rubbed his face.

"You spoke against the Almighty. You have forgotten Heaven. Forgotten us."

"I can't go back. That doesn't mean I've forgotten. I think..." Sunshine put his hand on Jeff's. "I think about home every day."

Looking genuinely upset, Jeff said, "I don't understand why you won't come home."

"Maybe you should leave before you do understand. If you want to go home, you should go. You've found me safe and sound.

Go home before...before you're away for so long you can't go back either."

Jeff stood and took a few brisk steps, then stopped and turned. He stared at Sunshine, clearly torn.

"Go."

"Tell me first. This man for whom you'd set aside the Almighty."

Sunshine shook his head. "It's better if you don't know. Besides, the Almighty knows all, right? If it were so much of an issue, I think he'd make it known to me."

"You assume so much."

"Pot meet kettle."

"What?"

Sunshine sighed. He wanted to curl up into a ball. How had anyone ever had this much patience with him? Although maybe he only lacked patience with Jeff because he didn't like to think about how he'd been. "You assume a lot, too," he translated.

They sat in silence on the bench.

His phone buzzed. He swiped it open to find a photo of several cookies covered in melted frosting. He almost cried. He rubbed his face and went inside.

Felix immediately said, "I'm sorry."

An apology over melted frosting? Sunshine shook his head, slipped an arm around Felix, and kissed his hair. "They're just cookies."

"I know." Felix sounded teary.

"Jesus Christ. Do you want a drink? I feel like I need a drink."

Felix nodded.

Sunshine riffled around and poured them both a finger of something brown and unlabeled into juice glasses.

"God, Sunshine, I just...my nerves, darling, they're just about shot." He downed the drink and grimaced. "Ugh. Anything a little smoother?"

"We're not at home and I don't think we should make ourselves too welcome." He had seen nicer bottles with the labels still on in the back.

"Goodness, you might be right. I've always had the worst manners...Papa must be ashamed of me. Would you mind running out to get something? I think I need to lie down."

Sunshine kissed his temple. "You're a very silly person, Mr. Specter."

"I come from a long line of absolutely ridiculous people," Felix confirmed. "Really, now, be a dear and run out."

Sunshine sipped his drink and found it to be terrible whisky. "Do you really want me to go?"

Felix nodded. "You know where I keep my wallet."

Sunshine didn't bother getting Felix's wallet, left the demon on the couch, and returned within half an hour with a very drinkable scotch. He poured them both a drink and went to sit on the couch. "What's the plan for tonight?"

"Oh, we'll leave things out and see who comes. Inform ourselves from there."

"That probably means I shouldn't make you another drink."

"No, no, of course not," Felix agreed. "I just...Well. You understand."

Sunshine nodded, as he knew was required of him.

"I thought I was done hiding!" Felix told his scotch as he sipped it. "I thought I was done being someone's secret."

"Specter, you know I—"

"Of course I know! Of course I do. God, darling, if there's anything I know, it's that." Felix drained his glass and burrowed under Sunshine's arm.

"As long as you know."

"Even if I am a shithead about it..." Felix closed his eyes and stayed quiet for a long time. When he stirred again, he seemed more settled.

They frosted the cookies and added sprinkles. Felix ate one, savoring it, as Sunshine devoured a few and then felt like a child, or a beast.

He brought one to Jeff, as a sort of peace offering. The angel hadn't left his room in some time and Sunshine found him dressed in his armor again, honing his sword.

Jeff said nothing and didn't take the cookie, so Sunshine left it next to him and went to bed. They had to get up in the middle of the night to catch the fairies.

Two a.m. found them in hoodies and sweatpants, crouched at the far end of the yard beneath a concealing spell, staring at a plate of cookies. Sunshine sat cross-legged on the ground and Felix had settled into his lap. He radiated heat, a small spell meant to keep away the November chill, so overall, the whole thing wasn't as bad as it could have been. Hot cocoa would have made it perfect.

It took about an hour for anything to happen.

It started with giggles and then three tiny figures appeared, crowded near the bench where they'd left the cookies.

None of the fairies stood above two and a half feet tall. One had fuzzy, moth-like wings, a second was a mossy green with cattails in his hair, and the last had wooly, sheeplike legs. The round, stubby proportions of their bodies did not speak of any of the petite species of adult fey.

"Toddlers," Felix murmured.

The trio of children consumed the cookies with delight.

"That's super cute," Sunshine whispered.

"Oh my god, I know. No wonder they're so naughty!"

Sunshine tightened his arms around Felix. "Now what?"

"Now you stop Jeff from doing whatever he's about to do," Felix said.

Sunshine looked where Felix pointed to see Jeff glowering at the fairy toddlers from the backdoor window. Sunshine hurried to intercept him.

The cookies still distracted the children.

Sunshine stopped Jeff from doing more than coming out the door. "Whatever you're thinking—"

"What are those?"

"Children."

"What sort?" Jeff demanded.

"They're Fair Folk. Even the little ones have powers, so whatever you're thinking, don't."

Jeff shook his head. "I have no business with fairies."

"Then why do you have your sword."

"That ghost—"

"Swords don't work on ghosts. Go inside."

Peals of laughter made Sunshine turn his head.

Felix had abandoned his concealing spell and walked directly toward the children. They swarmed around him, taking his hand with their sticky little ones.

One held up a fistful of squashed cookie and frosting toward him.

Felix's eyes had gone that cloudy gray again.

"Fuck."

The children tugged Felix toward the butterfly garden leaving smears of colored frosting wherever they touched them.

Sunshine ran toward them and managed to catch up to Felix just as the children led him through the twisted doorway of lavender and dill. They squelched through the doorway together.

It snapped shut behind them and the children looked at Sunshine.

The green child gave a squeal and ran, the moth-winged one sank surprisingly sharp teeth into Sunshine's wrist, and the sheep-legged one started to cry.

Felix stood there seeming only vaguely aware of the various sounds.

Sunshine shook the moth-child off his arm, doing his best not to hurt her.

His stomach sank as he heard Jeff demand, "Be gone!" to the crying sheep-boy.

Once freed of the moth-girl's bite, he turned to Jeff and gave him a shove back. "What are you doing!"

The sheep-boy kept crying.

Sunshine scooped up the moth-girl as she leaped toward him again and held her so her teeth couldn't meet his flesh again.

"I followed you."

"Obviously. Why?"

"You ran off in distress. Misguided you may be, but you are still one of us."

Sunshine sighed, then grunted when the girl's teeth pinched him through his sleeve again. "Stop!"

She bit harder.

Felix still stood there, his eyes grayed out.

"Stop it!" Sunshine demanded of the girl, setting her firmly back on the ground and holding her shoulders once he got his arm out of her mouth.

She gnashed her teeth at him and growled.

"You're being very bad," Sunshine told her.

She cackled and lunged for him once more.

He held her in place until she got frustrated and started to cry, too. When he let her go, she sank to the ground in a kicking, bawling tantrum.

It gave him the chance to check on Felix and shake him out of whatever state he'd been in. His chest loosened when the gray drained away from his eyes, leaving them dark and clear again. "You okay?"

"All I smell is fairies...and sugar." He looked around.

"Who is that!" Jeff demanded. "Is that the ghost!"

Sunshine and Felix stared at each other. The entrance had disappeared, which meant they were stuck in the Otherworld with Jeff and three fairy children.

Felix sighed. He twisted the band on his finger a few times, then slipped it off.

Jeff startled and dropped into a fighting stance, his sword pointed at Felix.

"Is that the appropriate response given the situation?" Felix demanded.

"You bear the Beast's taint. I can smell it from here."

Felix raised an eyebrow and glanced at Sunshine. "Can you smell his taint, too?" he asked, his lips twisted to keep from laughing.

"I've never smelled the Devil's taint, no."

"Sometimes I kinda think you sort of want to," Felix accused playfully.

"That'd be a step too far, even for me," Sunshine said.

Jeff glanced between the two of them. He pointed his sword at Sunshine. "This is the thing you were sent to kill. This was your mission."

Sunshine shrugged. "Things went sort of different than I planned. This is Felix."

"You're rutting with the Antichrist," Jeff accused, his voice so cold and dangerous it made Sunshine nervous.

He stepped forward a little, putting himself at an angle from Jeff and in front of Felix. "Animals rut. Animals mate. Stop talking about us like we're animals. Felix is my partner, my friend—"

"The reason you've turned your back on the Almighty."

"He's never made me choose between him and God. Will you?" Sunshine asked.

Felix touched his arm.

"You are bedding our enemy. There is only one greater adversary to Heaven."

"Move against him and you move against me," Sunshine warned. "And we have bigger problems."

"There is—"

"Can you get back to Heaven from here? Or Earth?" Sunshine asked.

Jeff glared, then his face softened. He blinked. "No."

"We have bigger problems," Sunshine repeated.

"Enormous problems," came an unfamiliar voice from behind them.

They all turned to see a tall, angular man with sharp teeth and moth wings. He gestured to the distraught children. "What havoc have you wrought among my children?"

Felix's had his eyes fixed upon the man's crown. A tiara made of thin, twisted silver rested on his brow. It was not the crown of the

Eastern or Western Court.

Sunshine could see the scars on the man's forehead where the silver touched his skin, some healed, some fresh. And some not even scars yet, but new burns leaking clear fluid down his face, glistening trails on his umber skin.

Sunshine knelt, the only sensible thing to do in front of a fairy who wore a crown.

Felix knelt, too. Naming himself as a prince of Hell would earn him nothing but hatred among the Fair Folk. He bowed his head, exposing the back of his neck. "Forgive us. We seek a way home. Nothing more."

"Nothing more," the man echoed. "Were they any thicker, I'd expect to taste your lies on the air. Such foul creatures find their way here from Earth. Deceivers all of them."

"Your children played in a human home. We thought them something else. A spirit that needed sending on. If we'd known—"

"If you'd known what?" the man asked. His voice sounded like cracking glass and the deep notes on a cello all at once.

"If we'd known it would come to this, we would have done something else."

"The cruelty of the fey is well known to you, isn't it?" the man asked. "You have crossed the Fair Folk before."

Sunshine forced himself to stay quiet.

Jeff hadn't kneeled but at least he hadn't pointed his sword at this man yet.

The man circled them. He drew the sheep-boy into his arms and kissed the boy's tight, dark ringlets. In a sweet singsong, he assured, "Hush, little one. No one will hurt you now..."

The boy quieted from weeping to sniffling as the man continued singing comforts. He buried his face in the man's shirt.

The girl grabbed the man's robe. "I wanted to play," she sobbed.

"Where is Milk?"

She pointed to a tree where the mossy green boy hid among the leaves.

The man brought him down, too, coaxing him down with a verse about little boys who climbed too high and never found their way home. "Follow me or risk your lives in the Wilds. Whatever I can do to you might well be kinder than what awaits you unattended here." He walked away without check to see if they followed.

Felix rose first. He helped Sunshine to his feet, though it felt more like an excuse to touch him than actual help.

"We're not following him," Sunshine said. "Are we?"

"He hasn't tried to kill, curse, or ensnare us yet. And I don't like our chances in the Wilds. No one knows what's in here," Felix said.

"The silver burns him," Sunshine whispered.

"Not all the time. It's not burning him now."

"I don't like this."

"Then you shouldn't have followed me!" Felix hissed.

Sunshine rolled his eyes. "Like I'd ever hear the end of it if I hadn't."

Felix turned him toward the retreating man and gave him a push. "Go."

Sunshine went.

Jeff hurried up and demanded to know what was going on.

"Just shut up and don't talk to anyone," Felix told him.

He lifted his sword.

Felix grabbed his upper arm before he could move it high enough to be a threat. "I will rip your fucking bicep off and eat it if you try to take a swing at me."

Jeff tried to yank his arm back but couldn't shake Felix.

"It's two against one," Felix warned.

Jeff looked at Sunshine.

Sunshine nodded.

Felix pried the sword out of Jeff's hand and shoved it into Sunshine's arms. "Hold onto that."

Sunshine wanted to give the sword back. Even though it was identical to his own, it felt wrong in his hand. It felt like wearing someone else's shoes.

As Felix continued behind the fairy, Sunshine dropped back to walk beside Jeff. "This doesn't have to be a big deal."

"He's the Antichrist."

"Technically, not yet. He hasn't ascended."

"He's still the spawn of the Beast."

"So?"

"So!" Jeff exclaimed so loudly Felix and the fairy looked back at them.

"It doesn't matter."

Jeff launched into a hissed rant about all the ways it did matter until he had made his point at least three times.

Sunshine shook his head. "None of that matters. You don't know him."

Jeff opened his mouth.

"I once thought as you do. I believed that he would doom the world. I thought I had to end his life. I tried. I even wounded him once, an unarmed little boy. Do you know what he did? He forgave me. He fed me and clothed me and gave me a home. He loved me anyway. How could someone evil commit so many acts of mercy?"

Jeff huffed but didn't argue other than to say, "You've lost your way."

Sunshine watched Felix, then caught up with him. He took his hand. "How fucked are we?"

"Depends on if Jeff can keep his mouth shut but at least a seven."

The man glanced back over his shoulder.

The little girl glared at Sunshine as she toddled along behind the older fairy, her little hand clasped onto his sleeve.

"Dire, peace," the man warned when he noticed her glaring.

"I wanted to play."

The man looked at Felix, then asked the girl, "Is *he* what you've been playing with?"

She nodded. "We had tea parties and picnics."

Felix's cheeks flushed.

A thin dribble of blood from the girl's bite had dribbled down Sunshine's hand and he hoped she wasn't venomous.

Felix let go of Sunshine and approached the man. "How should I best address you?"

The man raised an eyebrow.

"Will Your Highness do, or should it be Your Majesty?" Felix asked.

"Call me Nix. Or call me the Wild Prince, consort to the Meridian Queen, if you like titles."

The Meridian Court had not had a queen for thousands of years. The court itself had not existed for thousands of years. All that remained between the Eastern and Western Courts was the Wilds, a deeply hazardous land of trooping fey and monsters that no one could name.

"Nix will do fine, I think," Felix said. He smiled at Nix, who had eyes like chips of stone and dark hair, not black, but a rich, deep brown that tumbled in soft curls and waves around his face.

Nix smiled back. The harsh sharpness faded from his voice when he said, "My children took a liking to you. Especially Dire, it seems."

Felix looked at the girl. "I might have liked to play if I'd been asked."

"Our lady says princesses don't ask, they take," Dire informed him.

"Ah, well, I won't tell you how to be a princess, I have no experience with it," Felix said. To Nix, he said, "We thought they were ghosts. They've been coming into our friend's house."

"Ghosts."

Felix shrugged. "Until they ate all the butter, jam, and honey in the house."

Nix smiled at the children in his arms.

Felix beckoned for Sunshine to catch up. "I'm Specter. This is Sunshine."

"And that...?" Nix asked.

"That's Jeff."

"Jeff," Nix repeated as though the name didn't fit on his tongue right.

"I don't like it either. I don't like him very much, either, but given the circumstances, I've deigned to let it go," Felix confided.

Nix brought them along for a mile or so until they came upon a set of stone ruins supplemented here and there with tents and other semi-permanent dwellings. Nix brought them to a half-collapsed villa bolstered with trees, beams, ropes, and in a few places, bones. They passed through a thick tapestry of a bacchanal and into a spacious room decorated with low tables and pillows.

At first, Sunshine thought it was some kind of fairy flophouse, but he realized that this must be the children's room. Everything in the room was at their height and in the corner, he spied three little beds hanging from the ceiling.

Dire grabbed Felix and dragged him over to a table. "We can play for real."

Nix set down the other two, but neither went far, holding onto his legs. He took Sunshine's hand and examined the bite. Still holding Sunshine by the wrist, he brought him through another doorway, this one dressed with a gauzy curtain.

He wet a rag from a pitcher of water and dabbed the bite clean. It would bruise, certainly, but hadn't broken the skin any more than a cat scratch. Sunshine didn't want to know what her teeth would do to bare skin.

The fairy produced a small tin from within his robes and smeared a sharp smelling ointment over the bite, then tied a clean, bright green piece of cloth around his wrist.

"She's learned much from the queen," Nix said.

"Your queen must be fierce."

"She wouldn't be queen otherwise."

Sunshine looked around the room. It looked to be a bedroom, a lavish as could be had in a ruined villa. The bed had furs, the fire had wood stacked high beside it, and a battered wardrobe full of finery stood in one corner.

Nix looked at the wardrobe, too. "My lady sews with the deftest hand. Each garment she crafts for herself would make a lesser queen weep."

Sunshine didn't doubt that.

Nix touched the collar of his robe, his fingers smoothing over the creamy yellow embroidery.

Sunshine eyed the fabric. It looked warm and soft. Maybe wool, though probably not from a sheep. "Did she make that for you too?"

Nix smiled. "Yes."

One of the children peered up at him, no longer hiding his face in Nix's robe.

Sunshine waved.

The child stared back.

"Say hello," Nix prompted.

The child stayed quiet.

"That's okay," Sunshine assured.

"Your friend is a liar," Nix said, not accusatory but a simple statement of fact. He didn't sound nearly as disgusted by it as he had before.

"Specter? He's prone to exaggeration and drama, and, you know, he's kind of a flippant bitch, but he's..." Sunshine never knew what to say when describing the goodness beneath Felix's acerbic shell. "He's a decent man, through and through."

"Not a man I should worry about with my children?" Nix asked.

The fairy had relaxed since he'd come upon them. Of course, what parent wouldn't be upset finding their children in such a state, sobbing, hiding, and surrounded by strange men?

"Isn't it normally the other way around? Having to worry about fairies around mortal children?" Sunshine asked.

Nix's face tightened. "Mortals. If either of you is human, I've been gravely deceived about the inhabitants of that realm."

"You've never met a human."

"I've met precious few, most of them ensnared foundlings or twisted madmen. Humans that come to the Wilds are gravely lost.

Your trio is the first from Earth I've come across with their flesh and minds intact. You cannot be human," Nix decided soberly. Then his eyes flicked over Sunshine. "The sparkles sort of give it away."

Sunshine couldn't help but grin at him. "I'm an angel."

"A what?"

"It's not important, really. It's, uh...I'm not human, I have a few cool tricks up my sleeve. Not much to it other than that." He didn't know how to explain what an angel was without sounding overbearing.

Nix didn't look impressed.

"I'm a few thousand years old."

"Oh." Nix blinked a few times. "Is that common for your species?"

Sunshine nodded. "Yeah. We don't tend to reproduce so..." He shrugged.

"Interesting. And your friend?"

"Specter? You can ask him, he won't get mad," Sunshine said. "What about you?"

"Hmm?"

"You know, I don't know a ton about the Folk outside the Courts."

Unease flitted over Nix's face. "My lady would be sorely wounded if you thought her throne unworthy of recognition."

"Oh. No. I..." Sunshine didn't know what etiquette called for here. "I'll mind myself more carefully. I'd hate to offend any member of this Court."

"We may not have the same pompous airs as the Courts Beneath the Hills, but ours has its own glory," Nix recited.

Something about the way he said it made Sunshine worry the same way his silver crown and burns did. He kept his mouth shut and nodded.

"Praise our lady," the children echoed.

Sunshine liked that even less.

Nix glanced down at them. He gave them a gentle push toward the other room. "Go. Make sure your sister plays nicely with our guest."

They went, holding hands.

Sunshine wondered aloud, "Are they twins?" Dire seemed older, closer to four than three, whereas these two seemed just old enough to make simple sentences. Maybe two or so, or whatever the fairy equivalent was.

Nix looked at him.

"Just...they look the same age."

"They're a few months apart," he said.

Sunshine thought through a few scenarios where that was possible and decided it wasn't his business to ask how a couple would have two children so close in age without them being twins.

Nix looked confused for a few moments, then angry, then understanding broke on his face. "You think my lady carried them."

"I assumed. I shouldn't have."

"No. Other wombs carried my children."

My children. Not our children. Still, none of Sunshine's business. "They're very cute."

That brought the smile back to Nix's face, the warmest and most genuine expression Sunshine had seen from him yet. Then he smoothed it away and pointedly did not watch the children join their sister. "Come. I'll show you more of the Court while they play."

As they passed through the room, Sunshine made eye contact with Felix, who gave him a bright smile and a wave.

Felix popped up from the pillow nest built around him.

Dire called for him to come back.

"Watch your brothers," Nix told her. "Get them ready for dinner."

She nodded and started directing the younger two via a getting clumsily sang a getting-ready song.

As he walked through the doorway, Nix offered, "Join us for dinner."

Felix's grip on Sunshine's hand tightened. "I'm afraid we have to be getting home."

Nix looked him in the eyes. "You cannot go home without a doorway. Can you open one?"

"No, but—"

"I will bring you home. But first I must see to my children. Join us for dinner."

Felix swallowed. "Food here doesn't agree with me," he admitted weakly.

"What offense displeased your last host so?"

"My blood offered the slight."

Nix tilted his head, then continued on his way.

Sunshine and Felix trailed behind the prince as he circled through their Court. The other Folk greeted him, some with smiles, some with smooth, servile masks. The Court among the ruins had come to life with its dinner preparations, dozens swarming around to ready a long table down the center of the ruins.

Trees and stone arches twined to make a roof for their hall.

Nix watched a butcher pull the organs from a stag. His eyes on the glistening heart, he finally responded, "Is your blood like to offend again?"

"My blood can't help what it is. That answer lies entirely with you. Thought I think...I think if you were going to hate me, you would have realized it already."

"Who says I haven't?"

A thin smile stretched Felix's face. "Because I'm whole and uncursed."

Nix turned finally to look at Felix. "A fool I'd be to tamper with a man who comes as well guarded as you have. I hate to think what your guards might do if something unfortunate befell you."

"So much for under the radar," Felix muttered.

They moved on from the butcher.

"Precious few people travel with guards, or so I'm told. What makes you important enough for that?"

"He's...Sunshine's not my guard. We watch out for each other." Felix looked toward their linked hands.

Nix looked too, but it was like he saw a puzzle instead of affection. "Over dinner, you'll tell me more," he decided.

"It's not very interesting."

Nix held up a hand to dismiss the concern. "We don't get many travelers here and none so coherent. Your tale will likely interest me. Perhaps I will even repeat it to my lady."

During dinner, the throne sat empty. Sunshine tried not to think about the dark spatters on the flagstones around it, nor the dark substance crusted into the edge of the furs draped over it.

Felix pushed food around his plate and brought his glass to his mouth, but never drank from it.

Jeff ate without trepidation, though not at the table, and Sunshine realized he hadn't warned him about food in the Otherworld.

Ordinary food here presented little danger, other than being distractingly tasty. Sunshine had eaten peaches and cream here once and still craved it sometimes in a way that sort of reminded him of the handfuls of potent drugs people had shared with him over the decades. Coke sometimes he still got an itch for, the same as those peaches and cream. The real danger, for those not prone to addictions, came from cursed or enchanted foods. Ordinary fairy foods held magic well and so served as potent catalysts for spells of all sorts, whether it turned the world into a glamour, gave a person unquenchable bloodlust, or restored their sight.

Sunshine didn't know how Felix's ex, or her father, had gotten him to eat whatever had cursed him. He ate a few things off Felix's plate when no one was looking.

Felix, for the most part, played along with Dire's princess games, either out of good nature or because he didn't want to displease the girl. Her grasp of rulership and royalty seemed definitively medieval.

She bullied and threatened, and gave snippy orders to everyone she could, though most people ignored her and occasionally Nix offered a rebuke when she got too fresh. When she got tired of being ignored by adults, she turned her attention to the younger children.

Dinner turned into mild revelry with wine, music, and dancing, though Nix only watched.

Dire demanded that Felix dance with her and told him, "I'll make you my consort when I'm a queen."

Felix told her, "What if I'm already someone else's consort?"

"Then I'll kill her."

Hearing a little girl say that made Sunshine shiver.

Nix gave Felix an awkward smile. The sheep-legged boy had curled up on his lap and fallen asleep, while the other child played with a wooden dog under the table.

Sunshine wanted to ask when they could go home but knew it

wouldn't be well received. He ended up drawn into a conversation with the Court's smith, who wanted to know about his sword. Sunshine explained what he could about the green-silver metal with which God had crafted it, but ended up saying, "The Almighty isn't huge on explanations."

The smith asked to inspect it.

"It's Jeff's," he told her. "Better off asking him."

She looked at where the other angel stood, arms clasped behind his back, watching or, at least looking toward, the dancers with a vacant expression on his face. "He doesn't seem the talking type. And if it's his, why are you carrying it?"

Sunshine shrugged.

"Come on, let me get a look. I'll show you mine." She flashed him a topaz yellow smile and winked one of her several eyes.

Sunshine made sure Felix was still dancing with the fairy girl, then agreed to follow the smith. He let her inspect the sword and listened as she showed off the various blades she'd crafted.

She showed him one narrow, curved blade that he took a fancy to. He itched to hold it and she offered it like she knew.

As soon as his fingers wrapped around the hilt and he had it drawn from its sheath, he dropped it. It had sent an uncomfortable wind of lust through him, one that demanded subservience, pain, and humiliation to be sated. A far cry from how he usually went about things and not a sensation he wanted on a battlefield anyway.

The jeweled handle and fine leather scabbard, embossed with gold, showed this wasn't a weapon for a battle anyway.

The smith blinked at him, not all her eyes in synch, as he stooped to pick up the blade and return it to its scabbard. She took the sword back.

"It's beautiful," he said. "And powerful."

"My lady recruited me for my talent at the forge," she said. "I wonder how I would have fared had her eyes not fallen upon me..." She looked around the ruins. "My camp had nothing so fine. We weren't but one generation from wanderers. Our forge would never burn as hot. What would I have been without a forge?"

She returned the sword to a rack on the wall. She held out her hand.

Sunshine handed over Jeff's sword.

He paced around the rest of the smithy while she inspected it, though his head swiveled around when he heard the *tink* of metal against metal and found that she'd placed the sword on her anvil.

"I only wanted to test it."

He held his hand out.

She gave the sword back, more sheepish than begrudging.

He didn't want to carry around a bare sword all night and wondered if Jeff would hand over the scabbard.

He saw him still standing in the same place.

Maybe he could just give the sword back.

Declare a truce. That had worked for him and Felix.

He bid farewell to the smith and approached Jeff. "Hey."

Jeff looked over with only his eyes.

"I know I'm probably not your favorite person right now..."

"No."

Sunshine ground his toe into the dirt. He had on a pair of shearling-line moccasins, the kind meant more for putzing around the house than a trip to the Otherworld. "Listen—"

"No. There is nothing more to say."

"If you try—"

"I'm not stupid enough to attempt to take on you and the demon at once."

Sunshine took that to mean he needed to stick to Felix like glue until they got rid of Jeff. He didn't know what to do about this. If Jeff returned to Heaven, he might come back with more soldiers to even the odds. "He's really not a bad person."

"He threatened to maim and cannibalize me."

"You pointed a weapon at him."

"He is dangerous," Jeff insisted.

"He is," Sunshine agreed. "He had so much potential to do harm and yet he never acts upon it. A hundred and two years and he's never taken a life. He *helps* people. He saves them."

"The Antichrist acts through subtler means. He is a deceiver."

"What do you know?" Sunshine demanded. "They sent me down here to kill him and told me jack-shit."

"They sent you to kill an infant, something you failed to do. They sent me to kill an adult monster."

"I thought you were supposed to find me."

"Yes. As *his* captive. We thought we had to save you from being held prisoner. But you aren't. You never were. How quickly did you abandon your mission when he offered you pleasure?"

Sunshine knew that protest, logic, and appeals to emotion would get him nowhere. He sighed and went to sit.

"Such strife among your little band," Nix remarked.

Sunshine set the sword on the table, tired of holding it. "Family matters, I guess."

"I've heard they're complicated."

Sunshine raised an eyebrow. "But not for you."

"My lady makes things simple," Nix explained.

The way he said it made Sunshine nervous. The whole place made Sunshine nervous. He wanted to go home.

The sun started to climb above the horizon and people started to trickle home.

Nix retrieved Dire, setting Felix free from her attention. He put the children to bed, singing them a lullaby as they went, then returned to the dregs of the dinner. He stood beside Felix and Sunshine and said, "Come. Rest. I'll bring you home soon enough."

Felix nodded and stood.

Jeff shook his head. "I'll wait outside. I'm not tired."

They followed Nix into the ruins, past the children's room, and through a doorway into a third room. It held a few pieces of furniture, plain and sturdy. A bed, a chest, a mirror, and a stuffed chair, threadbare and old.

"Take your pick of pillows and cushions from the children's room. There's room enough for three if you don't mind my company."

"Is this your room?"

"When my lady doesn't call for me, I spend my nights here," Nix confirmed.

Felix burrowed into a pile of cushions he dragged in. He lay on his side beneath a blanket, tucked against a stone wall.

Sunshine had never seen him so compliant. He sat beside him and rubbed his back.

Nix shed his robe, brushed it clean, and laid it on the armchair. He did the same with his shirt and trousers until he wore only a thin, utilitarian undergarment of unbleached linen. It almost reminded Sunshine of an old-fashioned bathing suit. His robe, shirt, and undergarment had slits in the back that let his wings through.

Sunshine realized he'd been watching a stranger get undressed. "Sorry."

"For what?"

"I was staring. It's. You know, I spent most of my life without a body, so it never really sunk in, that I shouldn't want people to see it undressed, or that people don't like to be seen undressed."

"Some might have taken your watchfulness as interest."

Felix said, "Can you scratch my back? Right in the middle."

Sunshine obliged.

"Up a little."

Sunshine moved his hand up.

Felix hummed. "You're the best."

Nix folded in his wings in close, draped the blanket from his bed over his shoulders, and sat on the floor next to their cushion pile. He dug his toes into the fur rug. "Are you very tired?"

"Not exceptionally," Sunshine said.

"Would you mind if I asked a few questions?"

"No."

Nix grinned widely, showing sharp teeth like Dire's.

"Can I ask something too?"

"Yes."

"Can you fly?"

Nix laughed, a deep, thrumming sound. "No. Tell me of Earth."

"There's a lot to know."

"Tell me anything. Tell me of anywhere other than the Wilds. Earth or...whatever other realms there may be," he requested. "Tell me what an angel is."

Felix reached up and squeezed Sunshine's face. "This is an angel. Such a nice boy."

"Go to sleep before you get weird," Sunshine said.

Felix rolled over and nestled deeper into his blanket.

Instead of telling Nix about Heaven or angels, he told him about New York City.

Nix tucked his knees up against his chest and asked a dozen questions. After about an hour, he gingerly removed his tiara. He washed his face, dabbed the burned area clean then spread a thin layer of the same ointment he'd used on Sunshine's bite over it.

Sunshine watched him do that too.

Nix cleaned the tiara, wiping away a dried yellow crust from where his wounds had oozed. He set it to rest beside his robe.

Sunshine had heard of sackcloth shirts and spiked garters, self-flagellation, and other manners of self-harm. He couldn't guess the function of a crown that would burn its wearer. Iron burned all fairies, but silver harmed the wicked among them. Sunshine wondered what Nix had done to make the silver burn.

"My lady gives such thoughtful gifts," Nix said when he saw Sunshine staring at the crown. He looked younger, and tired, without the crown or robes. "I would retire. Perhaps we can speak a little more about your world tomorrow before you leave."

"I'd like that." And he genuinely would have liked to talk to Nix under different circumstances. He didn't know many fairies, and even fewer full-blooded ones born and raised in the Otherworld. He had only been to the Otherworld twice before.

"Goodnight."

They both settled into bed. Sunshine wrapped an arm around Felix but didn't close his eyes all the way. He wouldn't sleep, not even if he tried. Not with the threat of Jeff, fairies in general, and the absent Meridian Queen looming over him.

He wondered how much time had passed at home. They'd lost a whole week last time they'd come to the Otherworld, but Sunshine thought the fairies had done that out of spite.

Felix woke after a few hours and gave Sunshine a nudge with his elbow. They rolled out of bed, crept past Nix and the children, and examined the ruins under mid-morning light.

Jeff stood exactly where they'd left him.

Felix waved. "Morning."

Jeff didn't react.

Sunshine checked Felix's forehead. "Are you feeling alright?"

"Yes."

"I don't know, you just tried to make nice with him—"

"Would you rather I didn't?"

"Did you hit your head or something? Or should I be worried about some kind of fairy meddling?"

Felix pinched him.

Sunshine allowed it. He'd kind of earned it.

They walked around the ruins, which expanded for miles around them. Vines, trees, and other plant growth covered most of the area, and they could see a jagged border between the Court and the uninhabited portion where the fairies still worked at clearing things.

"Do you think this used to be the actual Court?" Sunshine asked.

Felix shrugged. He ran his fingers over some letters on a nearby stone pillar. "I can't read any of the fairy alphabets."

"Three Master's degrees and nothing to show for it," Sunshine clucked.

"Four."

"Four? You've got general arcane studies, supernatural and paranormal creatures, and Community ethics and society, and...criminal justice?"

"That was an undergrad. I have an MBA."

"Oh. Are you sure?"

"Positive."

Sunshine didn't argue. "Maybe it's time to go for your doctorate."

"Ugh, no."

"It's not like you don't have the time for it."

"Maybe when I retire," Felix conceded. "Besides, you didn't even go to school, what's it matter to you?"

"Oh, who doesn't want to say they're dating a doctor?"

"I wouldn't be that kind of doctor."

"Obviously. God, could you imagine? Worst bedside manner ever. People would get better just to get away from you."

Felix made a face. He gave a set of stone steps a once over, peered up to where they ended, then started to climb. He went up the stairs, balanced along a narrow, crumbled walkway, then hopped up to a mostly intact roof.

Sunshine followed.

Forrest surrounded them for miles, as far as he could see, on either side. The green remained unbroken by roads, clearings, buildings, or anything more than a small lake and, far in the distance, a long winding glint that must have been a river. Maybe more ruins lay concealed beneath the trees.

"So. What do you think of this Nix guy?" Felix asked after he sank down to sit.

Sunshine sat beside him. "He seems...okay enough. He hasn't done anything to us."

"That daughter, though, she comes out with some shit to say."

"Kids are weird."

"Babe, she drew blood," Felix reminded.

Sunshine shrugged.

"This whole place..." He shuddered. "That crown?"

Sunshine hadn't mentioned the curved sword to him. "Yeah, it's weird for sure. I hope we get out of here before that queen shows up."

Felix wormed his way up against Sunshine and under his arm. "What if we didn't go back?"

"What?"

"I don't mean I wanna stay *here*. But...you know. What if we went somewhere else? Somewhere better."

"Like where?"

"Civil rights are actually pretty good in Hell. The taxes are kinda high, but you know, he's...He's kind of made it *nice* there."

"So...Connecticut."

"Without the wealth disparity, yeah, kinda," Felix admitted.

"Do you want to move to Hell?"

"No. I don't want to move to Hell or Canada or anywhere. I want that fat fucking orange piece of shit to drop dead."

"They all do eventually. Remember when Nixon died, wasn't that nice?"

Felix nodded and sighed.

"Besides, what would happen to the agency if we didn't go home?"

"Oh, come on. Like we do anything useful. They'd be fine without us," Felix said.

"But who would give out the junior detective badges?"

Felix tittered.

They stayed up on that roof for a while, watching a quiet morning. The camp barely stirred. One man shuffled out from his dugout within a ruin, pissed in the woods, then returned to his bed. Jeff stood mostly motionless, though every so often he would pace around the perimeter of the Court.

"You think he's gay?" Felix asked.

"Who?"

"Jeff."

"Why...why would Jeff be gay?"

"I mean, aren't you-all supposed to be identical?"

"I...Well. Yes."

"So. If you're all identical and you're queer, wouldn't that make all of them queer?"

"I have no idea."

"So maybe you're not as identical as you thought," Felix said.

"Maybe..."

"Hmm?"

"I don't know. I know you've got this whole complex about being like a copy of some statue or random Roman guy, but you know, maybe Sky Daddy was a little more careful with you than that."

"Please don't call Him that. And it's not a complex."

"Mmm. Did you sleep?"

"No. Did you?"

Felix nodded. "Why don't you have a lie down? I'll wake you up if anything happens."

"I can wait."

"You get *weird* when don't sleep, my love. Just rest your eyes."

He hesitated.

Felix met his eyes, his face somber in a way rarely seen. He gave a small nod and Sunshine recognized it as permission, the trading of watches. He rested his head on Felix's thigh and curled up on his side.

Felix placed his fingers on Sunshine's neck and a dribble of warmth seeped over his body, just enough to take away the chill of the air. It was fall in the Otherworld, too, it seemed, though the leaves had not started to change colors. Maybe they didn't change colors here.

He fell asleep wondering about the life cycle of plants in the Otherworld. He woke to Felix rubbing his arm and saying, "Darling, something's happening."

He rubbed the sleep out of his eyes. "What?"

Felix nodded toward a commotion on the wood to the south.

The trio of guards prepared their weapons but lowered them immediately upon seeing the fur and velvet-clad woman who entered the Court. Behind her trailed a dozen people, three of them armed and wearing leathers, the other nine bound at the wrists and looking like they'd been through the wringer, smudged with dirt and blood.

The woman looked more or less ordinary. She lacked horns, or pointed teeth, or claws, or anything that made her seem outwardly dangerous. She had hair like summer wheat, braided and pinned to keep it out of the way, and wore a crown of woven of thistles.

The guards bowed, then scattered, waking the rest of the Court.

Nix hurried out of the ruins, smoothing his clothing and adjusting his crown. He bowed to the woman. "My lady. You grace us so much earlier than we expected. Forgive us the trespass, we'd planned your feast for this evening."

She waved a hand. "I'll have a bath first. That will give you time." She stripped off her velvet and fur cloak, and her leather tunic and leggings and tossed them into a heap atop her mucky boots.

"Of course."

She moved toward the ruin, then paused. She dug around in a basket one of her companions carried and said, "Another for your collection." She produced a floppy doll and handed it over. "Attend me in the bath."

He stared down at the baby doll in his arms as the woman walked away. He looked horrified for a second before his face smoothed and he carefully set down the doll on the pile of dirty laundry shed.

Felix stared at the doll, then stood straight up.

"Christ, it's not..." Sunshine squinted at the limp form.

"That's...that's definitely *not* a doll," Felix said.

They scurried down from their perch atop the roof and went to inspect the baby.

Felix knelt, put an ear to its chest, and drew back a few seconds later. "Poor thing's burning up..."

The baby wore a single, filthy garment and had several distinctly unpleasant stenches. Waste and something sour underneath all that.

They eventually found a festering wound on the baby's left thigh, a deep gash that was more crusted puss and scab than flesh.

"Spit on it," Felix said after a moment of staring.

Sunshine hesitated, not because he didn't want to help but because his mouth had gone dry with panic. "I don't know how much good it will do."

"Better than nothing."

It took him a few seconds to work up enough spit. When he did, he gently spread it over the wound, hoping it would at least do enough to keep the baby alive until someone with anything better than mildly healing saliva could help.

Felix placed a hand over the wound, then took Sunshine by the back of the neck and drew him in until their foreheads touched.

Sunshine could feel Felix drawing something out of him, magic or grace or his very lifeforce, whatever it was that let him use the handful of powers he had. He could have pulled back, or shut off the flow between them, but instead, he relaxed into it. He closed his eyes and mimicked Felix's pose, placing his hand on the back of the other man's head, locking them together.

After a few minutes, Felix sagged and pulled back. "I...That's it. That's all I can do. We're not healers." He sounded defeated and disgusted with himself. He let go of Sunshine and raked his hand through his yellow-green tinged hair.

Sunshine touched the baby. Her skin didn't burn as hot as it had, and she had lost that deathly pallor that had made her look like a porcelain doll. The wound still looked abysmal but maybe slightly less horrid than it had before. "I think it helped."

"What the fuck kind of place is this?" Felix whispered.

Jeff had come over to watch them. He stood beside Felix, looking down at them, and asked, "Is that a baby?"

"Yeah, why, do you want to murder it?" Felix snapped.

Unphased, Jeff asked, "Is it the Antichrist?"

Felix punched Jeff in the leg. "Go get some water or something. And a rag."

Jeff started to move, though to do what Sunshine didn't want to know.

Sunshine stood and took Jeff by the elbow, leading him away. "Come help me look. I think I saw a well over here."

They gathered water and a clean cloth in silence. It wasn't exactly companionable, but it wasn't hostile, either. Maybe the nearly dead baby had shocked Jeff out of his bad mood. Sunshine tried to think of his rejection as a bad mood. He didn't have the capacity to deal with it and this unplanned visit to the Otherworld, so Jeff's reaction had to be a mood.

It had to be.

Sunshine had gotten over the whole Antichrist thing and he'd looked for Felix for a lot longer.

He brought clean water back to Felix, who heated it and wiped away as much of the filth from the baby as he could. He helped as best he could, gently dabbing at the baby's face. Felix whispered foul-mouthed yet tender apologies to the baby the whole time.

When Nix reappeared, he looked harried and smelled faintly of burned skin. New redness had sprung up around his crown. He hesitated when he saw them tending to the baby. Quietly, he asked, "Is..."

"She's alive," Sunshine said.

Nix looked devastated.

"She needs a doctor or a...a healer or whatever," Sunshine said.

Nix glanced around the camp. "Jeshe is tending to one of my lady's warriors. She'll be by after."

"This is...This is more important."

Nix shook his head. "My lady expects her commands to be heeded."

"She's a *baby*," Felix insisted.

Nix whispered, "Please. Quietly."

Felix narrowed his eyes then looked at Nix's crown. "You *know* this is wrong."

"I do as my lady bids me. For a greater good. I must return to her." He produced a clean blanket from within his robe. "Please."

Felix didn't stop eying Nix, but he took the blanket and swaddled the baby. He touched the back of his hand to her forehead, brushing fingers with the fairy prince as he tried to do the same.

Nix withdrew his hand. He stood. "You'll join us for the feast."

The whole Court had scurried into a frenzied, rushed preparation.

"I'm guessing it's not optional?" Felix said.

"I can bring you home when my lady no longer requires my attention." He glanced back into the ruins, then turned away, his eyes lingering on the baby.

"We need to get the fuck out of here," Sunshine muttered.

"With a dying baby?"

Sunshine had not taken that into consideration. Of course, Felix had, though. Of course, he had. God, the one time that Sunshine needed him to be a flippant asshole and he wanted to bring a dying fairy baby home with them.

"Someone's got to—"

"I know," Sunshine immediately soothed.

"June could help."

"Let's just get her to the healer. I think she'll hold out a little longer."

The baby had not moved much, nor had she made a sound. She seemed to be unconscious or in some kind of induced sleep.

Felix rubbed his eyes.

"Felix, hon...You cannot take this baby," Sunshine whispered.

"I know! But I can't leave her."

People looked their way.

"Shhh."

Felix sucked a breath. He kept the baby cradled close to his chest.

"I think...I think Nix means well. He's taken care of the other three. This one will be fine with him," Sunshine soothed, his voice low and his hand on Felix's back.

Felix nodded. He leaned against Sunshine and continued cooing swear-laced comforts to the baby.

Jeff stood nearby watching them like they were an exhibit at the Natural History Museum.

It didn't take long for a short, plump person with brown skin and a frizzy halo of curls to make her way over to them. "Nix says you've...Oh, Jesus, not another one," she said. She wore the same hodgepodge attire as the rest of the court, old finery supplemented with leather and roughly spun fabrics.

Sunshine eyed her green suede shoes. He had to ask, "Are those Clydes?"

She looked down. "Oh." She grinned. "Yeah." She turned her attention back to the baby. "Here, let me see."

Felix hesitated.

"Fine, you carry her. My set up is over here. I'm Jeshe, by the way."

They followed Jeshe back to an airy, open tent. A fairy on crutches and his ankle wrapped hobbled out.

Felix glared at him.

Jeshe flapped a hand at Felix. "Over here."

Felix set down the baby on a wooden table, worn smooth surely by years of patients.

Sunshine couldn't get over the Clydes and how ordinary this fairy seemed. He dwelled on it while she treated the baby with some surprisingly conventional methods. Her tools seemed to be of fairy make but looked like perfectly ordinary scalpels, forceps, and other assorted medical tools for which Sunshine had no name.

Felix nearly lost his shit while she cleaned the wound, which she told him once had to be done and when he didn't settle down, she looked to Sunshine and said, "Get him to shut up or get him out of here."

Sunshine unthinkingly drew Felix into a hug, exuding as much calm as he could.

Felix sagged against him right away, which made Sunshine think that he'd needed it for more than just this.

He thought about how Felix had medications that an actual doctor had prescribed to him, instead of the ones he'd obtained through a dealer or a less than legitimate prescription. He didn't know what they were for or how often he needed them.

Felix sighed. "God, that's better than Xanax," he moaned softly into Sunshine's chest.

He rubbed Felix's back and turned his attention to Jeshe again. "So..."

She glared.

He stayed quiet until she had cleaned and dressed the wound, administered some sort of thin, clean tincture to the child, and washed her hands. When she finally turned to face him, hands on her hips, he said, "About the Clydes."

She looked down at her feet. "Yeah, I'm...Listen, I grew up in Chicago. I was a uh, a what do you call it? A changeling. What year is it back there?"

"Twenty sixteen."

Her eyes widened. "Fuck. Been a while then." She rubbed her nose. "Fuck."

"I..."

"No, it's..." She shook her head. "No one woulda been looking for me anyway."

"How long has it been?"

"Thirty years, I guess. Depending on the month. What's...You know what. Don't tell me. Don't tell me what it's like," she said. She turned back to the baby. "You're staying with the prince and all?"

"I guess," Felix said.

"Alright, give me a few minutes." She scribbled down a list of instructions, packed up two tiny glass bottles and several packets of herbs in a skin bag, and handed them over to Felix. "See that the prince gets these."

Felix tucked the bag into the front pocket of his hoodie. "Will she wake up?"

"I hope so."

Felix cradled the baby close. "You hope so."

"I was an EMT, not a doctor."

Sunshine put a hand on Felix's shoulder and steered him out of the medical area before he could argue. "See, she'll probably be okay."

"Did you see the shit that came out of her leg?"

"I sure as shit smelled it," Sunshine said.

"God, I thought I was going to be sick," he murmured.

Nix met them on their way back. He held out his arms, but Felix hesitated to hand over the baby. "I know you think poorly of me but please know that I do what I must."

"You're bound to her," Felix guessed. He finally gave the baby over.

"Is there a prince who is not bound to his queen?"

Felix handed over the bag and instructions from Jeshe. "She doesn't know if she'll wake up."

Nix touched the baby's face. "I can lift the spell," he pronounced finally.

"It's not...not a coma or something?"

Nix shook his head. "The squalls of a baby on such a journey must have taxed my lady's patience...Of course, Jeshe could not know. She has no sense for magic, even after so many years with us."

Felix and Sunshine exchanged a look. They trailed behind him back to his room, engaged in a silent argument about how urgently they needed to get home. It was an unproductive argument since neither of them could do much to leave the Otherworld.

Nix sat on his bed with the child for a long time, his eyes closed and his breathing still. The baby moved before he did, sluggish and glassy-eyed. She let out a pathetic mewl and Nix's eyes popped open. He smiled at her. "Welcome back to us, little one."

Once Nix had the baby fed and clothed, Felix cleared his throat. "So, uh."

Nix looked at him.

"You've been a gracious host—"

"I'll return you home when I can."

"Yes, and that's...much needed. It will be wonderful, but...You know. Sort of seeing how things are going around here..." Felix shrugged and trailed off, his hands in the pocket of his hoodie.

Nix stared at him. He looked upset but mostly confused.

"Just. This doesn't seem like a tenable situation," Felix suggested gently.

Sunshine barely managed to keep in the groan.

Nix shifted the baby in his arms. "Tenable," he repeated.

"It means—"

"I know what it means."

"Well."

Felix and Nix stood and looked at each other for minutes, uncomfortably silent. Sunshine wanted to walk away. He wanted to drag Felix away with him and take their chances finding some other fairy to open a doorway for them. The doing of it didn't require royal blood, just a little know-how. Fairies passed freely between their Otherworld and the human world with little difficulty.

Even the children had been able to open a doorway. They didn't need Nix or his unsettling queen to get home.

He moved but a twitch of Felix's fingers made him stand down.

The two princes stared at each other.

Sunshine rarely thought of Felix as a prince but at this moment, even in sweats, even with his hair utterly fucked from sleep, he looked like a prince. Not some pampered modern royal or a medieval tyrant, but a careworn civil servant, born into more responsibility than one man could handle.

Jesus, he looked like his father. Somber and eternal, Sunshine half-expected him to start turning into that awful thing that the Devil became, the thing that might have been more truly his form than the body he usually wore. He wondered if he'd still love Felix, if he'd adore him in the same way, if he became that same sort of thing. He wondered if Ira loved the Devil's monstrous form just as much as his person-shaped one.

"We can speak on this later. I have children that require my care." Nix turned away from Felix and, carrying the baby, walked into the children's room and called, "Stone, Dire, Milk, come and meet your new sister."

Sunshine touched the back of Felix's hand.

Felix looked at him. He smiled and for a second, Sunshine thought it would grow too wide, but it didn't. It was the same small, sweet smile Sunshine knew so well. "If he asks for help..."

"I know."

Felix shrugged like he was embarrassed.

Sunshine pressed a soft kiss to his mouth. He thought about teasing him but didn't have the heart.

Sunshine hadn't seen the Meridian Queen again but judging by the laden table and the general hubbub around it, she would make her appearance soon. He and Felix had exited the ruined palace and milled around, neither keen on straying too far. They contented themselves with people watching.

Felix abruptly looked to the ground.

Sunshine followed his gaze to see that Dire had attached herself to his arm.

She gazed up at him. "Are you going home?"

"Everybody has to go home at some point," Felix told her.

Still grasping his arm, she said, "Dada says I have to take you home." Relief barely had time to spread over Felix's face before she added, "But you have to promise to come back." She stared up at him, sharp little teeth bared in a hopeful grin.

Felix hesitated. He would have a harder time breaking a promise to a fairy and would probably end up cursed again.

"You have to come back," Dire insisted when he didn't answer. "When I'm queen, you'll be my consort."

Felix crouched and gently told her, "That's a long time away. Don't bind yourself so surely to the idea yet."

She dragged hard on his arm. "You have to promise."

"I can't."

"Why not?" she demanded.

"I'm promised to someone else."

The girl shrieked, "That's not fair!"

"Oh, shh, now," Felix soothed.

She continued to shout about the unfairness, demanded that Felix promise himself to her, and occasionally threaten to kill whoever he was promised to. Felix tried to quiet her but couldn't promise what she wanted, so she got louder and angrier until she was laying on the floor having a temper tantrum.

"Disappointing," came a quiet, ordinary voice from beside Sunshine.

He flinched and snapped his head over to find the queen standing beside them watching Dire's display.

Nix stood in her shadow, his face even as he stepped forward and attempted to pick up the thrashing child.

Dire kicked and shouted until she noticed her queen. She quieted, stood, and stepped out of Nix's grip. She bowed. "My lady."

"What cause had you for such a display?" the queen asked.

"I want him to be my consort."

"A monarch has a consort," the queen said.

Nix tried to tug Dire away, but she yanked her hand back.

"When I'm queen—"

"You? You are not even a princess. You can't even *behave* like a princess," the queen scoffed. She pushed the girl out of her way and toward Nix.

Felix had since straightened up. His spine straightened further, and his chin lifted slightly as the queen looked him over.

"Some exotic magic does come from you, and quite strong, too," the queen noted. "I understand her interest. Even common orphans can recognize quality when it's that obvious."

Felix flashed her a snotty smile. "A little good breeding goes a long way."

She seemed to like that answer because she smiled, though it was hard to tell with fairies. A smile might just mean she had decided to kill him slowly. "No one here knows anything about that. Savage things from the Wilds, all of them. Even my handsome little consort...The best I could find out here, but..." She sighed and glanced at Nix. "There's a reason he's a prince and not a king."

Shit. Sunshine wished Felix had a better sense for when to keep his mouth shut because the queen's eyes slid over Felix in a way that made Sunshine's stomach hurt.

Nix met Sunshine's eyes and they held as much worry as Sunshine felt.

The queen reached out to touch the sleeve of Felix's sweatshirt. She rubbed it between her fingers. "Soft but...It's not exactly flattering."

"I don't usually worry about looking drop-dead in my pajamas," Felix said with a shrug.

The queen gestured for Nix to come closer. "Find our guest something to wear. He'll join me for dinner. I'm curious to know more about him and how he came to our Court." She looked over Felix. "And why this is the first I'm told of it."

Nix bowed.

"We can speak more on that later," the queen noted. She headed toward the feast table, giving Felix one last smile as she went.

As soon as she had turned her attention elsewhere, Sunshine pushed him. "Do you have to flirt with every living adult you come across?"

"I flirt with a lot of the dead ones, too."

"This way, please," Nix said.

"I want to go home."

"I assure you I will take you home when—"

"Yeah, listen..." Felix glanced toward the queen. "I'm pretty sure I know her type and your lady is *never* going to not require your attention."

"She goes on hunting parties—"

"Hunting what?"

The fairy looked away. "I'll find you something to wear for tonight and—"

"What if I won't go?"

Nix said, "My lady would be displeased."

"I don't care if she's displeased with me," Felix lied. "I want to go home."

"She'd be displeased with me," Nix corrected with careful emphasis.

Felix sighed, scowled, and followed Nix inside.

Nix brought them into the queen's chambers. He opened a chest and inspected several garments, all of them old and made of heavy, stiff fabric. He set aside all of them until he'd taken out about half the clothes and produced a spring green tunic with yellow embroidery, and a set of fawn-colored hose. He looked at the clothes for a moment, then presented them to Felix.

Felix made a face.

"My lady gifted me these when she took me as her consort."

Sunshine couldn't imagine Nix, tall as he was now, being more than a young teenager at Felix's height. Maybe even a child. "Maybe that's..."

"Not the wisest course," Felix agreed.

Nix's brow creased slightly, not upset but confused.

"I mean, isn't...wasn't that special for you? Your outfit, your ceremony?" Felix asked. "Wouldn't it be strange to have someone wear *that* and sit with your partner? I don't even like to wear the same shirt if I bought it for a date with someone else."

"Special," Nix half-whispered. "So many things are special in the world." He looked between Felix and Sunshine and the steady, mostly neutral but slightly ferocious expression he wore slipped away, replaced with a teary-eyed look. "You are kind in neither appearance nor manner but...who else might I tell? A confession such as mine would endanger any who heard it as much as myself. No. That day was not special for me. You'll take that to your grave."

"Or?"

"Or I'll put serious contemplation into taking your tongue," Nix growled.

Felix grinned. "I'm a terrible secret keeper. You have secrets, tell them to Sunshine. He keeps all *kinds* of things to himself. He's got about a thousand secret ex-lovers."

Nix looked at Sunshine, caught somewhere between teary and startled. "I've never even met a thousand people."

"He didn't mean it literally," Sunshine assured Nix. To Felix, he said, "And they weren't secrets..."

"No, just things you never told me and probably lied about where you while they were happening. That's not a secret. Of course, not." Felix gave a bitchy, one-shouldered shrug.

Sunshine clucked his tongue.

Felix pretended to be snotty for about another second before he glanced back at Sunshine and gave him a little smile. Then he returned his attention to Nix. He took the fairy's outfit and set it on the bed. "Do you mind if I look through the trunk? I mean. Is anything off-limits?"

"Take whatever you wish."

Felix dug around for a while and finally straightened up with his arms full of garments. He tossed a few at Sunshine and Nix, then started to tug off his sweats. He paused. "Do I look like an absolute nightmare?"

"You could probably fix your hair. It looks slept on," Sunshine told him.

Nix provided a mirror, wash bin, and a few jars that he said contained 'hair treatments and tonics,' all of which Felix sniffed. It took him, in total, about half an hour to dress and arrange his hair in a way that pleased him. He finally spread his arms and asked, "How do I look?"

Sunshine had to answer, "Like a fancy wizard."

Felix had donned a brocade robe made of creamy white with heavy silver and black embroidery, tied around the waist with a broad black sash.

Felix grinned. "You always did know how to flatter a girl. You look like a, uh..." Felix shimmied his shoulders in thought. "A druid. Like very Dungeons and Dragons."

Nix hadn't put on the robes Felix had handed him. When Felix asked about it, he said, "I wouldn't want to hurt my lady's feelings and wear something she didn't make for me."

Felix didn't press the issue, just packed everything back into the chest and headed out. They passed by Jeff, who had refused to join the feast. Felix shot him a look but immediately turned his attention back to Nix, linking arms with him.

Sunshine hung back. "You should come sit."

"No."

"I mean, the queen will get upset if you don't, I think. It's not about playing nice with me or Felix. It's about not getting us into a dangerous situation."

Jeff grunted but came along with Sunshine tugged on his arm. "Where's my sword?"

Sunshine had hidden it, not thinking it the best feast accessory. Instead of answering, he said, "If you wanted, when we get back home, I could show you the city."

"No."

"There's this great little Italian place—"

"No. As soon as I can I'm leaving. If you come to your senses, you'll end that thing and come with me."

"Jeff...Listen. I don't want to hurt you. I really don't. I..." Sunshine frowned. "I love you. My whole soul *aches*—"

"We don't have souls. Humans have souls. We are *not human*."

Sunshine sighed.

Jeff stopped and grasped Sunshine's upper arm, but hard but firm. "What that *thing* is aside, you aren't meant to live like this. Stop...stop playing house with a monster. Come *home*."

"No."

"This place will never be yours. You know that. I *know* you do. You..." Jeff faltered. He put his other hand on Sunshine's other arm and stared at him, desperate about something. When he spoke next, his voice sounded tight and heavy. "You are missing from us."

Sunshine placed his hand on Jeff's cheek, cradling his face.

Jeff leaned into his touch, clasping a hand over Sunshine's. "Come back. We are not whole without you."

"I can't. It won't be the same. I'm too different. I don't...I don't belong there either."

Jeff yanked himself back, forcefully enough that he upset Sunshine's balance. He let out a wordless scream, then fled.

Sunshine watched him go. He stood for a while, then shuffled toward the feast.

Felix sat near Nix and the queen, putting on his haughtiest, most entertaining airs. Fairies, when they didn't hate him for being a demon, reveled in all the drama that Felix provided. Sunshine didn't think they necessarily liked him but found him entertaining at the very least. For some of the Fair Folk, finding something entertaining was as close as they got to genuine affection anyway.

The children, he noticed, had been seated elsewhere that night, a small table off to the side and out of the queen's sight. Even the baby had been left over there in a little basket. He wandered over to them when he saw Jeshe hovering around too.

She offered him a cup of wine, making a big show of watering it down the same as she had for the children.

He took it, stopped himself from thanking her, and asked, "So. What part of Chicago?"

She made a face. "I'll give you one guess."

"No, I've only been there like three times and I'm a terrible guesser. We saw an Andrew Llyod Wright house—"

"Only a couple of those."

"Alright, fine. How did you get back to the Otherworld?"

"Weird call," she answered.

"You were an...?"

"EMT."

He nodded. He watched Felix not eat and he watched the queen notice. He couldn't hear their conversation well, but when she held out a forkful of food to him with the expectation Felix eat from her hand, he saw the struggle between manners and self-preservation play out on his face. He took the bite and said something.

It made the queen laugh, at least until she noticed Sunshine watching them. She narrowed her eyes and he dropped his gaze.

He went to sit on the grass near the children.

Dire grimaced at him, but he ignored it in favor of accepting a bunch of grapes from the green boy with cattails in his hair.

"Milk?" he asked.

The boy didn't say anything.

"I'm Sunshine."

"Milk will do," the boy said.

A funny turn of phrase from such a little boy. He didn't say much else.

Jeshe said, "They don't talk much, the boys." She settled on a worn stone slab covered in moss near Sunshine. "No surprise, considering."

"I take it they made their way here the same as the baby?"

Jeshe nodded. "Stone and Milk came that way. Dire was born at Court. Actually, the only baby born at Court as long as I've been here."

"My parents were traitors," Dire declared.

"Adults are talking," Jeshe told her.

The girl glared at Jeshe but looked at the queen and stayed quiet.

"Give or take a handful of foundlings like myself, the whole Court is built from the queen's...recruiting campaigns."

"And Nix?"

"He was twelve when he came to us. But anything else is his story to tell...and I don't know the whole of what happened."

Sunshine couldn't imagine anything happy.

"He is..."

Sunshine glanced her way.

She shook her head.

"I'm a better secret keeper than most Fair Folk. Angels aren't supposed to lie, but that doesn't mean we can't," he offered.

She snorted. "Angels." She looked him over and shook her head. "No, he's just. He was a cute kid. He grew up handsome...in his way."

Sunshine knew what he meant. Nix had an intimidating air about him, like he was made more of shards of glass than flesh and bone. He held himself upright and moved with a smooth, calm stride that put Sunshine on edge. But he also looked at ease with a child in his arms and that appealed to some people.

He had moments where he looked hurt, too, and that, combined with the instability implied by the silver crown, appealed to Felix in its own way.

Sunshine could only see this going a few ways, most of them bad.

"Can you open a door between worlds?" he asked Jeshe.

"I never tried," she admitted. "The only thing worse than being a changeling in the Otherworld is being a changeling in the human one. I don't belong here, but I belonged there even less."

Sunshine drained his cup and poured more wine, undiluted this time. He regretted it as soon as he took a sip, but a few seconds later, he didn't know why he'd worried and took another. He watched Felix for the rest of the night, being less careful with his wine than required, and eating whatever bits of food Milk handed to him. Stone, the lamb-child, migrated closer and closer to him until he sat near Sunshine, within arm's reach, but never actually touched him. It reminded Sunshine of Specter's Dad, the cat, not the Devil.

The children, when they'd eaten and the rest of the feast had turned to music and dance, entertained each other, trading little magic tricks and playing pretend.

Stone, at one point, darted up to Sunshine and tapped him, then danced back, his small, dark hands covering his mouth as he stared.

Sunshine frowned. "What?" A funny disequilibrium tingled over him. He reached for the wine glass, though he shouldn't have given how unbalanced he felt, and realized he couldn't. It sat below him.

He continued to drift steadily upward.

Stone tugged on Milk's sleeve and pointed up at Sunshine.

"Kids..."

They giggled.

"Jeshe?" he called.

She looked his way. "Oh. They like you."

"I don't like this."

"They'll let you down by morning," she assured. "Or, at least, they always have."

"Can you pass me my drink?"

"I'll pass you some water."

He took the goblet of water she passed up. Even the water here had some indefinably better quality.

He started to spin as one of the boys started twirling underneath him.

"Oh, no, nonono," he muttered.

Jeshe knelt beside Stone and whispered into his ear. He stopped twirling and Sunshine stopped spinning. With Stone settled on her hip, Jeshe told Sunshine, "I'd start sleeping it off now."

"I can't sleep up here."

"You've had enough wine. You'd sleep anywhere at this point."

Gingerly, he laid back and found that the air supported him.

Stars.

He'd forgotten about stars. Not forgotten, of course not, but in the city, they didn't look like this. Here a dense carpet covered the sky, different shapes and patterns, even their moon was a different color.

He fell asleep looking at the stars, thinking that they looked happier like this.

He woke up when someone touched his shoulder. He groaned.

Two fingers pressed against his temple, a familiar trickle of magic that felt like Felix's but also like his own. "Wakey-wakey,"

Felix cooed.

"What time is it?"

"I don't know."

He opened his eyes. The sight of Felix's leg, pale and lightly fuzzy, greeted him. He pushed himself up, blinked a few times, and found the rest of Felix similarly undressed. "What, uh."

"I don't know."

"Oh."

"You're very welcome to sniff around and see if you can figure out what happened, but I'd just as soon take a bath and not think about it."

"That's. Are you...?"

"I." Felix raked his hand through his hair. "I don't exactly remember but...I believe I offered consent as best I could, given my state of intoxication. So. You know. The seventies again."

Sunshine had mud on his cheek. He could feel it starting to dry under the late morning sun. "Oh."

"You're upset."

"No."

"Tell me if you are."

"No," Sunshine insisted. "We talked about it."

Felix scratched his face.

Sunshine at up all the way.

"You're sure?"

"Of course I'm sure."

Felix squinted at him. "Then come help me find my clothes. I woke up over there." He cast a general hand toward the woods.

"Oh. Like...in the woods?"

"I mean. I found my way back."

"Did you see Jeff?"

"What?"

"Did you see Jeff? He ran off that way last night."

Felix stood slowly. "You don't think..."

"No."

"I mean, probably not, right?" Felix asked.

Sunshine took off the outermost layer of his outfit and draped it around Felix. "I don't think he would."

"No. I mean. Definitely not."

Sunshine nodded his agreement.

They walked toward the woods.

"Well. If I did, I'll give you a free pass to bone my dad."

"I don't..." Sunshine sighed.

"That sort of evens out, right? I don't think...I mean I don't have any siblings, really, that are actually *family*. The closest I've got is Elisa and that's more...Whatever it is between us. And well, I assume you're not interested in Bibi or Papa." Felix licked his thumb and wiped the mud off Sunshine's cheek.

"No. Listen, Felix, I don't want to have sex with any of your parents."

"I kind of feel like you want to sleep with my dad."

"No."

Felix pulled the robe closer around himself and gave a little shimmy of his shoulders. "It would *kind of* be funny."

"Please stop."

Felix stopped smiling. He tightened the robe, his fingers digging into the over-large garment like claws. He swallowed and watched the ground as he walked.

"Hey."

Felix shrugged.

"No, come on, hey." He put a hand on Felix's elbow.

"No, just help me find my clothes. Or. Like. Nix's clothes, I guess. Or whoever Elora killed to get those clothes."

"Elora?"

"Queen of the Meridian Court. Descended from King Minea himself. Yeah, I remember she went on about that for a while then...I don't know, she dragged Nix off somewhere." He frowned. "I don't think they came back after that. I saw you floating around up there."

"We shouldn't drink if we're going to be stuck here for much longer."

Felix offered his pinky.

Sunshine linked pinkies with him. He tugged him closer and put an arm around him. He kissed his hair.

"You're really not upset," Felix whispered.

"Are you upset?"

"I don't know. I'm hungover. And I don't even remember what I did...Or who I did it with."

"Ummm." Sunshine tugged him to a stop. He brought him in closer for a hug. He then sniffed him. "I don't think you slept with anyone."

"What?"

He smelled Felix's hands and face more directly. "This is not what you smell like after sex."

"What?"

"Just saying. You actually smell...kind of woodsy."

"Do you...do you smell me after I have sex?"

"Not usually intentionally but I mean, it's happened more than once," he said.

"I can't imagine under which circumstances you've intentionally smelled me after sex," Felix said.

"When you smell like me."

"God, you're so horny for someone who doesn't even like sex," Felix chided. He turned away but kept a hold of Sunshine's hand. "I woke up like over there so..."

After a half-hour of searching, they found Felix's clothes piled up on the ground a few yards away from a pond. At first, Sunshine thought they were tucked under a pile of branches until those branches stirred and sat up.

The tree-creature, mostly featureless save for the vague shape of a body and a face, smiled at Felix. "There you are."

"Here I am," Felix answered weakly. "Morning."

"You ran off last night."

Felix glanced around the grove. "Mmm."

"Did you find it?"

"What?"

"Sunshine. You ran off to look for it even when I said you'd be better off waiting until morning."

"Oh. Yes. Now, I, uh...I just need my clothes."

The creature gathered the clothes and handed them over. "No interest in picking up where we left off?"

"I...I don't think so. I act braver than I am after a few drinks and I...I'm working on it. Sorry to disappoint."

With a rustle of leaves and a shake of branches, the creature indicated no hard feelings. They patted Felix's head and wandered a few yards away, then turned entirely into a tree from what Sunshine could tell.

Sunshine grinned. "Leave it to you."

"Shut up."

"You tried to fuck a tree."

Felix lowered his voice. "I actually think I peed on them and that's what woke them up. And then it was...it was this thing where they thought it was water and I just...Jesus."

"Very classy, Mr. Specter. I wonder where you'll be finding sap later."

Felix grimaced. "Let's just find a bath."

Sunshine pointed to the pond.

Felix shrugged and made his way over. He set down the robes but let out a yelp when something thumped against his foot. He hissed out several swears then straightened up with a phone clutched in his hand. He most definitely had not come to the Otherworld with it, and Sunshine deeply doubted he had found it here.

"Is that your phone?"

Felix frowned, the nodded. "No service but..." He opened it and flicked through a series of recent photos which showed vaguely erotic but also somewhat hilarious acts between him and the tree. It seemed sort of like Felix had gotten pollinated. "Oh!"

"What?"

"I pulled this through."

"You what?"

"Through the place between worlds, I pulled it through, and once I realized what I'd done, I mean actually realized it, I tried to find you. I think I got lost or passed out, or something."

"Felix, you can't move between the words. You've never been able to."

Felix looked down at the phone in his hand. "Well. I did."

"Felix."

"Say my name again, I'm sure that will help."

"Well!" Something panicky and strange bubbled inside Sunshine. They didn't need anything else to deal with, he didn't need one more weird thing to think about.

"I took something from you the other day. We've never done that before."

"So?"

Felix moved in and cradled the back of Sunshine's head, drawing him in, his fingers buried in his curls. He smelled like sweat, dirt, mulch, and, yes, maybe a little bit like sex, barely there. He put their foreheads together and spoke practically into Sunshine's mouth as he said, "Sunshine, darling, together we can do things that would bring the world to its knees. I don't think it's outside the realm of possibility that we could move between realms. Not if we brought ourselves together."

"Wouldn't that, wouldn't it change us?"

"We've changed each other so much already, but I think we could do a little more without losing ourselves."

Sunshine swallowed. "I don't want it to be like this," he confessed.

"It won't be, darling, I promise, if I ever make you mine it will be because I love you, not because I'm afraid of a mad queen and your pissed off brother-clone."

"Promise?"

"I won't let it get that far," Felix vowed. "Trust me."

"Okay."

Felix pecked him on the lips. "Okay." He released him, then smoothed back his hair. "There he is. Let's get that pretty face of yours cleaned up."

They washed up in the pond with a cake of soap Felix had, after about an hour of attempts, pulled from his apartment. He said that it had been easier last time and couldn't pinpoint why.

Sunshine didn't want to think about it. Instead, he thought about something else while Felix chattered away while he washed him. He thought about Felix's soapy hands and those comically sexy pictures of him with the tree, he thought about being cozied up in bed, about what he wanted to make for breakfast, or lunch, or whatever mean it was time for.

He wrapped himself around Felix and drew him close. "Stop."

"Hmm?"

Felix curled up against him. "I don't feel great. Maybe the situation requires a bit of rest and recuperation. Though I don't want to go back to that Court."

"No. But where else can we go?"

"Mmm."

"At least that queen seemed to like you."

"She reminds me of Elisa," Felix said, his nose wrinkled. He gave a little shudder. "Ugh. I can't tell if she wants to fuck me or eat me. Either way, I'm *not* keen on her figuring out what I am."

"What are you?" Nix asked from the shore.

Felix grabbed on to Sunshine so hard his nails drew blood, then he splashed Nix and demanded, "What the fuck is wrong with you?"

Sunshine made himself put down the rock he'd grabbed.

"Jeshe said she saw you head off in this direction. Wandering alone in these woods is not well-advised for those unfamiliar with them. Even the trees themselves have whims."

Felix flapped a hand. "I met the trees."

"You met...Of course, you've met the trees." Nix sighed. His shoulders fell. "My lady found you intriguing last night."

"Oh?" Felix asked.

Nix seated himself on the grassy bank, his legs crossed.

"She'll keep finding me intriguing as long as I never let her know that I'm better than her."

Nix's eyes widened.

"She rules a Court of old furs and weathered stone. I could have an entire realm bent to my whim."

"Talk like that in front of her and I'll start to worry for my position at Court."

"Oh, no, Jesus, don't worry, I've got no intention of anything like that. Best she thinks I'm some snotty rich boy—"

"You are a snotty rich boy," Sunshine told him.

"Oh, don't flirt with me when we've got an audience, Mr. Sunshine, I might cause a scandal," Felix purred, trailing his fingers over Sunshine's chest.

Nix cleared his throat. "Surely you're more than that."

"Depends who you ask," Felix said. "But I have influence in my own way. If someone needed help, I know which ears to bend and palms to grease."

"Not here though."

"No. Not here," Felix admitted. "How's the baby?"

"Much as she was yesterday. My lady expects your presence again at dinner tonight."

"So if I asked you to take me home?"

"She found it less than amusing that I tasked Dire with doing so," Nix said.

Felix stood up, sloshed out of the water, and knelt beside Nix. He reached out a hand, then hesitated. "Can I?"

"Can you what?"

Felix eyed the crown.

"I'm not supposed to take it off."

"I won't tell."

"I can't lie."

Felix smiled. "Tell me no and I'll do it anyway."

Nix didn't say anything, he just stared at Felix looking like he wanted to cry or strangle him.

Felix gently lifted the crown away and placed it beside him. "It doesn't suit you at all."

"I hate it. I never wanted to be a prince."

"You came to the Court the same as your children did."

"I was old enough to keep myself alive. Others...others didn't fare as well. It wasn't until she made me consort that I could keep anyone else alive. Even then..."

"Go on."

"In the earliest days of our union, I thought myself...more

special than I was. I defied my lady too severely and she reminded me of what I had to lose. I railed, then, against her, half-mad with loss, until she brought me something else that she could take away."

Felix touched Nix's hand. "This is no way to live."

"Where else could I go? She'd track me from here to the mortal world."

Felix's eyes narrowed. "What about to Hell?"

"Where?"

"Hell. The realm of He Himself, the prince of darkness, who sits upon the Serpent's throne."

Nix shook his head.

"Uh. The Devil, Satan, the Beast, the Adversary," Felix rattled, "Lucifer, the Morning Star, the Lightbringer...?"

"I don't know any of those people."

"He waged the Obliteration."

Nix blinked. "Oh. Legends speak of a monster who led his legions against us. Dark creatures. We call them only the Maw and his Horde."

"Oh, the Maw, he'll like that one. Could she follow you there?"

"The Fair Folk move between our world and the mortal realm, but no others until death calls us away," Nix said.

Felix grinned. "Then I know where to go."

"But I can't get us *anywhere*—"

Felix cupped Nix's face in his hands. "Don't worry."

"You set before me an impossible feat. Here that means you've declared your intentions for love or war," Nix said.

"I am desperately useless in physical confrontations so I suppose it will have to be love, my Wild Prince."

At that, Sunshine snorted.

Felix glared over his shoulder, then turned back to Nix and patted his cheek. He dragged a robe over still-wet skin. "And you, Mr. Sunshine, exposing yourself like this! You ought to be ashamed. Is there no decency left in the world?"

Sunshine gave himself one last rinse, pulled on his clothes, and gathered up everything Felix had left behind as he sauntered back toward the Court.

Nix helped him carry a few things. "You trust him."

"Yes."

"And I would not be remiss in thinking you two lovers."

"No."

"I worry about my queen's intentions toward him. And...I wonder if I should worry about his toward me."

"He is a consummate gentleman in such matters," Sunshine assured.

Nix sighed.

"I'll tell him off if you want."

"No, I—that seems rude."

"He won't be upset."

Nix's cheeks flushed a darker shade of brown.

"Unless you're interested...?" Sunshine probed.

"I..." Nix swallowed.

"Do you like him?"

"He's...He's a strange man but..." Nix pressed his lips together. "I want him to talk to me. I want...I want him to look at me."

Sunshine smiled. "He's like that."

"I don't tell you this because I hope to rival you for his attentions. It's...I wish to be honest. Intentionally so, not out of requirement. I have few opportunities to do so."

"Nix, he might flirt with you, he might sleep with you, he could even fall in love with you, but you'll never be my rival. No one will ever to be to either of us what we are to each other."

"I don't understand."

Sunshine shrugged. "Me neither."

"And..."

"Hmm?" Sunshine prompted.

"I don't think it is that sort of interest that I have for Specter."

"Then definitely don't worry about it," Sunshine advised. "You have a lot to worry about already."

Nix let out a sad hum that reminded Sunshine of a cello. He had a fluid musicality to him that came out the most with his children. He seemed to have a song for everything, for going to bed, for washing their faces, for getting dressed.

Sunshine had heard of lullabies, but he hadn't fathomed that people had songs for all kinds of activities. A weird wrench of pain came over him and he was glad Felix didn't want children, at least, not with him. How could someone who'd never been a child ever be a father?

He chided himself. Bibi had never been a child and was a wonderful parent. Even Nix, in this horrible place, seemed to be having a better go at it than Sunshine ever could.

Maybe it was just him.

Maybe he should go home. What was the point of sticking around a playing house with a demon if he couldn't even do it right? He didn't belong here. He never would. Humans, and creatures like them, lead such narrow lives centered around families and social bonds, and he could only blend in, barely, on the surface. He had never known anyone on Earth the way he had known the others in Heaven.

He didn't belong in Heaven either, but at least there he could let his mind go and forget about it for a few thousand years.

Back in Nix's room, he dragged on his sweats and headed back outside.

"Where are you going?" Felix asked, once again completely naked. He snagged Sunshine's wrist.

"To find Jeff."

"He'll be fine."

"Yeah, unless he finds a tree that doesn't want to fuck him," Sunshine snarled and yanked his arm back.

Felix pursed his lips. "Oh, so we're doing that. I asked you—"

"I don't give a shit if you fucked a tree, you fuck everything!" He stormed out, nearly taking down the curtain in the doorway.

He made it to the trees before he realized he didn't want to find Jeff either. He didn't need another tirade about everything he was doing wrong.

Half-heartedly, he wandered into the woods, found a log, and sat against it. He tucked his knees up to his chest and rested his forehead on them. He needed to go home. Not to Heaven, but back to his bed in New York. He needed to sleep somewhere safe, no ghosts or fairies or worrying about Felix or politics. No angry daughters of long-lost friends, no scared old men lecturing him about how he'd had easy.

He needed the sheets to smell right.

He needed his kitchen, to cut up predictable things and cook them in predictable ways, where the only unknown would be a new spice blend, not any of this bullshit.

He let out a groan that made birds fly away when he realized he didn't know where he'd left the sword last night. He dragged himself up and trudged back to camp, checking where he'd fallen asleep, then retracing his steps until he remembered he'd stashed it under Nix's bed.

"Is that what I was sleeping on?" Nix asked when Sunshine pulled it out.

"Mmm."

He could hear Specter singing about speckled frogs in the other room.

"Did you find your companion?"

"I don't even know where to look."

"I will ask my lady if she will lend one of her hunters to the task. Even I'm not sure what he might run into out there if he strays too far."

"Great."

Nix smoothed his robe, then walked away.

Sunshine took the sword to the blacksmith and asked for the proper materials to clean and hone it. It had a few dings and scrapes, and something sticky near the handle. He wondered what Jeff had gotten up to.

He stayed at the smith's for hours, helping her do more little chores like that. He had no skill with a forge, but he could clean armor and sharpen knives. He even figured out how to mend arrows with minimal instruction.

It felt good to do something like this.

No. It felt empty. He could let all his thoughts drain out.

As the sky started to darken, someone kicked his foot. "They found Jeff."

He stared at Felix. For a good few hours, he'd forgotten Jeff and Felix had existed.

"He's kind of freaking out."

"Got any benzos?" he attempted to joke.

Felix didn't smile.

He set aside the leather armor he was cleaning and wiped his hands on his sweats, which by now had seen better days. "Listen..."

"I don't really want to."

"Please."

Felix sighed. "I don't have any high ground to stand on for stuff like this so I'm not asking for you to, like, grovel or apologize or whatever you're trying to do. I just...I don't think I can talk about it without getting upset and I think if I get upset, we'll fight, and I really, *really* don't think I can fight with you right now."

"So?"

"So come calm down Jeff."

Sunshine nodded. He followed Felix to where a handful of the queen's hunters surrounded Jeff, bound in ropes and seething about it.

"He put up a fight. He'd be good sport," Elora told Felix, "If you're not too attached to having both of them."

"They're a matched set, it wouldn't do to split them up," Felix said.

Sunshine knelt in front of Jeff and gestured for the hunters to give them space. Everyone shuffled back a few steps, which wasn't exactly what he'd had in mind. "I'm just going to settle you."

"Don't you *dare*."

Sunshine locked his arms around Jeff. "I'm sorry. If I don't, they might do something worse. Just relax."

"*Don't*."

"It's okay. The fight's over. Just breathe."

Jeff writhed and bucked against him, which made Sunshine kind of feel like he was strangling him.

He repeated the same soothing directions he usually gave to Felix and oozed out as much calm as he could. It didn't seem to have an effect, not until he squeezed Jeff even harder and begged him, "Please, I want to go home, too. Please stop fighting me. I don't want to fight."

Jeff gave a weaker thrash, then sagged against Sunshine.

"I'm sorry. I'm sorry for everything. I'm sorry I failed you all. Let me help now." He slowed his breathing and gave one more push. "You're okay."

Jeff slumped finally, not unconscious but dazed.

Sunshine kept holding him.

People cleared away.

Watching him mumble pathetic nonsense to Jeff was not as amusing as hugging him into submission it seemed.

Felix stayed. He watched, his arms folded and clutching his huge sweatshirt around himself.

Sunshine would have bet he was digging into his ribs so hard there'd be red marks on his skin. "Will you help me bring him inside?"

"Nix doesn't want him around the kids if he's going to be like this."

"I'll keep him settled."

Felix nodded, then went to hoist under Jeff's other arm.

They brought the angel inside, deposited him on the pile of cushions in Nix's room, and spent a long time standing around not saying anything to each other.

"Should we untie him?" Sunshine asked.

"I wouldn't."

"You untied me," he reminded, trying to make it warm, trying to remind Felix how things had been.

"Maybe I shouldn't have. Maybe I should have sent you back."

"You couldn't have."

"Maybe I should have killed you," Felix said. "Maybe I should have let you kill me. Or done it myself. I still think...you know, this whole thing still really feels like an elaborate suicide attempt."

Sunshine wanted to insist he not talk like that, but it would only make Felix keep things to himself.

"Maybe he's right. I've...I've sort of ruined you, haven't I? You're not a very good angel anymore. Maybe I'll find a way to ruin the world too."

"Felix."

"Maybe you should have let me jump in front of that train."

"Specter," he insisted, a whine creeping into his voice.

"No, I know. I *know*. I know. I just...I do actually have meds I'm supposed to be taking and I think..." He let out a sigh. "Fuck."

"Can I hug you?"

"I'd be despondent if you didn't."

Sunshine squeezed him.

"I'm just very on edge and I sort of...You know. I thought I could do this, and I fucked that tree and now I'm just..." He groaned.

"I don't know if you even can fuck a tree."

"I don't know either, I tried to go back and look at the pictures, but I have no fucking idea what we're doing." He let out a shaky, wretched little sob into Sunshine's chest. "I just wanted to sleep with like, some nice sex worker and make sure my dick works the way I want it to, but I just ended up with bark and leaves all over me and I had all this *pollen in my mouth*."

Sunshine rubbed his back. "It's okay. You can have sex with someone when we get back to New York."

"Well, now I don't even want to."

"Alright, well, then..."

Felix let out another sob. "I just *want to be normal*."

"Fuck."

"I know, it's so fucking pathetic, I'm a hundred goddamn years old and I still just want the other kids to play marbles with me and I just..." He trailed off incoherently into Sunshine's sweatshirt, although at one point he did surface enough to say, "And your shirt fucking stinks!"

Sunshine rubbed his back and waited for it to pass.

Finally, Felix pulled back roughly, scrubbed his face with his sleeve, and demanded, "Jesus fucking Christ, could I go like a *fucking week* without a fucking breakdown?"

"You feel better?"

"No, I feel like shit!"

Sunshine nodded.

"If he doesn't get his shit together, I'm going to tell Elora she can have him."

"Please don't."

Felix softened a little. He rubbed his face. "You know I wouldn't."

"I know."

Felix continued to curse under his breath and seem generally annoyed with himself until he went to bed early and played games on his phone until it died. When he woke the next morning, he seemed a little more himself.

Disquiet lingered in Sunshine's stomach, but he managed to keep it together.

For a week, they had snuck off to the woods to practice reaching the strings between worlds. They went under the guise of a morning walk, though no one seemed to care either way what they did.

Felix had pulled through many things: clean clothes, granola bars, a baggie of uncategorized pills that Sunshine did not question. He had sent through a few things too, like a note to Bobby not to worry and to stay away from the butterfly garden. He didn't know if Bobby received it, he did not yet have that kind of control over this newfound power.

He also had a remarkably low tolerance for touching the strings themselves. After a minute or two, he always pulled his hand back, and it took him forever to find the right string. Sunshine didn't remember it being so difficult, but then again, his brain had been empty then and he was a full-blooded angel.

Felix presently had Sunshine's hand in a death grip, which he always did during these sessions. He needed the contact to draw out Sunshine's power and, Sunshine guessed, to steady himself as he touched the things that lived beneath the skin of the world. With a hissed curse, he ripped his hand away from Sunshine's, abruptly cutting off the flow between them. It felt like he'd had ice water dumped down his back.

He flinched, shuddered, and rolled his shoulders. "What?"

"I fucking hate this."

He took Felix's sleeve and tugged on it.

Felix collapsed next to him and wormed under his arm. He opened his hand to reveal a squished handful of grapes. "Want one?"

"No, thanks."

"I can't do this. I'm not...I'm not supposed to be doing this," Felix admitted quietly. "There's no way I'll be able to get us all through. I could get myself, maybe. But both of us and Nix and four little kids? I'd be lucky if we all came out alive. I don't even *hope* I'd get us through with all our parts."

"A week is hardly enough time to become an expert."

"I can't even touch them without wanting to throw up."

Sunshine tightened his arm around him. He thought about what to say and how to say it. "Remember how I asked you to sleep somewhere else if you kept sleepwalking?"

"Mm."

"If you can get yourself through, you should go."

"I'm not leaving you here."

"I'll survive being here, Felix, I don't know that you will."

Felix huffed.

"Be reasonable, for once."

"I hate when you get like this."

"You're useless here. I mean...you're walking on eggshells around that queen, making weird tragic-helpless goo-goo eyes at Nix, sneaking pills—"

"I'm not sneaking!"

"Mmm."

"I'm...you know. I know you can tell. I just, you know, it's embarrassing, Sunshine. I'm embarrassed that I'm an unstable freak."

"You are *not*."

Felix made some muffled, grumbling sound of protest. He turned his face into Sunshine's side and groaned miserably. "What am I supposed to do?"

"Go get help."

"Would you leave me here?"

"I'm not you, don't judge yourself by the actions you think I would take," Sunshine said, which was not something he'd thought of on his own, but something that someone much smarter had said to him.

Felix seemed to know it because he wrinkled his nose. He sighed, then stood. "I think I've got one more in me."

Sunshine held out his hand.

Felix linked hands with him, screwed him his face, then gingerly pushed his hand through the skin of the world. He stayed painfully still for a few minutes, then he let go of Sunshine's hand. He didn't draw back from the in-between. "You meant it?"

"Go."

Felix swallowed, then he was gone.

The world felt warped and empty where he had been. Sunshine reached out to touch the air and it felt wrong, not because there was anything wrong with it, but because Felix been there and now, he wasn't.

"Good," he said to himself.

He stood for a minute, then brushed off his clothes, and walked back. He wandered the Court aimlessly for a good half-hour before he resigned himself to doing nothing and went to sit with Jeff.

Jeff didn't do much these days. He sat around in a few different locations for hours on end. He'd move, eat, and speak in mumbled, short phrases if pressed.

Sunshine sat next to Jeff. He offered him water, which he looked at and drank when Sunshine nodded. "How are you today?"

"Tired."

"Didn't sleep well?"

Jeff shook his head.

"I know this is hard."

Jeff scowled.

Sunshine touched his arm and despite the scowl, Jeff put his hand over Sunshine's arm. He leaned against him. "You'll be home soon."

"It will never be the same."

"Change is hard and scary, but it isn't always bad."

"We'll never be whole again. The same thing happened to the notaries."

"What do you mean?"

"The one that went to the Pit. She...She didn't come back for a long time and when she did, she came back twisted. The notaries suffered for it. We suffer without you."

"Well, what happened to them? What happened to the rest of us?"

"The notaries cast her out. Drew away from her until she was a writhing puddle, alone on the ground. They had to. She would have poisoned all of us eventually. Now she haunts the Citadel, a shell of a thing."

"The Almighty opened the Citadel?"

"What choice did He have? Cast her to Earth? Leave her in Hell? She could not stay as part of us again. It's the kindest convalescence He can give her."

That, Sunshine thought, would be his fate if he went back to Heaven. Stuck in the Citadel with a notary who had usurped the Serpent's throne and done her time in the Devil's dungeon for it. Shit, that might be worse than falling.

His stomach clenched.

Things had really gotten fucked up between Heaven and Hell. This couldn't have been how things were supposed to be. Had the Almighty imagined this when He'd cast out Lucifer? Had Lucifer thought things would go this awry when he'd started the war in Heaven?

"We shouldn't be messed up in this kind of stuff," he

confided. "It's above our pay grade."

Jeff sniffled. "I hate it here."

"I know. I used to hate it too. Earth isn't so bad though when you get used to it."

"I don't want to find some *thing* to rut—"

"Fuck off, Jeff," Sunshine said, more tired than angry, or even annoyed, with this attitude. "Sex is not this big a deal up there, I don't know what's got you harping about it all the time."

"Because it's keeping you here."

Sunshine couldn't help but chuckle. "It's been almost eighty years since I decided that going home wasn't worth killing someone over. The sex came significantly after that."

Jeff didn't respond.

"Can we stop fighting?" Sunshine asked. "I'm not going to let you kill my friend and I'm not going back to Heaven, but this doesn't have to be ugly. I really have missed all of you."

"I feel like shit."

"Me, too."

They sat for a long time. When a meal rolled around, they ate together but away from the others, quiet but companionably so.

Nix watched them from the table, the subtlest expression of concern on his face until he returned his attentions to Elora.

Watching them together made Sunshine's skin crawl. Nix attended to Elora's every need, he did everything she suggested, even if it made his crown burn. The children went more or unless unattended until Elora retired for the night and Nix slunk back out of the villa. He woke hours before the rest of the Court to make sure the children had a bath and breakfast, and he always came back out to put them to bed. When he couldn't watch them, they watched each other with occasional aid from other Court members.

Jeshe seemed to have taken unofficial watch over the baby but sometimes she cried for a long time before someone could get over to her.

The crown burned the hottest when the baby cried, and Nix could hear it but stayed by his queen's side. Sunshine could smell the burning flesh then and even Jeff had expressed concern about the state of the burns on his face.

Today, when the baby started to fuss, Sunshine went over. He didn't know what to do, so he mimicked what he'd seen others do.

"You!" Elora called.

Sunshine glanced her way, frowning.

"Yes," she confirmed.

He approached, the baby still in his arms. "Your Majesty?"

"Where's your master? He hasn't missed a dinner yet."

"He...He had other matters that required his attention."

"What in my Court could require *his* attention?" she asked.

Sunshine suddenly wished he wasn't holding the baby.

A courtier plucked her from his arms as if reading his mind.

"He took his leave from Court."

Her face shriveled, withering like a corpse in the desert before his very eyes. "Leave! Who granted him permission to *leave!*"

Sunshine could only stare at the leather of her face. Her whole body had shifted into something distinctly less human-like. She looked like something that had died in a bog. He scanned the area as best he could for a weapon, wishing he hadn't taken to hiding the sword from Jeff.

The table had knives. He could reach one if he had to.

Before Sunshine could stammer an excuse or think of a lie, Elora turned to Nix. She grabbed him by the hair and dragged him out of his chair.

He went without resistance. "I'm sorry, my lady."

"Pathetic. You have no right to jealousy, not when you cannot even offer your loyalty."

"I'm sorry."

"You show yourself for what you are. Pick one."

"No, *please*," he begged, his voice rough and heavy. "Please."

"Pick or I will pick."

Sunshine had a horrible feeling about this. He positioned himself in front of the children and said, "Nix didn't help Specter leave."

The queen glared.

"He didn't. He couldn't. You command his loyalty too strongly. Specter asked him and he said no every time. Nix didn't help."

"No one was talking to you."

"But I'm talking to you. I act Specter's stead; my words are as his. How would he think of this Court if he came back to see such..." Sunshine paused to think of the right word and to give it weight, "Barbarity?"

She released Nix and reached for Sunshine.

He grabbed her by the arms. "I have seen royalty and this display is not what my prince would seek in a queen. You're embarrassing yourself." He didn't expect to change her mind, just redirect her anger.

It worked. She thrashed out of his grip and struck him across the face, her fist closed. He didn't move to defend himself. Instead, he took the punch, a solid one at that, to the face and reeled back, making a show out of it. He dropped to his knees, which might have oversold it, but Elora looked pleased.

"Speak out of turn again—" she began.

He stood and put out an arm to stop Jeff. He said, "She's failed the first test. I told him she wasn't worthy of his interest. Come."

Jeff frowned.

Sunshine leaned against him as though he needed support but used his weight to steer Jeff away from the scene.

Elora had forgotten about Nix and the children. She stormed away, spitting at Nix for him to ready her leathers and sword, to find her a horse. She clattered out of the camp shortly thereafter on a white stallion Sunshine had never seen before. She had a sword and a bow and Sunshine wouldn't have wanted to be anywhere near her path, even if he'd been fully armed and armored.

Although, maybe a good spear would have evened the odds. Mounted warriors always came up short against spears.

Nix approached Sunshine once the sound of hooves faded.

Not knowing what else to say, Sunshine said, "Didn't know you had horses."

"Oh." Nix looked toward the forest. "No. We transfigured Gallow."

"Jesus Christ," Sunshine said.

"You acted unwisely."

"I saved your ass."

"And made yourself a target in doing so. Where is Specter?"

Sunshine shrugged. "I don't know. He'll return."

"He really intends to wed my lady? She'll press me for the truth," Nix shared, his inflection careful.

Sunshine picked up on his intention. Nix could not lie, but Sunshine could.

"His judgment is yet withheld but that display would not have impressed him," Sunshine offered truthfully. "Does she want to marry him?"

"She wants to marry someone else who has truly royal blood. She wants a true Court. She knows..." Nix looked around. "She named me Nix because she knows that's all she has here. Nothing."

Sunshine wanted to ask if Elora really would have hurt the children, but that was just a reflex, some way to grasp onto something saner than this place. He didn't doubt at all that she'd hurt those children, that she'd continue to hurt them. He didn't even want to know what she'd done to Nix.

He put a hand on Nix's shoulder and gently squeezed, hoping the gesture of comfort translated.

Nix patted his hand, briefly intertwining his fingers with Sunshine's. "Come. The children should get to know you better. I know Milk and Stone are somewhat fond of you."

"Oh."

"Dire is not but her whims are wild even for a fey child."

"I did sort of notice."

Nix sighed. "I try."

"That's important."

When they entered the villa, the children swarmed Nix. He greeted each of them, then went to check on the baby. She slept.

"How's her leg?"

"Mending. Slowly. But mending. Jeshe thinks she will keep it."

"That's good."

Nix nodded. He touched the baby's chest lightly and smiled

down at her. "She needs a name. My lady has not yet selected one for her."

"You don't name them?"

"More generous names I would give my children if I could," Nix said. "Sunshine. That's a beautiful name. Whoever named you must have loved you."

"He does."

Stone wiggled out of Nix's arms and toddled over to get a toy. He dropped on to a cushion and, laying on his belly, pushed the toy back and forth over the carpet. He hummed to himself.

Jeff stood in the doorway, not interested in the children.

Nix sat by Stone and gestured for Sunshine and Jeff to join him.

Sunshine sat, though Jeff didn't.

"We can speak of lighter things. You told me of a city."

"New York."

"Do you have more to share? It seems a vast place."

"I have a thousand stories to tell."

"We'd love to hear them," Nix said. Milk cuddled into his lap, his thumb in his mouth.

Sunshine ended up talking more about Pickering than New York, and Nix shared a few lighter tales about the Court. They spoke for hours, they even took their dinner alone in the villa, as Elora had not yet returned.

When Sunshine mentioned that she'd been gone a while, Nix said, "It can take hours to sate her temper."

Sunshine wanted to say something kind, offer him hope, but assumed the less Nix knew to repeat the better.

"You mentioned tests before and that my lady had failed one."

"Oh. Yes." Sunshine hadn't thought that one through. He'd only wanted to distract Elora. Honestly, he might have stolen the idea out of some medieval poem Bibi had read to him. It felt medieval, a visiting prince in disguise seeking a bride, leaving his trusted servant to observe the woman's true behavior.

"She'll ask me about them."

"If she knows the tests, then she can cheat."

"Wise."

Stone placed a wooden doll on Sunshine's leg and glanced up at him. He balanced the doll carefully, then knocked it over. He did this several times, then moved on to the table. At one point, Nix reached over and grabbed the doll and pretended it was flying away, making an accompanying sound effect.

Stone giggled, then reached for the doll. He stretched up on his toes and whined, then finally said, "Mine!"

Nix relinquished the doll then. "It is yours. It's almost time for bed. Few more minutes."

Stone didn't seem to pay attention, but a few minutes later, when Nix started cooing a lullaby, he cleaned up his toys.

Nix had the children wash their hands and faces, clean their teeth, and change into loose, plain nightshirts. He sang them through all of it and sang them to sleep, and it made Sunshine miss Phaedrus and Hiram.

They'd taught him how to do so many things.

He'd spent so many nights observing their family workings, not joining unless they insisted. Still, they'd given him endless patience. Phaedrus had pulled him aside one evening when Felix and Hiram had gone out and shown him a children's primer.

"I bought this to be Felix's first book, but he went ahead and learned to read without it. I don't want it to go to waste," Phaedrus has said.

Sunshine had thumbed through the pages, staring at letters he saw everywhere but didn't understand. "I can't read."

"I know, darling. I know Felix can get a little catty, but some night when he's not home, I could teach you."

"He's...He's not home now."

Phaedrus had smiled at him. "I know."

Sunshine had stared down at the book. "Could we start tonight?"

"If you're ready."

Sunshine still had that book. It was close to falling apart.

"Are you staying up for a while longer?" Nix asked.

Sunshine shook his head and pushed himself up. "No. I'll come to bed."

Jeff remained behind. If he slept, he slept in the children's room most nights, near the door. He said it made him feel safer to have eyes on the entrance.

Nix and Sunshine got ready for bed, though it didn't feel as weird as it should have. The worst part was watching Nix take off his crown.

"I..."

Nix looked his way, the burns across his forehead angry and weeping.

"I'm sorry."

"Wickedness always has its price."

"Still. It's cruel."

"Cruelty oft shows its face in this life."

Sunshine tried not to stare as he cleaned his crown and did what he could to soothe his wounds. Sunshine wondered if they would kill him someday.

Once they'd both settled into their beds, Nix asked, "Can I tell you a secret?"

"Yes."

"Sometimes...Sometimes it burns me when I think of what I'd do to her. It is one thing to make a choice when your hand is forced, but I think of what I'd do of my own free will and it is monstrous."

"Thoughts are different than actions. We all have upsetting thoughts."

"It doesn't upset me. I like to think about it. I think I'd like doing it."

Sunshine rolled on his side to face toward Nix, using his arm as a pillow. The nest of cushions felt empty. "Is it such a bad thing to hurt someone who hurts you?"

"The crown thinks so."

"But what does metal know?"

Nix sat up a little bit. "What do you mean?"

"I mean. Silver burns evil fey, right? But how does it know who's evil? By what moral standards does it judge a person?"

"I don't know. Maybe if I had been raised in a beautiful Court full of song and knowledge, one where they had books and scrolls and Nightingales to sing the ballads, as the Meridian Court did all those years ago, maybe then I would be able to think on these things, I might have a shadow of an answer for you," Nix said. "But I'm..." He smiled. "I'm well-named."

Sunshine scooted to the edge of the cushions. "I don't think so."

"You're well-named, too."

"Tell Specter."

Nix smiled.

They laid there and smiled at each other.

"We always talk about me. Tell me about the Court," Sunshine said.

"Oh, by all the stars, I don't know what I could tell you that you haven't seen already," Nix sighed.

"Oh."

After a quiet few minutes, Nix proposed, "I could tell you

about before the Court."

"If you'd like to."

Nix slipped out of his bed and sat on the floor, blankets pooled around him. "I had a mother and a father, as some little boys do. I had a brother. Older. We never stayed in one place for long, our little band. Maybe a dozen, maybe twenty of us moving from ruin to cave to grotto. We went all the way south to the ocean once...I tasted the sea." Nix grinned. "We spent months there. We would swim every day, diving down to gather shellfish and crabs. My parents always promised we'd go back. We couldn't spend too long in one place, or go there too often, or we'd spoil it.

"We spent a lot of time by the water. Of course, we had to. A river or a lake. Once this scummy little pond with a nasty old kelpie in it. We didn't stay there long." Nix smiled. "My mother tried to teach me to hunt, but I'd get too nervous at doing something wrong and my wings would flutter too loud and scare our prey away. My brother could stay quiet better. So I stayed back with my father. He made the most beautiful pottery. I was a fair hand at it by the time I was ten or so. I made clay toys for the other children."

"That's sweet."

Nix went on for a while, sharing little snippets of his childhood. He never spoke of how he'd ended up at Court.

After a few hours, Dire came in, her face snotty and flushed, her nightshirt wet on the seat and lap.

Nix looked at her and said, "Oh..."

She started to cry.

"No, no," Nix immediately assured. "It's alright. Accidents happen."

Sunshine remade the child's bed while Nix got her cleaned and changed, but she wouldn't go to bed. She started to cry when Nix tried to put her to bed, which woke the other children, who then also refused to go back to sleep.

Then the baby started to cry.

Nix did his best before he started to sniffle too. He had a child in both arms, and one clinging to his leg, all of them crying and none of them letting him get to the baby.

Sunshine picked up the baby and did his best to mimic what he'd seen others do. It didn't take much to settle her down, just closeness and a little rocking.

"Get her basket, bring it to my room. There's no helping things when they all get like this," Nix said. "You might want to sleep out here."

Sunshine didn't want to sleep out here. He loathed that the villa had no doors; he didn't even like sleeping in Nix's room. He knew the villa had more rooms, beyond Elora's suite, but Nix said they hadn't been reclaimed yet, so Sunshine guessed they were full of rubble and plants. He almost would have rather taken his chances in one of those than sleep next to the entrance.

He brought the baby into Nix's room, put her back in her basket, then gathered up more cushions and blankets at Nix's behest. Half an hour later, they were all on the floor together in a dense, very warm pile of bodies.

"You can go," Nix said once the three toddlers had stopped crying, but before they had fallen asleep. "You won't get a good night's sleep like this."

"I haven't slept well since I got here. I definitely won't sleep well without Specter." He also didn't think he could get up without upsetting the children. It'd be better to stay where he was, and he didn't necessarily find being smothered by all these warm little bodies unpleasant. It almost felt like being at home, but sweatier and with an odd dairy smell.

He didn't think he would sleep at all but nodded off when Nix started to sing to Dire, who was still upset about wetting her bed.

He woke up with two little hooves in his back, positioned exactly over his kidneys. He gingerly moved away from that to find he had nowhere to go. In the night he had rolled over and pressed right up against the stone wall of the room.

It took some maneuvering, but he managed to roll over and sit up without waking any of the children.

Nix rubbed his eyes but did not open them. "It's so early still, little love, go back to sleep," he murmured and burrowed further into the blankets.

Sunshine managed to get up and out of bed.

"I said go back to sleep," Nix said, opening his eyes now. His fingers curled around the leg of Sunshine's pants. When he saw his mistake, he immediately let go. "I thought..."

"I know."

"Don't stray too far. My lady's ire may not yet be soothed when she returns."

Sunshine nodded.

He woke up Jeff to go for a walk. He needed to move and stretch after sleeping like that.

Neither of them spoke for most of the walk, but that was fine. That hostile, surly disapproval didn't roll off the other angel the same way as it had before.

"Have you ever been swimming?"

"No."

"We should go to the beach. Not here. I don't think I'd like the beaches here, but we could go down to the Sound sometime. The waves are incredible. I used to go down there with this girl I was seeing—"

"A girl," Jeff pronounced with such judgment that Sunshine's stomach hurt.

"A woman, a woman. She was an adult," Sunshine quickly clarified. "Her name was Nancy. It was like...I don't know. Seventy-eight, seventy-nine. She was staying with her aunt at the Weller for the summer. She drove this shitty little VW Bug and she drove like a maniac. I mean she drove crosstown and didn't stop at a single light...She was a lot of fun. We had a lot of fun that summer. She was engaged the next time she came to visit her aunt, but that was fine. She keeps in touch sometimes. Christmas cards."

Jeff said nothing. He started to peel the bark off a stick he'd found on the ground.

Their walk consumed most of their morning and by the time they returned to the Court, everyone else had woken and started the day. A small, bird-like woman with enormous wings said she'd spotted their queen on her way back, so the camp had a tense feel to it.

Sunshine found Jeff's sword and returned it, though Jeff held it with a loose sort of disregard. He went to the blacksmith and requested a knife.

"I'll trade you," the blacksmith proposed.

"I don't have anything to trade," he told her.

Her eyes scanned over his body. "You have a lot to trade."

He held in a grimace.

"Lots of meat on those bones. All your fingers, too, and teeth."

He made a face.

"What about a toe or two?" she proposed. Her fingers poked his ribs and stomach. "A rib. I could take it out no problem."

"No problem for you or no problem for me?"

She grinned, her topaz smile glittering in the glow of the forge.

"Listen, uh...What about something a little less gruesome?"

"What did you have in mind?"

"Help around the forge for a day or something like that."

"Mmmm. Maybe. I'll think about it." She dismissed him with a wave of her hand.

It took two days for her to make up her mind. By that time Elora had returned, blood-soaked and hideously cheerful. Sunshine had spent most of his free time helping with the kids since Elora had demanded a lot of Nix's time, a good deal of it in private.

The poor fellow stank of burnt flesh most of the time these days and Sunshine genuinely worried that the crown might kill him.

When the smith approached and said she wanted Sunshine to follow a hunting trail out into the woods, find a cave, and bring back a pelt from some sort of elk-type thing she vaguely described it as large and very furry. A fetchgroat, she called it.

It didn't take much into talking Jeff to go with him, though Jeff didn't feel like company so much as a rain cloud. It took about three hours to follow the path along to the cave and Sunshine started to worry as they got close to the cave.

Jeff pointed out the remains of a small animal. "I thought this was a deer."

"Yeah."

Sunshine adjusted his grip on the bow the smith had lent him for the task. She'd also lent him a knife after he'd pointed out how hard it would be to skin an animal without a knife. He edged closer to the cave.

It stank like rotten meat.

Jeff pulled his shirt up over his nose.

Sunshine inched into the cave until his foot slid on something.

Jeff caught his arm before he could fall. "I'm going to throw up."

"Well, don't." He looked down to see what he'd stepped in. A slick of crushed maggots and blood coated the bottom of his Sherpa slippers.

A few yards in, they found the remains of a large, hairy animal that had rotted away to a bloated pile of fur, bones, and maggots.

Jeff tapped the antlers on the floor. "If this is the deer..."

"That's a huge deer." The smith had described it more as an elk, but this thing was the size of a moose. Sunshine held his breath and crouched down, poking through the remains with an arrow. The skull showed long, sharp teeth that looked like they belonged in a wolf.

"We should go."

There was nothing of the hide to salvage. He stood, put his hand on Jeff's shoulder, and led them out of the cave.

Outside the cave, he took some time to try to scrape the fetid rot off the bottom of his shoes. He couldn't get a lot of it out of his treads until he found a little stick and cleaned them out. He'd have to get a brush and scrub them later.

He scuffled around in the dirt for a second longer, trying to at least dry the muck, then headed back toward the Court.

"Are you sure that's the right turn?" Jeff asked when they turned left at a fork.

Sunshine looked at the rail-thin path going right. "I...Yes."

"I...I just remember thinking it was such a narrow path," Jeff said.

Sunshine looked at the skinny path. "No, I don't think it's that one."

Jeff pressed his lips together.

"I mean...You know what, there was that big rock right before the turn. We can go that way for a bit and see if we find it," Sunshine offered.

Jeff nodded and set down the narrow path.

They walked for a while and the rock didn't turn up. "It's not here."

"We've only walked for a few minutes. It wasn't that close," Jeff insisted, pressing on.

Sunshine followed if only to catch up with Jeff and drag him back to the right path. He bumped into Jeff, who'd frozen in the middle of the path.

"Stop." Jeff's hiss came sharp and quiet. He had his hand on his sword hilt.

"What?" Sunshine whispered.

"We went the wrong way."

"I know but—"

"Shh."

Sunshine edged closer.

A monstrously large and hideous thing stood between the trees, its face lowered over the remains of a smaller animal. It didn't have antlers like the thing in the cave, but it did look like some unholy elk, it's snout narrow and full of teeth, its legs long and muscular, with clawed feet instead of hooves. A heavy tail swung lazily from side to side as it ate, ripping away bits of its prey.

He kept his hand on Jeff's shoulder as he took a single, quiet step back.

They silently edged backward like that until they came to the fork in the path again, at which point they started to run and didn't stop until they got back to the Court. Sunshine headed to the smith's and threw the bow and quiver of arrows on the forge where she heated a bit of metal.

With a shout, she jumped back and brandished a pair of tongs at him. Then she laughed when she sat who it was.

"Funny fucking joke," he snapped.

She doubled over in laughter.

He stalked away.

He was still in a shitty mood when Nix found him later keeping an eye on the children with Jeshe. There was a particularly mossy area of Court where they'd bring them to play without worrying too much about them hurting themselves on all the stone.

Jeff generally made a lazy circle around the area, casual but clearly on patrol. Sunshine didn't know if he cared about the children, acted out of instinct, or just needed to keep moving.

Sunshine had the baby on his lap as she slept. She slept a lot, which Jeshe said was normal for a baby, especially one who was still healing.

Nix sat beside him.

Sunshine smelled him first so the abrupt collapse of another body beside him didn't startle him. "You have to take that thing off."

"I couldn't spurn my lady so."

"It's going to kill you."

"It hasn't yet." Nix sagged against Sunshine. "How is my littlest one?"

"She ate. She pooped. She slept."

"Good, good. I'm glad the medicine for her leg hasn't upset her stomach too much." Nix touched the girl's hand.

"Are you okay?"

"Okay." Nix rolled the word around in his mouth. "That's not a term here. Okay. You say it all the time and I've derived some meaning from context, but I don't understand it well."

Sunshine opened his mouth.

"No, don't explain it to me. I'm too tired."

Jeshe came over a little while later and demanded Nix come to her tent. He returned smelling of herbs.

A few nights later, while getting ready for bed, he started crying while he started to lift the crown. With quick, shallow breaths, he pulled it away one millimeter at a time. By the time he had it off, he was pallid and sweaty, tears and snot streaming down his face.

He dropped the crown.

Sunshine caught him before he hit the ground too. He sat him on his bed.

"I'm sorry, I just...A little lightheaded."

"Stay still."

Nix swallowed.

Sunshine had watched him clean his burns enough times that he knew what to do. He did it for him as carefully as he could. He applied the ointment, then wrapped a bandage around the fairy's head.

"Those are for the baby."

"Shh."

"She needs them."

"So do you." Sunshine thoughtlessly smoothed them down a little.

Nix let out a terrible whine of pain.

"Fuck, I'm so sorry." He leaned back on his heels, then got up and started digging through the pile of things Felix had left behind. He found the baggie of pills stuck tucked into the pocket of a pair of jeans. He peered at them. "Would you like a Vicodin?"

"I don't know what that is."

"A painkiller."

"Yes."

"They're, uh, they can be kind of dangerous—"

"I said yes."

Sunshine got him water and handed over two Vicodin, which he judged to be the right amount for someone of Nix's side and injury level. "These things work great though."

Nix swallowed them without even looking.

A little while later, he had oozed into his bed, bundled up in the blankets. His thoughts dribbled out of his mouth and he hadn't let go of Sunshine's arm since he'd started talking.

Maybe two had been too many.

"You're a good friend, Sunshine," Nix said, lacing his fingers with Sunshine's and squeezing.

"I try."

"I know Specter's coming back for you. I can't imagine him leaving you behind. Whatever required his attention...He'll come back."

"He usually does."

"I don't want you to go. I don't want him to go either. I wanted...I wanted to hear about something other than this place so badly. I'm sorry. I should have brought you home right away."

"It's alright."

"It's *dangerous* here," Nix insisted.

Sunshine patted his arm. "We muddle through, the two of us."

"I'm sorry."

"It's okay."

Nix snorted. Then he giggled to himself.

"Nix?"

"Hmm?"

"You shouldn't put that crown back on until you heal."

"She'd be so mad."

"Fuck her. Don't put it back on," Sunshine insisted. "Wait until you heal, okay?"

"Okay."

"Promise?" Sunshine asked.

"Yes," Nix said, then he looked at him, grinned, and giggled. He didn't let go of Sunshine until he fell asleep.

Sunshine made sure he was tucked in, checked on the kids, then went to sleep.

In the morning, Nix shook him awake, his head still bandaged. Panic harshened his features so that Sunshine flinched away.

"What! What happened?"

"You have to release me."

"I'm...I'm not holding you."

"You asked me to promise and I did." He swallowed. "I can't put it on."

"You shouldn't put it on."

"Sunshine, you don't *understand*," Nix insisted.

"I understand that it's going to kill you."

"That's a possibility, yes, but I'd rather take my chances than have my lady see me without the crown she gave me."

"Nix."

"*Please.*" Nix grabbed his hands and dragged him closer, on his knees beside Sunshine. "She will hurt my children."

Sunshine saw no good way out of the situation. He believed Nix but he also didn't know how much the fairy's body could withstand. "Let me look."

Nix didn't let go of his hands right away.

"Just let me see." He gently pulled his hands back. He peeled back the bandages, cleaned and treated them again, but when he tried to apply a new bandage, Nix pulled back. "Do you trust me?"

"No."

Sunshine smiled. "Fair enough. Did you mean it when you said I was a good friend?"

"Yes."

"So let me be *your* friend. Let me help."

"You don't understand how things are here. You can't help. No one can."

"Let me bandage you again. Get back into bed. I'll go and talk to the queen."

Nix shook his head.

"Yes," Sunshine insisted. "I'll talk to her. I'll tell you're not well because you *aren't*. Just play it up if she comes to check on you. I'll watch the kids for a few days."

"You don't understand how things are here."

"Can we try, at least?"

"If she hurts one of them over this, I swear I'll gut you myself. I'll feed you to your prince, make him eat you until he's sick—"

"Alright. Settle down." Sunshine squeezed his shoulder and

started to bandage his forehead. He pushed Nix back into bed.

"I swear by all the stars—"

"Do you want me to tuck you in, too?"

Nix narrowed his eyes and huffily got under the covers.

Sunshine went not to Elora but to see Jeshe. He asked her to go see Nix and give him something that would knock him out.

"Why would I do that?"

"So he can actually rest."

She frowned.

"Have you seen his face lately?"

She sighed and dismissed Sunshine. "I'll see what I can do."

Sunshine was in the middle of feeding the children when she came in, softly argued with Nix, then came back out and told Sunshine, "It should last a day or two."

Sunshine didn't know if that would buy enough time to matter, but he hoped it was better than nothing. He smiled and continued setting out breakfast for the children. Dire demanded to know where their father was.

"He's asleep. He doesn't feel well," he told her.

She wouldn't eat her breakfast and Sunshine gave up trying to convince her. If she wanted to be hungry, that was her business.

It took him hours to get them ready for their day and he still got it all done by the time Elora sauntered out of her suite. She did a double-take when she saw Sunshine then looked around the room.

"Where's Nix?"

"He's not feeling well."

"What?"

"I think he's sick. He felt warm when I tried to wake him up, so I let him sleep."

She squinted at Sunshine. She looked normal again, no trace of that decrepit monster from before. She wouldn't have looked out of place somewhere like Wisconsin or a rural English farm, blonde, well-muscled, and heavily freckled with a plain kind of prettiness to her. "I'll be the judge of that."

Sunshine followed to see what she would do.

She unsuccessfully tried to rouse Nix, alternatively shaking him and threatening him. The most he did was barely open his eyes and moan an incoherent word. After that, she punched him incredibly hard on the arm, which got another moan. Then she stepped back and asked, "What did you do to him?"

"Nothing."

She narrowed her eyes. "You'll attend me until he wakes, then." She snatched Nix's crown from where it lay beside his robe. "Put it on him."

"No."

Slowly, she said, "Then pick a child to wear it."

Sunshine looked down at the crown in his hands. "No."

"Then I'll choose." Elora tried to grab it back.

He stepped back and brought it close to his chest.

"Him. Or them," she reminded.

He shook his head. "You can't make me do things like you can make them. I am not your subject."

"Not yet," she reminded.

"No," he agreed. He didn't know exactly how this queen had such a firm hold over her people. She had the most control over Nix, who had nowhere to flee but wilderness with three small children and a baby.

Nix could have killed her. He had enough hate in his heart to do it, Sunshine knew that by now. Something stopped him, though. Fear, he had that in spades, but it wasn't enough to stop him from protecting his family. Something else stopped him, must have bound him from doing harm to her.

Such things happened, especially with fairies. Just as he'd promised Sunshine not to put the crown back on, he must have promised something to her.

"I'll attend you until he wakes but remember who comes back for me as you make your demands."

"Your master has been away for many days now. What makes you think he's coming back for you?"

"Because he always does."

She smiled.

He smiled back.

"A bath and my meal. And my pot needs emptying."

He barely stopped himself from rolling his eyes. She thought she was so terrifying because she spent all her time bullying helpless people. Still, it was better to let her think she made him worry or she'd try to make a point. "Of course, my lady."

He asked Jeff to keep an eye on the children, then went to carry out Nix's morning duties. Taking care of her was worse than the children because at least the children tried to help. She expected literally everything done for her, every inch of washing, and stitch of clothing. He was surprised she even walked on her own and didn't need to be spoon-fed her breakfast.

Attending her made for a series of abysmally boring days and taking care of the children and Nix made for short nights. Jeshe stopped by each night to assess the burns and dribble some water or broth down his throat. Three passed in total before Nix woke, hungry but overall cheerful once he set eyes on each of his children.

Elora demanded he resume his normal duties as soon as he'd bathed and eaten.

His smile died as soon as he saw her.

"Our newest members will pledge themselves tonight," she informed him. "I knew the pledge means so much to you, so I delayed it."

Nix dressed himself, unsteady but staunchly refusing Sunshine's assistance. When he reached for his crown, he did it with his jaw clenched. His burns had healed somewhat but still needed time.

When he touched the crown, he frowned at it, then turned it around. "What did you do?"

"Nothing. I release you. Put it on."

Nix placed the crown in his head, wincing slightly as he settled it.

Sunshine had tampered with the crown, painstakingly gluing a thin film of plastic bag and strip of cloth to the twisted metal, making sure that nothing showed when someone wore it. He hoped it would be enough to keep the metal from touching Nix's skin.

"Good?" Sunshine asked.

"You should excuse yourself from the pledging. You might find it distasteful."

"I could hang with the kids."

"The children will be in attendance."

"Oh. Should I wear something nice?"

"Wear something you don't care about."

Sunshine looked down. He'd cycled through the same two pairs of pants the whole time he'd been here, a now-ratty pair of sweats and jeans that Felix had brought over for him. They weren't his jeans, and they didn't fit how he liked. He changed into the sweats for good measure and left his slippers behind since he'd just managed to get the last of the gunk out of the treads.

Nix left to accompany his queen when she called for him.

Sunshine carried the baby, still unnamed, and Jeff trailed behind with Milk, who had fallen asleep. The children didn't keep the same schedule as the rest of the Court and when Sunshine saw the captives lined up before Elora's throne, he hoped Stone and

Dire would fall asleep too.

Dire's face lit up and she grinned viciously at the captives. She tugged on Sunshine's sleeve when he didn't pay enough attention to Elora's demands for their loyalty.

One by one, she passed down the line, asking each individual to swear fealty and obedience to her crown. The first three knelt and accepted.

The fourth spit on Elora and a second later, she gurgled then collapsed when Elora plunged a knife into the woman's throat.

Jeff let out a startled "Ugh," of displeasure and looked at Sunshine.

Sunshine shook his head, no idea what to do. The whole Court had their eyes fixed on Elora.

If they'd all sworn the same fealty to her, no wonder this place was like this.

His heart pattered, rumbling through his whole body, but especially in the hollow of his stomach.

Elora moved on and the remaining captives all knelt.

Three fairies came forward and brought away the dead woman's body, smearing her blood on the faces of her fellow captives.

Milk, thank god, hadn't woken up, but Stone had silently watched the whole thing.

He didn't cry or blink, just held on to the leg of Sunshine's sweatpants.

Someone came and smeared a swath of blood across the baby's face.

"Don't wash it off," Jeshe advised quietly when she saw Sunshine tug his sleeve down and reach for her face.

He withdrew his hand.

"Come eat."

Sunshine followed her to the table and noticed a strange cut of meat, barely cooked, among the other foods.

He decided to avoid any meat he hadn't seen pre-butchery from then on. He couldn't eat anything that night anyway.

He'd seen dead bodies, seen people die before, but that didn't make it less disturbing.

Jeff pushed a few round, green fruits around his plate. Sunshine didn't know what they were called but they reminded him of something between a tomato and cucumber.

"Have you ever...?"

Jeff looked at him.

Sunshine glanced toward the blood still pooled before the throne. "First time?"

Jeff shook his head. "No." He pronounced it with gravity.

"Have you?"

"I don't know. Maybe. You?"

"No. What happened?"

"A man tried to rob me. I disabused him of the notion that it was possible to take something from me. I...I fled after that. I don't recall the state I left him in exactly, but it's possible he didn't survive."

"Oh." Sunshine had gotten into a few close encounters like that but knew that the worst he'd done was broken bones and some light organ damage. Those had all been extraordinary circumstances, though. Normally Felix caused a showy enough distraction that they could run away, and the handful of times they'd gotten mugged, Felix had just tossed a fistful of cash at their assailants, grabbed Sunshine, and run in the opposite direction.

For a supposedly deadly pair, they ran away a lot.

That hadn't happened in a long time. Manhattan wasn't what it used to be. Sunshine didn't miss a lot of things, like getting mugged or harassed, or vice raids on the Diamond, but did miss some things.

Nostalgia always made things seem better than they had been. Going to grindhouses to see all those low-budget horror movies and softcore pornos had not been exactly romantic, but he'd always tagged along, happy to have been gently bullied into it. They'd even gone to adult theaters sometimes before Giuliani had turned Times Square into Disneyland.

He couldn't help but smile thinking of all the things like that they'd done together and how he'd still needed to tell Felix that just because he hadn't explicitly come out didn't mean he was in the closet.

He shook his head and tried to think about something else. He settled on thinking about *Star Trek* because he'd seen it so many times that he could easily replay episodes in his head. He and James Kelly had spent a lot of time discussing *Star Trek* while Felix and June caused trouble.

Sunshine went on to spend most of the time not thinking about things. Or rather, pointedly thinking about things that didn't matter.

Right now, he was cleaning the blood from under Elora's nails and thinking about baking competitions. He was not thinking about how he was pretty sure it was Nix's blood, because he'd seen scratches all down Nix's back last night. They had strayed dangerously close to his wings and thinking about how easy it would be to shred those delicate wings had made him want to throw up.

Elora yanked her hand back with a hiss. "Careful."

"Well, next time don't get so much blood under them."

She yanked her hand and splashed him. "Go away."

He went, gladly.

The children were in bed already, snuggled beneath the covers.

Elora would probably call for Nix later when the water had cooled and she wanted him to towel her off or oil her skin or go down on her, or whatever it was they did when they were alone.

Sunshine pushed back the curtain to their room and found Jeff and Nix sitting on the floor. Nix had the baby's hands wrapped around his fingers and Jeff was calling gentle encouragement as the baby wobbled back and forth on her feet. She bounced up and down a few times, then fell on her bottom.

"Oops," Nix said. He tried to stand her up again, but she wouldn't put her feet under her. He cuddled her close and kissed her cheek. He looked up at Sunshine. "She's done with you?"

"I annoy her."

Nix smiled.

Sunshine sat down next to them. "She's still favoring her right leg."

"Wouldn't you?" Jeff asked.

Sunshine shrugged. "Hard to walk if you won't put weight on one leg."

"She's too little to walk," Nix said. "She's learning how to stand up."

Sunshine had no idea how long he'd been at Court, but it had been months at least. The baby hadn't been a newborn when she'd come to Court, but now she was starting to crawl around.

He knew he could ask Nix how long it had been, but he didn't want to know. Two months, six months, he didn't care.

He put the baby to bed when Elora called for Nix, then stayed up playing dice with Jeff and recounting episodes of *General Hospital* for him. He sort of worried he was giving Jeff a warped view of how the human world worked, but Jeff found the stories enthralling in the same way people enjoyed true crime documentaries.

In the morning, Elora made them draw her another bath.

She tried to find tasks, meaningful or otherwise, to keep them busy, to eat up Nix's time the way she'd used to, but between him,

Jeff, and Nix, they actually got things done. Sunshine could tell it bothered the shit out of Elora but she hadn't yet reached the point where she'd yell at Nix for doing something genuinely useful like making teacups instead of sitting there waiting for her to come up with something stupid for him to do.

Nix had taken up pottery again, making little clay dolls and marbles for the children, and some dishware for the house. Everyone had a cup with their name painted on the side now, though no one but Sunshine could read what he'd painted, so sometimes Dire ended up drinking out of a cup labeled 'Jeff.'

Jeff went out hunting a lot. He had taken a liking to a bow hunting in particular. He spent most mornings stalking through the surrounding forest and usually came back with something for dinner, so when he was inside fletching arrows one morning, Sunshine asked, "What's up?"

"It's raining."

Sunshine cocked an ear toward the door. He could hear a heavy patter against the stone. He peeked outside and saw the entire Court full of puddles and mud. One miserable soul darted between doorways. "Oh boy, it's really coming down."

A few minutes later, Nix got up and said more or less the same thing, but he said it with a sense of dread.

"What's that face for?"

"Winter...winter can be difficult," he said, "with all of us inside together. Too cold and wet to go out and play, or hunt."

Sunshine could see how being trapped inside with Elora and the children would be miserable. He put a hand on Nix's back, careful to avoid his wings. "It'll be alright."

"What's it like to lie so freely, Sunshine? Does it make your heart lighter?"

"Um."

"It must. I can only think you do it out of kindness. I know you aren't a cruel man."

"Nix, geez."

Nix sighed and put his hand out the door, letting rain patter against it. He drew back and dried his hand on his shirt. "Have the children eaten?"

"I just got up."

Nix touched his shoulder then went over to the hearth, dragging over a pot and sack of grain.

Sunshine brought him the other ingredients before he asked for them.

Elora woke earlier than usual and stormed out of her room in a rage over how loud the children were while they played. "Bring them outside or make them silent," she demanded.

"It's raining," Nix told her.

She grabbed him by the face, her nails digging hard into his cheeks. "Do you think these two will stay forever?"

He swallowed. "No, my lady, of course not."

"A year and a day from his departure before I can claim them," she reminded. "Either they'll be mine or they'll be gone. Remember that." She released him with a push.

"You can't claim us," Jeff told her.

"Your master had abandoned you. A year and a day from his departure and his claim on you will be worn away," she told him.

Jeff opened his mouth to argue, likely to tell her that Felix was not his master, but Sunshine coughed loud enough that it interrupted him.

Elora glared in his direction. "A bath. Breakfast," she demanded.

She had a lot of anger but a short attention span. She'd target whoever she saw, not exclusively the person who'd pissed her off.

He went to fetch her tub. It took ages to fill and heat the tub and Elora watched every minute of it, picking away at him with little jibes.

He ignored all of it, mentally replaying a walk to work one crisp spring morning several years ago. It had been a particularly beautiful morning and he had come across a stray dog and her litter of puppies. He'd ended up late to work because of it since he'd taken the time to call a shelter and make sure the animals all got caught.

The stray had been pissed, growling the whole time, and the puppies had cried, but he'd gotten an update from the shelter a few months later saying all the dogs, even the mother, had been adopted and was doing well. He'd seriously considered taking a puppy but knew he couldn't commit to the care a puppy needed.

As he hauled the last bucket over to the tub, he wondered how Garfield and Specter's Dad (the cat) were doing.

Elora implied that his mother must have fucked a stump to produce offspring as dull and stupid as him.

The more he ignored her the harder she tried to intimidate him. So far, she'd done nothing but threaten and call him names, detailing all the things she'd do when he belonged to her.

Today, though, she slapped him across the face because the

water was too hot.

He blinked a few times, trying to orient himself emotionally. It hadn't really hurt. He smiled at her.

She hit him again. "Stop smiling!"

He smiled wider.

The third time she hit him he started laughing until finally, she shoved him. He fell into the tub, knocking it over, and he lay on the floor, soaked, as he laughed and coughed so hard he nearly peed his pants.

Elora let out a hideous scream and demanded that they get him out of her sight.

Jeff had to carry him out of the room, leaving Nix to clean everything up. When he finally stopped laughing, Jeff asked, "What's wrong with you?"

Sunshine shook his head. "You wouldn't understand."

"I'm worried about you."

"No, no, don't worry. I'm fine. It's just...it's *really* funny."

"What about being trapped in a hostile camp ruled by a mad queen who holds her people enthralled amuses you?"

Sunshine rubbed his face. He started to peel off his wet clothes. "It's not that. It's...Listen, you don't want to know."

"Assure me you haven't lost your mind."

"So. Felix and I. We're involved, you know that, and I've always liked it so much when he was just the right kind of mean to me. And it's just...He's so *nice*, like he's such a nice little daddy's boy underneath everything. And I...God, I wanted him to hit me. I wanted him to do it so bad, like he really meant it. I wanted him to just...hit me and pull my hair and make me his, take me like...Like. Like a fucking animal, like just *mark me* so people would know he'd done that and that I'd liked it."

Jeff stared at him, wide-eyed and grimacing slightly.

"He'd pull my hair and I'd melt, and you know, he always tried to do what I wanted, he tried to like..." Sunshine held in a giggle. "He tried to spank me a few times and he couldn't even do that. It was so cute."

"I don't see the humor in this at all and I do not feel assured that you're of sound mind," Jeff warned.

Sunshine pressed his lips together. "No, it's just...It's really funny. That she's so fucking mean but she has no fucking idea that I'm *into it*. Like she thinks she's hurting my feelings but she's just flirting with me and she has no idea."

Jeff held out a towel. "You're ill."

"Oh, don't kinkshame me, Jeff," Sunshine scoffed. He toweled off and got dressed, then wrung out his clothes and left them to dry by the hearth.

It wasn't that he found Elora's threats of pain and domination arousing, or that he desired her in any way, but it was like being threatened with a nice date with someone he wasn't attracted to. Not his idea of a great time, but not unendurable. It was like the time he'd had to double date at El Bulli with some Spanish olive oil heiress Felix had been seeing; she'd brought along her cousin, who'd only talked about the perfection of Spanish ham and soccer the whole time.

It was just like that, or like getting hit on by some loser at a bar.

It had to be.

He stared at the fire and pulled his robe a little tighter around himself.

Then he made himself smile again and went to play with the kids. They liked his watered-down retellings of shows and movies, even the admittedly awkward times he'd tried to explain an episode of Seinfeld to them.

It made him sort of feel like he shouldn't watch so much TV. Maybe Bibi could recommend a good book to him.

Nix, when he returned, didn't take things lightly. He fussed over the mark she'd left on Sunshine's cheek and the scrape on his arm from the stone floor. He persisted until Sunshine had hugged him, promised him it wasn't his fault, and asked what was for dinner.

"I don't know," Nix confessed.

"Let me cook."

"Are you sure?"

"Of course."

Nix tightened his arms. "I don't know what I'd do without you anymore."

"Don't worry about that."

"I'm scared."

"Don't be."

"You keep asking me for impossible things," Nix reminded.

Sunshine patted his back. "Someday they won't be."

He made the closest he could to shepherd's pie, and everyone devoured it, so he went to bed a little happier than he'd expected.

Now that they didn't have to go to bed so late, or get up so early, he and Nix stayed up sometimes talking about nothing in particular. Amusing parts of their day, a story from the past, or quiet hopes for the future. Never anything more immediate than, "Maybe it will be nice tomorrow, we can take the kids for a walk," though. Anything more than tomorrow was too far away.

Occasionally Jeff came to sit by the door and listen, though he never shared.

He probably didn't have anything to share.

Tonight, Sunshine finally worked up the nerve to ask, "Are your wings really like moth wings?"

Nix tilted his head. "How so?"

"I mean...moths and butterflies, they're so fragile."

Nix grinned. "I wouldn't still have them if they were as delicate as a moth's. Neither would Dire! By the stars, with how often she throws herself on the ground and has a tantrum..."

"Oh."

"They are...they're sensitive and it's easier to damage them than the rest of my body. But they can heal."

"I just, you know, I always heard that if you touched a moth's wings, they'd never be able to fly again."

"I can't fly anyway," Nix said.

Sunshine shrugged.

"Do you want to touch my wings?"

"Oh, I..." That seemed so intimate.

Nix didn't wait for an answer. He slid out of bed onto the floor, unlacing the back collar of his underclothes so it slithered down his back, around his wings. He turned around, exposing his back to Sunshine. "Go ahead."

"Are you sure?"

"As long as you promise to be careful."

Sunshine barely touched them, but still, his fingers came away powdery. He felt like he shouldn't have, especially when the wings twitched and the muscles in Nix's back tightened. "I'm sorry."

"It doesn't hurt."

He gently the back of one finger along one wing.

Nix giggled and his wings twitched again. "Satisfied?" He looked over his shoulder at Sunshine.

"Do you want me to fix your shirt for you?"

Nix turned around, holding Sunshine's gaze. His clothes pooled in his lap. Here and there, pale pink scars decorated his chest and arms. He touched one. "Climbing a tree that was too tall for me." He touched another. "Not paying attention when I went to visit the smith. I walked right into a red-hot piece of metal." He touched a third on his stomach, right below his belly button, half-obscured by a trail of hair. "Trying to shave."

Sunshine giggled.

"I knew I'd get more hair when I grew up and I distinctly did not want to grow up. I thought if I could get rid of the evidence..." He smiled, then licked his lips.

Sunshine knew he could have touched that scar if he'd wanted.

Nix grabbed a blanket and dragged it across his chest, his face flushed. "I. I'm sorry."

"No, it's...Don't worry about it."

"I shouldn't..." He swallowed. "I don't even *feel* that way about you. I. I don't have an interest in men but..."

"Go ahead."

Nix rubbed his face. "I only think sometimes that even if I don't like men, that if we made love, you might at least be kind to me."

"I mean, I would, but I don't think that's what either of us really wants."

"No," Nix agreed.

"Turn around, I'll fix help with your shirt."

Nix turned and Sunshine tied the laces on his shirt again, taking care around his wings, still afraid to touch them.

To the back of Nix's head, he said, "You know...it doesn't have to be about sex. If you just...You know, if you just wanted to sit with me for a little bit."

"You wouldn't mind? Or feel misled?"

"No."

Nix scooted closer to him and rested his head against Sunshine's shoulder. "What if I slept next to you?"

"That's fine."

"I've always had this stupid fantasy that someday I'd sleep next to someone without feeling sick to my stomach. I didn't think it'd be like this. I didn't think it'd ever happen."

"Funny how things work out."

Nix hummed softly. "Funny is one word for it."

It hadn't gotten cold enough to snow, but the rain came down in heavy, bitter sheets that turned the world outside into an ugly mess.

They were all clustered around the hearth in Elora's suite, even Jeff, because the wind could reach them as much in here.

Elora sat closest, wrapped in furs and blankets, and had allowed that the children could sit beside her as long as they weren't troublesome.

Nix sat a little further back, still close to the queen. She'd originally had him come sit beside her to clean and file her nails. She had a carefully shaped piece of pumice she used for shaping her nails and Nix had told a sweet little story about gathering pumice from where it had washed up on the beach.

"My brother let me think I was so strong, giving me all the pumice to carry while he filled up his bucket with other stones. I don't even remember what we needed them for anymore, I just remember him saying I must be so strong from working all that clay with Dada."

Elora took her hand back to warm it by the fire. "Why do you insist on making noise all the time?"

Nix didn't say anything after that.

They sat silently in the room, the fire crackling, the building pounded by wind and rain, and the stone scraping over her nails.

Sunshine and Jeff shared a blanket. Jeff sat practically on top of him, as close as he could get.

"You might as well cry to climb inside me at this point," Sunshine said when a cold wind slipped through and Jeff scooted closer.

"It's *cold.*"

"No shit, it's cold. Go get another blanket."

"There are no more blankets."

Sunshine grunted. "With all the shit you're out there killing, we don't have more blankets?"

"Shut up."

Sunshine elbowed him.

Jeff pushed him back.

They nudged and pushed back and forth, not fighting but fooling around.

"Stop that," Elora said.

Sunshine looped an arm around Jeff's neck and pulled him close, ruffling his hair, then releasing him when he started really squirming. "Yeah, Jeff, quit fooling around."

"Me...!" Jeff pushed him.

Sunshine shoved him back, giggling when Jeff laughed.

"I said stop!" Elora snapped.

He and Jeff went quiet for a moment, then looked at each other. "Yeah, Jeff, she said stop it," he muttered.

Jeff pressed his lips together but after a second, he elbowed Sunshine in the ribs.

"Ow, hey, now that hurt!" he protested but couldn't keep himself from laughing.

"Enough!" Elora barked, her face briefly lined and leathery again.

They both quieted down, hunkering under their shared blanket.

Nix offered them one of the furs from his lap.

Sunshine asked, "Was your brother a lot older than you?"

"He was grown when I was born, but that's oft the way of our people. Children come rarely and are children for so few years that...that it's almost like we were never children at all," Nix said.

Sunshine thought back to what Jeshe said, that she'd known him as a boy and that she hadn't been here for more than a few decades. Fairies could live for centuries, even thousands of years, so in the grand scheme of the Otherworld and from Sunshine's personal perspective, Nix was still incredibly young.

He never really counted his years in Heaven toward his age, not in a meaningful sense. His existence there was so different from his years lived on Earth. Oh, if asked, he would say he was thousands of years old, but that was to impress people and buy a little credit with the other immortals.

"How..." He tried to think of the least offensive way to ask the questions. "How long have you held Court here?"

Elora looked at him. "You mean among ruins?"

It was the first time anyone had dropped the pretense. Maybe Elora was the only one who could get away with it and live.

He said, "The buildings are ancient, surely, but I can't imagine the Court matches their age."

"A hundred years we've settled here, hundreds before that I traveled the Wilds. I searched..." Her face softened, that plain and human-looking freckled face again, no trace of the monster that slipped out from time to time. "I searched for anything. Any scrap of civilization, of kin, or *anything* that might be left. I am the last of my line, or close to it."

"Oh."

"I found ruins. So many ruins. This Court had glory once. Greatness. I'll restore that. I've done more in a hundred years than others have done in the thousands since the Obliteration. Do you know what it is to make something from nothing?" she asked.

"Ex nihilo," Jeff said. "The Almighty fashioned us from nothing."

Sunshine hadn't counted on Jeff chiming in but was glad he had. It was better than anything Sunshine himself would have come up with.

"From nothing I'll make a new world," Elora declared.

No adult answered, but the children quietly said, "Praise our lady."

She scowled at the children but didn't lash out.

Nothing made her happy.

No surprises there.

The baby stirred, starting to fuss. Sunshine started to get up but froze when Elora looked at Nix.

"I thought you liked these things," Elora said. "You've so readily given them away."

"I cherish all your gifts, my lady," Nix said.

"Are they less precious to you now that you have so many? Once you attended to them thoroughly."

Nix hurried to get up and take care of the baby. "They are as dear to me as always, my lady."

"As dear to you as clay pots, at least," she noted but said nothing else to Nix. "Your master paid heed to the children before he left."

"He likes kids."

"He has his own?"

"No."

"He intends to?"

"I imagine it relies heavily on him finding a suitable spouse to raise them with."

"Hmm. Maybe Nix will still have some purpose at Court if any sort of arrangement arises," Elora said. "Though I wonder at the length of your master's absence."

Sunshine said, "Wherever he is, I know he's doing his best. He wouldn't be away unless he had to be."

She sighed. "Nix, my nails still need filing."

Nix was in the middle of changing the baby.

Before she could lash out at him for not immediately attending to her, and before he could start to feel bad about leaving the baby, Jeff went to finish changing her diaper. He brought the baby back and bounced her on his thigh.

She laughed.

Sunshine didn't know how she managed how to be such a happy, agreeable baby but she laughed more than she cried.

Jeff eventually asked to know about the next series of happenings on *General Hospital*. Sunshine talked so much his throat started to hurt and his voice rasped.

Nix brought him a cup of warm water with honey and took a turn telling stories. He dragged up a sort of cute tale about how the Blue Lady, one of their goddesses, had come to the aid of a pair of lovers in enemy tribes whose lands were separated by a vast river. She told them how to build a bridge, which would hold them, and only them. It turned out the goddess had swollen the river to its enormous size to separate the tribes when nothing would soothe their conflict.

Nix ended it with, "And they wed upon the bridge with their families watching from both sides. Lariel's brother set foot upon the bridge and the Blue Lady allowed it because he had no hate in his heart, only joy for his sister and new brother. One by one, their families came to meet them and embrace the pair, giving their love and blessings."

Elora scoffed. "That isn't how it ends."

Nix tilted his head. "What do you mean?"

"I mean the story doesn't end there," Elora said. "One of Tauren's uncles stabbed Lariel's sister when she spurns his advances and the Blue Lady drown them all."

"Oh. My mother must have left out that part."

Elora scoffed again.

Sunshine wondered about her parents. Who had raised her? Surely, she hadn't been created out of the malice of the very Wilds themselves. She must have had parents. and something must have happened to them. Cautiously, he asked the queen, "What kinds of stories did your parents tell you?"

The question startled her. She glowered at Sunshine. "My parents told me no stories. They told me truths. Hard ones."

They spent two days like this.

When the rain stopped, every member of the Court sluggishly went about putting everything back into order. They shoveled away mud, branches, and leaves that had found their way in, repaired the skins that they'd put over the firewood, checked to make sure nothing had spoiled their food stores.

Jeff went out to hunt and came back with a pair of large fowl.

Nix held Elora's train out of the mud and water as she prowled the Court.

Sunshine carried wood into the villa, washed the laundry, and hung it by the hearth to dry, and thought about dinner. He hadn't cooked a proper meal in ages. He could do basics here with the open fire and a pot, but he wanted to bake something.

He wanted cookies.

Chocolate chip, with walnuts, gooey and warm from the oven.

He poked at the fire and wondered how he could make them here, then gave up. He thought about penne a la vodka and wondered if he should tell Felix that he'd learned that recipe from Anthony DiMarco, too.

He'd spent so long purposefully not thinking about Felix that doing so felt like a papercut. At first, nothing more than the knowledge that he'd done it, then a deep, throbbing sting as his nerves realized he was hurt.

He couldn't quite pull himself back together after that. He didn't cry or break down, but he went to bed early, no longer interested in stories or games. Even Elora noticed though she found it more amusing than anything.

Jeshe was the only one who seemed to know what to do with him in this mood because she was the only one with any perspective on what a relationship like theirs on Earth could be like.

"I never had a problem with queers," she told him abruptly one morning when she stopped by the check on the baby and he'd invited her to stay for breakfast.

His head had swiveled toward her, no idea why him passing her a bowl of porridge had prompted that remark.

She seemed to take his wide-eyed disbelief as worry at being outed more than a flinch from an outdated way of saying things. Of course, how could she have known? "Like I said, I don't judge. Being a queer, that's your prerogative. You and Specter were obvious. It's gotta be hard for you, not knowing when he'll be back."

"Oh."

"You never talk about it."

"He always comes back." He had never been away for this long.

"But you've gotta miss him."

"Of course," he said.

"Just saying. If you want to talk, I'm here. You don't have to worry about me giving you a hard time about it," she said. "I know things are rough for your type back on Earth."

"Oh. Well."

"Judging by how Jeff is about it..." She shrugged. "If you need to talk."

"That's kind of you."

She nodded.

He took a few bites of porridge, fed some to the baby, then had to say, "You know."

"Hmm?"

"We don't really call people queers anymore. At least, straight people shouldn't. And even then, it's more of an adjective these days than a noun."

"What?"

"Like. You can say that I'm a queer person. But you shouldn't call me a queer."

"Huh. Go figure. I guess a lot must have changed."

He nodded. "You don't ever think about going back?"

Jeshe shrugged. "Ah, not really. This place has its issues, but I'd rather be a black woman here than back on Earth. And Elora leaves me alone for the most part. I'm not saying I condone what she does but..." She sighed. "I'll take her over the shit that happens on Earth."

"I understand. Or, you know, I think I do."

"Besides, in another hundred years or so this place might be nice!" Jeshe said with a smile.

"Maybe."

He went back to feeding the baby and not thinking about Felix.

Jeff had once again brought back a pair of fowl for dinner. Sunshine wondered if he wasn't in danger of wiping out the local bird population but didn't know how to voice it. It would have felt bizarre to complain about food, especially with the weather as nasty as it was most days. A roast bird made for a nice dinner when it was so cold his fingers hurt.

He wished it would snow.

Jeff ripped feathers from the bird, littering the ground outside the villa with handfuls of feathers.

Milk grabbed a handful and threw them in the air, spinning underneath them.

"Oh, let's not do that," Sunshine murmured and started to pick the feathers out of his hair.

Milk reached for another handful and tossed it toward Stone.

Dire threw herself directly into the feathers, laughing and rolling around in them.

Sunshine's skin crawled. He finally lost it when a feather floated down onto the baby and she immediately put it in her mouth. "I said enough with the feathers!"

The children scurried away.

Sunshine scooped up the baby and took the feather out of her mouth, praying she hadn't already contracted salmonella.

The toddlers had gone to hide behind Jeff.

"They're dirty, I just don't want you to get sick. I'm not mad."

The trio stayed put. Stone had buried his face in Jeff's back.

Jeff glanced at them and then at Sunshine.

"Shut up."

The baby started to squirm, so he turned her to face out. She wanted to see everything and got fussy if she was facing away from where most people were.

She kicked her legs and bubbled a few nonsense sounds.

One last feather floated down and she reached for it.

Sunshine went to grab it before she could, but beyond the feather, he saw something that made his stomach drop. He went cold all over at the sight of a too-tall, horrible figure standing in the middle of the Court ruins.

It couldn't be anyone else, not with that inky hair and milk pale skin, not with limbs that should have been on a spider, not a person.

He practically ran over and threw himself against the Devil, squeezing him tight. He had never been thankful to touch that spindly body, but right now, the Beast felt like salvation.

Lucifer cooed a funny little sound of surprise. He patted Sunshine's curls. "What's this now? Which one are you?"

"It's me," he said into the Devil's shirt.

"Ah. Good. Felix said he has two now."

"Is he...he's here, right?"

"Mmm, I think he's looking for you...Ah. Felix!" Lucifer called.

Sunshine turned to see Felix bound out of Jeshe's tent.

He took Sunshine by the face. "There you are! Jesus, oh...Oh. Your hair! Sunshine, why is your hair so *long?*" he demanded, combing his fingers through Sunshine's hair. "Christ, that isn't the baby, is it?"

"We don't have time."

"What do you mean?"

"I mean we should go *now.*" He handed the baby over to Lucifer without thinking. "Before everyone wakes up."

"Of course, of course, darling but...But your hair."

Sunshine grabbed Felix's hand and dragged him to the villa, handing him a child, then going inside to get Nix.

He hadn't come to their room last night, so Sunshine crept into Elora's room. Nix slept curled up on one side of her bed. Sunshine barely touched him and whispered, "Let's go."

Nix rubbed his eyes.

"Come on."

"What's wrong?"

"Shhh. Come on."

Nix eased out of bed.

Sunshine took him by the hand as soon as he stood and led him out of the villa to find Lucifer holding the baby on his hip and an unconscious Jeff over one shoulder. Sunshine decided not to question it, scooped up Stone and Milk, and handed one to Nix.

Dire had already attached herself to Felix.

"Are you ready?" Sunshine asked Nix.

"Ready for what? I'm not even *dressed,*" Nix pointed out, settling a rather startled Stone on his hip.

Sunshine hadn't registered that.

"Nix?" Elora called from inside.

"Go," Sunshine demanded of Lucifer and grabbed on to him, dragging Nix in close too. "Don't let go, no matter what."

"I–"

Felix completed the huddle, crowding them all around the

Devil who, with a beleaguered sigh, brought them through the in-between.

A moment later, they stood in the great hall of the Devil's place, which looked much different than the last time Sunshine had been here. Of course, that had been over a hundred years ago.

It was cozier, more like a sitting room than the hall of a palace. At least a dozen cats lounged on various couches and stuffed chairs around the throne room. A black one with a white splotch had curled up on a cushioned rocking chair.

Milk wiggled out of his arms and ran over to one of the couches, Dire started to physically climb Felix like he was a tree, and Stone started to cry. The baby had her fist twined in Lucifer's hair, but he was taking that in stride well enough, though he had dumped Jeff rather unceremoniously on the floor.

"Now tell me, Felix, how did going to get Sunshine turn into *this?*" Lucifer asked.

Felix ignored his father, pulled Dire off of him and deposited her on the floor, and came over to Sunshine, once again grabbing him and demanding, "Why is your hair so long!"

"Well. It grows," Sunshine said, not sure what other explanation Felix expected.

"I know, but how did it grow so *fast?*"

"It didn't."

Felix's eyes had gotten huge. "How long was I gone?"

"I don't know."

"Not...Not a long time right? I...I couldn't find you, you know, with the time differences between home and here *and* the Otherworld, and then I didn't even know *where* in the Wilds you were, it's not like I had a map," Felix insisted. "I looked all over and I had to go back to your apartment to...to fucking take hair out of your hairbrush to find you but you keep everything so fucking clean, I had to get it out of the drain!"

"I clean my drain."

"The sink drain," Felix clarified. "With one of those gross metal snakes."

"I'm sorry."

"I...Just. Sunshine!" Felix grabbed on to him. "I was only gone a week!"

Sunshine didn't know what to say. He wrapped his arms around Felix, sliding his arms around his ribs and burying his face in his neck. "We should get Nix something to wear."

"Please," Nix said, his voice barely there.

"Oh my god, shit, you're right." Felix pulled away from him, then doubled back and squeezed him again. "You're okay?"

"I'm fine."

Felix pulled back and looked around, scanning over the people around him. Dire had fixed herself to his leg again, holding onto his pants and demanding his attention. "Uh. Dad!"

"I'm two feet away, you don't need to shout," Lucifer said. "Who did we just kidnap?"

"Uh." Felix looked around. "Stone, Dire, Milk, and Nix, Wild Prince of the Meridian Court."

"And this?" Lucifer looked at the baby.

"She doesn't have a name."

"Alright. Well." Lucifer turned and headed upstairs. "This way, please."

They all trailed behind him, stepping around the cats.

"Did you get more cats?" Sunshine asked.

"I don't *get* any cats. They come here."

Felix said, "You're okay, though, right? Sunshine. Come on. You look...You look weird."

"Maybe I'm actually Jeff."

"That's not funny!"

"It's a little funny."

"It's not! Jeff *freaked out* when he saw my dad, by the way."

Sunshine shrugged, trying not to think about how he'd run into Lucifer's arms. "How are you?"

"I'm fine."

"You look tired."

"Well, I was up for a week trying to find you!"

"Not all week?"

Felix sulked, "No. Dad made me go to bed."

Sunshine grinned. He looped his arm around Felix's shoulders and kissed his hair. The smell of him sent a shiver down Sunshine's spine and hit his gut like a rock. "I missed you."

"You know I didn't mean to leave you there like that."

"I know."

Felix whined.

Lucifer pushed open the door to a bedroom. He cleared his throat. "Uh. I think this room might suffice for our guests presently."

It had a crib and dozens of toys, a bookshelf lined with narrow, colorful books.

"We'll get some beds, I have plenty in storage, but uh. The

crib. We only have one of those," Lucifer said. He placed the baby in it and handed her a stuffed toy, which she immediately grabbed on to with a grin.

The toddlers descended on the other toys.

Nix stood in the doorway looking like he was going to cry.

Sunshine went over and put his hands on his shoulders. "It's okay."

"Where are we?"

"Uh. The Devil's palace in Hell."

Nix blinked several times, and his answer came out slightly choked. "I don't know what that means."

"It means you're safe here, okay. It's, uh." Sunshine smiled. "It's Specter's dad's place."

"This was my room," Felix said. "For like two weeks, anyway," he muttered. "And this is my dad."

Nix looked over Lucifer, his brow slightly knit.

In his most current form, Lucifer didn't look like anyone's dad and he certainly didn't look like he should be addressed a man, but the Devil had no real gender, not even when his body looked like it did.

Lucifer grinned and waved, but when he saw that Nix still looked like he was going to cry, he excused himself by saying, "Here, you three catch up, I'll go get some pants for your friend."

Nix wrapped his arms around himself and flinched when Lucifer trailed a finger over his wings.

Felix scowled.

Sunshine grabbed a blanket. "Here, tuck your wings in," he said before he draped it over Nix's shoulders.

Nix clutched the blanket close. "I shouldn't be here."

"Well, you couldn't stay there," Sunshine pointed out.

"I could have."

"I couldn't leave you there," Sunshine said. "I couldn't go without knowing you were somewhere safe." He touched Nix's face, his eyes on the circlet. Elora never let him remove it in her presence. He lifted the crown from Nix's head and threw tossed it onto a nearby chair. "It's...it's over."

"How can you say that? Now I...I have *four children*, Sunshine, and no home. No food, no goods, not even clothes. How is it over? Do you know how furious she'll be when I go crawling back?"

"You're not going back," Sunshine insisted, too forceful even to his own ears. He had his hands on Nix's shoulders, holding him too hard. "You never, *ever* have to go back there."

Nix shook beneath his hands. "You don't understand."

"I understand that..." Sunshine took a deep breath to steady himself, to keep himself from shouting. He loosened his grip on Nix. "We're friends, Nix. I couldn't leave you there, and I won't abandon you, either. We're going to take care of you and help you get your feet under you again. Okay?"

Nix shook his head.

"I mean it."

Lucifer cleared his throat and stepped through with an armful of clothing. He offered them to Nix, who clutched them to his chest. "Why don't you take a minute, hmm? Get cleaned up, get dressed. The bathroom is one door down," he suggested gently.

Nix bowed gravely. "You're too kind, my lady."

Lucifer smiled.

Nix looked at his children, who didn't seem to care that they'd been transported across realms.

"Go ahead," Sunshine said.

Once Nix had left, Lucifer crossed his arms. "So we kidnapped a prince."

Felix shrugged.

"I'm assuming his...his what, his mother? Isn't particularly kind-hearted."

"Oh, she's not his mother."

"His wife?" Lucifer asked, his nose wrinkling.

"Wife, abusive harpy who groomed him from childhood, what's the difference, really?" Felix said.

Lucifer grimaced. "Fine. I do like to know when I'm going to be kidnapping people of importance, though, even if it is warranted."

"Okay, well, we kidnapped him, he definitely saw his family get murdered, and he's been living under the threat of deadly violence for at least a decade," Felix said. "So he can stay here, right?"

"Well, yes...hang on." Lucifer looked at the children.

"Well?" Felix pressed.

Lucifer sighed. "You couldn't have bothered to mention any of this while I was very helpfully whisking you around Earth so we could go get the two, not six, people you said need to get?"

"I had other things on my mind."

Sunshine sat down.

Not in a chair or anything, just directly on the ground.

"Is he alright?" Lucifer asked.

"Are you alright?" Felix asked at almost the same time, then scowled at his father. He knelt next to Sunshine.

"Yeah. I just. I thought I was going to throw up or pass out or something."

Felix touched his forehead.

"I'm not sick."

"You're all clammy and gross."

"No, I'm fine, I'm okay. I just need to sit for a minute. Why don't you go check on Jeff and make sure he hasn't, like, committed ritual suicide or started stabbing the staff?"

"I'll put him in the dungeon," the Devil proposed cheerfully.

"Please don't do that," Sunshine said. "Maybe just...you know. A locked room."

"The dungeon is full of locked rooms," Lucifer said.

"Please."

"Yes, fine, I will put him in a locked room *not* in the dungeon. And then I will go do something despicable somewhere because this is seriously going to hurt my reputation..." Lucifer wandered out of the room, murmuring horrible acts to himself.

"Please go make sure he doesn't eat Jeff."

"No, no, he's been really good, he's fine. He's on vacation."

"What?"

"Yeah, he took time off when I stumbled through the nowhere place into his kitchen and promptly threw up all over his boyfriend."

"You threw up on Ira?"

"All over him. Like in his hair and everything. I felt so bad. Then I passed out. So Dad took some time to help me out. Isn't that sweet!"

"Can...can he do that?" Sunshine had a vague notion of the Devil accruing sick time like an hourly worker.

"Sure, Ira took over for a couple of weeks. Cute, right?"

"Super cute," Sunshine agreed. "You passed out?"

"Yeah, apparently touching the strings can outright drive humans insane, or kill them, but you know, I'm only half so I've got more wiggle room." Felix touched his face again and made a pitying face that lingered somewhere between love and guilt.

"I'm okay."

"Alright but maybe I just...I missed this face. I was worried sick all week."

Sunshine let out a weak chuckle.

Felix cuddled up next to him. "Can I tell you that I don't love your hair like this? It's giving me weird Michael Landon vibes but like...not as cute."

"Well, that's what happens when you leave me somewhere with no shampoo or conditioner for several months."

"I don't know, he was on a prairie and he made it work."

Sunshine sniffled.

Felix squeezed him harder. "It wasn't...it wasn't really months, was it? I mean. Not...not too many months, right? Not so long that you're not okay, right? Like...she didn't *do* anything to you did she?"

"No, I, I, uh. I told her you'd left me behind to test her character to see if she'd make you a suitable queen."

Felix covered his mouth and smothered a giggle. "No, you didn't."

"Ask Nix."

"What kind of tests did you give her?"

"No, I didn't give her tests, I just told her she failed one every time she did something shitty."

Felix tittered. He nuzzled his face against Sunshine. "I love you so much. You smell like..." He sniffed.

"It's beeswax and animal fat," he sighed. "My skin was getting dry from being near the fire all the time."

"Oh, you poor baby. Ira said I could use the big bathtub whenever I wanted. Let's go have a bath."

It felt wrong somehow.

"Or we can just sit here. Or we can go to bed. We can do whatever you want."

"Let's sit for a minute."

About fifteen minutes later, they had to wrangle children as a pair of servants carried in a bed frame and mattress. The servants assembled the bed, made it up, and bowed to Felix on the way out.

Felix elbowed Sunshine when they bowed. "It's good to be the king," he said. Then he grabbed Dire, kicked off his shoes, and jumped up onto the mattress to bounce it with her.

She let out delighted peals of laughter, especially when Felix told her to spread her wings and helped her pretend to fly around the room.

Nix came back half-dressed and Sunshine cut a pair of slits up the back of the shirt for him.

"You doing okay?"

"There's that word again." He turned and rested his head on Sunshine's chest. "Maybe some breakfast would be in order."

Sunshine looked at Felix, who wandered out of the room and returned a little while later to say, "Hasbani will come up with something to eat in a little bit. Pancakes. Thought that would be fun for the kids."

Nix stepped back and looked at Felix. He smoothed his clothes and bowed. "My apologies for my conduct. Your aid is not as unwelcome as—"

Felix grinned. "No worries! You and the kids relax, okay? Get acclimated, maybe find a cat to play with, they're all pretty friendly. I think there's a litter of little fuzzies downstairs. Sunshine and I will be a few doors down. And honestly, if you need anything, just ask anyone. You're a guest, okay?"

Nix gave a smaller bow. "I'll do my best to be a better guest than I was a host."

Felix took Sunshine's hand and led him out of the room.

"I feel like I shouldn't be here."

"Probably for about a dozen reasons. Let's just take a minute to breathe, though. And get that animal fat smell off you." Felix brought him into an enormous master bathroom and started fill in an inset tub big enough for several adults. "I'm pretty sure my dad and Ira are like constantly banging in here."

"Ew."

"I don't know, I think it's kind of nice. That they still like each other after so long. Do you think we'll be like that?"

"I...Will you be offended if I said I hope not?"

Felix tittered. "Get undressed."

He threw his clothes into a pile and tested the water with his hand. He slipped in. "Are you coming in?"

"Oh, I took a shower this morning," Felix said, then rolled his eyes. "Of course, I'm coming in, give me a second."

Sunshine sat and watched as Felix gathered up an armful of bath products, lined them up by the side of the tub, then shimmied out of his clothes and into the tub.

"Alright, so none of these are labeled," Felix said, sniffing one of the bottles, "So I'm not sure which one is shampoo but this one smells like Ira's hair."

"Leave it for a second. Come here."

Felix sloshed over.

Sunshine grabbed him and tangled them together, as much skin as he could get, and closed his eyes. Between the weightlessness and warmth of the bath, it was almost exactly right. It was almost how Heaven felt.

They breathed together.

"I'm never leaving you anywhere again."

"I told you to go," Sunshine said.

"Sunshine, I could have lost you."

"Don't be ridiculous. You will never lose me. Ever," Sunshine said. "You did exactly what you were supposed to do."

"I feel awful."

"Don't. I'm fine."

"Just promise you're okay."

"I'm okay. Nothing bad happened. I just had to spend a couple months with a mean girl and the man she was holding hostage with threats of violence against his children and maybe some kind of fairy magic," Sunshine said. "Oh. And I saw a lady get stabbed in the throat."

"Fuck me."

"No, it's fine, I mean. Not that she's dead. But I'm fine. We're fine."

Felix sighed. "What about you and Nix?"

"He's a friend."

"Mmmm."

"If he liked guys, it'd probably be a different story, but he doesn't, so we're friends," Sunshine said.

"I wouldn't be mad," Felix half-pouted.

"Can we not?"

"No, I'm. I don't know. We haven't been apart for this long in…ever. And Nix is, like, actually really hot. His face looks a lot better, by the way! But like we're still new to this and I really didn't mean to leave you there and like, I'd done whatever with that tree right beforehand, which I talked to my dad about that—"

"Felix."

"Hm?"

"We are not new to this. We are new to some *parts* of this. I have followed you in abject adoration for decades now."

"Abject?"

"Yes."

"How so?"

"Huh?"

"Abject. It's not a good thing. It means self-abasing, or it means to the most extreme degree about but in the context of something bad. People say abject misery, they don't say it for good things," Felix pointed out.

"Oh. Both. Definitely both. I'd very much like to be abased to the most extreme degree possible," Sunshine confirmed.

"Stop flirting, I'm trying to talk to you."

Sunshine smiled. "Hold your breath."

"What?"

"Please." He took in a deep breath and waited for Felix to do the same, which he did with narrowed eyes. Sunshine pulled them underwater, eyes closed, one warm muddle of person and water. He stayed under as long as he could, which was much for longer than either of them should have been able to hold their breath.

Felix had splayed his fingers over Sunshine's chest, not pulling any power from him this time, but feeding in his own. He slowed things, not time, but themselves, putting them into a calm bubble with barely-there heartbeats and a trickle of oxygen moving through their blood. Sunshine put his forehead to Felix's and didn't breathe, didn't think, didn't do anything except exist together in this warm, quiet world.

When they surfaced, Felix didn't bring up Nix again, he didn't ask if Sunshine was okay again or insist that he hadn't meant to be gone for so long. He moved a little more gently from then on. He took care of Sunshine. He washed his hair and said, "Maybe it's not so bad at this length if we shaped it up a little."

Sunshine kept his eyes closed, his head leaned back.

At one point, Felix asked, "Did I get soap in your eyes?"

"No."

"I know I'm a bit of a walking billboard for hysterical crying fits, but sometimes it feels better if you let it out."

"It feels like I'd never stop."

"We have time, darling. You're safe and very loved."

"I didn't think about it. Or I tried not to. Close my eyes and cover my ears and it's not there, right? But some of the stuff she said was awful. I didn't let her get under my skin, I couldn't, because once she did, she would have ripped me apart. But the shit she came up with! She didn't do it right."

"What?"

"I always liked it so much when you were mean to me, but she didn't do it right. I pretended it didn't bother me because I like being picked on, or when you pull my hair, but..." He opened his eyes. "You always knew I liked it. You did it for me. Not to me."

Felix kissed his palm.

Sunshine needed that. He needed something gentle. Maybe for longer than he thought. For a woman who'd rarely laid a hand on him, she'd done a lot of damage.

"I'll be careful," Felix promised.

He said it because he knew Sunshine needed to hear it.

"I know."

After their bath, they went back to check on Nix but found him and the children all piled in the enormous bed together, asleep or just very still. They backed out of the room and headed downstairs.

Felix handed Sunshine a kitten and sat him at the kitchen table. "Ok, so your options are super limited because processed food isn't really a thing here, so I can like fry an egg or make toast or bake a potato. Or I think there's oatmeal."

Sunshine had eaten his share of hot cereals for a while. "Is there peanut butter?"

"Yeah, like the oily Whole Foods kind."

"I would love a peanut butter and jelly sandwich."

Felix made a face like he thought Sunshine might be joking, then said, "Okay," and got to work.

"How's Garfield?"

"He's fine. He thinks he's a cat now. He likes to eat their dust bunnies."

The kitten Felix had handed him started to chew on his thumb.

Felix set a sandwich in front of him. "I could make tea."

Sunshine nodded.

He ate three sandwiches, two out of hunger and the third for the sheer enjoyment of it. He sipped chamomile tea and traded recaps of their time apart. For someone who only had a week to talk about, Felix had been up to a lot between finding Sunshine and warding Bobby's house so fairies couldn't get inside anymore.

"We have to go back for our stuff at some point," Felix said. "But honestly if I need to stay one place for a hot second. I feel all...glued together. Dad says I'll get used to it, but I don't think I want to."

Sunshine didn't like the idea of staying in Hell any longer than strictly necessary, but he also didn't know how long that would be. Elora could move between Earth and the fairy realm, but she couldn't get to them here, not unless she converted to a different religion, died with sin or guilt in her heart, and escaped her cell.

"He says Nix can stay in Hell," Felix said.

"Does Nix want to stay in Hell?" Sunshine asked, his skin crawling at the idea of leaving four children here.

"Oh, come on, I saw you hugging him," Felix said.

"Hugging me?" came a slippery voice from behind Sunshine, accompanied by the feel of spindly fingers trailing through his hair.

Sunshine flinched and yelped, dropping the kitten and spilling tea all over the table.

Felix sighed and grabbed a towel from the oven door.

"He *ran* into my arms."

"Stop feeling up fiancé," Felix sulked as he sopped up the tea.

Lucifer ruffled Sunshine's hair. "He likes it. Have you two considered a venue, yet?"

"I told you we're not getting married."

"Felix, you cannot be engaged to be married if you have no intention of getting married," Lucifer pointed out.

"Oh, says the person literally kicked out of paradise for not following rules."

"I think you're confused."

"I'm...!" Felix scowled.

Lucifer brought another cup of tea over for Sunshine, then sat next to him. "So clearly he's not a position to discuss this rationally. We have a gorgeous gallery at the University and, you know, if I do say so myself, an attractive palace with lovely grounds, so there's an indoor-outdoor option depending on the weather."

Sunshine looked around the kitchen, which felt undersized for a palace, and said, "I don't think this kitchen could handle the catering for a wedding."

"Please don't encourage him," Felix said.

"I'm not—"

"How many people were you thinking? I haven't seen the guest list."

"There is no guest list, we're not getting married," Felix said.

"Then you're not engaged."

"Listen, what would you know! You're not married."

"I most certainly am."

"Well. I mean. Not really. When was the last time you even saw your wife?" Felix asked.

"Last time she and Imogen went on a trip together," Lucifer said with a shrug. "Have you been in the garden lately? We put in wisteria a few years ago."

"Dad!"

"It's just really pretty. It could be a really small ceremony—"

"Listen, I already know. Alright! It's all already planned it's just *not happening*," Felix said.

"Hon, let's leave it," Sunshine said.

"Tell *him* to leave it."

Sunshine made himself look at the Devil. "Please."

"Oh, of course, of course, I'm sorry, Sunshine, *really*, it's just...you know."

"I have no idea."

Lucifer smiled. "No. Of course. How could you?" He touched Sunshine's face. "I'm so proud though. He was such a little baby, and I was so worried. And now he's all grown up and you two are so beautiful together. You're going to make the most beautiful little apocalypse." He looked at his son and put a hand on his arm. "Hiram and Phaedrus did such a nice job with you. I knew they would."

Felix sighed. "Dad."

"What?"

"I love you."

"I love you too, little one."

Sunshine couldn't sleep. He wasn't even tired, though he should have been. The excitement from the day had him keyed up still. Felix had wanted to go to bed early and Sunshine had gone along, happy to lie next to him. He'd expected a little more, but Felix had yawned, curled up into a ball, and fallen asleep.

The week had taken it out of him, and Sunshine guessed he hadn't slept much.

Now, the curve of his spine pressed against Sunshine's chest. He'd wiggled as close as physically possible and held Sunshine's arm against his chest.

The quiet of the night unsettled Sunshine.

He didn't think Hell should be quiet. It should have echoed with the moans of the damned or awful something like that, but all he could hear were the distant sounds of the city and the occasional cat.

Felix released his arm and burrowed further into the blankets.

Sunshine took the opportunity to ease out of bed. His arm had gone tingly and he needed to pee.

After a trip to the bathroom, he listened outside of the guestroom where they'd locked Jeff, who had resoundingly told them all to go fuck themselves earlier in the day. Sunshine had asked to go in and Lucifer had simply said, "No," and walked away.

Jeff had eaten the food Imogen had brought in for him and she'd only smiled at Sunshine when he'd asked why she had blood on her mouth.

"Don't worry, he's not her type," Ira had assured. "He probably just got fresh."

Ira's assurances had comforted Sunshine more than anything else. He looked trustworthy, far less unsettling than his companion, with his circlet nestled among bouncy, cherubic curls, his face open and innocent, and standing a good half-foot shorter than everyone around him.

He always sulkily reminded people that he was not anywhere near as young as he looked, grumbling, "I'm over a hundred, I'm just *short*."

Sunshine wondered if Lucifer liked people thinking he was fucking someone barely pubescent, if he liked making their skin crawl. Even Sunshine, who knew for sure and with a lot of reassurance from people he trusted that everything between Ira and Lucifer was above board, found that the two of them unsettled him.

He headed downstairs, trying not to think about anything dire, and then went to let a handful of cats who'd crowded by the door outside.

The cats trotted out into the garden.

Sunshine followed.

The sheer blackness of the sky made him feel like it might devour him. A single star winked like a dead pixel. The palace sat on a hill in the center of the city and from the front steps, Sunshine could see the lights of the Eighth and Ninth Precincts, and the darkness of the Seventh, a narrow slice of city delineated by the lights at the top of the massive walls that kept the souls from the rest of the city.

He wrapped his arms around himself and padded down the steps. He didn't want to go inside but he didn't want to look at the city.

He wanted to forget where he was.

He could barely see a thing but then as he took a few steps off the path to the gate and toward the garden, gentle light came up around him to illuminate his path.

Small smudges of light emanated from stones strategically placed around the garden, making it so he wouldn't trip but preserving the intimacy of the darkness.

If there had been stars it would have been a perfect place for a midnight picnic.

He paced, the clover and moss cold and wet under his feet.

It was beautiful out here, carefully tended but not rigid.

"I told you it was nice," said the Devil.

"Holy...! Holy fucking shit," Sunshine cried as he spun and clapped a hand to his chest. "Why the *fuck* are you always behind me?"

Lucifer smiled, all the more ghastly for being underlit. "You make it so easy to sneak up on you I'm starting to think you like it."

Sunshine grunted. "Why are you awake?"

"Oh. Ira kicked me out."

"For what?"

"Talking too much," Lucifer admitted. "I do have difficulty ceding control of things to him."

"Felix was happy you took time off for this."

"Really? He repeatedly asked me not to."

Sunshine shrugged. "You know how he is."

"No. Not really. We aren't as...familial as we could be. Sometimes he feels like a stranger to me and he looks at me..."

Lucifer sighed. He tucked a bit of hair behind his ear, twirling it around his finger several times first. "You don't want to hear this."

"Is that what's got you worked up about the wedding...or the not-wedding, I guess?"

Lucifer let out a startled laugh. "I'm a bad father. I have been a miserable parent to every child unfortunate enough to bear my blood. Most of them never want anything to do with me except for a few favors here and there. I deserve that. I would deserve it if he didn't want me there. Birthday presents and sporadic visits and guilt don't make up for it. I deserve it, but it hurts."

He sounded honestly miserable about the whole thing. That had to be his best trick, making people believe that he had feelings, that he wasn't just some uncanny amalgamation of evil and perversion.

Sunshine knew the Devil didn't mean any of it, that he said these things to toy with Sunshine, that he wanted something out of this interaction, some way to feed this moment into his infinite machinations to breach Heaven and defeat the Almighty.

Despite all that, Sunshine said, "He's not excluding you."

"Yes, I've probably done it to myself. I push away everyone."

"No, I mean, he's really not excluding you. We're not getting married. There *is* no wedding."

"You wouldn't want me there either. I have less reason to believe you than him."

Sunshine couldn't help himself. He said, "I thought I was your favorite angel."

"I would gladly cannibalize every other angel on sight, so take 'favorite' with a grain of salt," Lucifer reminded.

Still, he didn't look right. He looked miserable.

Not knowing what else to do, Sunshine changed the topic, "How's Ira? Is he still having seizures?"

"No. Goodness, no. You don't think I'd let him take the throne if he wasn't well, do you?" Satan asked. "He had a brain tumor."

"Oh, holy shit. But he's okay now?"

"Benign. Easy enough to remove it, too. He's all healed up, healthy as anything."

"Oh. Good. I'm glad."

"I don't know what I'd do without him. I mean. I do. Of course, I do. I've lost people before, but he's so special to me. It would be worse," Lucifer said.

"It's never easy," Sunshine agreed.

Lucifer took a few steps forward then glanced back to see if Sunshine had followed, which he had. "Tell me about this other angel."

"Jeff?"

Lucifer closed his eyes as if to gather his patience. "Did Felix name him, too?"

"Oh, no, if Felix had named him it would be worse than Jeff."

"I mean, for a human, it's not so bad, but for an angel? Hideous. Tell me about what's happening with Jeff."

They walked the garden as Sunshine filled Lucifer in on the appearance of this second angel. Normally, Sunshine would have kept as much as possible to himself, but he knew he and Lucifer had at least one common goal: keeping Felix alive and well.

Lucifer offered to kill or incapacitate Jeff in a variety of thoughtful ways, all of which Sunshine refused, until finally, the Devil said, "Well, then I'm out of ideas, so I don't know what you want from me at this point!"

"I just want him to not kill Felix."

"If you just wanted that you would let me murder him."

"Okay, well, I also want him to, like, not hate me or Felix."

"Dead people don't hate anyone."

"Fucking...are you like this on purpose?"

Lucifer gestured around. "I do generally have death on my mind."

Sunshine had temporarily forgotten where they were. The middle of the night in Hell had that same mystic, uncanny feeling as it did on Earth. Anything could happen at three a.m. and any two people might find themselves together without reason or judgment. "No, I don't want him dead. I just. I want him to like me."

"You want him to love you," Lucifer said. "You're an angel."

Sunshine gave him a sideways look.

"It has been millennia, but I do remember that much. I do...I do still have that much. We all want to be loved. Men, beasts, angels, hideous unthinkable monsters. I made things down here to be without love and they still learned how to do it. Anything that has enough of a mind to think of others as it thinks of itself learns to love others as it loves itself," Lucifer said.

"He'll never love Felix."

"Not unless he learns not to fear him. You learned that. Maybe Jeff can, too."

Sunshine sighed.

"Or I could tear his bones from his flesh."

"No."

Lucifer shrugged.

They'd walked long enough that the sky had started to redden. Just as Hell had no stars, it had no sun, just some unseeable source of light and warmth that made life possible.

"Thanks for listening, though, I guess," Sunshine made himself say.

Lucifer smiled at him, a normal and almost human smile. "You really are my favorite angel. I meant it when I said you could be a prince. Even if you don't ever fall."

"Uh. Thanks."

Lucifer sighed. He looked toward the palace. A bit of that melancholy from before crept into his face.

Maybe he really did remember love. He had been an angel and the other Fallen still loved. Maybe somewhere in him, he honestly did love Felix in his own twisted way.

Sunshine asked, "Can I do you a favor?"

"I believe you owe me two of those already."

"That's what I'm asking. Can I do you a favor?"

Lucifer narrowed his eyes.

"If we ever do get married, I'll make sure you're invited. Like, really invited. To all the same parent stuff as Phaedrus and Hiram. Rehearsal dinners and...I don't know, dress shopping and picking out entrees."

"You want me to use one of three favors ever promised to me by an angel, a servant of Heaven, on a thing so frivolous as a wedding invitation?"

"Or you could accept that Felix would invite you anyway *if* there was a wedding, which there presently is not."

Lucifer narrowed his eyes. "I want flowers. And a plus-one."

"Plus-two. Georg would be invited. You'll have to work out who gets to wear the mother-of-the-bride dress with Phaedrus, I don't know how they're going to lean on that one."

Lucifer's face changed. He looked like he was going to cry, his horrible eyes red-rimmed and shiny. He nodded. "That's your second favor," Lucifer agreed. He touched Sunshine's face and leaned in to kiss the corner of Sunshine's mouth. "Thank you."

Sunshine rubbed his arm. He didn't know what the fuck had happened, but he wouldn't have to think about it unless Felix decided he did want to get married, in which case inviting Lucifer was a given anyway.

The way this deal settled over him felt less ominous than last time.

He headed inside to see about making something for breakfast. He desperately wanted to use a frying pan.

Lucifer stayed in the garden and when they saw each other later at breakfast, they gave each other awkward, but not forced, smiles.

By the time everyone came downstairs to eat, Sunshine had prepared a feast. French toast, eggs, and home fries, bacon and sausage, and a pile of sauteed mushrooms for Lucifer.

Felix looked between Sunshine, the mushrooms, and his father's beaming face, but said nothing. "Should we bring something to Jeff?"

"Oh, I know, hang on. Don't feed him for like...two weeks, and then to gain his trust—" Lucifer began.

"No," Felix, Sunshine, and Ira said together.

Nix said nothing. He hadn't said much all breakfast, instead trying to wrangle the children and, it appeared, keep himself from crying. Stone and Milk were giving him a hard time about eating and the baby was unusually fussy. Anytime someone tried to help, Nix grew bristly and over-protective, telling them, "I can do it," in that deep, lighting crack voice of his.

Lucifer looked impressed.

Dire, at least, had wrapped herself around Felix's leg, though she hadn't eaten much either.

The baby went from fussing to full out crying.

Lucifer stepped in and picked up the baby, looking revoltingly at ease with a baby in his arms. He bounced her in a particular way and said, "Changing realms can be tough on little tummies. Give it a few days, they'll adjust."

Nix pressed his lips together. He reached out to take the baby back, but as soon as he did, she started crying again but louder.

"I'm actually not, like, bad with kids despite what you might have heard," Lucifer said.

Nix kept ahold of the baby.

"Yeah," Ira said, "He even made a law saying not to have sex with them."

"You can't have sex with a baby, you can only rape them," Lucifer said. "Babies have no capacity to give consent."

Nix stepped back.

"Do you always have to be so condescending?" Ira asked.

"I thought it was more pedantic," Lucifer said. To Nix, he said, "Honestly, I can help. What's her name?"

"She doesn't have one."

"Well. Either way. I can help."

"He's not bad," Felix assured.

Nix looked at Sunshine.

"It's okay," Sunshine said.

Nix eventually handed over the baby. Lucifer bounced her again, cooing to her about how she just needed a few days to get used to things. The fairy didn't take his eyes off Lucifer.

"You should give her a name. I know fairies are funny about it, but honestly," Lucifer said.

"It has not been my privileged of late to name my children. That belongs to my queen."

"Yes, this queen...I thought nothing remained of the Meridian Court," Lucifer said as though he had not been the one to decimate it.

"It rises again beneath my queen."

"Is she still your queen?"

"I swore my fealty to her crown. I swore obedience."

"That is a pickle. What do you intend to do?"

Nix glanced at Sunshine, then back at the Devil. "So long as I am your captive, I'm at your mercy. Were I free, I'd seek my way home."

"Consider yourself very much my captive, then."

Nix nodded. "Yes, my lady."

"We've got to do something about that," Felix said.

"Do nothing," Nix advised.

"You'll trade one captor for another?" Felix asked.

"If she proves to be gentler than my last, I have no protest."

"Don't you want to be free?" Felix pressed.

"Maybe this isn't a breakfast conversation," Sunshine proposed.

Ira stood, kissed Lucifer, and said, "I've got work to do."

"Stay out of the Seventh," Lucifer warned.

"The Seventh needs tending, too. Am I your proxy or not?"

Lucifer grabbed Ira's wrist and stared him in the eyes. "What the Seventh needs can wait until I'm back. Stay out of there."

"I'm not—"

"Ira, please," Lucifer said. "Stay out of the Seventh. We have new souls there and they are still learning their place. I need you to come home to me."

Ira smiled. "Mmm, fine, alright. You know, one of these days that isn't going to work on me."

Lucifer let go of him, kissing his hand before he did, and watched him leave.

"I told you it's kind of cute, right?" Felix whispered to Sunshine. He started gathering up dirty places and put them in the sink. "I'll do them later."

Sunshine made a plate for Jeff and headed upstairs. He gently bullied a servant into unlocking the door for him, even when she insisted that someone had already brought him food and that she wasn't supposed to open the door for anyone else.

He just kept smiling and asking her to open the door, until she'd thrown the key at him and run away like he'd pulled out a gun.

"They're afraid of angels around here," came a small, feminine voice.

He looked around but saw nothing.

"Down here."

He looked down to see a small black cat with a white splotch. She wound around his ankles and then sat down and looked up at him.

"Terrified ever since that upstart redecorated," the cat told him.

"Uh."

"I lost a mouse through that door the other day. Let me in, while you're at it."

He unlocked the door and held it open for the cat, who slunk through without another word. He closed the door behind him, unhappy when he heard the lock click, and flicked on the lights. "Jeff."

Jeff sprung him from where he'd hidden himself on the other side of an overturned bed. He'd piled all the furnishings in the room into one corner, creating a barricade. He emerged holding a fork which Sunshine initially took to indicate his hunger until he realized he was holding it like a dagger.

"I brought breakfast," he said but hurried to set down the plate when Jeff started rushing toward him. He couldn't find a suitable place and ended up backing away, trying not to drop anything. "Hang on, just wait a second, fuck," he said.

"Let me out!" Jeff pressed the tines of the fork against Sunshine's throat.

"Give me a second!"

Jeff pressed harder for a second, then stepped back.

Sunshine put the plate on the first flat surface he could find, a turned-over bookcase. "Shit, what are you doing?"

"Let me out."

"Do you stab everyone who comes in here?"

Jeff bared his teeth and grunted.

Sunshine walked over and pulled an armchair out of the pile of furniture. "Come sit down."

"Let me out of this room."

"I will, as soon as you show me you're not going to go on some kind of murder rampage."

"We are in Hell. These things deserve to be murdered."

Sunshine sighed. He shifted around the pile and found another chair. He dragged it out and sat in it. "Come on, eat, before it gets cold."

Jeff threw the plate against the wall. "I don't need their poison!"

"Hey! I made that."

"What?"

"Yeah! I made that. No one is trying to poison you." Sunshine sighed and went to pick up the food, but just stared at the mess when he couldn't find a garbage can. "What's gotten into you?"

"We're in Hell. Are you so blind—"

"Yeah, who made Hell?"

"What?"

"Who made Hell?"

"Uh."

"Who sends souls here?"

Jeff narrowed his eyes.

"Say what you want about the Beast but the demons, they just work here. It's a day job," Sunshine said. "It's just a place."

"You don't mean that."

"It isn't anyone's fault that they get born here. Half the people here don't even work the souls, they're like...shopkeepers and librarians. Maids." He tried to scrape the food and plate shards into a pile.

Syrup streaked the wall.

"I actually thought you might like the French toast," Sunshine sighed.

"You've lost your mind."

"I'm not the one who's been stabbing butlers with forks." He sat down in the comfier looking armchair. "Can we talk?"

"There's nothing to talk about."

"Listen, I'm not calling the shots here. If I let you out and you start acting like a maniac, he's not going to lock you in a guest room this time. You know you're *alive*, right? And that can end? No going back to Heaven. No nothing. You try to go up against him and it will be a shit show."

"Better to—"

"No. Listen. We're just two-bit soldiers. He's a deathless, unquestionable ruler of an entire realm. Also, I'm pretty sure if you act up, he's going to make me do something fucked up to you, so I'm gonna need you to reel it in and act like a person. Not even a civilized person, just anything other than a fork-stabby nutjob."

Jeff narrowed his eyes.

"Please."

Jeff collapsed into the other chair, his head in his hands. "What am I supposed to do?"

"I literally just told you. Stop trying to stab people—"

"No, I mean—"

"I know what you meant. Don't think about it. Pretend he's someone else." He glanced around the room and saw Marlow gnawing the head off a mouse. "Pretend he's that cat. Literally anything he says or does, pretend he's a cat."

"What? Why?"

"I mean, you wouldn't stab a cat with a fork. Would you? Even if it said something weird or licked you somewhere you didn't want."

"I should...let him lick me."

"No, just pick him up and move him. Like a cat."

Jeff frowned.

"Just like a cat," Sunshine promised.

Jeff sighed. "Go away."

"Fair. I'll give you some time. Do you want something to eat?"

Jeff shook his head.

Sunshine headed out and tried to get Marlow to follow, but she ignored him. He made sure he locked the door on his way out. He didn't want Jeff running around unsupervised.

Someone skated a finger up his spine and said, "Boo."

He kept in the scream and whirled around.

"You make it so easy," Felix said. "You want to go for a walk?"

"Hm?"

"I figured we could get you something to wear cause we're all wearing my dad's hand-me-downs. And maybe a haircut, too, huh? I wanna be able to see that pretty face of yours."

"I think it's very young David Bowie."

"You think that, but it's not. Come on. You at least need new shoes cause those ones actually have blood all over them and they kind of reek." Felix wrapped his arms around one of Sunshine's. "Come on, it will be like one of those shopping montages in a teen movie."

"Do I get a makeover?"

"Absolutely!"

The Ninth Precinct of Hell felt less like the realm of eternal torture and more like a gentrified neighborhood in a small city. Even the Eighth had cleaned up a lot since the last time Sunshine had been here. It had a homey, cozy feel to it. The narrow alleys between houses on the outskirts no longer teemed with rough workers and garbage but housed cheery flower gardens, murals, or clotheslines. Some even sported little carpeted cat-trees draped in a half-dozen cats.

Of the tidy, well-cared for neighborhoods, Felix said, "I can't tell if he does it because he cares or because most of the people in Hell are capitalists. The real torture is that they're being flayed by people who make a living wage."

"Do they still flay people?"

"I don't keep up on the latest torture methods, that's way outside my purview. Here, let's check in here." Felix tugged him into a store that had a truly bizarre collection of clothing on its racks. The styles ranged from the genuinely ancient to things that seemed like they belonged in an edgy, futuristic sci-fi movie.

Sunshine did his best to find something quasi-normal, though he was sorely tempted by a draped tunic in a becoming shade of pale turquoise. He looked at it for too long and Felix pulled it off the rack.

"No, I—"

"It's Hell, you can wear whatever you want! Come on."

"I think your dad will make fun of me."

"For wearing a tunic? You know he has tits now, right? He doesn't exactly *do* gender norms."

"...I know."

"Just try it on."

In the end, he did try on the tunic and allowed Felix to put it on the pile of more standard shirts and trousers he'd selected. He tried not to think about how much he'd liked it because that required reflection on how much he did to fit in on Earth. He didn't look like he'd walked off the set of *Goldfinger* or anything, but people noticed his skin. And his eyes. Orange wasn't exactly standard issue up there. Dressing in anything other than the safest fashion of the era only made him stick out more.

He stood in line, his arms full, thinking about fashion and gender and how it stung to be looked at when he hadn't meant to be.

He got out of line.

"Hmm?"

"I. I want to try on a few other things."

Felix opened his mouth, then scanned his face. "Okay. I'm gonna keep our spot." He had his own armful of clothes, mostly black, aggressive pieces that made him look like an assassin or some BDSM vampire. "Do you want me to hold those?"

"I might put some of them back."

"Oh, don't, here, I'll take them, I'm just going to charge it to the palace anyway." Felix pulled the clothes out of his arms.

Sunshine rejoined him a short time later, a few more daring pieces clutched against his chest. He worried about how sweaty his hands were, if it would ruin the fabric.

Felix ran his fingers over the embroidery on a silk kimono. "It's pretty."

He tried to make himself not blush. He didn't know if it worked, but Felix didn't point out that he'd gotten red.

The person who checked them out carefully packaged all their purchases and called for someone to hand-deliver them to the palace. She also gave Felix the name of a good barbershop a few streets over. She referred to him by various royal titles and seemed thrilled to get to sell him things.

She didn't even notice Sunshine.

Probably a good thing. Angels didn't fare well down here.

A haircut and several new pairs of shoes later, they headed back to the palace.

Sunshine had proposed lunch, but Felix declined on the principal that he could only be fawned over so much in one day.

"Plus," he said as he combed his fingers through Sunshine's newly trimmed and tidied curls, "I told him to leave enough to hold onto for a reason." He playfully tugged Sunshine's hair.

His stomach tightened in the most marvelous way.

He happily trailed along behind Felix back to the palace. His stomach gurgled a few times. He did like to eat lunch around now, and normally that would have taken precedence in his mind, but he hadn't seen Felix in months.

Months.

Fuck.

It had taken a while for that to sink in.

In the privacy of their room, Felix kissed him, and Sunshine wrapped him up in a hug, not able to do anything but crush him close for a few minutes.

"You okay?" Felix asked.

"I don't know."

"Do you want to lay down for a little bit?"

"Yeah."

They climbed into bed and nestled close, face to face. Occasionally they traded kisses. Sunshine put his hand under Felix's shirt to let it rest against his skin. This terrible layover in the Otherworld aside, the past few months had done right by Felix. He'd lost that gaunt, haggard look he'd carried for the duration of his curse, his no longer lips dry and tinged blue, his eyes no longer constantly sunken and circled by bags the color of a fresh bruise.

"This was supposed to be such a standard case," he said.

Felix snorted. "Tell me about it. Bobby feels awful, by the way. I told him not to worry, that we'd get dinner soon."

"What are we going to do about Elora?"

Felix groaned. "I can't think about that right now. We're supposed to be having a steamy reunion not planning to right injustices in the Otherworld."

"I don't think anything I've ever done has been categorized as steamy."

"Oh, for shame, Sunshine. You can be incredibly steamy when the occasion calls for it," Felix assured.

"Why are you planning a wedding?"

"I...Oh. That's..."

"If you don't want to get married."

Felix sat him. "I don't know. Because I like to think about it. I like to pretend. Does it bother you?"

"It makes me worry that...that I'm keeping you away from something you want."

Felix smiled, then laughed. He didn't stop laughing, collapsing in on himself, arms wrapped around his middle and kicking his feet, tears coming to his eyes. When he finally stopped, his breathing came ragged and he practically launched himself on top of Sunshine. "You know what I love about you? How fucking simple you are. There's a beauty to it, the way you see the world. Like. I love that you see me so clearly and that you still think the veil of normalcy can fix whatever's broken in me. No, Sunshine. I am...I am anathema. Oppugnant."

"I don't know what that means."

"It means no matter what I do, pretending to be normal is never going to change the fact that I am literally the fucking Antichrist and that our society is built on a system of white supremacy and colonialism fueled by toxic Western ideals propped up by government and organized religion. I *cannot* be normal. A wedding...it speaks to me. It does. To that part of me that still wants the other kids to play with me. But a wedding, in the context I know, is the summation of everything I'm not. And everything I don't want to be. I really don't. I'm making peace with that."

Sunshine stared up at him. "I don't think you're broken."

"I know. You think I'm beautiful."

"So. No wedding?"

"No wedding."

"I promised your dad he could come if there was. He used a favor on it and everything."

"You made sure it was if, right? And not when."

"I made sure."

"Oh, conning a conman, that's dangerous, Sunshine," Felix teased. "Do you feel better?"

"I think so. I still don't know what oppugnant means."

"Look it up later, there's a dictionary around here somewhere." He started unbuttoning his shirt, letting it slide away a little at a time.

Sunshine couldn't look away.

"If I could rebuild the world, I'd rebuild it to be full of people like you."

"Idiots?"

Felix grinned. "Exactly. Idiots. I want a world full of people who are so stupid they want to love and be loved more than they want anything else."

Sunshine tugged Felix's shirt out of his hands.

Felix curled him against him, his ear against Sunshine's chest. "It doesn't have to be steamy."

"Hmm?"

"We don't have to do anything."

"I don't mind."

"I don't want you to not mind. I want you to want to."

He put his arms around Felix. "Things still feel weird."

"Okay. What else did you and my dad talk about?"

"Bryan Ferry."

Felix sat up.

"Yeah, turns out he's a big Roxy Music fan."

With narrowed eyes, Felix started to climb out of bed.

Sunshine caught him and brought him back. "Unless you're going to get me lunch, you're not going anywhere."

"I'm not making you lunch anymore. We've had our touching reunion so it's back to our usual dynamic."

He nipped Felix's ear and didn't let him go. "Make me lunch and then you can fuck me silly."

Quietly, Felix's suggested, "Maybe we should flip that order around, I'm no good on a full stomach. I get cramps now. I'm not twenty-five anymore." He burrowed into Sunshine's arms. "Besides, I thought we weren't. You're giving me mixed messages and that makes me nervous. It's going to take me forever to get anywhere at this point."

"So then you're going to make me lunch."

Felix pinched him and squirmed away. He stormed out, snatching his shirt as he went.

Sunshine snuggled under the covers to wait.

Twenty minutes later, Felix returned with a grilled cheese sliced into triangles, one perfectly golden side facing up.

Sunshine checked the underside.

"It's not burnt!"

Sunshine got out of bed to eat and asked, "Do you want half?"

"No."

He held out a triangle.

Felix chomped off the corner. He flopped onto his back, sprawled out on the bed. Through the mouthful of sandwich, he said, "I fed the burnt one to Garfield, he went apeshit for it."

Nix, Lucifer, Felix, and Sunshine sat at the well-worn kitchen table. The children slept upstairs and had for hours. Nix had sat quietly, his hands folded in his lap during the entire discussion, which had circled uselessly around the same two topics: Jeff and Elora.

Lucifer offered morally objectionable ways to deal with both of them, ranging from brainwashing and torture to outright murder, some methods needlessly gruesome.

Felix and Sunshine walked him back from each solution but couldn't decide on their own course of action.

"Listen, if you don't want to actually *do* anything to her then why are we even talking about it?" Lucifer asked.

"Because we live on Earth and she can get there," Felix said, "And I don't think she's going to take kindly to us kidnapping her consort." He looked at Nix for confirmation.

"My lady does not allow slights to stand unaddressed. She has taken eyes for cross looks and...and children for cross words."

Lucifer once again said, "Then you should act against her before she'll act against you. Or stay here."

Felix said, "I'm not staying here. I can't stay here."

"I sent you to Earth to keep you safe, to give you a chance at a human childhood but you're not a child anymore, little one. You could easily make a life for yourself here. You'd do wonderfully at our university or library. Even the Record's Office..." Lucifer trailed off and shrugged. "You'd have a fine life."

"No. I wouldn't. I can't stay here. What would they do to Sunshine?"

"Nothing I didn't allow."

Felix snorted.

"Listen, he's got all those muscles. What good are they if he can't defend himself?" Lucifer asked.

Sunshine scowled. "I don't want to live here, regardless of whether or not I could slaughter people who'd make an enemy of me."

"So then kill the mad queen," Lucifer repeated. "And go back to your trash island."

"I'm not murdering anyone."

"I'm not demanding you personally get your hands dirty. I know you're too sensitive for that—"

"I'm not...!" Felix groaned and grabbed his hair, letting his head hang forward.

Sunshine rubbed his back.

"Do you carry some affection for this woman?" Lucifer asked.

"No."

"Then why object so strongly?"

"Because believe it or not, you're not supposed to kill people for no reason," Felix said into his lap.

"But you have a reason," the Devil reasoned. He looked at Nix and skated his fingers over the ghastly rope of scars across his forehead. "I bet this one can think of hundreds of reasons."

Nix lowered his eyes.

Lucifer stroked his cheek. "Who are we to decide your queen's fate? Should that not rest with those to whom she's done the most harm?"

"We have all sworn fealty to her."

"Every creature in her Court?"

"Except the children," Nix said. "None of them could speak when she brought them to Court and...I think she forgot about them after that."

Lucifer grinned. He leaned forward and kissed Nix's forehead.

The fairy shivered.

"What say you, Wild Prince? Do we bring your lady to stand trial?"

Nix drew back. He opened his mouth, then closed it.

"Go, think, Wild Prince. Return to us with your decision while we decide what to do with the angel."

Nix wrapped his arms around himself. He swallowed and looked at Sunshine. "Can I...Can I speak on the angel's behalf?"

"He means Jeff," Felix clarified.

"I know," Lucifer said.

"What do you have to say about Jeff?" Sunshine asked, genuinely curious.

"Jeff always helped when I asked. He never shouted at my children. It would sadden me if an unpleasant fate befell him. I don't think he's earned that. At least...not by my count."

"Consider it noted. Go, think on your queen's fate. And rest. You look exhausted."

Nix stood, bowed to Lucifer and Felix, and excused himself.

Lucifer leaned back in his seat when Marlow jumped up onto his lap. He stroked her from ear to spine. "What do you think we should do?"

Sunshine waited, expecting the cat to speak again.

She purred.

"We could—" Lucifer began.

"Don't you dare say kill him," Sunshine said.

"I was going to say single combat, but I lost that last time I went up against an angel, and she was only a notary. Felix, maybe you should fight him. Might be sort of poetic."

"Well, I suck at poetry," Felix said.

"Oh, no, I don't think so!" Lucifer insisted. "All those little ones you used to write in your journals?"

Felix turned an awful shade of red.

Sunshine worried that Felix might pass out or be sick, but underneath that, a question wiggled around the back of his mind. He meant to ask Felix if he was okay, but the question that came out was, "What kind of poems?"

He thought of the boxes of Felix's old journals tucked away in his closet. When he'd first seen one of Felix's well-worn notebooks, leather-bound with thick pages, it had been scrawled with letters, runes, and doodles he couldn't interpret anyway.

Felix let out a screech, an awful sound more suited to a dying animal. "You read my fucking diary!"

Lucifer held up his hands, palms toward Felix. "Oh, peace, little one, you'll strain something doing that."

"They're supposed to be *private*; they have *locks on them*."

Lucifer climbed on the table, crawled over, and crouched in front of his son. He grabbed Felix by the face. Slowly, he said, "I can see your soul. I can *hear it*, Felix, I can hear everything that goes on in that sweet and oh-so-human mind of yours. Humanity holds no secrets for me. Locks mean nothing when your very soul speaks to me."

Felix had stopped trying to pull away.

Sunshine stared, not sure if he should or even could do something to help.

Lucifer let go of Felix on his own. He smoothed back Felix's pale hair and checked to make sure he hadn't left a mark on his face.

"Dad," Felix rasped.

Lucifer slipped off the table and pulled Felix into a hug. "I'm sorry."

Sunshine shifted uneasily. He wanted to take Felix out of Lucifer's arms. He wanted to lock him up somewhere safe because as much as he knew that a parent shouldn't hurt their child, it didn't mean they wouldn't. Of all the parents in the world, Lucifer was the most fundamentally wrong. It seemed a perversity that he could even produce children.

Despite all that, Lucifer was not the worst of parents.

"Don't look at my soul," Felix requested softly.

"Why not?"

"Because I'm the fucking Antichrist, I don't want to know what's in there."

"Oh, no, little one, it's a beautiful soul. Even the dark parts are still pretty."

Felix stepped back. He rubbed his nose. "I don't *want* to have dark parts."

"Goodness means nothing if it's not a choice," Lucifer said. He gestured toward Sunshine. "Look at that thing. Does his goodness mean anything? Does he choose to do it? Or is it simply all he can do?"

Sunshine frowned.

"He has no capacity to choose and therefore his actions mean nothing. You can choose and that means everything," Lucifer said.

"I choose things!" Sunshine protested.

Lucifer looked at him. "Oh, shoes or which slice of pie is not what I mean by a choice."

"No, I...I choose things. I do," Sunshine insisted. "I didn't kill Felix. That was a choice."

"No, that's...he may have made you to be a soldier, but it's a hard soldier that can kill a baby."

"The others all did it. And I didn't choose not to kill a baby. I chose not to kill a man. I chose that over Heaven itself."

Lucifer blinked a few times. "I'll admit, I do not hear angels the way I hear humanity. I. I assumed your head was as empty as your face. Pleasant and pretty but...pointless. Ooh, that's a lot of alliteration, I'm sorry. Goodness." He swallowed, played with his hair, and then straightened up. "You choose."

"Stop saying it like I'm the only angel who does."

"Well, there's me and the Fallen, but you are not one of mine. You still belong to our Father. I suppose there's also Rivka, but that wasn't free will so much as a corruption of purpose. No, few angels make choices. They simply act." His eyes went wide, and a far-away look claimed his face.

He stayed like that for several uncomfortable minutes.

Felix took Sunshine's hand and rested his head against his arm. He whispered, "It creeps me out when he does that."

Sunshine nodded.

When Lucifer did come back to himself, he patted them both on the head and walked out of the room. They didn't follow and he called, "Come with me!"

"Where?"

"For a walk. Sitting around hasn't gotten us anywhere. Maybe a walk will do us better. Fetch the other angel. Jeff. It's his name, and I should use it even if I hate it. Go get Jeff."

"I don't know if he'll come."

"I'll wait. We all have plenty of time."

Sunshine went to get Jeff, who still lurked behind his furniture barricade. He hadn't tried to stab any of the staff in the past few days, so Sunshine had decided to take as many small victories as he could get.

"Come for a walk," Sunshine said.

"A walk where?"

"I don't know. Around. Lucifer wants to talk to you."

"On first-name basis with the Beast now," Jeff grumbled.

"Just come for a walk."

"Where?"

"I don't know, Jeff, just a walk! Please." He held out his hand.

Jeff glared at it. He pushed past Sunshine to the open door and strode through it. He stomped down the stairs and right up to Lucifer where he conferred softly with Felix in the foyer.

Sunshine clambered after him, grabbing his arm and pulling him back as he got right in Lucifer's face, poking him in the chest. "Hey," Sunshine warned.

Jeff yanked his arm back.

Lucifer smiled at him. "Jeff. Or...is it Jeffery?"

The question gave Jeff pause. He opened his mouth, then stepped back. He looked at Sunshine. "I don't *have* a name."

"But I have to call you something."

"Call me nothing, Beast."

"We already have someone called nothing, that's going to get confusing. If you're having reservations about committing to Jeff, I did have some ideas."

"You may not name me."

"So just Jeff, then?" Lucifer asked. "Come. I wanted to walk with you."

Jeff shook his head.

"You're a guest—"

"You locked me up."

"That is what happens, generally, when one attempts to stab

me. Your sword, by the way, is under the care of your..." Lucifer looked at Sunshine.

"Brother-clone," Felix supplied helpfully.

"He's not my brother," Jeff said.

"We're not clones," Sunshine said.

"No, but how does one relate two drops of water when they're not in the ocean? I have no idea. I think it's quite confusing that he's just started making you in batches. Uh. Littermates? That does sort of lend the idea of a little more individuality, which I think you deserve, considering the difference in your reactions." Lucifer reached out to touch Jeff's face.

The angel slapped his hand away.

Lucifer rubbed the red mark that came up on his skin. "That was really hard. Oh, he's not playing around, this one." He gave Sunshine a pat on the head as if to reassure himself that there was at least one angel who wouldn't attack him.

Then he started to walk, heading outside and through the gardens. He pointed out a pair of little pink birds to Felix and said, "That's Momo and Apple, they bring each other seeds."

The smallest hint of red lightened the sky.

"Cute," Felix said.

"I don't know if they're boys or girls, the pink ones are all pink, but the boys have this little white spot underneath their wings and I haven't gotten close enough to find out."

"I'm surprised you have any birds, what with all the cats."

Lucifer let out a sigh and agreed, "Oh, it used to be ghastly, little dead things all over the palace. Ugh. But I had a very long talk with the cats, and we came to an agreement."

Sunshine asked, "Can they all talk?"

Lucifer looked at him. "What?"

"I mean, did you talk to all of them or did you have to appoint some kind of cat council for the ones who can talk? And then they told the rest of them."

Lucifer stopped walking. "Cats can't talk. Even in Hell."

"The other day Marlow said..." He trailed off when the other three looked at him. He put his hands in the pockets of the loose, rust-colored trousers he'd gotten on their shopping trip. Felix had picked out a jade green top to go with it and Sunshine felt sort of smart and fashionable, instead of just like he was wearing clothes.

"What did she say?"

Sunshine shrugged.

Lucifer narrowed his eyes and let out a small hum. He started walking again. "But anyway. It's a spell that keeps the cats from the birds. Some university professor worked it out for me, if you go into the cat keepers' room, there's a little painting of her. Sometimes they treat it like a shrine when the cats are particularly moody. It was too much work to put bells on all of them and keep them on. Oh, Felix, look there's the wisteria I told you about. It is pretty, isn't it? June got it to grow down here for me."

Felix admitted, "It's pretty."

Sunshine thought it was gorgeous.

Lucifer brought them out of the gardens and down into the Ninth.

Jeff stopped at the gate.

"Come into the city. No one will hurt you," Sunshine said.

"Why?"

"To see what Hell is," Lucifer said. "Or stay here." Then he kept walking, the hem of his loose shirt fluttering around his body, moved by the brisk breeze that danced around them every so often.

Every so often the wind would give a huge gust and blow the Devil's loose clothes all askew.

Sunshine found himself staring, almost hoping for a glimpse, though of what he didn't know. Something monstrous. Something that would reveal him as the Beast.

"You're going to give me ideas if you keep looking at me like that," Lucifer said, dropping back to walk beside him.

"Oh, no, I—"

"There's no tail or horns or anything. Not on this body anyway."

Jeff had dropped back by several yards at this point, more like a stalker than part of their group.

"Don't do anything to him," Felix warned over his shoulder, but soon enough got distracted by a child on her way to school, judging by the backpack, who'd run up to him and demanded to know if he was really the Antichrist.

Her parents caught up with her and apologized.

Apparently, word spread fast in Hell, and the citizens were thrilled with the prospect of a long-hidden prince who might destroy the human world. From what Sunshine could gather, the people of Hell wanted badly for their monarch to have an heir.

A real heir, they said, because they didn't think the grandson he'd selected, or Ira, would be able to stand against Elisa or Tabitha if they came seeking the throne. They seemed to think Felix might be up to the job.

Sunshine had never met the grandson Lucifer had selected, but he knew he was the current king in Triviai. He made the newspapers occasionally but lived an intensely private life. Most high-profile immortals did; it gave the human world less on which to speculate. Few people without direct ties to the Community knew anything about its members and bought into conspiracy theories about unnaturally young-looking people injecting the stem cells from aborted babies instead.

He wondered what the tabloids would say about Lucifer.

He listened with one ear as Lucifer pointed out various things about the city with a quiet sort of pride.

Jeff trailed behind at a snail's pace and Felix wandered in front of them, peering into window fronts and petting stray cats.

"Why do you do it?"

"Oh, well, without a good sewer system it would be absolutely abysmal," Lucifer answered as though he thought Sunshine might be confused.

"Isn't that the idea? Is this not the Pit?"

"But not for my citizens. This is not their punishment, it's their home. Shouldn't it be clean and safe and comfortable for them? Shouldn't they have everything they need? I made them, you know. I'm responsible for them."

Sunshine wrinkled his nose, not because he hated the sentiment, but it felt wrong from the Devil.

"I'm more than my title. You know that, right?" Lucifer asked. "Oh, I am more my job than most people are, of course, but it is not all that I am."

"I..."

Lucifer raised his eyebrows.

"Maybe."

"I'll take a maybe." Lucifer gave Sunshine a pat on the back, then went to catch up with Felix. He did it with an unusual exuberance, catching his son around the shoulders and bringing him in for a hug.

Felix let out a surprised laugh. "Dad!"

Sunshine couldn't help but smile. Whatever they were, they loved each other. He stopped and waited for Jeff to catch up. When he did, he said, "So it's not so bad."

"It smells."

Sunshine nodded. Hell did have a strange sort of smell to it and the food had a tang, almost ashen, easier to taste coming straight from the Otherworld. "Everyone smells it differently, I think. I smell...milk. Not sour milk, but the milk where you smell it a couple times before you decide it's okay to drink. That and animals, but I think that's the cats."

"It smells like rotten meat."

"That is different," Sunshine agreed. "I didn't even notice the first time I came. I was too distracted. I was too scared. I didn't think I'd make it back alive."

"Sunshine!" Felix called. "Breakfast?"

"Is anywhere open?"

"Everywhere in the Eighth," Lucifer said. "A few places in the Ninth."

"What about that place we went last time? That little place?"

Lucifer nodded and steered them up a street.

Jeff protested the idea for the first ten minutes of the walk there, then it took ten more minutes to get him in the restaurant and seated.

Once he sat, he crossed his arms and refused to speak or eat. He stared, cold and long, at the waitress who came to take their order.

She had eyes like pennies and a short, curly shock of hair circled by a crown of horns that went all around her head. She bowed to their table and her voice wavered when she asked, "How can I serve my Prince and their guests?"

She looked at Jeff, then Sunshine, then looked at the floor. She gripped her little notepad so hard the edges bent.

Lucifer asked, "Are you alright, Geri?" He looked her over.

"Of course, my Prince."

He narrowed his eyes.

"Forty years, Geri. Hasn't that earned your Prince some honesty?" he pressed.

"I was born after the Ravens, I've just never..." She looked at Jeff and Sunshine again. "People are saying..."

"That there are angels in Hell," Lucifer finished. "Yes. Two. One, at least, is tame." He patted Sunshine's curls and said, "You know, I thought you were identical but really, seeing you together..." He eyed Jeff, then returned his attention to Geri. "There are no revolutions brewing, Geri, rest assured."

Geri nodded but still held onto her notepad for dear life. She brought it up and asked, "What...What can I get you?"

"Water, to start, and a few minutes with the menu."

She nodded and scurried away, returning with a bottle of iced water, then immediately leaving.

Probably because Jeff stared at her.

Sunshine elbowed him. "What's your problem?"

Jeff answered, "It's vile. Them pretending to be human."

"Acting like people doesn't mean they're pretending to be human," Felix pointed out. "Humans are not the only people with corporeal forms and civilizations."

"The purpose of the Pit is not civilization, it is the cleansing of souls. All else is indulgence."

Lucifer smiled. "Sometimes...Sometimes I wonder why I left but spending time with an angel always reminds me *exactly* why." He reached out and touched Jeff's hand, then pulled back before Jeff could flinch away. "Why are you here?"

"Because you knocked me unconscious and held me captive here."

"I locked a door. I did not bind you to this realm. And yet you remain. Why?"

Jeff narrowed his eyes. "I—"

"Dad, let's not—" Felix began.

"I'm not...I couldn't move from that Otherworld but..." Jeff grinned, a moment of maniacal elation on his face for an instant. To Sunshine, he said, "Come with me."

"No."

Jeff reached for him anyway.

Lucifer wound an arm around Sunshine and gathered him close. "No."

"Fine!" Jeff snapped. And then he was gone, rattling the table when he went.

Sunshine stared at the space where he had been. A strange ache seared through his chest and came out as an unpleasant whine. He reached out to touch where Jeff had been but there was nothing. No trace of the body that had existed there a minute before. He pressed his lips together and clenched his jaw.

"Sunshine, I..." Felix stood and moved to sit next to Sunshine.

Sunshine twisted in his seat and pushed Lucifer. "Why did you do that!"

"I didn't do anything."

"You...You made him go. You...!"

"I only reminded him that he could," Lucifer answered gently.

"Why?" Sunshine demanded, his throat clenched tight so his voice barely escaped.

Felix had not yet sat down, hesitating by the chair, staring at Sunshine and picking his nails.

Lucifer smiled, not his usual too-wide grin, but a trace of a smile. He sighed and clucked his tongue. "You can't make him love you. You could keep him with you for a thousand years, but love is his to give, not yours to take."

Sunshine dragged in a breath. He grabbed a handful of Lucifer's shirt, not sure what else to do.

Lucifer put his hand over Sunshine's. "It's okay."

Sunshine shook his head. It wasn't. The closest he'd come to home in a hundred years and now he was gone. He was gone and he hated Sunshine, and he hated Felix, and Sunshine could never go home again.

Lucifer hugged him. "It's okay."

He pulled back at first, then pressed his face against Lucifer's chest and started to cry.

"He gets like this when he doesn't sleep," Felix suggested softly. The chair creaked when he sat down. He put a hand on Sunshine's thigh.

The Devil didn't let go, not in a restrictive way, but in a comforting one. He rubbed Sunshine's back and when Sunshine managed to sob, "I want to *go home*," Lucifer tightened his arms and answered, "I know, darling. I know."

He let out a shaky breath and pulled back. He wiped his face and couldn't even look at Felix. To Felix's general direction, he said, "I'm sorry. It's not—"

"Don't be sorry, my love," Felix assured him. "We all want to go back to a place we can't. It's part of growing up. We all want to be safe and warm and loved again."

He rubbed his nose and still couldn't look up.

Felix kissed his cheek. "Did you look at the menu? What did you want for breakfast? Was there anything you didn't make for that smorgasbord the other morning?"

"I want a knish."

"No dice there, I'm afraid," Lucifer said. "Not a significant Jewish Quarter down here. No Chinatown or Little Italy either...Trash Island does have its appeal in some respects."

"First thing when we get back," Felix promised. He kissed Sunshine's cheek again. "You're throwing me through a loop with this crying thing. It's making me reevaluate our whole schtick."

"I'm sorry."

"No, no, it's probably good. Healthy. For you to finally cry. For me to finally take care of you for a change."

Sunshine took his hand, cozying their fingers together. "We

always take care of each other."

Felix rested his head on Sunshine's shoulder. He picked up the menu. "What about...what is a sheepherder's breakfast? Do you guys have sheep down here?"

"We have something like sheep down here," Lucifer said. "Try it. It has eggs."

In the end, they ordered something else. Nothing special. A quiet breakfast.

By the time they walked back to the palace, it had grown fully light. Lucifer went to his study to do some reading on judicial proceedings in the Otherworld and to see if he could drum up a neutral party from one of the other Courts to oversee things. One from each would be best, he said.

Sunshine and Felix went to bed since they'd neglected to do so at the appropriate time.

Felix snuggled right up to Sunshine and wrapped around him, the same as he always did, so Sunshine guessed there weren't any hard feelings about his display earlier. "Love you."

"I love you, too," Sunshine said.

"I promise I won't wake you up, even if I get really bored. I can tell you need to sleep. You get so funny when you're tired."

"Funny how? Funny like I'm a clown?"

Felix snuggled a little closer. "Shut the fuck up, Sunshine, I'm never watching a single one of those gangster movies again, not now that I know you were skulking around with all these Italian mama's boys—"

"A few Jewish ones, too. Even an Irishman once."

"Shut the fuck up."

"What can I say? I love a man who loves his parents."

With a yawn, he said, "I resemble that remark."

"My own personal hardboiled—"

Felix cut him off with a kiss. "Go to sleep or I'll have to do something to you."

Sunshine snuggled deeper under the covers. He meant to say something back, but he yawned and fell asleep instead.

The calendar in Lucifer's study gave a dozen dates and Sunshine couldn't figure out which one belonged to his reality. Some months and years he recognized, but others listed months that didn't exist and years that hadn't happened or had happened centuries ago.

Felix pointed to one that read November 25, 2016 AD, and said, "That's us."

"That's it?"

Felix nodded. He stretched and set down his copy of *On Liberty*. "Yessir." He pointed to another one. "That's the date here. Third day of the Fourth Month, One hundred and one A.R."

"What's AR?"

Felix smiled. "After the Raven."

"Oh."

Felix pointed to an aged parchment that listed a series of time periods in Hell's history. Before the walls, the building of the city, after the walls, the Bleeding Scourge... Felix tapped one. "So I was born in 32 AWP – After the Wasting Plague. Roughly. The dates don't line up down here and up there. The next big event after that was the Raven coup d'état." Felix skimmed his finger to a spot higher up on the list. "You were probably born around here." He pointed to The Building of the City. "Dad says that's when God made most of the new batches of angels. It's like a two-hundred-year span."

"Oh."

"You dirty old man, taking advantage of a sweet young girl like me."

Sunshine took Felix's hand when he held it out.

Felix kissed his knuckles, then pressed his cheek against them. A minute later, he let go, stretched again, and rubbed his eyes. He went back to the book, scribbling notes about the consistencies between fairy, human, and demonic judicial proceedings.

Sunshine wandered off to make tea.

The children had taken over the throne room. The three of them had scattered toys everywhere, aided by the cats.

Nix sat on the throne with the baby. He hadn't recognized the plain, cushioned rocking chair as the throne, which admittedly most people didn't. The only thing that gave any indication was that the rockers were carved like snakes.

The original throne was somewhere in storage and Lucifer had said he took it out for special occasions.

Dire hurried over when she saw Sunshine and grabbed his hand, dragging him over to the toys and shoving a stuffed deer-sheep-thing into his arms. "This is Thimble, he has to go to the ball."

"Oh. A ball for sheep."

"He's not a sheep, they're called woolbucks. The princess says they live outside the city, but we can go see them soon," Dire said.

Sunshine took a little knit vest and put it on the stuffed sheep. "That'll be a fun trip."

"He can't wear that to a ball!" Dire scolded.

"What do you wear to a ball?"

Dire groaned and took Thimble back. A few minutes later, she forgot she was irritated with him and said, "The princess says there's misperia in the garden for the wedding."

"A mis...oh. Yes. Have you gone out into the garden?"

Dire looked at Nix. "Dada says we aren't allowed to go outside."

Sunshine looked at Nix. "Dada, did you say that?"

"She can't lie," Nix reminded tersely.

Sunshine approached the rocking chair. "The baby still not sleeping?"

"She's sleeping."

"Then why do you look like shit?"

"Because *I'm* not sleeping."

Sunshine put a hand on Nix's shoulder.

"Every time I close my eyes, I start to worry one of them has wandered off."

"The doors have locks," Sunshine suggested.

"You think a lock can keep Dire anywhere? It wasn't...At home, I knew at least they didn't go far enough that trouble would find them. Or. I thought so. And I knew the others would keep an eye on them. But here? I don't even know what could be out there."

Sunshine said, "It's pretty safe out there."

"This is the realm of the wicked dead, or have I misunderstood something?"

"Oh, well, kind of, yeah, but...Just come outside." He took Nix by the hand and tugged at him.

Nix tried to take his hand back, curling one arm to keep the baby closer.

Sunshine pulled harder and smiled. "Please."

Nix groaned and stayed seated. He took his hand back. "I don't want to go."

Sunshine left it alone, at least until Felix wandered downstairs. "I thought you were making tea," he said.

"Kettle's on."

"Ugh."

Dire threw herself around Felix. "Come help get Thimble ready for the ball. Sunshine couldn't help."

"Well, he's very new to the idea of having fashion sense, so you'll have to be patient with him," Felix said.

Sunshine glanced down at his outfit, self-conscious about his clothes in a way he never had been. He wasn't wearing something he'd blatantly stolen from a display or magazine and the sudden fear that he looked silly overwhelmed him.

He must have looked stupid in a draped tunic, no matter how much he liked the color. It wasn't the ancient Mediterranean. He looked like a fucking Argonaut.

"But isn't he doing a nice job with it?" Felix asked the little girl. "Why don't you tell him how handsome he looks?"

Dire looked at Sunshine suspiciously.

Felix looked at him, too, an open, affectionate smile on his face. "So handsome, my very own Perseus. You'll have to save me from the Kraken later. Find a rock to chain me to..." He smiled wider. "Or the other way around, if you'd prefer."

Dire saved him from having to say anything else by asking, "What's a crack-um?"

"The Kraken, my dear, is a sea monster," Felix began.

Sunshine turned his attention back to Nix, who looked miserable. "Come for a walk."

Nix barely looked at him.

Sunshine plucked the baby out of Nix's arms and deposited her in Felix's lap. He turned back for Nix. "Come on. Come outside. I can't believe you've just been *inside* this whole time."

Nix bristled and pulled away. "I've been busy. I have four children."

Felix looked their way and made a face at Sunshine. "Your boyfriend sounds pissed," he noted.

Sunshine ignored him. He put a gentle hand on Nix's upper arm. "Let's go for a walk."

Nix pressed his lips into a thin line but followed Sunshine outside. He let out a curse at the sight of the sky.

"You kind of get used to it," Sunshine promised.

Nix didn't answer.

Sunshine walked, heading over to a far part of the garden with a bench where they could sit and talk. He settled himself on the bench, double-checking to make sure his tunic covered everything even though it wasn't so short he needed to worry about that. He gestured for Nix to sit beside him.

Nix remained standing, his arms folded.

"You're upset with me."

Nix didn't answer. His face didn't even change.

Sunshine kept in a sigh. "If you don't talk to me, I can't help."

"Help," Nix repeated.

Sunshine took his hand, which Nix lifelessly allowed, his face still neutral. "I thought we were friends."

"So did I." His face changed ever so slightly.

"Nix!" Sunshine protested.

Nix yanked his hand back and moved away. "Don't try to compel me."

Sunshine stood and edged a step closer. "Com...Nix. Come on. Will you just come *talk* to me? Please?"

"What could we say other than what's been said? We thought we were friends. The circumstances changed and revealed otherwise."

Sunshine smiled. He shouldn't have because Nix looked upset, which given his tight control over his expressions, meant he was borderline distraught. He smiled because he knew exactly what had happened. He hugged the fairy. "Nix."

Nix didn't pull back right away. He relaxed for half a second first.

Sunshine didn't let him go. "Don't be jealous of Felix."

"I'm not."

"Oh, is this a fairy who's learned to lie?"

"I'm not jealous of him. I'm jealous of *you*. I'm *envious* of him," Nix pointed out. He sighed and settled into Sunshine's embrace. "I'm scared. I can't do this alone. I can't. Four children and...Nothing else. What will become of us?"

"You have me."

"No. Specter has you."

"I can have friends and a boyfriend at the same time, you know. Most people do."

Nix sighed. He pulled back and looked at Sunshine. "But I need...I need more than a friend. You." He pressed his lips together. "You cared for my children. You shared my bed. You shouldered burdens that were not yours and became...a partner. I know you will never choose me over Specter. I know that. I'm not asking you to."

"I."

"We cannot both have you the way we need."

Sunshine wanted to tell him he was wrong, but it would have been a lie and a pointless one. He would never choose anyone over Felix. He didn't even think he could. "I'm sorry."

"Circumstances changed."

"I'm still your friend, though. Alright? I'm not...I'm not going to abandon you. Or the kids. I can...I *will* help. We will figure this out."

"How?"

"I don't know. I'm not the smart one."

Nix sighed. He sat on the bench and rested his head on Sunshine's arm when he sat, too. "I miss you."

"Just because we're not right on top of each other all day doesn't mean you can't come get me. I'll still help with the kids."

Nix neither accepted nor rejected the offer. He stayed quiet for several moments and finally said, "I'm scared."

"Is that different than before?"

"I knew the rules before."

Sunshine held his hand. "Lucifer is...He has a soft spot for kids. You can trust him when it comes to that at least. He won't hurt them."

They sat for a while, holding hands.

"What do you say? Should we bring the kids outside?" Sunshine proposed.

"Before we do..."

"Hmm?"

"He knows how fortunate he is to have you, doesn't he? As if your fates are written by your very names..." Nix swallowed. Quietly, like an apology, he said, "I love you."

"I love you, too."

"So do the children."

"I love them, too."

They went to get the children and brought them out. The three toddlers descended upon the space, screeching and running like they hadn't been outside, well, in weeks. Even Dire abandoned her usual pursuit of Felix's attention in favor of hiding among the plants and attempting to stalk her brothers like prey.

The baby shoved a fistful of dirt into her mouth right away.

Felix watched them, his arms crossed loosely over his chest. He elbowed Nix lightly. "See? It's not so bad."

"The grounds are beautiful."

"Mmm. The wisteria really is nice..." Felix stared at it. "Nix."

"Yes?"

"Can I ask you something personal?"

Sunshine eyed them.

Nix's face remained calm. "What do you wish to know?"

"You and Elora. You're her consort. In what capacity, exactly? I mean. She made you a prince, she made you her consort but...You two aren't married, are you?"

Nix said, "I believe my lady felt taking a common lover too far beneath her station. She named me a prince and took me to bed, but we exchanged no vows of wedlock."

"Ok. So." Felix raked a hand through his hair. He put his hands on his hips, then in his pockets, then back on his hips. "I...I don't think having the kids go up against Elora on a trial will work out. Dire still wants to be just like her and the boys barely talk."

"Ah."

Felix looked between Sunshine and Nix. "I kind of had this idea. About the trial. If you two are okay with it..."

"I can't speak against my queen. Literally."

"I know. But, uh, what if you happened to have a relatively coherent and somewhat handsome, granted in a very specific way, husband who could speak on your behalf and also happened to be a highly favored prince of a powerful realm? Do you think that would influence the court's opinion? Cause...Cause I sort of think it would. I kind of think that would shake out," Felix said. He glanced at Sunshine. "Right?"

Nix said, "I don't understand. Aren't you and Sunshine together?"

"Oh, no, it's fine. Polyamory is legal in Hell," Felix offered easily. It was probably simpler than explaining his stance on marriage. "Like I said, the kids are useless at a trial. No offense. I mean, I love them, I do, they're super cute. But..."

"But...?"

"But the Eastern and Western Courts would not want another Obliteration on their hands. The Otherworld is beautiful and wild and deeply enchanted, but my father has an army of the damned. He terrorized the Otherworld once over deals and wishes. Over a blow to his ego. Thousands of years and the Meridian Court has not recovered. What would he do to those who condoned what happened to his son-in-law? Let me speak for you and let me do it from a position that matters," Felix said. He looked again at Sunshine. "I mean. If you guys think..."

Sunshine shrugged. "Do you think it will work?"

Felix nodded. "I do. I think legally it's a little sketchy but politically it's a smart move. And it will afford some future protections for Nix and the kids."

Nix looked unsettled.

"Listen, I'm not asking you to like...*marry me* marry me. Like. It'd be political. You know, affectionate, but political," Felix assured.

"I...What would be expected of me?"

"Expected? Uh. Nothing? Like. I guess that you don't act against me or my best interests, but I don't think we need to formalize that," Felix said.

"My lady had expectations," Nix reminded, his tone laden with implication.

"Oh! Jesus Christ, no, God. I don't want to fuck you. I mean. Not like that. Christ." Felix looked scandalized. He looked at Sunshine. "What awful things have you been telling him about me while I was away!"

Nix watched the children. "You'll take them as wards?"

"Yeah, we'll name the baby and everything."

"I mean, will you provide for them? For their care. And provide well."

Felix's eyes narrowed in thought, as though he were doing difficult sums in his head. "Yes. I mean. As long as they don't all want to go to an Ivy League."

"And our lodgings?"

"That depends on what you want. I don't think going back to the Meridian Court will be an option while Elora still lives there. You could likely find a place at the Eastern or Western Court, but I'm not sure how that would work out," Felix said. "If we get Elora banished from Earth, which is my intent, you can come back to the city with Sunshine and I. Find you a nice little place somewhere. I do have some property in Connecticut..." Felix drifted off. "We talk about it. Do you want to go talk about it? I can show you pictures of the house."

"Connecticut is kind of far," Sunshine said without thinking about it.

"Like three hours tops," Felix scoffed.

"I think Nix needs more than a few friendly faces that are hours away," Sunshine pointed out.

"Mmm. Earth will be a big change. What about here? Do you like it here?"

Nix sniffed. "I..."

"You know what! Don't answer me yet. Just. Think about it. Okay?" Felix insisted.

"I will think on the matter," Nix said. "Likely without cease."

Felix assured, "I'm not trying to stress you out."

"Of course not, Your Highness."

Felix made a face, his mouth slightly twisted, not displeased but amused. "I think Dire's trying to eat one of the birds."

Nix sighed and hurried over to stop her from reaching into a nest of baby birds. She would, without doubt, eat one if left unattended.

"You stress everyone out," Sunshine told him. "Have you talked to anyone else about this?"

"No. Why?"

"It's...It's something your father would do," Sunshine said, trying to keep his voice light.

"You heard all of Dad's plans, they mostly involved cannibalism and murder," Felix said.

"But he schemes. This is a scheme."

"Is that a problem?" Felix asked, his back straightening and his chin lifting.

"I just don't know how you came to this solution."

Felix's shoulders softened. He shrugged. "We have been talking about getting married a lot. I guess I figured if I was ever going to have a meaningless set of documents define my legal relationship to another person, I should at least do it for a good reason. And you're already in my will so..." He gave a bit of a smile. "And I know you'd break into a hospital to get to me if you needed to."

Sunshine took his hand.

"Taking care of Nix and the kids is a good reason. Right?"

"It's a great reason."

"And you're so lovey-dovey with him, so, you know..."

Not sure what Felix was implying, Sunshine frowned.

"You care about him. And I care about you. And there's four actual babies on the line here," Felix said. "Someone has to do something."

"Marrying him is certainly doing something," Sunshine agreed.

"Besides, I am a prince. You had to know that I could never marry someone so far beneath my station as you," Felix reminded. He slid up against Sunshine and wrapped his arms around Sunshine's ribs like a vice. His forehead rested against Sunshine's chest, warm through the thin fabric of the tunic.

Something seared through Sunshine's chest and at first, he thought it was pure emotion, a combination of affection, melancholy, and fear. For some reason, it was centralized and didn't seem to have anything to do with his heart or throat, where he usually felt the physical manifestations of strong emotions. Then it got worse and started to seriously hurt. He stepped back, pressing a hand over the spot.

He looked down, checking for blood without even thinking about it. It was that kind of pain.

"What?" Felix asked, a little sulky at first. Then his eyes went wide. He looked slightly green as he fumbled with the shoulder clasp on the tunic, exposing most of Sunshine's chest to show an irritated patch of skin the size of a palm in the middle. "No. We weren't even...I wasn't even *touching you* there."

Sunshine couldn't get a good look at the spot. He took Felix's hand and felt nothing but skin and bony fingers. Nothing out of the ordinary. He waited.

Felix didn't pull back. "It doesn't hurt."

"It shouldn't hurt. The wards are gone. And they never hurt me."

"What is that?" Felix demanded more like Sunshine were a cat that had dragged something inside.

Sunshine gingerly examined the spot. It was tender and slightly raised.

"What the fuck *is that?*"

"I don't know."

"Sunshine!"

"I don't know!"

Felix whined. He touched the area.

Sunshine felt an inquisitive little buzz of magic skate over his skin.

Felix frowned, his eyes squinting. He started to chew on the skin around one of his fingernails.

"Well?" Sunshine asked after a minute.

"Well," Felix sighed. "I definitely did it."

"Were you mad at me?"

"No."

"Did you want me to be upset about you proposing to Nix?"

"No!" Felix scowled. "Definitely not. Why would I want that?"

"I don't know why you do most of the things you do, Felix," he reminded. "I am very stupid after all."

"Stop flirting. This is serious." He laid his palm over

Sunshine's chest. It neither burned nor ached.

"How did you feel when it happened?"

"I've never done magic by accident before. Not even once, not even when I first came into it."

"But how did you feel?"

Felix licked his lips. "I." He sighed, then let out a frustrated groan. He rubbed his face. "I just thought." His face turned pink.

"Babe, what?" Sunshine prompted, not able to keep the smile out of his voice. He looked so silly when he blushed like that, sort of sweet and overwhelmed all at once. Not at all like who he pretended to be.

"That I love you. That we could do it. Together. Make the world a little better." His skin had gone red and pink with blotches. If he got any redder, he would actually look like a demon from some low-budget horror movie or a fantasy videogame. "That maybe it wouldn't be so terrible."

"Aww, babe." Sunshine smiled. He took Felix's hand. "I love you, too."

"I'm." He took a breath and let it out slow. "I'm not ready for that."

Sunshine pulled him in closer, looping an arm around him.

"I still don't know what I was even trying to do."

"It's okay."

"It's really not."

"You'd never hurt me," Sunshine assured.

"I *did* hurt you. I hurt you all the time," Felix reminded. Still, he rested his cheek against Sunshine's chest and that pain didn't return. The area from before stung, sort of like a scrape, but that was all. "Maybe I am too much like him," he breathed.

Sunshine thought and finally said, "Maybe that's not a bad thing."

Felix pulled back and studied him critically. He'd gone back to his usual anemic pallor. "Did I fry your brain or something? Are you sick?"

"All I'm saying is...You know, he is doing a good job, all those infernal machinations on Earth aside. His realm and his citizens seem well-cared for. Maybe that part of him isn't so bad."

"I did. I finally broke you. Or did you finally give in to your weird fear-lust and screw him?"

"Why is everything sexual with you? I'm just plain afraid of him."

"Ahh, I don't know, there's definitely some sort of sex-thing in play between you two," Felix said. "You can add him to your list of men you've slept with but never told me about."

"You know it wasn't just men."

"Excuse me?"

"And it wasn't just sex. It usually wasn't sex. Sometimes it was dinner or drinks or day trips to the beach that I never told you about. I did things without you all the time."

"Sunshine, honestly, I'm scandalized!" Felix said.

He pointed out, "You did things without me too."

"But I always told you about them."

"You were on bad terms with a lot more people than I was."

Felix rolled his eyes. "Alright, so I might have been...somewhat more abrasive toward people with different ways of thinking in the past. I have scaled it back though. Haven't I?"

"You do act more like a person recently, even when people disagree with your radical views on civil rights and social programs."

Felix snorted. "So you'll walk me down the aisle, right?"

"One of your several parents won't want to do that?"

"Fuck, you're right. I have to tell Papa and Bibi. Fuck. Shit." He groaned and slithered out of Sunshine's arms. "You think Nix will agree to it?"

"I think he's a single parent of four small children with no job, no money, and nowhere to go. I don't think he has much of a choice."

"Maybe I should put it in writing that he doesn't have to have sex with me."

"I don't think he can read."

"Alright, well step one: we'll teach him to read. Step two: we'll assure him of his rights in our marriage via a formal contract. Step three: we'll get married. Step four: we'll forbid Elora from ever setting foot on Earth and go back home cause ever since you mentioned knishes I've been dying for a cheese one."

"Are you sure you're ready to be a dad?"

"No, Jesus fucking Christ, no. Not at all. I'm not going to be their dad! I'll...I'll be like a fun, rich uncle...who's married to their dad."

"You know he needs more than just money and a roof over his head. He needs help."

"Yeah, but help doesn't mean me being their dad. Help means...an au pair or something. A preschool that can handle fairy children. Therapy. For sure therapy."

Sunshine looked over at Nix, who he was still trying to

persuade away from the bird's nest, though he had so far managed to keep her from eating any of them. "For sure therapy. And maybe a big fenced-in yard."

Felix nodded.

The following morning at breakfast, Nix asked to speak with Felix in private. They disappeared for about an hour and when they returned, Felix looked at the Devil and said, "I need to tell you something and before you get excited, listen to the whole thing."

"Okay," Lucifer said.

"I'm getting married to Nix for reasons that are neither romantic nor sexual."

"Financial, I assume," Lucifer agreed calmly.

Felix narrowed his eyes. "You're not going to freak out?"

"I'm holding a baby, Felix, I don't think that would be appropriate. Are you sure about this arrangement?"

"Yes."

"Both of you?" Lucifer looked at Nix.

Nix lowered his eyes. "I'll be most privileged to have your son as a husband, my lady. He assures me I'll be well cared for," he told the floor.

"A welcome change, I'm sure," Lucifer said.

"So you said something about the University gallery being nice?" Felix asked.

Lucifer finally looked at Felix, his eyes slightly widened. "Yes."

"Well, we don't have a lot of time to plan this, but I assume being the eternal monarch of an Otherworldly realm can speed along the process." Felix made a dismissive, impatient gesture.

"You're having a wedding."

"Uh. Yes? I just told you."

"No, I mean, you're...doing the whole thing? The whole ceremony and process and all that?"

"It's likely the only wedding I'll ever have. Might as well do it right."

"A real wedding?" Lucifer asked.

"Yes. A real wedding. And you're invited. Let's get this ball rolling."

Lucifer grinned.

"God, don't do that when you're holding the baby," Felix chided.

"It'll be a good party at least, even if it's not what any of us expected," the Devil said.

"You need to take me to tell Bibi and Papa."

"Can it wait until after breakfast? The little one and I are in the middle of a serious conversation about whether peas and carrots are better together mashed or in chunks."

Felix settled himself at the table and helped himself to some eggs. He reached for the potatoes, couldn't reach, and asked, "Nix, can you grab me that?"

"Of course, my lord."

Sunshine gave Felix a sharp look.

Felix immediately looked appalled. "Don't call me that."

Nix looked, briefly, terrified, then his face smoothed over. "I apologize, my prince."

"Nix, don't," Felix said. "It's not like that."

"How do I best address you?" the fairy asked.

"Specter is fine, same as you have been," Felix said. "Or, you know, by my given name if you'd like. Which...Which is Felix, by the way. I don't think I ever did properly introduce myself."

Nix bowed his head slightly. He spooned potatoes on to Felix's plate and passed it back.

Fifteenth day of the Fourth Month, 101 AR

Several things had gone wrong in the impromptu announcement of Felix's wedding. For one, Dire had taken the news extremely poorly had refused to speak to Nix or Felix since, screeching like a wildcat every time one of them tried to speak with her. She sobbed regularly about the betrayal. The word had also somehow gotten around that Sunshine and Felix had broken up, resulting in several dozen texts and calls to the both of them revealing all their friends' thoughts and feelings about their relationship.

Most people thought Sunshine was better off and that Felix needed to get his shit together.

That had put Felix in an awful mood, not one of his petulant, bitchy ones but a wretched melancholy. Hiram and Phaedrus hadn't taken well to this arrangement, so that didn't help things either.

On the bright side, the gallery had been secured as a location, Nix and Felix had worked out the exact terms and expectations of their marriage and committed it to writing even though Nix couldn't read, and they'd found a good caterer who could accommodate their last-minute requests.

They had flowers and decorations planned, the cake picked out, and the invitations had gone out and, for the most part, come back.

A few people had declined, a few stragglers hadn't responded yet, but they had forty confirmations of the sixty or so invitations they had sent out.

The last piece was garments.

Sunshine and Specter both already owned appropriate suits for the occasion. Felix had settled on black tie optional, since it was a smaller ceremony and so last minute. He could wear one of the various bespoke dinner suits he already owned. It wasn't exactly the white-tie fanfare that would be expected of a prince's wedding, but Hell had looser rules about etiquette and fashion.

They just liked a party.

Rumor had it that the citizens of Hell were planning celebrations to coincide with the wedding. Lucifer was considering declaring a Revel but didn't want things to get out of hand. A Revel could easily turn into a days-long affair and they still had to manage Elora.

They were currently at the tailor having an appropriate

garment made for Nix. Suits and ties were not common attire in the Otherworld, and they were having a hard time settling on what Nix should wear.

Nix repeatedly offered to wear whatever Felix wanted and Felix insisted that Nix should wear something he was comfortable in.

Sunshine browsed the ties, trying not to hover.

He didn't have a dinner suit, but he also didn't want to dress like another groom and there was no wedding party, so he'd settled on a good, charcoal suit that he already owned.

A new tie might be nice, though.

He looked over to see Nix stock-still, his eyes on the floor, and silent.

Felix was staring at him.

Sunshine watched for a few minutes.

"I really need some kind of direction here," Felix prompted.

Sunshine went over and put a hand on Felix's arm. "Babe?"

"Mm?"

"I could like kind of go for a coffee."

Felix stared at him. "What?"

Sunshine shrugged. He gave a small smile. "Please? There's that little place down the street we walked past. You could just run and grab it."

Felix scowled, then said, "Fine."

Once Felix left, Sunshine took Nix's arm and circled around the store with him, looking at a couple different things. He didn't make any comments or ask any questions.

"I don't know what he wants," Nix said, nearly whispering.

Sunshine said, "He wants you to pick out something to wear."

"But what?"

"Whatever you want."

Nix looked around the store. "There's so much."

The store had formal options from all different eras and cultures and a few things distinctly not from Earth. Demons were like magpies and their lengthy life expectancies made fashion a mess down here.

"Honestly, whatever you want."

Nix twisted a length of his shirt around his fingers. Another hand-me-down. He'd politely declined offers to get him anything else. He'd declined offers for anything, really, other than bare necessities.

Sunshine said, "You know you don't have to do this."

"He's made that clear."

"I know you're in a rough situation right now but honestly, Nix, if you don't want to do this, don't. Like. For you and for him. For me. I've picked up enough messes, this doesn't have to be another one."

"It's an acceptable solution to the severest of the problems at hand, but...I worry. My daughter won't talk to me. I don't think his parents have taken kindly to the idea."

"And?" Sunshine prompted.

"I never thought I would be free. I never thought I'd sleep beside someone I loved. I never thought I'd make love to someone for whom I held any passion. I never thought I'd have a family the way I remembered having a family. Now I am sure I never will."

Sunshine had to try not to laugh when Nix said, 'make love.' He managed it. "How do you know that?"

"I don't doubt that he'll care for us well, that we'll have affection between us, but this isn't what I wanted. I don't think being with him will be worse than with my lady but—"

"Nix, hang on. You know Felix is not expecting you to have sex with him."

"He mentioned."

"He means it."

"He assured me of my right to refuse."

"Okay, and did he assure of your right to have sex with other people?"

Nix frowned.

"I mean, he and I aren't breaking up over this, obviously, so he's not expecting you to choose between him and chastity," Sunshine said with maybe too much emphasis on 'obviously.' "You can see other people."

Nix kept frowning.

"On Earth, we call it dating. Maybe you guys call it courting? Whatever it is, you can pursue relationships with other people. I'm not saying that won't be a doozy as a single father, but you know, he's not asking you to be his or no one's."

"We hadn't spoken about that."

"You should know I wouldn't let him do that to you."

"I didn't know you held so much influence over him. Princes can be capricious."

Sunshine agreed, "Oh. He is definitely capricious. Mercurial, someone called him that once and I think that's perfect for him. His shape changes but his substance never does."

"But you influence him."

"We influence each other. And besides, he doesn't need me to influence him into not keeping you in a shitty marriage. He really just wants to help. Does that make you feel better?"

Nix nodded.

"So are you ready to pick out something to wear?"

Nix pointed toward a section that held gowns, mantles, robes, and kaftans fit for a formal event. "I think I saw something over there. Red with gold threading."

"That would look great on you."

By the time Felix returned with a coffee for Sunshine, Nix had selected a handful of shirts, trousers, and robes to try on, just to get a feel for the styles and fabrics.

In the end, they commissioned a custom robe of red and gold damask to accommodate his wings, with trousers and a shirt to complete the outfit.

"You're going to look great," Felix said, running his fingers over the fabric one more time. To the tailor, he said, "You're sure you can get this done on time?"

"Anything for my princes," the tailor vowed. He had four arms, too, so Sunshine thought he had a pretty good chance of keeping his promise.

"You didn't even drink your coffee," Felix pointed out as they left.

"It's still too hot. I burned my tongue."

"Yeah, but it's still full."

"I waited too long. It's cold now."

Felix rolled his eyes. He put his hand on the cup, warming it to an appropriate temperature.

He took Felix's hand. "I didn't really want a coffee."

"Yeah, I kind of figured that one out."

"I'm gonna drink it though, I promise."

Nix walked in front of them. He wanted to learn his way around Hell on his own, so he usually took the lead navigating them around the city when they went out. Sometimes he'd glance back and ask for directions, but he seemed to have an excellent sense of direction. They were heading back to the palace now and it was the easiest place in Hell to find, so he walked ahead of them with confidence to his stride.

He looked happier than he had since Dire had stopped talking to him.

"I have to ask Dr. Reza for references for children's therapists when we get back," Felix said. "She's gonna have a field day with this marriage, by the way. I was thinking maybe we, like all three of us and just me and you, we could do like some counseling. Keep everything kosher before it gets a chance not to be."

"I've never been to therapy."

"It's not so bad." Felix leaned against him and wormed under his arm, almost pushing Sunshine off balance.

"Christ," Sunshine breathed.

"Don't, I'm very delicate right now!" Felix warned. "I think Bibi and Papa are going to try to talk me out of this and I don't know what else to say other than what I already said."

"Which is?"

"The truth about the situation."

Felix had gone alone to talk to his parents, so Sunshine didn't know how it had gone other than less than spectacular. Hiram and Phaedrus were not the type of parents prone to shouting, insults, or other types of outbursts, but they did worry very much about their son. He'd given them plenty of reasons to worry and a surprise marriage did seem like the sort of erratic, desperate thing Felix would do in the throes of one of his more heightened episodes of dysregulation.

He tightened his arm around Felix's shoulder. "I think they'll get it once they meet him."

"What if they don't? I know he's having a hard time and, you know, this is a sham of a marriage, but I still want him to feel like part of the family."

"You're taking this really seriously."

"Well! It's sort of a serious thing."

"No, absolutely, but it's not like you to admit it."

Felix groaned and gave no further answer. He went upstairs to lie down when they got back to the palace.

Stone and Milk hurried over to their father and Dire hid behind the sofa.

With one boy on each hip, Nix discussed what had happened with the children with Imogen, who'd gamely offered to watch them when no one else was available. Her exact words had been, "If I can manage Lucifer for all these years, I can manage actual children, too."

To Sunshine, Imogen said, "That Reinhart and Phaedrus are out in the garden."

"They're here?"

She shrugged. "They wanted to talk to Felix."

"Oh, I better go say hi." He looked at Nix. "Uh. Did you want to come meet them?"

"I'd rather not."

"They're so sweet, they'll love you. Come meet them."

"I got the impression they were not pleased with this wedding."

"That's because Felix is impulsive and unstable."

Nix visibly paled.

"Not in a bad way! I mean. Bad for him, obviously. With the rest of us he just gets bitchy," Sunshine assured. To Nix, he said, "Come on. Imogen, do you mind watching the kids a second longer?"

She shrugged. "No."

Nix gave the boys each a kiss and set them back down, saying, "I'll be back soon. Go play."

As they walked out, Nix looked borderline ill.

Sunshine offered, "Do you want to hold hands?"

Nix took his hand.

A quick walk around to the back garden brought them to Hiram and Phaedrus. Hiram looked about as happy as a cat on a hot tin roof and was not looking at the plants Phaedrus was pointing out to him. Nix tugged his hand back as soon as he saw the pair.

"Hi!" Sunshine called.

They both turned, Phaedrus with an open smile and Hiram with a tighter one. He looked exhausted. He had looked steadily more and more tired as the years had worn on. He was, after all, far too old for a human man, held together with the Devil's magic and sheer will.

Felix was right. He shouldn't have been running a university.

Nix hung back as Sunshine went over.

"Sunshine!" Phaedrus cried. They wrapped their arms around Sunshine and gave him a long hug. "Felix said you'd been through a bit of an ordeal. I hope everything is alright."

"I'm doing pretty well, all things considered."

"I'm so glad to hear that, darling. Honestly." They squeezed him tighter.

Hiram came over and hugged Sunshine as well. "Maybe it's better we found you first."

"I kind of think so, too," Sunshine said.

Phaedrus and Hiram both looked at Nix, who lingered yards away, his face stony and his back stiff.

"Is he well?" Hiram asked.

"He's fine."

They looked again at Nix and exchanged a look.

"Come here, let's talk." He gestured for Nix to come over.

Nix approached.

"Uh, Nix, these are Hiram Reinhart and Phaedrus Queen, Felix's parents. You two, this is Nix."

The three stared at each other.

Awkwardly, Hiram said, "He told us your name."

"And not too much else, I'm afraid," Phaedrus said. They looked over Nix again, their eyes intentionally missing the scars on his forehead. "I am horribly interested to know what happened. Felix is always so light on the details. I think he thinks we'll worry if he tells us what happened, but I worry so much more imagining what might have."

"It is nice to meet you," Hiram offered.

"What did happen? This is so sudden," Phaedrus said.

"It's a long story," Sunshine warned. He smiled at Phaedrus. "And I probably won't tell it very well."

"Oh, no, darling, you do wonderfully," Phaedrus assured. "So thorough."

Sunshine related what had happened, to the best of his ability, though he did temper the details somewhat. He watched Felix's parents grow more concerned as he told it and knew holding back a few things had been the right choice.

Nix responded to their reaction, drawing in on himself, standing straighter and tighter until Sunshine thought he might snap. He looked again like that terrifying creature that had found them in the woods.

He didn't look at all like someone a parent would want to marry their child, he looked vicious and cruel and far too capable of violence.

When Sunshine ended the story with Felix's impromptu solution, Hiram and Phaedrus stared.

Phaedrus spoke first. "Darling, you poor thing. That's horrible." They hugged him again. "Atrocious. He left you there!"

"I told him to go. He had to, otherwise, we'd both still be there," Sunshine said. "And the kids would still be there."

"He didn't say anything about children," Hiram said.

Phaedrus released Sunshine and turned to Nix, cautiously moving a little closer.

Nix tightened.

Sunshine put a hand on Nix's arm to find him shaking. He'd left out how close he had Nix had grown and some of Elora's worse behaviors, not sure how to explain it. He also knew that it was not his place to reveal the things that had been done to Nix. "It's okay."

"That word again," Nix growled.

"He didn't say anything about children," Hiram said again.

"Of course, he didn't, why would he!" Phaedrus said. "Why would he tell us anything more than 'come to Hell, I'm getting married to a fairy prince I met a few months ago'!"

"He can't be a father," Hiram insisted and then looked scandalized with himself. "I mean, he's a good person, he really is, but he barely takes care of himself. And, Sunshine, what...what about..." Hiram looked lost. "We thought if he were going to marry anyone...Have I finally lost my mind?"

"Of course not, Hiram." Sunshine smiled, still not able to understand how Felix acted after all these years. "He and I have spoken about it. A marriage wouldn't do anything for our relationship. Neither of us sees a wedding as...a commitment to each other or a culmination of our feelings. It would just be a piece of paper. But if that piece of paper can afford protections to people who need it, why not put it to good use?"

"It's political," Phaedrus said.

"I'm assuming he didn't mention that," Sunshine said.

Phaedrus put their hands on their waist. "He certainly did not."

Sunshine laughed. He couldn't help it. He tried to cover his mouth and stifle it, but honestly, it felt good to laugh.

Nix didn't seem to find anything funny.

"Where is he?" Phaedrus asked.

"He's lying down."

"Oh." Their face softened. "Is he well?"

"A little delicate. He said you'd want to talk him out of it."

"We did come here with that intention," Hiram admitted. "I wish he'd told us."

"You know how he is," Sunshine said.

"He really can't be a father," Hiram said. He looked at Nix.

"My children already have a father," Nix said, each word precise. "They do not need another."

"I think we've gotten off on the wrong foot," Phaedrus suggested.

Sunshine tried to think of something to get Nix to relax. "Is anyone hungry?" Without a sun it was hard to guess the time, but the sky seemed at peak redness, so it must have been about midday. "Or how about something to drink? Tea. They drink a lot of tea around here, there must be a dozen different types in the kitchen at least."

"Tea sounds wonderful, Sunshine," Phaedrus said.

Hiram nodded.

Nix followed as they went inside, slightly apart from the group.

The boys again hurried toward him when he came inside, but they hesitated at the sight of Hiram and Phaedrus. They stopped walking and linked hands, staring at the strangers.

"Oh, god, they're so little," Phaedrus breathed into their hand, their mouth covered.

"Dire will be four soon. Milk and Stone are two. The baby's not a year yet. Maybe nine months? Ten? We're not sure, really," Sunshine said. He saw Dire scowling out at them from behind the sofa. "Boys, come here, come meet my friends."

They looked at their father, who gave the smallest of nods. They inched closer and stopped about half a foot away.

Sunshine crouched down. Softly, he said, "You know how Dada's getting married?"

They nodded mutely. Their nods didn't always indicate full understanding, just acceptance of the situation at hand.

"Well, these are Felix's parents. They're his Papa and his Bibi, just like the princess is his dada, too."

They nodded again.

"Can you say hi?"

Stone waved but looked at the floor. Milk looked at them but didn't wave. He was staring at Phaedrus, his eyes fixed on their face.

Sunshine smiled and put a hand on Milk's shoulder. "You can say hi. They're very nice, I promise."

Phaedrus and Hiram waved.

Stone retreated to his father's side, burying his face against Nix's leg.

Milk kept staring at Phaedrus.

"He's never seen anyone else green before," Nix said.

Phaedrus moved a little and Milk fled to his father's side.

Sunshine watched him go, then said, "They're shy."

Hiram nodded.

He stood and made his way to the kitchen. Phaedrus followed. "I'll get started," they said. "You go get my son."

"Should I say it like that? Cause I don't think he'll come down if I do."

Phaedrus snorted. "Go, please."

Sunshine went. He rolled into bed next to Felix and plucked

the phone out of his hand. He kissed him.

Felix grunted.

"Hi."

"Hi."

"What's wrong?" Sunshine asked.

"Everything."

Sunshine kissed him again and snuggled up to him. "Do you feel better now that you laid down for a bit?"

"No."

Sunshine frowned. "Why not?"

Felix groaned. "You ever know what you have to do but you don't want to do it?"

"Sure."

"Well. I'm gonna do it."

"The wedding—"

Felix shook his head. "It's not about the wedding. It's about after. It makes no logical sense for you and I and Nix to live separately. And it's not like he can live on his own anyway. He has no life skills when it comes to our world. How would he even figure out how to pay for groceries? I can't leave him down here." He drew in a breath, then let it out as another groan. "New Avondale is a Community town. It's small and safe and we'll have enough land for the kids. They can put a fence in by the end of the month."

"Felix."

"I think we have to."

"What about the business?" Sunshine asked.

"We can open a Connecticut office. It makes sense to expand. Take on a few employees there. Connecticut has enough Community members and it's close enough to Massachusetts that we'll get cases there, too. There's a few places around town for rent."

"Is that what you've been doing up here? No wonder you don't feel better."

"I think we have to. I think it's the right thing to do."

Sunshine squeezed him. "You've been doing that a lot lately."

"It sucks. I don't want to move to Connecticut."

"Nobody wants to move to Connecticut," Sunshine assured.

"But I think I'm going to do it."

"Cause it's the right thing to do?"

"Cause it's the right thing to do," Felix grumbled. "And like some kind of idiot, I want to do the right thing."

"Think about all the drivers you'll be able to scare."

"I'm gonna get pulled over all the time."

Sunshine kissed him. "You know how much I love you, right?"

"I guess."

"Cause it's a lot."

Felix scooted up against him and kissed him, more than just a casual peck on the lips. It was warm and asked for reassurance.

Sunshine was happy to give it to him, nestling as close as he could get until they were one mess of limbs and half-off clothes. He rolled on top of Felix, pressed between his legs. On instinct, he gave a bit of a thrust, a thoughtless movement born of little more than the need for pressure and friction.

Felix pulled back.

Sunshine eased up.

"I could try," Felix offered quietly.

"You would hate that," Sunshine reminded.

"Fucking whatever, then what the fuck do you want to do?" Felix grumbled.

"I mean...do you *want* to?" Sunshine asked.

"Not really, I just thought you wanted to. I don't know."

"I'll never expect you to do anything that makes you uncomfortable," Sunshine assured. He'd said it before, but he liked to remind Felix. He knew Felix had done things he hadn't liked to impress or satisfy other people. "And I definitely wouldn't spring it on you like this."

"All your secret liaisons taught you that much, at least."

Neither of them spoke for an awkward second.

"I'm probably game for whatever you'd like to do to me. In having no particular sexual proclivities of my own, I'm usually willing to try something out and see how it goes," Sunshine said.

"Wanting to get hit counts as a sexual proclivity if it gets you hard," Felix reminded. "Are you asking me to fuck you?"

"I'm saying you could. If you wanted to."

"I'll think about it."

"I'd probably like it."

Felix rolled his eyes. "You'd probably really like it if I pulled your hair or tied you up."

"Is that an offer? I am still waiting for you to abase me."

Felix put the back of his hand to his own forehead. "Oh, you must forgive me. I am so fragile these days, Mr. Sunshine, I don't have the strength."

"Then let me be nice to you," he proposed.

Felix twirled one of Sunshine's curls around his fingers.

"You're so good to me."

"I am adequate. You're just used to jerks."

Felix giggled and kissed him again. "Well, come here, then."

Before Sunshine closed the space between them, he said, "Thank you."

"For letting you blow me?"

"For talking to me. I know it isn't easy for you."

Felix rolled his eyes. "Just shut up and blow me."

"I but live to serve, Your Highness." He kissed Felix one more time and then kissed his stomach.

Felix squirmed when Sunshine ran his tongue over his stomach and wiggled his way out of his pants when Sunshine tugged on them. He took care of Felix and Felix did the same for him, then they snuggled close, trading soft kisses and quiet pillow talk.

He ran his fingers through Felix's hair. "We should do something with it for the wedding. You've got to at least tint it a little. Smooth out that last bit of green and your roots."

"I know."

"Are you ready to go downstairs?"

"What?"

"Bibi's making lunch."

Felix tried to sit up.

Sunshine dragged him into a hug. "Don't get worked up. Don't. Come here. You were in such a good mood a second ago."

"Do they know we're up here together!"

"We're all adults."

"Go brush your teeth."

"What?"

"We can't go eat lunch with my parents if we smell like we sucked each other off," Felix hissed. "Go brush your teeth."

Sunshine kissed him one more time. He tossed Felix his clothes and wiggled into his own. They brushed their teeth, though Felix did it with a little more vigor.

When they came down to the kitchen, Phaedrus said, "Oh, there he is. Needed some convincing, did we?"

Felix flushed.

Sunshine took a plate and served a helping of the chicken, vegetable, and rice dish Bibi had prepared. He handed the plate to Felix and made one for himself.

Felix stayed squirrelly for a while.

Nix hadn't relaxed either.

Hiram didn't seem any better off, but at least Phaedrus wasn't bothered.

"Sunshine, tell me more about this Meridian Court," they requested. "I can't believe there's anything left there."

Sunshine told them everything he could remember, happy to have something to talk about, and even happier to have a plate of Phaedrus' cooking in front of him.

When he exhausted the topic, he nudged Felix's calf with his foot. "Tell them about the house."

All three of the other adults asked, "What house?"

Felix bared his teeth at Sunshine. "I'm going to literally murder you."

Nix paled.

Sunshine hurried to assure, "He doesn't mean literally. Felix, tell them about the house."

"Yes, I'm very curious," Phaedrus said.

"I bought a house. I was gonna..." Felix pushed food around his plate. "It was supposed to be for quiet weekends and when you guys retired but I mean, obviously this is a more pressing matter, so we're..." He glanced at Nix. "You know, with everyone's consent and blessing, we're moving there."

"When are we retiring?" Phaedrus asked.

Felix intentionally didn't look at his father. "I don't know, you guys can't run that university forever," he mumbled. He shoved a forkful into his mouth.

"Felix, you haven't got to worry about us," Hiram said.

"Yeah, well, I have since I was twelve so that's gonna be a bitch of a habit to break," Felix snapped.

Hiram put a hand to his chest. "Felix! Why I never..."

"That is a bit much," Phaedrus agreed.

"Well!" Felix demanded.

"Babe, come on," Sunshine said.

Felix groaned. He pushed his plate away and rubbed his face. He stood.

"Where are you going?" Phaedrus asked.

"To dye my hair!" Felix said as he stormed out.

When he'd trudged upstairs, Sunshine said, "That went a lot better than I thought it would."

"Incredible, really," Phaedrus agreed.

Nix made a small sound and they all looked at him. "Is...Does he have a temper? If *that* went well...I hate to ask, but I think I have to know. For the children's sake, at least."

"Oh, no, he's a good boy," Hiram assured, "It's only that his nerves get the better of him sometimes. He does have a terribly nervous temperament."

"He'll come back down in a few hours," Phaedrus said, "Like nothing happened."

Nix looked at Sunshine.

"He's not going to hurt you or the kids. It's not that kind of temper."

"Do you promise?" Nix asked.

Sunshine didn't know the exact rules for promises to fairies. He didn't know if he could make a promise about another person's behavior. "He's a good person."

Nix nodded.

"Where's the house?" Hiram asked.

"Connecticut."

"Oh, that will be nice," Phaedrus said. "They have good schools. Strong education culture in New England, that's important for the children."

Nix looked like he might have rather died than say it, but he asked, "What are schools?"

Phaedrus and Hiram let out a collective sigh of pity and horror.

"Oh, bless you, all of you, I can't imagine," Hiram said.

"You poor thing," Phaedrus said.

Sunshine felt better about things once Hiram and Phaedrus explained schools to Nix and he immediately took to the idea. Once he found out there were schools for adults, he positively lit up. His wings even gave an excited little flutter.

Later, Sunshine went upstairs to help Felix with his hair. They tinted it with a little bit of pale pink, enough to even out the greenish tinge and give a hint of color.

"It's going to wash out by the wedding," Felix huffed. He scowled into the mirror a little longer, raked his hands through his still-wet hair one more time, then turned away.

They'd made a mess, staining a few towels and getting pink spatter all over the bathtub. Sunshine thought it gave the bathroom a lived-in look, which most of the palace lacked. Most of the palace was lifeless, an empty monument to what Lucifer thought his life would be here. Sunshine wondered about what he'd been like then, young and recently fallen. He'd had hope or aspirations of some kind, building a palace like this, full of bedrooms and studies.

He wondered what kind of palace Satan would build now.

"Maybe for the wedding you can have a professional dye your hair," Sunshine suggested, giving a stain one less futile scrub.

"You're practically a professional at this point." Felix pulled his shirt back on and stretched.

"I am not."

"Sure you are. Maybe we won't even open another office, we can open a beauty parlor."

"And play into conceivably every stereotype this small town in Connecticut is going to have about you, your husband, and your live-in boyfriend."

"I still plan on calling you my fiancé, so be prepared for people's minds to be absolutely blown," Felix warned. "And you're also definitely Nix's boyfriend, too, so stop pointing fingers at me for making it complicated."

"It's not like that."

"It's not sexual, it is one hundred percent romantic," Felix said. "I didn't say he was your fuck buddy."

"Can we not add more layers to this right now? Cause it's already enough to explain."

Felix shrugged. "I call it how I see it."

Sunshine clucked his tongue. "And you're never wrong."

"I might, on some occasions, make small errors," Felix conceded. "Ooo, like that time I thought the person who lived under us sold drugs, but they were actually embezzling. Or when I thought Tammy Halwell's little sister was actually her secret child from a teenage pregnancy."

"Or when—"

"No, no, I don't need you to weigh in on this."

"Okay, so are you ready for dinner?" Sunshine asked.

"Yes."

"Are you ready to act like a person at dinner?"

Felix sighed. "Yes."

"Promise?"

"Yes."

"Okay. Come here, give me a kiss."

Felix kissed him. "Maybe like seventy-five percent person."

"What's the rest?"

"Bauhaus albums and drug cravings."

"Bump it up to eighty percent person for me."

"I can't, but I can throw in five percent homosexual yearning from the Romantic movement to bring the drug craving down a little," Felix offered.

"If that's your best offer, Mr. Specter, I suppose I have to take it."

"It's a very strong five percent, you might find it quite to your benefit."

To Felix's credit, he acted entirely like a person at dinner and for most of the days afterward, with the exception of his usual tendencies toward the dramatic.

First Day of the Fifth Month, 101 AR

Three mornings before the wedding, the tailor personally delivered Nix's outfit, and the one's they'd had made for the children, all four arms laden with crisply wrapped boxes. The tailor practically glowed as he handed over each box. Everything had been done to perfection and Sunshine had started to wonder if he shouldn't have gotten a new suit.

It wasn't his wedding, he reminded himself, and his suit looked fine.

It looked better than fine. He cleaned up very nicely.

The tailor had asked if they wouldn't mind sending him a picture of the wedding. He'd wanted to hang it up in his shop. Hell hadn't had a royal wedding since Lucifer had married Tabitha, and that had been a different sort of affair altogether. Hell had been different then, full of marauding clans wearing furs and mounted on what passed for horses in Hell.

The horses here were undeniably horses, but they were huge, occasionally scaly, beasts with too many legs and teeth that could slice through a man's arm like a carrot. Sunshine had thought horses a silly thing for Ira and Georg to be afraid of until he'd seen one down here.

Felix had agreed to send along the photograph, then dug out the bowtie he'd gotten for Garfield.

The salamander tolerated it after a few sniffs and one half-hearted attempt to scratch it off.

"That's super fucking cute," Felix pronounced.

Sunshine opened his mouth to agree but the sound of shredding fabric turned his head. He looked over to see Dire tearing a shirt in half. She dug around for something else, but Nix snatched her away from the boxes before she could.

She dug her teeth into his arm, coming away with blood on her mouth.

"What are you doing!" Nix demanded.

"I hate you!" she screamed. It was the first thing she'd said to him in weeks.

Felix watched for half a second, then scooped up the boxes and the torn shirt and moved them out of her reach. The shirt wasn't the first thing she'd destroyed lately. She had scratched Nix across the face the other day, leaving a mark on his cheek, and she'd ripped a cattail out of Milk's hair when he'd tried to play with a doll she'd abandoned.

Stone and Milk huddled behind Sunshine, which they had taken to doing when Dire got like this.

"It's okay," he assured the boys.

Dire bit Nix again.

This time he let out an actual cry of pain, much different from the milder grunts or hisses that her attacks usually provoked. He pushed her away, hard enough that she fell onto her back.

She started to bawl and kick her feet.

Nix stared at her, his left hand wrapped around his right forearm. Blood seeped between his fingers.

Sunshine had no idea what to do.

Something had to be done, though.

He ushered the boys into the kitchen and Felix followed with the baby. To the boys, Sunshine said, "I'll be right back." He looked at Felix, who nodded without being asked anything.

Nix hadn't moved, blood oozing everywhere.

Dire continued to scream.

Sunshine hadn't expected so much blood. He put a hand on Nix's arm and said, "Come upstairs."

He didn't know what good going upstairs would do other than they had towels upstairs and there was so much blood.

Nix shook his head, staring at his daughter, who had screamed so much her face had gone a horrible shade of red.

"Nix, please."

"I have to help..."

"You can't help anyone if you're bleeding like that. Come on."

He shook his head again. "I can't."

Sunshine ducked back into the kitchen for a clean dish towel. It took some convincing to get Nix to let go of his arm and he tried not to react when he saw the ragged bite. It needed to be cleaned, it probably needed stitches. It needed more than a towel, at any rate. He wrapped it anyway because he didn't think he'd get Nix anywhere anytime soon. He couldn't even get him to sit down.

He had locked himself into place, staring at his screaming daughter, covered in blood.

Sunshine gave him as much calm as he could, letting it trickle between them.

Eventually, Nix's posture softened. He leaned into Sunshine's power without question, maybe without even realizing what Sunshine was doing. He agreed to sit on the couch after a minute. When he walked by Dire, she tried to kick him.

Once he had Nix seated on the couch, he scooped up Dire,

despite her screams and attempts to bite him, too, and brought her to the bedroom she shared with her father and siblings. He set her on the bed and told her what he usually told Felix when he got worked up like this: "We're not going anywhere until you get yourself together."

She screamed that she hated him, too.

He said, "I know you're angry," and left it at that.

After about five minutes, her screams turned into regular sobs.

He went to sit next to her on the bed and she immediately crawled into his lap, smearing him with snot and tears. He told her she was okay, which probably wasn't true, but he didn't know what else to say.

"You're safe," he settled on. "I'm right here."

It took about ten minutes altogether for her to stop crying, which not as bad as it could have been. He wiped her face and asked, "Why did you do that?"

"I *hate* him."

"He's your dada. Even when you're mad, you can't hurt him like that. Why are you so upset?"

"I don't want him to get married."

Sunshine sighed.

"*I'm* apposed to get married."

"You can't get married. You're too little. It's illegal."

She rubbed her nose and smeared snot everywhere. "What's illegal?"

"It's against the law. Against the rules. We'd get in trouble."

"I'll get in trouble?"

Sunshine felt the need to explain, "No. Not you. You're too young to get married. You don't know what it really means. And you can't do the things that married people do together. So the person who married you would get in trouble."

She frowned at him.

"And you can't marry Felix anyway, even if he and Dada weren't getting married, even if you were grown up."

She bared her teeth at Felix's name. "I hate him, too."

He put an arm around her and held her close. "I know things are scary right now. A lot of things are changing. That's hard. It's really hard, but Dire, you've got to know that your Dada loves you so much. All these changes? They're hard for him too. He wants you to be safe and happy. He's trying so hard for that."

She shook her head.

"What?"

"No, he doesn't."

"He loves you," he said.

She didn't say anything else.

After a while, he moved her off his lap and said, "Stay in your room for a little bit. I have to go check on everyone."

She stayed where he left her.

He headed back downstairs to find Nix still on the couch. He could hear Felix entertaining the other children in the kitchen with pots and pans. He sat next to Nix and said, "She's settled down."

Nix swallowed.

"I really think you need to go to a doctor."

"It will heal."

"Nix."

He shook his head.

Sunshine sighed. He didn't even know where to go for something like this. Hell had medical care, yes, but Sunshine had no idea how to access it. "I'm going to get Felix. He's going to take you to a doctor."

Nix shook his head.

"It's not really an option."

"I can't. I can't...I feel like I can't even breathe," Nix said. "I can't believe I did that. Did it really happen?"

"She's okay. She really is. Now we need to make sure you're okay."

"I'm *not* okay."

"Alright," Sunshine said. "Sit tight for a second."

After a quick conversation with Felix, they decided they'd call for someone to come to the house.

By the time Lucifer and Imogen came home from their business in the city, they'd cleaned up all the blood, gotten the bite cleaned, stitched, and bandaged, and given Nix a couple of sedatives so he could rest. He currently lay on the couch, swaddled in several blankets, snoring lightly.

Felix had given him the pills when he hadn't been able to move past having pushed Dire away from him. The fairy had asked repeatedly if it had really happened.

They stayed in the throne room, Nix and Felix on the couch, Sunshine on the floor, leaning against Felix's legs, and the children all upstairs taking a nap.

Dire had already been asleep when Sunshine and Felix had brought the other three up. The boys cuddled up to their sister like nothing had happened.

Despite their efforts to clean, Lucifer and Imogen smelled the blood when they came inside anyway.

"Probably not a great idea for a four-year-old to have teeth like that," Lucifer remarked.

"You know, I don't think there's a lot we can do about it," Felix said.

"There's at least one thing you can do about it."

"Dad."

"I'm not saying to do it. I'm saying there *are* options," Lucifer said airily. "Pretending they aren't there doesn't make them go away."

"It kind of does," Felix said. "If we all pretend that removing a child's teeth is not an option, it definitely goes away."

"It could be done painlessly, they're only milk teeth."

"Go away," Felix said.

Lucifer shrugged and went.

Felix slumped back down onto the couch. To Sunshine, he said, "How are we going to get her into preschool?"

Sunshine covered his mouth to hide a nervous giggle. "We'll figure it out."

"It's not funny."

"I'm not laughing cause it's funny."

Nix stirred and sat up a little, rubbing his face.

Felix put an arm around his shoulders and drew him close. "Go back to sleep."

"Is that possible?" Nix asked. "That she would be denied entrance to a school because of her behavior?"

"It's not going to come to that," Felix said. "She's just having a hard time with everything. Right? She isn't usually like this."

Nix yawned into the crook of his arm. "She's never...before we announced the wedding, she's never acted that way toward me before. Strangers, yes, but only if she feels threatened by them. I'm not blind. I won't pretend she isn't cruel sometimes, but..." He touched the bandage wrapped around his forearm. "But she's never bitten anyone this hard before. A bruise or a little blood, but never like this."

"You've never married her future consort before," Sunshine said. "She's taking it hard. How's a three-year-old get this obsessed with marriage?"

"My lady often spoke of finding a suitable husband. Less while you were there, likely because she thought she'd secured your master's affections. Children listen much more intently than we allow ourselves to believe," Nix said.

"I am a catch," Felix said. "On paper, at least."

"She's so young and her mind is already so thoroughly twisted by her time at Court. They all are. I." Nix pulled away from Felix. "I worry. I worry that nothing can save them."

Felix started to assure, "Elora can't—"

"You misunderstand," Nix said. "From themselves. From a life so steeped in discontent and fear. In neglect."

Sunshine wanted to say the children hadn't been neglected, but he knew there had been times when Nix couldn't attend to them as he should have. It wasn't his fault, but it was true. He didn't know what that could do to a child.

"You love them," Felix said. "That's what matters. You love them and you have us here to help you. We're going to take care of them."

"I don't think it's enough."

"I was eavesdropping," Lucifer announced from the stairs.

They all turned to look.

"Of course, you were," Felix said.

He carefully descended the stairs, making sure not to disturb the cat that had perched on his shoulder. "Can I tell you a story that might make you feel a little better?"

"Any comfort you might give would be welcomed," Nix said.

Lucifer seated himself in front of the couch, facing them. The cat leaped from his shoulder onto the couch. "A child was born to me once, many years ago. He was not conceived out of love. He was born too early and we all thought he would die. I thought he would die. I looked at him and thought that even if he lived, he would be so small and weak that the world would be cruel to him. And it was. His mother was slain by her own father and brother shortly after his birth. He was brought to me in a blanket covered in blood by a vampire who had markedly little experience with humans, let alone children. I do not know what passed in the week it took her to travel to me. He was brought to me weak and thin, and I thought again he would die.

"I kept him with me. I held him and fed him and sang to him. I made sure he was clean and warm. And then an angel came. The same one that had tracked him to his mother's house, the same one that would find him later and nearly kill him. The same one that hunted him for twenty-six years. This angel came to my palace, a beautiful thing in beautiful armor. He carried a shining sword and all I could see was my son, my weak little son impaled on that sword.

"We fought, this angel and I. I became the Beast. I defended my son. I did not kill the angel, but I scared him away, I think. He retreated, for reinforcements or to rally, or out of fear, I don't know. But he went and I returned to my son, who had seen all this. He cried when he saw me. He didn't stop for hours. For days, whenever I went close to him, he cried. He knew what I was and even born of my flesh as he was, he could not tolerate it.

"I brought him to Earth and gave him over to the care of people who could do what I couldn't. As long as he stayed in Hell, this would happen, over and over and over. The angel would come, many angels, even, and I would fight them all and he would live beneath a wheel of violence. These people could hide him as I could not. They raised him and loved him and kept him safe. Even hidden, though, he lived under a shadow of death, hunted by so many who would end him for nothing more than being what he was. He grew up in a world that didn't love him, either, for many reasons. He grew up with every reason to be a wicked thing. A cruel man with harsh passions. Do you know what he did to the angel that hunted him?"

Felix's eyes had gone shiny and bloodshot with the telling of the story. He scrubbed at them with his sleeve, which didn't make anything better. He couldn't look at his father.

Sunshine couldn't look away from Felix. He had never heard Felix's earliest days laid out so clearly before him. He had known about them, they all had, but never like this, never paired with the context of what a childhood actually was, or what children were really like. He had never known children until now, he had never loved one until now. He had always thought of them as strange little things, never people in their own right.

"I don't know," Nix admitted. He didn't look comforted at all by Lucifer's story.

Felix let out an ugly, phlegmy gasp and covered his mouth with his hand.

"He captured the angel. He leveled a weapon at him and then he let him live," Lucifer said. "He called a truce and took him in and taught him how to be a fucking person like he was some kind of street cur that needed love and a bath instead of a vicious, mindless killer."

"Shut the fuck up, Dad," Felix growled, his voice wet and strained.

Nix looked between Felix and Sunshine.

"I think he turned out alright," the Devil said. He gave a cheery smile.

"Jesus fucking Christ, no wonder I'm so fucked up," Felix said into his hands.

With gentle concern, Lucifer reminded, "You knew these things."

"But no one ever said it like that," Felix insisted.

"Come here, little one."

Felix rushed forward and folded himself into his father's arms. He didn't cry but he did make a hideous, snot-filled noise.

"It's alright," Lucifer assured, his spindly arms wrapping around Felix, his loose black clothes blending with Felix's similarly dark garb, making them look like one lanky, pale creature for a moment.

"Yeah," Felix agreed. He sniffled.

"Oh, we're so emotional today," the Devil noted. "It's all alright, though, little love, you'll be okay."

Felix nodded.

"Your children are young, and you love them, and you're aware of the shortcomings in their lives so far. This gives you an advantage. You have willing assistance from two people who have overcome many of the unfavorable circumstances that accompanied them. That's another advantage. Have some hope, Wild Prince," Lucifer said.

"I do feel...better. A little." Nix looked at Felix, who had extracted himself from his father's embrace. "I didn't know."

"Well, it's not the stuff of casual conversations," Felix said from where he'd settled on the floor between Sunshine and Lucifer.

"Would you have rather I hadn't heard it?"

Felix shook his head. "No, I suppose it gives you context. Really. It's not as bad as he made it sound. My parents gave me a good childhood, all things considered." He nudged Lucifer. "All of them."

"Ah, you give this old monster joy." Lucifer stood. "And now he must go. My captains and I meet soon. Perhaps you'd do better to amuse yourselves. There is a wedding coming up and this mood might not be well suited to it."

When Lucifer had gone, Felix quietly said, "I think if I drank, I would have a nervous breakdown."

"Let's take the kids out when they wake up," Sunshine proposed.

"Is that wise?" Nix asked.

Sunshine shrugged. "I don't know." He wanted ice cream. He felt he deserved ice cream after everything.

"My lady spoke always of consequences for poor conduct," Nix said. "She dispensed them willingly enough."

Sunshine blew a raspberry. "Well, let's rip all the pages she wrote out of your parenting book."

Nix said, "There is no book."

"Not a literal book."

"Ah. Yes. I understand," Nix said. "They aren't pages I would much miss."

Sunshine started thinking of what kind of ice cream he would get. Things tasted different here, but they still tasted pretty good, all things considered, once the palate acclimated.

"I don't know. I'm not saying we...we do anything drastic, but we should do something," Felix said. "She really hurt you this time. She should at least apologize. A real apology."

"She might be incapable of that. She cannot lie," Nix reminded.

"We should talk to her, at least," Felix said.

Nix looked unsure.

"Felix is an expert when it comes to apologies," Sunshine said. "I'll follow his lead on this one."

"You're very good at making me feel like I need to apologize," Felix said. He looked at Nix. "When she wakes up, we'll talk to her."

"What if she won't apologize? The Fair Folk are prideful."

Felix pulled one knee up to his chest and rested his chin on it. "The essence of a good apology is not just the expression of regret for harm done but the promise to refrain from the action that caused the harm in the future and adherence to that promise. She should acknowledge she hurt you and say she won't do it again."

"She would be bound to her word on that. Is it still meaningful if she has no choice?" Nix asked.

Felix grinned. "No." A strange sort of delight flashed in his eyes.

"You mean to force it anyway," Nix guessed.

"No! Goodness, not at all. But I am sort of excited to have something to think about other than this fucking wedding. You're lucky the bride's parents pay for the wedding," Felix said, "Cause without Daddy's money this thing wouldn't come together nearly as quick. A wedding, a trial...then back to Earth. You'll like it there, I think. I hope. The house is nice. They're putting in a fence right now."

"I'm not looking forward to the move," Sunshine admitted.

Felix flapped a hand. "The house is furnished. The family ran out of there so fast! We just need to move our personal things."

"We can just leave everything else behind like that?"

"I talked to Amity, he said it would be okay for us to sublet the rooms for a while. You know, until the kids are grown up." Felix flashed a grin at Nix. "Or until Nix finds a nice lady he'd rather share the house with."

Nix dropped his gaze.

Felix nudged Nix with his foot. "How 'bout it?"

"Oh, Felix, don't play matchmaker. He's gone through enough without adding that on top of it," Sunshine said.

"You are an awful thing!" Felix scolded. "Nix, can you believe him?"

"I can't imagine I'll have good prospects."

"Babe, have you looked in a mirror? Someone's gonna snap you up," Felix assured. "Climb you like a fucking tree...God." He let out a hungry little sound.

Nix looked somewhere between flattered and embarrassed.

Sunshine elbowed him. "How the fuck are you this horny all the time?"

Felix flopped on to his lap. "Poor breeding, I suppose, and even poorer raising. I was so thoroughly raised without shame and you do know what they say about wicked things like me."

"I have heard the rumors. Can any man sustain such libertine ways?"

"Libertine!" Felix giggled. "You flatter me, Sunshine. How dearly I would love to be a libertine."

Sunshine couldn't stop smiling at him.

Felix smiled back at him.

"I want ice cream."

"I know. I saw you staring through the window last time went out." Felix draped one arm across his face and wrapped the other around Sunshine to rest his hand on Sunshine's back. "You and Nix take the boys and the baby out for ice cream. I'll have a word with Dire. We'll join you forthwith if she and I can come to an understanding."

"Are you sure?" Sunshine asked.

"Of course. Fun uncles can have serious conversations," Felix said.

Sunshine placed his hand on Felix's chest.

Felix peeked at Nix with one eye. "Is that agreeable to you?"

"I don't know."

"I won't do anything but speak with her. I'm not the kind of person prone to coercion or violence when it comes to children."

For once, Nix didn't look at Sunshine. He met Felix's eyes. "You swear?"

"I swear."

Sunshine hoped going for ice cream would lighten the mood because things had started to feel much too serious.

"Very well." Nix rubbed his face. "It's not as though I have a better idea."

"Hey." Felix sat up and scooted closer to the couch. He put his hand over Nix's. "Being a parent is hard. You're doing a good job."

Nix held his hand. "Now that I've met your parents that eases my conscious a little."

Felix beamed. "I love them so much."

After lunch, they took the children, all of them, for a walk. They didn't mention any particular destination. At an intersection, Felix handed Dire a bag containing the shirt she'd ripped and told her, "We have to go this way."

She glared.

"We'll meet up with Dada and Sunshine after. Come on. We have to get that shirt fixed." He gestured for the others to keep going.

Sunshine took the first step and Nix followed after a moment.

"They'll be fine," Sunshine assured.

Nix sighed. He adjusted the baby on his hip.

"We should give her a name."

"She should have one," Nix agreed. "But I've only named one of my children and I no longer have that daughter. I worry about the luck of it."

"Name her after the trial," Sunshine proposed.

Nix looked at the baby, who smiled up at him. "She's such a happy baby."

"Maybe she knows how lucky she is to have such a good dad." Sunshine glanced back to see that Dire and Felix had gone, rounded the corner on their way to the tailor.

Their small group attracted a lot of attention as they walked. An angel and a bunch of fairies, not exactly standard for Hell.

A few people gave them scathing looks. Sunshine did his best not to glare back.

A family at the ice cream shop moved away from them, to the

far corner of the store.

Sunshine didn't care, not went he saw the jars of all the different toppings they had.

Milk and Stone pressed right up against the class on their tiptoes, staring like the buckets of ice cream were the most miraculous thing they'd ever seen. They grabbed Nix by the shirt and pulled him closer, point out all the different colors of ice cream and wanting to know what flavors they were.

The girl behind the counter answered all their questions willingly. She smiled a lot and offered to let them try whatever flavors they wanted.

It took a good half an hour for them to make up their minds, and it took Nix even longer. Sunshine ordered his own, an unnecessarily decadent sundae that Nix eyed with envy and finally copied when he put in his own order.

Sunshine fished out a handful of coins from his pocket and handed them over.

He'd never seen the boys so excited. They fed each other bites and made a general mess of their faces and clothing in the process.

It took about an hour for Felix to join them, but he'd texted to say they were on their way.

When they arrived, Dire walked up to her father and set a shirt box on his lap. "It's fixed now."

Nix touched the box.

"I don't want you to get married."

"I know."

"Felix says you don't want to get married either."

Nix looked at Felix, who stood slightly behind Dire.

Felix met his eyes, gave a guilty shrug, and went back to looking at ice cream.

"No. I don't."

"I don't understand."

"Sometimes we do things because we have to."

Dire guessed, "Like the things you did for our queen?"

Nix nodded.

She turned to look at Felix, her little face angry. She told him, "I hate you."

"That's okay," Felix said. "Feelings are okay. It's not okay to hurt people. Tell your father what we talked about."

Dire glared but turned back to her father. Her expression softened. She wrapped her hand around a few of his fingers. "Dada, do you accept my apology?" She said it like she'd rehearsed.

"I do."

"It means I'll try not to do it anymore."

"That's good to hear."

"But I get so mad."

"I know," he said.

"Feelings are okay," she intoned, "Hurting the people you love isn't. I love you, Dada."

He set the box on the table and pulled her into a hug. "I love you, too. Even when you're angry."

She curled up on her father's lap.

Felix came over with two ice cream cones. He offered a vanilla one to Dire.

She glared at him.

"Nobody hates me too much for ice cream," Felix said. "Try it."

"Go ahead," her father said.

She took it and her face grew considerably less sour as she ate.

Felix sat next to Sunshine. He held it out toward Sunshine.

Sunshine licked it then made a face. "Oh, what flavor is that?"

"It just said green on the label. I think it's just a bunch of green stuff mixed together."

"It tastes like lime and spinach."

Felix smiled. He licked it. "And maybe a little zucchini or something." He offered it to Sunshine again. "Do you taste zucchini?"

Sunshine licked it. "No."

Felix kept with it. He offered some to Nix, who declined.

Stone and Milk both tried it and made faces at the flavor.

"Cucumber," Sunshine decided with Felix forced one more taste on him.

Felix ate the rest of it and seemed to enjoy it. He called it refreshing. When he'd finished, he licked his thumb and rubbed it on Sunshine's face. "You had hot fudge..."

"Thank you." Sunshine wiped his face reflexively and examined his finger.

Felix nodded at the kids. "I think they're going to need a bath."

Fourth Day of the Fifth Month, 101 AR

Sunshine had felt sick with nerves all day. He had been put in charge of getting the children clean and dressed. Felix had been whisked away by Hiram and Phaedrus to prepare and Nix had been taken under the wing of Ira and Georg to get ready.

Lucifer watched Sunshine fuss with Dire's hair.

The boys and the baby were clean and dressed, for the most part. Milk kept taking off his shoes, since he'd never had any before and said they pinched his toes. Stone couldn't wear shoes, so using him as a good example was out the window.

Dire had agreed to wear shoes only because she'd gotten the gaudiest pair available in her size.

"Do you want help with that?" Lucifer asked.

"Don't you have somewhere else to lurk?"

"No," Lucifer said. "Felix asked me to help here."

"Oh."

"I make Hiram very nervous," Lucifer admitted. "Felix thinks it's better if we don't spend too much time together lest he be entirely fraught by the ceremony."

"I know this was important to you."

Lucifer gave him a smile. He came to sit on the bed next to Dire and Sunshine and took the comb from Sunshine's hand. "Do you mind?"

Sunshine shook his head.

"I am pleased to see Felix acting with such a becoming combination of kindness and cunning and I'm glad to see my family grow. I am a grandparent many times over, but I am as poor a grandparent as I am a parent. But I'm a little closer with Felix so perhaps I'll be privy to some small family moments," Lucifer mused. His fingers worked through Dire's hair, pulling and weaving half a dozen strands. "I am excited for him. And for you. I know you and Nix are close. But when I asked to be included in his wedding, I meant his wedding to you, specifically to you."

"Oh."

"He loves you so much, Sunshine," the Devil continued. "Get me a ribbon."

Sunshine could only find a hair elastic.

Lucifer took it without complaint. He secured the braid he'd done and started on another. "Sunshine." He had his eyes fixed on Dire's hair. "I know we have a difficult history."

"I almost killed you."

Lucifer grinned. "Yes. And I almost killed you once, too, if memory serves."

"Yes." He handed Lucifer another hair tie.

Lucifer secured the second braid. "Go down the hall two rooms and get the small, green box on the nightstand. Bring it back."

Dire eyed him, then went.

She liked Lucifer and seemed to hold the Devil in the same kind of esteem as she'd held Elora. In fact, meeting Lucifer had appeared to have dulled her opinion of Elora. Once she'd asked why Nix couldn't marry the princess instead of Felix.

Lucifer didn't look at Sunshine. "I am glad I never killed you, Sunshine. I thought about it a lot. I am glad Felix couldn't kill you either. I am glad he loves you."

"Oh. Me too."

"I'm not just glad that he loves someone that treats him well, or that he has a good friend, or that you weather his shortcomings in mental health," Lucifer continued. "I am glad that he loves *you*."

"Oh. Me too."

Lucifer let out a little giggle. He finally looked at Sunshine and took his hand. "I don't think you understand how much it means that he is mine and you are Our Father's, and you love each other."

Sunshine looked at Lucifer. He understood exactly what the Devil meant for once. He understood the expression on his face and the tightness of his grip.

"You ran into my arms not so long ago. Would you be opposed to finding yourself there again?"

"That is absolutely how a serial killer would ask for a hug."

"I do fit that definition in some ways," Lucifer said.

Sunshine scooted across the bed and hugged the Devil. It felt wrong because Lucifer's was body was not exactly the right shape or size for a person and because angels shouldn't have been hugging the Devil like this.

It also felt nice.

Sunshine considered that he could easily slip a knife between Lucifer's ribs right now. He thought that doing so would legitimately surprise him. A few months ago, he would have considered that dealing the Beast such a wound would have been the right thing to do.

The Almighty had never asked Sunshine to kill Lucifer.

The Almighty had never spoken to Sunshine.

He was real. The angels had all seen Him, but He concerned

himself with Heaven about as much as He concerned himself with Earth.

Sunshine tightened his arms around Lucifer.

Dire returned with the green jewelry box.

Lucifer opened it to reveal dozens of tiny pieces of jewelry and let each child pick out a piece or two to wear. He called them trinkets, but Sunshine was sure they were made with real gems and precious metals.

"My daughter outgrew these thousands of years ago," he told Sunshine. "They serve no purpose and therefore have no value." He placed a thin, golden bracelet around the baby's wrist and checked to make sure it wouldn't slip off accidentally. "The hour approaches and I believe we're all meant to be at the ceremony before our grooms arrive. You should get dressed."

Sunshine got dressed and they headed out. Lucifer peeled away from the group before they went inside, saying he was needed elsewhere.

The children scattered as soon as they stepped inside, running around to look at everything.

The wedding didn't exactly look like weddings he'd been to before. The ceremony was in the same place as the reception, at the gallery of the University. Various pieces of art, most Hellish but many human, decorated the walls. A few statues stood in corners, marble ones that seemed direct mockeries of the Renaissance with their deformed bodies and grotesque expressions. Small tables with dark table clothes stood off to the side and guests milled around the room. It felt more like an intimate fundraiser for a secret society than a wedding.

There were no seats except the ones around tables.

He didn't see either groom.

People they knew from Earth gave him pitying looks. No one believed that he and Felix hadn't broken up, or that they wouldn't soon. No one believed Felix could balance two relationships or that Sunshine should put up with him marrying someone else.

He tried not to think about it.

June came over and put a hand on his arm. "How are you holding up?"

Sunshine pressed his lips together and didn't say any of the cruel things he'd thought.

"He's got to be an awful mess planning this wedding. I don't know how he pulled it off so fast," June continued. "I know he takes it out on you when he's upset."

"He only takes it out on me because I let him," Sunshine said, then realized how terrible that sounded.

June seemed to understand what he meant. He smiled. "But you're doing okay?"

"I'm fine. I'm...I'm ready to go home. More than anything, I'm ready to go home." Then he realized he'd have a new house on Earth, more new things to get used to. He'd been longing for his apartment, but that would be sublet soon enough with the price Felix had advertised.

"Click your heels three times," June joked. "I heard there's a baby."

Sunshine pointed to the baby carrier. He'd set it down at a table with his name on it. "She's sleeping."

June went over to look at the baby, declared her to be adorable, and left it at that.

"Where's James Kelly?"

"Oh, he wouldn't come down here for a million dollars!" June laughed. "And he said he knows he'd just be grumpy about me staring at Lucifer all night." He slipped his phone out of his pocket. "He'll feel better if he knows you're here, come here, come take a picture."

June took a selfie of them and sent it to James Kelly with the caption, *See? Sunshine will keep me on my best behavior.*

Sunshine checked the time. The ceremony wasn't due to start for about fifteen minutes and he had no idea what to do with himself. Most of the people here were either important people in Hell or more Felix's friends than his.

He'd lost track of the children, too, and scanned the crowd.

Stone was trying to reach the wedding cake, Milk had taken a painting off the wall, and Dire was speaking with one of Lucifer's Captains, marked clearly by the badge she had pinned to her blouse.

He went for Stone first, scooping up him and telling him the cake was for later.

The boy stared at the wedding cake, which smelled of buttercream and vanilla even from a foot away.

"You can have a big piece later, okay?" Sunshine said.

Stone nodded.

He went to put the painting back on the wall and asked Milk not to touch any more of the paintings.

"What about the stone people?"

"Those are statues," Sunshine said.

"I can touch them?"

"As long as you don't break them," Sunshine said.

He scampered off.

Sunshine didn't know if he should go stop Dire from bothering the Captain, but the woman seemed happy enough to talk to the girl. He adjusted his arm around Stone, who'd rested his head against Sunshine.

Hiram and Phaedrus joined the guests, which likely meant the ceremony would start soon.

Everyone started whispering to each other about them. Hiram was just a human mage, no matter how long he lived, so the fuss wasn't really about him. It was about Phaedrus. Whether people liked their books or not, or even knew all the pennames Phaedrus had published under, they were famous and somewhat controversial.

He waved.

The couple waved back but couldn't make their way past the people who had come over to talk to them.

At the exact minute stated on the invitation, Lucifer stepped out among the crowd and went to stand on a small dais, likely one used to give speeches or lectures on most days.

People went silent.

Everyone with allegiance to Hell knelt or bowed. Some demons touched their foreheads to the floor. Phaedrus inclined their head forward slightly. Sunshine had never seen Phaedrus kneel before Satan. He couldn't imagine Phaedrus kneeling for anyone. Of the demons, Ira alone remained upright.

The earthly guests looked around uncomfortably.

"Rise," Lucifer said and the demons stood in eerie unison, "And join us. We are here today to witness the legal union of two creatures in wedlock and to witness the legal assumption of guardianship of these two creatures over four children."

The demons let out polite applause.

The people from Earth stayed quiet and looked at each other.

Lucifer produced three sets of documents and set them on the table and laid two pens beside it. "Greet them with me," he requested and turned to face the door.

Felix and Nix walked out together.

Sunshine's heart sped up a little.

Felix cleaned up well, but he never lost that dark edge, always looking exactly like what he was even in a perfectly made dinner suit. He looked wicked and dangerous, black-eyed and too pale. The pink tint to his hair softened the look.

Nix stood perfectly straight, his eyes forward. He was taller than Felix by at least a head and broader than him too. The band of scars on his forehead subtracted nothing from his beauty. The gold and red robe brought to mind an emperor or a mighty sorcerer.

They would scare the shit out of the PTA.

Sunshine couldn't wait to see it.

The children asked to be picked up so they could see, so he moved them forward to get a better view.

People parted for him.

"Step forward when called to confirm your identities," Lucifer said. "His Highness Felix James Specter-Reinhart-Queen, most favored son of the Serpent's Throne."

Felix stepped on to the dais.

"His Highness Nix, Wild Prince of the Meridian Court."

Nix joined Felix.

The baby let out a coo at the sight of her father.

"You have convened already and laid out the terms of your agreement. By signing on the first set of lines, you affirm that you are here of your own will and that these terms are agreeable to you. By signing on the second set, you take guardianship of the four children, marked here by their fingerprints, until either they are adults by the standards of their race or seek emancipation. One set for your household, one for the Record's Office, and one that I believe will suffice on Earth when presented to the proper authorities."

Felix took up the pen and signed all three, his hand swift and precise. He whispered something to Nix.

Nix took the other pen and made a few shaky marks where Felix indicated.

Lucifer placed his seal and signature on the bottom of each document, and Georg stepped forward to sign it as well, acting in his role as the Master of Records.

When they both set down their pens, Lucifer said, "We declare you wed and the children with guardians."

"We're done?" Felix asked quietly so that only people close to the dais could hear.

"It is concluded," Lucifer said. "Join your guests."

The demons clapped again as the newlyweds turned and stepped off the dais. The people from Earth joined in uncertainly.

Hiram and Phaedrus hugged both of them. The children flocked to their father.

Lucifer stepped down beside them and put a hand on Felix's

shoulder. "Some people do celebrate a little more."

"Should we do a round of shots?" Felix asked.

"Felix," Hiram sighed.

"I'll be right back," Lucifer said and made his way toward a sleek bar of dark wood. The snake-faced woman behind it immediately stepped forward.

Sunshine moved a little closer.

Felix peeled away to stand before him. "Are you terribly thrilled for me?"

"All your friends are looking at us."

"Because they think I'm an asshole who dumped you for a sexy fairy prince," Felix said, "Or that I'm too greedy to let you go be happy with someone who'd actually love you and I'd rather condemn you to a perpetuity of unhappy adultery."

"I think our adultery is going to be very happy."

"I don't even think it counts as adultery given that it's written into our agreement that we're allowed to see other people."

"Ah."

Lucifer returned with a small, carefully balanced tray of shot glasses.

Felix took one and handed it to Sunshine, then took one for himself. He clinked glasses with his husband and parents, then said, "Cheers," as they slugged back the clear liquid, though Hiram sipped it a little more politely.

Vodka.

Nix let out a wheeze.

"Oh, no, I'm sorry!" Felix said. He put down his glass and took Nix's. "I should have warned you."

"That's horrible." Nix pressed the back of his hand to his mouth.

Sunshine had thought it was pretty smooth, all things considered, but then again, it tasted like rubbing alcohol compared to fairy wine.

Felix rubbed his husband's back. "I'm so sorry."

Lucifer smiled. He took Nix by the arm. "Come, let's find something more suited to your palate. And you too, children, I think you'd like Shirley Temples," he said as he led them away.

June asked if he could hold the baby now that she was awake.

She went with him happily, reaching for his horns.

Felix stayed next to Sunshine.

Sunshine took his hand.

A little tension slid out of the demon's body. He grinned

nervously at Sunshine. "He said you helped him practice writing his name."

"I remember what it's like."

Felix ran his thumb over Sunshine's hand. "I'm gonna be super hungover for the trial tomorrow."

"I told you not to schedule them back-to-back."

"When have I ever listened to you?" Felix asked.

Sunshine watched the toddlers edge away from the bar with bright red drinks clutched in their hands.

"I could use about six more shots," Felix said.

"Babe."

Felix signed and nuzzled his face against Sunshine's arm.

Sunshine kissed the top of his head.

"We've got to make the rounds, me and Nix. It would be rude not to."

"I know."

"Don't be a stranger, though."

"Oh, I don't think I could stand the looks. I'm just going to tuck myself into some corner where I can't be looked at," Sunshine said.

"At least yours are looks of pity. I feel just about withered by the ones I'm getting," Felix said.

"Give me a kiss before you go."

Felix kissed him. "And cut me off later! Nix won't."

Sunshine smiled and watched him go.

For most of the evening, he kept the children out of the most major of their mischief and sat with June and the baby.

June had firmly resolved not to get in any trouble while he was away from James Kelly and seemed to think that Sunshine and the baby could provide him the best way to do so. They chatted about mutual friends and acquaintances and rather gleefully talked shit about mutually disliked people.

Lucifer approached them after dinner when the band began to play and waiters with cake and coffee circled around. He stood before June. "Junius, you've avoided me."

"I'm trying not to get into trouble."

"You think I'll get you into trouble?"

"You got me into the most trouble I ever been in in my life," June reminded.

Lucifer smiled. "One dance won't do any harm. Even that jealous vampire of yours couldn't begrudge you that."

"He's just afraid," June said. "Don't you remember being

young and afraid of everything?"

"One dance before you return to that wretched island of garbage and misery—"

"You sent me there," June reminded.

"Please."

"Alright, but we both know it won't be one dance," June said.

"It won't be more than dancing," Lucifer promised. He held out his hand.

June handed the baby to Sunshine. "So much for staying out of trouble." He took Lucifer's hand.

"That was almost us," Felix said from just behind Sunshine.

Sunshine startled, then scowled at him.

"A thousand more years of not being able to touch and that would have been us," he said. He sat next to Sunshine. "All star-crossed and yearning, quietly resigned to distant affection and an empty space in our heart. Being in Hell would make June so miserable and Dad literally can't stay on Earth. Can you imagine? At least we could pine within arms' length."

"Don't get melancholy."

"I'm not. I'm actually really thrilled that you got your shit together and took that ward off," Felix said.

"Me, too."

Felix's eyes had gone glassy with how much he'd had to drink. He pointed to Nix and Hiram on the dance floor, both with perfect posture and timing as they moved with the music. "Papa's teaching Nix how to dance." He put a small white box in front of Sunshine. "I know it's not our wedding..." He nodded to indicate Sunshine should open it.

Inside, he found a cupcake.

"Butter pecan," Felix told him.

He took up a fork and tried a bite and nearly melted. "Oh my god, it's fucking delicious," he mumbled around the cake, covering his hand with his mouth so as not to be a complete monster.

Felix scooted closer and put his head on Sunshine's arm, watching him eat.

It took Sunshine several minutes to notice the scraping sensation over his skin. He had felt it before when Felix had left that weird red mark on him. He put an arm around Felix and pulled him closer. "I love you."

"I love you too."

He didn't let go of Felix until the pain had swelled to a peak and then subsided into a dull, persistent throb. It only took about five minutes. If he hadn't been drunk, it probably would have hurt a lot worse. He probably would have reacted instead of just leaning into it.

"I'm gonna have...three more drinks. Okay. Cut me off after three."

"Okay."

"You want to come dance?"

His chest felt wet. "I'll be right out. I need to use the bathroom. Watch the baby?"

Felix nodded.

"And drink some water." He pushed a glass toward Felix and wandered off to find the bathroom.

In the bathroom, he locked the door and unbuttoned his shirt to find red beads welling through his undershirt.

He hung up his jacket and tie, double-checked them for blood, then pulled off his undershirt to see what had happened.

As though it had been carved into his skin with a fine blade, in the center of his chest, lay Felix's seal. The stag, the orb, the serpent, little drops of blood welling to the surface.

He sighed. "Shit."

Someone knocked on the door.

"One sec."

"Sorry," June called back.

Sunshine went over to the door and opened it. He grabbed June by the wrist and pulled him inside, then locked it again.

"Sunshine, what..." The demon's eyes went wide, and he put a hand to his mouth. "What did you do?"

"I didn't. I mean. Felix did it. I...I don't think he meant to but..." Sunshine looked down again at the mark.

"Geez."

"It just sort of happened."

June grabbed a handful of paper towels from the sink and handed them over. "You're bleeding."

"I just. I think I need a Band-Aid." Sunshine pressed the paper towels to his chest.

"Let me get Lucifer."

"No."

June sighed. "Well. Do you feel different at all?"

"No. It just kind of hurts."

"You didn't...Did you fall?"

Sunshine shook his head. "No."

"Are you sure?"

"Yes."

"Fuck, alright, well, then I don't know that is or what he did," June said. "Lucifer would know."

"Can you just find a Band-Aid or something?"

"Oh, yeah, I'll run down to CVS!"

"Get an undershirt while you're there."

June scowled. "I'll be back, I guess."

It took about twenty minutes for June to come back with a large piece of gauze, some tape, and a clean undershirt.

They bandaged the mark and Sunshine made June promise not to tell anyone.

When Sunshine found his way back to Felix, Felix said, "What happened? You're all sweaty."

"I...I think I drank too much."

"Oh. Are you alright?"

"I'm fine."

"Are you sure?"

"Yeah, I'm fine, I just needed to..."

Felix nodded. "Boot and rally," he said sympathetically.

"Sorry."

"It's okay; if you were getting married, I probably would be a bigger mess."

"Did you still want to dance?" Sunshine asked.

"Are you okay?"

"I'm fine."

Felix looked uncertain.

"You've been promising to teach me to waltz for fifty years at this point and honestly, if Nix learns and I don't, I'm going to be upset."

"That's fair." Felix stood and gave Sunshine a long hug.

They left the baby with Phaedrus, who was entertaining the other three children with some story or another.

"Alright, so this is not a waltz," Felix said as he settled his hands in the appropriate places on Sunshine's body, "It's a foxtrot."

"That's fine."

"I'm gonna lead."

"Obviously."

"Just do what I do but backward."

Sunshine didn't think that would be sufficient explanation and with anyone else, it might not have been, but they were so used to each other that it was. It helped that this dance only had a few steps done over and over again.

He peeked at Hiram and Nix, who were doing something similar but much more complicated.

"Turns out he's a really good dancer," Felix noted.

"He sings all the time. It makes sense."

"I thought he and Bibi would hit it off, but I think Papa's taken a shine to him. Which is nice. I expected Papa to have a hard time with this wedding. You know he gets a little old-fashioned about things sometimes."

"A sudden, financially advantageous wedding for non-romantic reasons is perfectly old-fashioned."

"I really forget how old he is sometimes. Oh, oh, this is a waltz. Are you ready?" Felix asked.

They danced two more together, then Felix went back to dancing with his husband. Sunshine danced once with Hiram, then went to mind the children so Phaedrus and Hiram could spend some time together.

June and Lucifer wandered in his direction.

June asked, "What, are you doing quick changes now, too?"

"What?"

"Weren't you just wearing like...that whole soldier costume y'all wear when you come down from Heaven?" June asked.

"No."

"Oh." June frowned.

Lucifer had let go of June. "Where did you see him?"

"Oh, I don't know, by...by the door, I think." June blinked a few times, more than a little tipsy. "I thought it was...I don't know, some kind of joke or something. Like a weird best man roast or..."

"Watch the children," Lucifer said to June. He grabbed Sunshine by the arm.

"I..." June pressed his lips together. "Is something wrong?"

Lucifer touched June's face. "You're still firmly not in trouble, Junius. Watch the children. The angel and I need to speak."

June nodded.

Lucifer caressed June's cheek before they went.

Once outside, Lucifer said, "Find him."

"What?"

"You can find him, can't you? The same way that he finds you. Whichever one of them it is," Lucifer spoke fast and low, his fingers wrapped around Sunshine's arm.

Sunshine had forgotten. It had been so long since he'd tracked anything. He nodded and closed his eyes. It took him a while to settle.

Lucifer's nervousness didn't make it easier.

Finally, he said, "It's Jeff."

Lucifer bared his teeth. "Where?"

"Let me find him."

"Sunshine," the Devil growled.

"He's not stupid. If he left, he knows he's outnumbered. He'll wait until people start to leave. The best place you can be is keeping an eye on Felix."

Satan let out a whine.

"Go ahead. Just...run if you hear me scream."

Lucifer went to play his hair, pulled his hand away before he could disturb the braids, then nodded.

Sunshine headed off toward Jeff, who had circled around toward the back of the building. Maybe he was trying to sneak in or hide somewhere. That made Sunshine pick up the pace, though he wasn't exactly dressed for a jog. His shoes slipped more than once on the cobblestones and made a lot of noise, so he didn't have stealth on his side.

Luckily neither did Jeff, not dressed in golden armor and carrying a shining sword.

He was also sitting down by a pile of garbage.

Sunshine stood in front of him. He cleared his throat.

Jeff looked up. He moved and Sunshine flinched, dropping a little more firmly into a protective stance. Jeff had only tossed his sword at Sunshine's feet.

"Hey, uh..."

"I came here to end this."

"Yeah." Sunshine kicked the sword away from them and hoped he wouldn't regret it.

"I can't. It falls to you."

"I'm not going to kill him; we've been over this."

"No," Jeff said. "Me."

"Jeff."

"I went home. I went home and it was...wrong. It wasn't the same."

Sunshine crouched next to him, keeping away from the garbage.

"They welcomed me back and I was with the rest of us, and they loved me. He loved me. But it wasn't right. I wasn't right."

Sunshine sighed. "Jeff."

"I am ruined."

"That's a little dramatic."

Jeff finally looked up at him and it was obvious he'd been away from Heaven for a while. He looked like shit. Tired and beaten up, with either bruises or deep bags under his eyes.

"Was it that bad?"

"They don't understand anything," Jeff said. "It was like...like sharing my consciousness with a pillow."

"Maybe give it another chance. Give it some time."

"I gave it time!" Jeff insisted.

Sunshine took Jeff's hand. "Listen. I can't kill you. Why don't you come inside, and we'll get you something to eat? That always makes me feel better."

"I don't want to eat. I don't want to do anything." Jeff gripped hard onto Sunshine's hand. "I'm angry all the time and I want it to end. I want...I want you to end it. Please."

"No."

Jeff yanked his hand back and shoved Sunshine. "You made me like this, you did this to us. At least you could fix it."

Sunshine didn't know what to say so he just sat there.

Jeff stood up, kicked a bag of garbage, and screamed.

Sunshine could only think that if he had a piece of cake, he'd feel better, but he knew it wasn't true. Cake couldn't fix this. It would just be a distraction and he didn't think Jeff loved food the way Sunshine did anyway.

He needed his own distraction, his own way to acclimate to a life outside Heaven and Sunshine knew he couldn't do it the same way as Sunshine had.

Sunshine stood, brushed the dirt off his pants, and watched Jeff kick a bag of garbage until it split.

He let out one more cry of rage then stood there breathing heavily.

"Come inside."

"I don't want to see that *thing*."

"Which one?"

"Any of them," Jeff said.

"What about the kids? They ask about you."

"No."

Sunshine put his hands in his pockets. "So are you going to stay out here by the garbage or...?"

"I don't know what to do!"

"Well. I'm going inside." Sunshine turned and walked away.

About thirty seconds later, he heard Jeff catch up with him.

Then the footsteps stopped, followed by a choking noise.

He turned to find Lucifer with a knife to Jeff's throat.

"Oh, fuck, don't!" Sunshine managed.

Lucifer hesitated to draw the blade the rest of the way. Blood had already started seeping down one side of Jeff's neck.

"Stop, stop it!"

Lucifer stepped back but didn't lower his blade much.

Jeff kept a hand pressed to his throat and whirled to face Lucifer.

"You screamed," Lucifer accused as he sidestepped Jeff's lunge.

"No, that was him."

"Ah. Well. Everyone inside heard it too and now they're all worked up," Lucifer said. He took one large step back and to the side as Jeff stumbled forward. "Are we fighting or...?"

"He's gonna bleed to death!"

"Give me your tie," Lucifer requested. He held out his hand.

Jeff swayed on his feet, looking between Sunshine, Lucifer, and his own blood. "No," he said, though what he meant by it was anyone's guess.

Sunshine fumbled to get the tie off as quick as he could and handed it over.

To Jeff, Lucifer said, "Come here, let me fix it." He stepped forward when Jeff stayed still.

Jeff grabbed Lucifer by the wrist and dragged him close. "Finish it."

Lucifer looked at Sunshine.

"Don't," Sunshine warned.

Lucifer sighed. "Angel, if you'd like to die by my hand, then so be it, but not tonight."

Jeff asked, "You'll do it?"

"We can enter into a formal contract concerning such things at a later date, but I am not working tonight." He pulled Jeff in, pushed his hand away from the cut on his neck, and said, "Oh, that's not bad at all. You could do that shaving."

"Do you shave with a machete or something?" Sunshine demanded.

Lucifer wrapped the tie around Jeff's neck. He wiped his hands on the linen shirt beneath Jeff's cuirass. "I'll have my butler bring you to a doctor shortly. Do you prefer to wait here...?"

"I'll wait here."

Lucifer shrugged. He put his hand on Sunshine's arm. "Come, Felix was looking for you."

Inside, it took a while to reassure Felix that he hadn't been the one to scream and that everything was fine.

Lucifer sent Imogen out to handle Jeff's medical care.

The wedding, which had been winding down anyway, petered out. By the time he and Felix left, Jeff was nowhere to be seen.

That seemed to worry Nix in particular. When they found Jeff outside the palace, sitting on the steps with Imogen standing behind him, arms crossed, Nix smiled. "I was worried."

Jeff looked up.

"You left us so suddenly."

Jeff blinked.

"He won't come inside," Imogen said.

"So leave him outside," Lucifer suggested. "Angel, seek me tomorrow should you have business with me. I have my own matters tonight."

His own matters seemed to be nothing more than escorting Ira and Georg, both of them drunk and in a silly mood, inside and upstairs.

Jeff's face didn't register anything.

Felix edged around Jeff and followed after his father. "I'm going to bed," he told Sunshine.

"Drink some water."

Felix rolled his eyes and walked away. He would have stalked away any other time, but he was carrying Milk, who'd fallen asleep, and that probably made it hard to storm off.

Sunshine made to sit beside Jeff, but Jeff said, "No."

Sunshine stopped.

"Leave me alone. Both of you." He looked at Nix. "I can here to end this farce, not to make amends or say farewell."

Nix frowned. "Are you sure that's the wisest course?"

"Would you recognize it if it was?" Jeff asked. "What could you possibly know about doing the right thing?"

"That's enough," Sunshine warned.

"No," Nix said, "He' right. I'm uncertain about many things. I'm easily goaded by fear and coerced by threats. I don't act with any concern for right or wrong, not anymore."

"Go inside. Leave me alone," Jeff said again.

Nix gave him a small bow before he went.

Imogen followed the rest inside.

"I said go," Jeff said.

"I know. But...You're not going to let him kill you, are you?"

"Why wouldn't I?"

"Because you hate him."

Jeff shook his head. "I hate nothing. I hate everything. I cannot act against that half-breed monster without acting against you, and I cannot act against you. Despite everything...I still want you to come home. I want us to be how we were. But that can never happen."

"No," Sunshine agreed. "But that doesn't mean suicide is the answer."

"Then what is?"

"Time. Friends. Maybe a hobby. Therapy."

"You acclimated so easily."

Sunshine snorted. "Easily? I was here for a quarter of a century before I really met Felix and by then I was so...I was desperate for anything close to what I'd left behind, I took whatever companionship someone offered me. Even if it came from a monster."

"It's not fair."

"That's the thing about being a person."

"I'm not a person!"

"Ah, kind of seems like you are now. Mindless servants of the Almighty's will usually don't have moral dilemmas or suicidal thoughts."

Jeff heaved a sigh.

"Give it a while, at least, before you decide that being a person is so bad that you'd rather die."

He sighed again.

"Do you want to come inside?"

"No. It's...It's nice out here. I like being outside."

"That's a start."

"Go. Go be with your monster."

"His name is Felix."

Jeff rubbed his face. "I know."

Sunshine sat next to Jeff.

"I said—"

"I know. But you don't get to tell me what to do."

They sat outside for a long time without saying anything. A few hours at least, until Sunshine started to yawn. The next time Jeff told him to go to bed, Sunshine felt like he could. He dragged himself upstairs and curled up in bed. He hadn't been laying down for more than five minutes before Felix cozied up to him.

By morning, Jeff had at least come inside, likely due to the incoming guests for the trial. They had cleared out the toys from the throne room and brought the real throne upstairs, though Sunshine could still see the rocking chair tucked in the corner of a nearby parlor and covered with a sheet.

During all of this, Jeff, much like the cats, had seated himself on the stairs to watch.

"Good morning, Jeff," Felix said. He sounded surprisingly cheerful for someone who'd woken up in the middle of the night to throw up and sat in the bath moan for an hour afterward.

"Don't call me that."

Felix stopped, put one hand on his hip, and sipped his coffee. "Finally pick something better?"

"It was never my name. Only something people called me."

"Ah. How jellicle of you," Felix said. "Are you here to kill me or just here for the trial, or what?"

"I didn't know where else to go."

"Mmm. Coffee?" Felix asked.

Sunshine watched from the kitchen. He couldn't stop watching Felix anytime the other angel was in the same room as him. He didn't trust him not to finally snap and make one more attempt on Felix's life.

"No," the angel said.

Felix shrugged and walked away. He went to direct how the throne room might be arranged for the trial.

Lucifer had gone to retrieve Elora from the Otherworld.

All morning a slow trickle of various guests from the Eastern and Western Courts had come. Erithacus, the king of the Eastern Court had sent his son, Oliver. Maeve, queen of the Western Court, had sent one of her more steadfast courtiers. Both monarchs had declined to make an actual appearance, though Erithacus had declined due to a previous engagement, while Maeve had hinted that she thought the whole might be a trap. A representative for each of the Otherworld's four deities had come as well, though they hadn't been selected by the gods themselves, just sent from the various religious orders that served them.

Three judges from Hell's courts had come, too, as well someone from the major arcane universities, and someone from the Grand Hag Council.

Georg had set up someone near the throne to take notes.

Lucifer had called in a lot of favors for this, Sunshine guessed, but it must have taken a lot to banish someone from an entire realm. Even if she was only the queen of a ruined court, she was still a queen. She might always be queen of nothing, or someday she might be powerful. Fairies held long grudges.

Sunshine went to stand next to Felix. He pressed a hand against the center of his chest to quell the persistent, painful itch.

"You keep doing that," Felix said.

"Heartburn," he lied without thinking about it. He knew he couldn't hide the seal from Felix's forever, but he wasn't ready to deal with Felix's reaction yet.

"You want me to make some tea?"

"I'm okay."

"Mmm. If you say so." He cast his eyes over the room one more time. He had them adjust the chairs a little bit more so they'd make a semi-circle fanning out from the Serpent's Throne. There was a chair in the center for Elora, and one for Felix, who brought the charges against her. The chairs faced each other, separated by about six feet.

"Should we put in a table?" Felix asked.

"What?"

"So we're not staring at each other."

"Table could work," Sunshine said.

Felix called for them to bring in a table.

Waitstaff circled around, bringing refreshments to the guests as they explored the Devil's palace.

Well. Some of them explored. Some of them stood in a tight cluster in the foyer and refused anything they were offered.

"Go make nice with our guests," Felix suggested. "I think it would be too pandering if I did it."

"It's not if I do?"

Felix shrugged.

"You seem really okay right now?"

Felix smiled. He took a sip of coffee. "Am I that much of a mess that it's worth pointing out when I'm okay, instead of the other way around?"

"It's been a fucked-up couple of years."

"Maybe a quiet couple of years in the middle of nowhere will be a good change."

"Maybe," Sunshine agreed.

"I don't know if it can make me worse."

"Felix, you could be so much worse," Sunshine said.

"Your bar is so goddamn low."

"Specter, honestly. Are you fishing for compliments or do you genuinely hate yourself that much?"

"Both."

Sunshine nudged him, not even hard enough to make his coffee spill. He grinned, glad to see Felix in a good mood.

"Ahh, stop."

Sunshine blew a soft raspberry against Felix's cheek.

Felix giggled. He took one more sip of coffee and handed the mug to Sunshine. "Go take a tums or something. Dad should be here soon. I've got to get ready."

Sunshine stared down at the dregs of coffee as Felix walked off to talk to Georg. The Master of Records had taken charge of organizing the affair in the Devil's absence; he organized everyone and shuffled them into place as efficiently as a hung-over person could.

Sunshine headed upstairs to the balcony, where Nix and the other uninvited members of Lucifer's household would eavesdrop on the trial.

Nix had been invited but had declined. He said he didn't want to see Elora and he didn't want the children to see her either.

"Where are the kids?"

Nix gestured to the bedroom.

Sunshine peeked in and saw Jeff with them. Dire had a lot of questions about where Jeff had been.

He sat down, legs crisscrossed, peering through the rails.

Nix sat beside him.

Ira sat on his other side. "How are you holding up?"

"Oh, I didn't even drink that much."

"Really?" Ira asked. "June said you got sick."

"Oh. Well. I mean. I didn't drink that much after that," Sunshine said.

Ira nodded wisely.

A few minutes later, Elora and the Devil walked in together.

Lucifer didn't have to drag her in, but she didn't look pleased, either. She narrowed her eyes at the arrangement in the throne room and stopped walking. She stepped away from Lucifer.

Nix scooted back from the railing before she noticed him. "Don't tell her I'm here," he whispered.

"Do you want me to stay with you?"

Nix shook his head and retreated to the bedroom. He closed the door.

Not a moment later, Elora's voice rang out, "Where is he?"

"Don't worry about that," Lucifer assured.

"You said—"

"I lied to get you here. I didn't think you'd come otherwise. Was I wrong?"

She made for the door.

Lucifer waved a hand and it snapped shut. "We can leave when we come to an agreement about what's to be done. Come. My son has business with you."

"And what business do the rest have?"

"Queen Elora, lady of the Meridian Court, you're on trial for crimes against your consort and his children," Lucifer said. "These esteemed guests are here to ensure I temper my judgment. I would have dealt with this so much differently, but my son is soft-hearted and fair-minded."

She glared at Felix, her face faintly lined with rage. "What business does he have with me? What does it have to do with my consort?"

Lucifer went to sit.

Felix stood. "Your consort is my husband. His children are mine. When you acted against them, you acted against me."

She snorted. "Tell me this is some farce."

"No." Felix gestured to the other chair. "Sit. Hear the charges against you."

"I don't consent to this."

Felix frowned and gaped at her slightly. "Consent is not a word I thought I'd find in your vocabulary. Please. Sit. Let's make this painless."

"These people are not fit to try me."

Lucifer, from his throne, said, "You stand before people who are beyond your peers, Elora. Consent to this trial or I will be the only one who decides your fate."

The guests whispered among themselves.

Elora looked at them.

"Sit and you can become acquainted with my guests," Lucifer said. "I won't ask again."

Elora glared for a moment longer, her face growing more and more dried and twisted by the minute.

At Lucifer's request, each guest stood and announced themselves.

Elora grew a little more relax, or at least, her face went back to normal, as she found out who would judge her.

Sunshine watched Felix try his hardest not to pick his cuticles.

Once the guests had introduced themselves, Lucifer had Georg come forward and read the list of offenses Nix had named.

"Bring Nix to make these accusations himself," Elora demanded.

"Nix has sworn fealty and allegiance to your crown, hasn't he?" Lucifer asked.

"He has."

"Would this preclude him from speaking against you?"

"It could," she admitted through her teeth.

"Does it please the court that my Master of Records read the charges? Nix has relayed the charges to Mister Schreiber and signed the document listing them," Lucifer said. "His husband has also signed it and is here to represent his interests."

Georg passed the charges around so everyone could inspect it if they wanted and no one protested it.

Sunshine saw Oliver, the prince from the Eastern Court, frown at the document. He was human-raised and the most likely to have sympathy for Nix. "I'm sorry. Does this say infanticide?"

"Yes, Your Highness," George answered.

"That's killing a baby, right? Like...an already born one?"

"Yes, Your Highness."

Oliver returned the document and settle back into his seat.

The look on his face made Sunshine feel better.

Outright killing Elora would have been dicey and maybe difficult, but it would have been a definitive end to things. She didn't really have anyone who would take up arms to get her back. Turning this into a trial could see things go sideways for them.

The fairies could decide Elora was in the right of it. They could want them to give Nix and the kids back to her.

They didn't want to cross Lucifer again, Felix was probably right about that, but Sunshine had seen fear turn into bitter hatred. They might want to fuck over Felix just to hurt his dad.

Sunshine wished he knew more about the fairy deities. He didn't know how their representatives would swing.

No one looked openly hostile.

George read the charges aloud when Elora admitted she couldn't read them.

Ira let out a sympathetic, "Oh, poor things," a few times.

Sunshine wondered why Nix had left so much out.

"Did you do these things?" Lucifer asked.

"Excuse me, Your Highness," Maeve's courtier said before Elora could answer.

Lucifer looked their way.

"Call me Ravvin, if it please you, Your Highness. May I speak?"

"Provided it's relevant."

"Asking someone who cannot lie does not exactly go in the spirit of this sort of thing, does it? Is there no evidence to be presented? No testimony to be given?" Ravvin said. "This proceeding is so...human. I'm unfamiliar, I admit, with many human things, but to try someone who cannot speak in her own defense..." Ravvin shrugged. "Perhaps you can enlighten me."

"The purpose of this is not to ascertain guilt, but to decide a sentence," Felix said.

"So you will not hear her testimony, then? Or that of anyone allied to her?" Ravvin asked.

"You're asking her to incriminate herself," one of the human mages pointed out.

Felix scowled in her direction. "What's your point, Blakely?"

"It's not exactly fair," the mage answered. "Innocent until proven guilty."

"This isn't a thesis defense, alright? No one needs you to play Devil's advocate."

Blakely looked at Lucifer for half a second, turning pale when Lucifer smiled at her. "No. Clearly not. But, come on, Specter, you've trotted us all out for this, asking us to judge a perfect stranger based on guilt alone. You've given us no context."

"For killing a baby? You need context for that?"

Blakely met Felix's eyes. "How many ethics violations do you have stacked up, Specter? How many laws do you bend in that little office of yours?" she asked. When Felix looked unimpressed, she asked, "How many papers did you write against arcane interference in human problems? You think that never cost someone their life? Doctor Coal certainly—"

"Get his name out of your mouth." He didn't look irritated or angry. He lifted his chin and swallowed. "You don't get to drive him out of three different jobs, then use him against me."

"You're asking us to decide this woman's fate based on *your* context, Specter. And your father's." This time Blakely didn't look at Lucifer. "Give us a little more or admit this is an outright farce."

Lucifer sat low in his throne, his fingers steepled. He tilted his head slightly when Felix looked at him and arched one brow.

"Is it the position of our guests that they would prefer more context?" Felix asked.

A few whispers stirred among them.

Lucifer beckoned Georg over and murmured to him, then said,

"My Master of Record will pass out slips of paper. Inscribe an X should you wish to have context for crimes of Her Highness. Leave it unmarked should you not. We will count the slips and decide that way."

Lucifer waved a hand and had refreshments brought to the guests while they waited.

Sunshine wondered if he could get snacks to be part of jury duty in the United States. He didn't think so.

Ira and Sunshine helped Georg go through the study and cut up slips of paper, as well as round up enough pens and pencils for everyone.

Fifteen minutes later, Georg was counting the slips, sorting them into marked and unmarked stacks. He looked down at the slips, gave Felix an apologetic look, and said, "They want to hear it."

Felix sighed. "Fine."

Elora smirked.

"We'll go through the charges. You'll explain why you did them, every single one."

"I can do that."

Lucifer said, "The first charge, please, Mister Schreiber."

George stood, cleared his throat, and said, "Murdered all the adults in the familial group Nix traveled with as a child, including his parents and brother."

"I was on a campaign to grow my Court. I offered that they could come join me peacefully. They declined my offer."

"What gave you the right to make that offer?" Felix asked.

"I am the Queen of the Meridian Court, the last of the line. Who else could do it if I could not?"

"So you killed his family," Felix pressed.

"The ones that fought me. Should I have let them kill me?"

Felix pressed his lips together.

Georg looked at him.

He nodded.

Georg read the next charge. "Bringing Nix to the Court against his will, stripping him of his name, and coercing his allegiance."

The fairies whispered among themselves, sounding scandalized.

"His true name?" one fairy asked.

Elora shook his head. "His common one."

The fairies collectively sighed.

"Explain that," Felix said.

Of course, Elora could.

For every charge, she had an answer that must have sounded

rational to her, or people with the same rather medieval mindset.

Even Lucifer gave a sympathetic shrug once or twice to one of her explanations.

When Georg read, "Infanticide," Sunshine's stomach tightened. He was glad Nix wouldn't hear this part.

"My consort favored the child over me. He acted always in her favor. He became underhanded and rejected my directions, undermined his obligation to me at every turn. I could not tolerate a disobedient consort."

Felix rubbed his nose. "So you killed his baby?"

"I gave him the choice. I could return the child to where I found her, or I could kill her. He chose that my hand would end her life."

"Where did you find her?" Lucifer asked, sounding more curious than judgmental.

Elora answered, "Her mother's arms."

"He chose for you to kill her instead of returning her to her mother?" one of the mages asked.

"Yes. He believed a knife to the throat a kinder fate for the babe. I cannot say why," Elora said.

Felix sat up straighter and looked at the fairies, most of whom shared his look of disbelief. "Where was her mother?" Felix asked.

Elora's smile faltered a little.

"Where was she, exactly, Elora?"

"In the same grave where we put the rest of her family."

"So you offered to bury her alive in a mass grave or slit her throat," Felix said.

"One could see the choices in that light," she said with a shrug.

Felix looked at Georg, who read the next charge.

Once Elora had given sufficient context for her actions, Felix stood and addressed their guests.

"In light of her actions, it is the request of myself and my husband that Elora not be allowed to enter, visit, reside in, or otherwise occupy the same realm which he, I, and our wards will occupy."

"All of Earth?" Oliver clarified.

Felix nodded.

"You stole my consort and four other members of my court. I want them back, or I want something in return. I don't care to ever set foot in your filthy realm, or this one, but I will not leave this slight unaddressed."

Lucifer waited, asked, "Anything further?" then had the guests escorted to the dining room to discuss their decisions. Georg went in with them.

Elora remained in her seat, Lucifer remained on his throne, but Felix wandered upstairs to wait. He kissed the top of Sunshine's head and went to speak with Nix.

Sunshine heard Nix say, "Don't tell me anything. I don't want to think about it."

"I wanted to talk to Jeff, too, actually," Felix said.

Sunshine turned around.

Felix met his eyes, then closed the door.

The last thing he heard was the other angel saying, "I don't want to talk to you."

Ira made a face. "What's that about?"

"With Felix, I'm never sure."

Ira smiled.

He looked so much better than he had at Felix's birthday party in the spring.

"Oh! He said you had a tumor."

Ira laughed. "Yeah. I'm better now." He lifted his curls on one side to show a shorter patch of hair with a scar running through it. "Who would have guessed? Lu thought someone was doing something to me. Poisoning me, or some kind of spell or something. He was so worked up about it. I don't think anyone's ever looked happy to find out their lover has a brain tumor."

"Still. That's a lot to go through."

Ira shrugged and smiled. "He always says I'm resilient."

Sunshine smiled back.

Ira grinned. "You know you have the best smile. I just...I want to smile back whenever you smile."

"I think it's beatific," Sunshine said.

"It's infectious, for sure."

It took a while for Felix to come out of the room. He gave Sunshine another kiss, this one on the cheek, then went back downstairs.

He conferred softly with his father, then went to sit in his chair.

Elora wrinkled her nose at him.

He scowled back.

He only managed to stay seated for about half an hour. After that he paced around, sometimes coming back to his seat, sometimes going to stand huffily next to the throne, and sometimes just standing with his hands on his hips in the middle of the room.

After about an hour, Georg poked his head out of the room and said to Lucifer, "Darling this is going to be a while. Maybe something to eat?"

Lucifer nodded.

"You should eat, too," Georg said.

"Thank you, Mister Schreiber," Lucifer said. He stood and stretched, his bones cracking hideously. He looked upstairs. "Does the gallery care to join us for a meal?"

Elora looked too.

Sunshine wished she hadn't seen him. He didn't want to go downstairs or have to speak with her. In the end, he went down to the kitchen and brought food upstairs for Nix and the kids.

"The food here is foul," the other angel pointed out, picking apart the sandwich.

"You get used to it."

"You might."

Sunshine had lost his appetite. He took a bite and all he could taste was the ashen aftertaste of Hell-grown food on his tongue. "You're not really going to make a deal with him, are you?"

"Didn't you do the same thing?"

"Yeah, but not to...to you know. Do what you're doing."

"My business is my own, Sunshine," he said. He put his hand on Sunshine's arm. "I know you are ruined now for Heaven and that your only choice is to make what life you can here. I judged you too quickly."

Sunshine could only nod. "I wish I knew a way to have both. To have my life here and still be able to...to visit or something."

"I think you'd find it much as I did. Beings there are too pure. Untouched. They don't understand. No matter how much they love you or try, they can't. And you'd be left as the notary was."

Sunshine swallowed. He twisted his hand so he could hold the other angel's. "I'm sorry you came looking for me. This really didn't shake out for you at all."

He only sighed and tightened his grip on Sunshine's hand. "What is done cannot be changed."

"Not unless you want to tangle with the Temporal Parliament," Sunshine tried to joke.

All he got for his effort was a sigh and shake of the head.

Dire asked to go out to the garden, saying she was sick of being inside.

Nix told her, "Later."

Sunshine expected her to lash out, but she only stomped her

foot and bared her teeth before going to play.

Nix watched her go. He looked like he'd aged overnight. His wings drooped. Whenever they twitched, a little shower of power escaped.

"You okay?"

"I don't believe so," Nix said.

"You should try to get some rest, you look exhausted."

"I couldn't sleep last night. Or the one before. I won't be able to sleep now, either, I think. Not knowing she's here."

Sunshine extended a hand toward him.

Nix came to sit beside him on the bed. "I'm frightened," he confessed in a whisper. "I know what she asked."

"It won't happen."

"You don't know that."

"Felix didn't go through all this just to hand you back to her," Sunshine said. "And I won't let it."

"I hope you're right."

He put his arm around Nix.

The fairy leaned against him.

"Your wings are all dusty."

"It happens sometimes."

"Stress?"

"I think so. Or dry weather." He swallowed. "This place Felix will bring us. Connecticut." The word sat strangely on his tongue. "Tell me about it."

"It's...I don't even know how to describe it."

"Try. So I can think about something else."

Sunshine did his best to describe Connecticut, though he thought most of what he had to say was lost on Nix. Finally, he said, "You'll just have to decide for yourself."

Nix didn't answer.

Sunshine shifted a little to get a better look.

He'd fallen asleep.

Sunshine let him sleep. He needed it.

Felix came in sometime later, opened his mouth, then softly asked, "Is he...?"

Sunshine nodded.

"Well. It's time."

Gently, he gave Nix a shake. "Hey. Are you ready?"

"No."

"Come on," Felix urged gently.

"I can't. Tell me what they say. Don't make me go near her."

"Alright," Felix agreed.

Sunshine stood and went back to the balcony to watch.

Felix settled into his seat, tearing his cuticles.

Elora didn't seem bothered by the wait at all. Sunshine had never counted patience as one of her virtues before. He thought she'd have raged or tried to attack, but maybe she liked being here. Maybe she saw this as validation. After all, a queen would get a trial like this. Anyone else who crossed the Devil would just be dead.

Georg exited the dining room last. He had a piece of paper in his hand, folded and sealed. He ran his finger over the seal, which made Sunshine uneasy.

"Tell us," Lucifer said, "Before I get a kink in my back and I won't like any answer."

Georg turned to Felix and Elora. "The jury convened for this trial has considered all that was said. They have come to a compromise. Do you accept their authority on this?"

Felix shrugged.

Elora didn't answer either.

"You have to agree to accept the ruling or it doesn't mean anything," Georg pointed out.

"I consented to this already," Elora reminded tartly.

"I accept their authority," Felix answered.

Sunshine rocked on his toes.

A hand settled on his shoulder. "Peace," the other angel advised.

Georg broke the seal. He glanced at Lucifer, who nodded. "Elora, for as long as Nix, Felix, and their children live on Earth, you are forbidden from it. You may not go there, nor send people there to seek them, their kin, or their companions. Do you agree to this?"

"Have I any choice?"

Lucifer smiled at her. "There's always a choice."

"I agree," she said.

"Felix."

Felix glanced up, his head cocked to the side like he hadn't expected anything else. It was fake, though. Sunshine could see through that and Lucifer probably could too. "Yes?"

Elora smiled though.

"Your father decimated the Court of her ancestors. You returned and stole courtiers from her again. Five creatures seems a small number to a larger court or kingdom such as this, but she has so few. You took all the children from her court. This cannot stand."

Sunshine tightened his fingers on the railing so hard it creaked.

"You must select two members of your house to return to the Meridian Court with Elora until such time she dismisses them."

"Do they have to swear allegiance to her?" Felix asked. "I won't make anyone swear fealty to her, but I'll send...ambassadors."

"All my courtiers swear fealty," Elora said.

"No. I won't make anyone do that. Being bound to you is a cruelty no one deserves."

Sunshine couldn't believe Felix hadn't outright rejected the idea. He couldn't send anyone back to the Court. Nix would never let any of the children go and sending him back would be a death sentence. And what was this bullshit about ambassadors?

He let out a displeased grunt.

Ira looked up at him, eyebrow raised. Softly, he said, "Breath, Sunshine. It's not over yet."

He shot Ira a nasty look.

"Peace," Jeff counseled.

"They don't have to swear fealty," Georg said. "That's not part of it. They just need to go with her and stay at her Court until she tells them to go."

Felix glanced up at the balcony. He took in a breath and shrugged. "Fine."

Georg tilted his head.

Sunshine started toward the stairs, more than ready to drag Felix out of there and lay into him.

Jeff didn't let him go. He kept a hand on Sunshine's arm and pulled him back. Sunshine tried to wrench his arm free, but Jeff shook his head. "Wait. We are gifted with patience. Use it."

Sunshine hissed, "Fuck you."

Jeff ignored him. He turned his eyes back to the scene below, and so did Sunshine.

Elora had narrowed her eyes at Felix. She didn't like how easily he'd agreed. No one did.

Sunshine sure as shit didn't like it. He hated it when Felix got like this. For all that he said he wasn't like his father, there were moments when it couldn't be denied. He was sneaky and backhanded. He was a liar.

Sunshine trusted him but that's because he was an idiot.

A lonely, desperate idiot, looking for something to obey.

"I'll send one of my angels with you." He looked up, directly at

Jeff.

Jeff's hand tightened on Sunshine's arm, not hard but reassuring.

"And which of the children?" Elora asked. "Or will it be Nix?" She had a horrible smile on her face. "I've had new crowns made for all of them."

Felix turned to face her. "My house is large, Elora. I'll send you home with my newest angel, as a sign of goodwill, and I'll send you with my eldest sister." He smiled. "As a reminder of what we are."

Lucifer stood up. He looked at least a foot taller than he had before, which made him grotesquely elongated. "She is *not* yours to give."

One of the mages let out a squeal when Lucifer's fingers lengthened to talons.

"She is of my house, is she not?" Felix asked.

"She is not yours."

"But she is of my house."

Lucifer stepped down from the throne. His mouth stretched.

Felix went to meet him. He looked over the hints of the Beast peeking through his father's more human veneer. "If you keep her in that apartment any longer, she's going to hurt herself. Or lose her mind."

Lucifer stared down at his son. His voice came out thick and layered, the voice of something ancient and terrible. "You think yourself so high above the rest of my children. You think I'll let you do whatever you want."

"Dad," Felix said softly. "She's been in that one apartment my whole life. I'm the only one that visits her. You certainly don't. She's more mine than yours."

"She's my daughter," Lucifer growled.

"She is. She absolutely is. Do you think Elora could do anything to her? Do you think anyone in the Otherworld stands a chance against her?" Felix asked. His voice stayed calm and gentle. "Dad, I know you love her. But I also know you don't know what to do with her and trapping her in an apartment where she can see New York City happen around her and never go outside is not the right thing to do."

Lucifer glared down a moment longer. He let out a growl, but it sounded more pained than angry.

"It's all she talks about, getting out of that place."

"She'll tear apart the Otherworld."

"So tell her to behave or you'll put her back," Felix said. "I think she knows you're serious by now."

Lucifer blinked.

He grew a little shorter.

"Is she that unhappy that you think a ruined court and mad queen a kinder fate?" Lucifer asked. His fingers looked like fingers again.

Felix shrugged. "You're her dad. She did something wrong and you sent her to her room. But you can't keep her there forever."

Lucifer nodded. "Very well." He waved a hand.

The door to the palace slammed open.

Several people shrieked and most of them flinched.

He looked entirely himself as he said, "Go, all of you. We appreciate your service. Go. Quickly. My people will see you home."

People started to hurry out, not in any mood to test his temper or see if any more of the Beast would show its face tonight.

"I don't want—" Elora began.

"I don't care what you want," Felix snapped. "It was my choice to make. If you want to keep your courtiers, maybe you shouldn't be such an awful piece of shit to them."

Her face withered.

"Fucking try it," he goaded. "Go ahead, start something. It won't matter what the jury decided cause you won't live to see it."

She didn't do anything more than glare.

It didn't surprise Sunshine. Bullies picked on people weaker than them, abusers selected people they could coerce and control, and Felix was neither.

When they had all gone, except for Elora, Felix touched his father.

"Felix, don't."

"Dad, you know—"

"I know. Of course, I know! But...I didn't expect this of you."

"Are you mad at me?" Felix asked.

"No." Lucifer shook his head. He touched Felix's cheek. "I'm not angry. I love you, little one, but you should go too. I think I need to be alone. Send me the angel. He, the queen, and I will go to fetch your sister."

Felix nodded.

Sunshine held on to Jeff's arm when he started down the stairs. "You don't have to do this. He's got no right to send you there. You're not...Elisa's his sister but you're not one of his. He can't send you away."

"No. But he can ask me to go. And I can say yes." Jeff put a hand over his. "I told him it was easier there. I'm not displeased."

"You just came back."

"We'll see each other," Jeff said. He smiled. "Elora can't send me anywhere, but I can still move as I please."

"You're really sure about this."

Jeff nodded.

"I don't want you to go."

Jeff shrugged. "I want a lot of things, Sunshine. Maybe next time we see each other, things will make more sense to me."

Sunshine hugged him until Jeff stepped away. "Maybe you'll be a good influence on her."

"I am an angel. I can only be a good influence." He went to stand beside the queen and the Devil.

Sunshine thought about how long it had been since he'd thought of things that simply. Maybe it was okay. He didn't think Elora could get worse and Jeff had been contemplating suicide up until just now.

In a blink, they were gone.

All the life went out of Felix. He looked like he might be sick. "Ira," he whispered. He cleared his throat. "Ira. Will you help me bring them up? I think between you, me, and Sunshine, we can get there in one piece." With shaky hands, he took a plain silver ring from his pocket and slipped it back on his finger.

"He doesn't really want to be alone," Ira assured. "You know how he gets."

"I know. But I think we need a little space. Tell him to find me when he's ready. And make sure he does it."

Ira smiled. "I will."

Felix stepped around Sunshine to get up the stairs and didn't look at him.

Sunshine moved in front of him. "You didn't tell me."

"Tell you what? What was I supposed to say?"

"Felix, you knew this was going to happen."

"No," Felix said. He finally looked up. "I thought it was going to go a lot worse."

Sunshine faltered a little.

"I think Oliver pulled for us a lot in there. He still lives on Earth part-time, so he knows the Community. He knows that my family is a lot bigger than it looks, even if we aren't close. That 'from my house' bit had to be his," Felix said.

"I hate when you get like this."

"And I hate when you act like I had a choice. What should I

have done?" Felix asked. "I didn't see you coming up with any bright ideas. Oh. That's right. You can't."

Sunshine huffed and pressed his lips together. He turned away.

Felix grabbed his wrist. "I'm sorry."

"No, you're not."

Felix let go of him. "Fucking...! What do you want from me? You want me to let Jeff enter some weird suicidal deal with my dad? You want me to send one of the kids back, or pick some random sibling or cousin that I've never met? I did the best I could with three minutes to think of something."

"We could have talked about it."

"And come up with what?"

Sunshine didn't have an immediate answer.

"Jeff hates Earth. Elisa hates that apartment. They're both strong enough to stand up to Elora," Felix insisted.

Sunshine sighed.

"So cut it out."

"Nice, coming from you."

Felix rubbed his face. "Are we fighting right now?"

"I don't know."

"Well, figure it out, cause I think I'm also fighting with my dad and I can't do both," Felix said.

"Felix, you're not in a fight with your father," Ira said.

"Not right now. But I did just get him to do all this for me and then give his eldest child, his only child with his wife, to a nutjob. I went behind his back. He's never...He's never taken me seriously before. Not like this. I changed everything."

"Not everything," Ira said. "He loves you."

Felix sighed.

"And he needs someone to keep him on his toes!" Ira said.

Felix sighed.

"Come on, I'm his proxy. I promise you're not fighting with him. He's just...old. And weird. I mean, I got him murdered and he wasn't even annoyed."

Felix let out a harsh, uncomfortable snort of laughter. He glanced at Sunshine.

"I'm annoyed," Sunshine said. "But I don't want to fight. We can talk about it later."

Felix nodded. "I can handle annoyed." He took Sunshine's hand. "As long as you're not too terribly annoyed with me."

"Honestly, Specter," Sunshine sighed.

He was annoyed. And hurt. But Felix had annoyed and hurt

him before and they'd always found their way through it.

As the mark on his chest let out a particularly strong itch, he recalled that Felix wasn't the only one who'd kept something from their partner. He made himself keep his hand down, not wanting to draw attention to his chest again. Felix would see it eventually, but Sunshine didn't know what to do about that yet.

They gathered their things, which would have to be sent up later, and got Nix and the kids. They squeezed in tight and held on to each other for dear life as Felix and Ira pulled them through the place between worlds, with a hefty boost of Sunshine's power.

They tumbled unsteadily onto the lawn of a large farmhouse.

Ira let out a small moan of nausea.

Felix covered his mouth.

Sunshine put down Garfield and the elemental tottered away a few steps, then sat down and let out a small puff of smoke.

"Maybe I'll stay for a few days," Ira suggested weakly. "That way he has to come talk to you."

Felix nodded, dry heaved, then gagged.

Nix stared at the house.

The toddlers had already scattered across the lawn, not as bothered by the unsteady landing as the adults.

Dire was up a tree, Stone had found his way under the porch, and Milk had somehow tangled himself in the garden hose.

The baby started to fuss.

"Is that a house?" Nix asked.

"That's *our* house," Felix said.

Nix sniffled.

Sunshine winced when the baby started to cry. Nix looked like he might start too, so Sunshine reached out his hands and said, "Here, let me hold the baby. She'll settle down in a second."

"Irideae," Nix said.

The baby quieted immediately. She stared up at her father like she'd heard a loud noise.

"What?"

"That's her name. Irideae."

"It's a good fairy name," Felix said.

"It was my brother's name."

"Irideae," Sunshine said. "Nice to meet you."

Nix cried a little bit anyway, and so did the baby, and so did everyone, generally that first night in the house.

ABOUT THE AUTHOR

Dan is an author and educator who has lived in Connecticut for their entire life. They received a degree in education and later wrote their Master's thesis on representation of women in same-sex relationships in contemporary Spanish literature and cinema.

www.ingramcontent.com/pod-product-compliance
Lightning Source LLC
Chambersburg PA
CBHW071207210726
48293CB00002B/322